BOOK 3

ROCK F*CK CLUB

MICHELLE MANKIN

Copyright 2018
By Michelle Mankin

Without limiting the rights under the copyright reserved above, no part of this publication may be reproduced, stored in or introduced into a retrieval system, or transmitted, in any form, or by any means (electronic, mechanical, photocopying, recording, or otherwise) without the prior permission of the above copyright owner and publisher of this book.

This is a work of fiction. Names, characters, places, brands, media and incidents are either the product of the author's imagination or are used fictitiously. The author acknowledges the trademarked status and trademark owners of various products, bands, and/or restaurants referenced in this work of fiction, which have been used without permission. The publication/use of these trademarks is not authorized, associated with, or sponsored by the trademark owners.

License notes
This book is licensed for your personal enjoyment only. This ebook may not be resold or given away to other people. If you would like to share this book with another person, please purchase an additional copy for each recipient. If you're reading this book and did not purchase it, or it was not purchased for your use only, then please return to your favorite retailer and purchase your own copy. Thank you for respecting the hard work of this author.

Cover created by Michelle Preast IndieBookCovers
Photo by Wander Aguiar
Cover Model Matt
Formatting and interior design by Cassy Roop Pink Ink Designs

Sign up for my bimonthly Black Cat Records' newsletter. There's a giveaway each month and a chance to win an autographed paperback and swag.

Link to subscribe: http://eepurl.com/Lvgzf

ABOUT THE AUTHOR

Michelle Mankin is the *New York Times* bestselling author of the Black Cat Records series of novels.

Rock Stars & Romance. Love & Lyrical Ever Afters.

Love Evolution, Love Revolution, and Love Resolution are a BRUTAL STRENGTH centered trilogy, combining the plot underpinnings of Shakespeare with the drama, excitement, and indisputable sexiness of the rock 'n roll industry.

Things take a bit of an edgier, once upon a time turn with the TEMPEST series. These pierced, tatted, and troubled Seattle rockers are young and on the cusp of making it big, but with serious obstacles to overcome that may prevent them from ever getting there.

Rock stars, myths, and legends collide with paranormal romance in a totally mesmerizing way in the MAGIC series.

Catch the perfect wave with irresistible surfers in the ROCK STARS, SURF AND SECOND CHANCES series.

Romance and self-discovery, the FINDING ME series is a Tempest spin off with a more experienced but familiar cast of characters.

Exploring the sexual double standards for women, the ROCK F*CK CLUB series is a what-if the groupies called the shots instead of the rock stars.

When Michelle is not prowling the streets of her Texas town listening to her rock or NOLA funk music much too loud, she is putting her daydreams down on paper or traveling the world with her family and friends, sometimes for real, and sometimes just for pretend.

OTHER BOOKS BY MICHELLE MANKIN

BRUTAL STRENGTH series:
Love Evolution
Love Revolution
Love Resolution
Love Rock'ollection

TEMPEST series (also available in audio):
Irresistible Refrain
Enticing Interlude
Captivating Bridge
Relentless Rhythm
Tempest Raging
Tempting Tempo
Scandalous Beat

**The MAGIC series
(also available in audio):**
Strange Magic
Dream Magic
Twisted Magic

**ROCK STARS, SURF AND SECOND CHANCES series
(also available in audio):**
Outside
Riptide
Oceanside
High Tide
Island Side

FINDING ME series (also available in audio):
Find Me
Remember Me
Keep Me

ROCK F*CK CLUB series
(also available in audio):
Rock F*ck Club #1
Rock F*ck Club #2: A Postseason One Novella
Rock F*ck Club #3

CONNECT WITH MICHELLE MANKIN

on Facebook: https://www.facebook.com/pages/Author-Michelle-Mankin/233503403414065
On Twitter: https://twitter.com/MichelleMankin
On her website: http://www.michellemankin.com/
On Instagram: https://instagram.com/michellemankin/

Sign up for the Black Cat Records newsletter where I give away an autographed paperback and swag every month: http://eepurl.com/Lvgzf

The Gods of Rock Tour.

4 summer concert venues. 10 famous rock stars to f*ck.

Two at a time. Maybe even three.

I know what I like and how to get it.

I'm Marsha West. Raven Winter's best friend.

A sidekick no longer, I'm in the starring role.

I'm going to f*ck whoever I want. However I want. Whenever I want. I have my reasons for being the way I am and doing the things I do.

I've warned WMO they might have to stretch the rules to keep their TV-MA rating for me.

It's Rock F*ck Club. Season Two.

What could go wrong?

Squire or nobleman, servant or king, love is the tide that shapes the fate of us all.

– Tides of Conquest

BOOK 3

ROCK
Fuck
CLUB

PROLOGUE

"Tilt your ass up," he commanded gruffly.

"Ok." I widened my stance.

"More." He tightened his grip on my hips. His fingers pinched my skin as he drew me backward and rammed his steely length in deep.

"Alright." I spread my arms wider on the glass window in front of me and lifted higher up onto my toes.

"Yeah, baby." He groaned. His breath was a hot brand on the back of my neck. "That's it." His next thrust glided in deeper, and his heated hands went higher. Finding my tits, he shaped and squeezed them. A reward for my compliance, I supposed. But his reward didn't do anything for me.

"Faster," I urged. "Fuck me faster." Panic seeped into my voice. If he didn't pick up the pace my brain would kick in.

"Almost there, babe." He abandoned my tits and smoothed his long, unfamiliar fingers down the length of my spine. At my hip, he

16   MICHELLE MANKIN

glided his hand around to the front. Skimming over the crease between my thigh and leg, he went straight for my pussy and cupped it.

I sucked in a breath. I was past the point of being interested in foreplay. I just needed him to fuck me.

Fast.

"You feel so good." He let out another deep groan as he drove inside. "So tight."

"Stop talking." My fingers curled into frustrated fists on the cool glass. On the Avenue of the Americas fifteen stories below, it was rush hour. People spilled out of the buildings. Workdays done, they hurried home to their families. Families that loved one another. Families that cared for each other. Homes that were a refuge for them rather than a combat zone.

Nurture. Approval. Grace. My best friend Raven Winters had grown up with those things in a two-parent loving home that contrasted sharply the criticism and harsh discipline that had characterized my own.

Don't think, I told myself, squeezing my eyes tightly shut, curling my fingers into my palms and trying to stop it. *Feel. Be in the moment. This moment.*

My hookup grunted again.

Focus, Marsha. On his hard cock inside you. On the thrill of the now. On being needed desperately.

At least I was during the time it took a man to fuck me.

Little talk. Less expectations. Being fucked by a random guy in a public space was a setup that usually worked for me.

But not today. My brain engaged, it was already too late for me. I couldn't come once my mind switched on. I would have to fake it.

"Give it to me, big guy," I mewed. Wetting my parting lips, I turned my head and glanced over my shoulder at him through my

ROCK *fuck* CLUB BOOK 3   17

lowered lashes. "I need that big…mmm…wonderful cock of yours."
Untrue. What I really needed was for him to give it to me fast, so I
could go to my room and finish off alone. The only guaranteed way for
me to come anymore was using the one night I had spent with Hawk
Winters as my inspiration.

"Yeah. Oh, yeah." He started to hammer his cock into me.

"So good." I faked another moan, frosting the glass with the lie and
my humid breath. To the left, the door to the gym suddenly rattled.
Turning, I saw a large silhouette through the opaque glass. Someone,
a male someone, cursed and muttered about their keycard not working
properly. It probably would have worked, only I had dead bolted the
door. I might get off on the public sex part, but I had zero interest
in being arrested. My hookup didn't seem to mind the interruption.
His thrusts became more regular. He was really into it now. Totally
in throes. The tight flesh over his hips smacked my rounded ass. He
didn't even notice I wasn't playing along anymore. Not that it would
have mattered. This wasn't about me for him or him for me.

It was about self-gratification.

An inferior substitute for lovemaking. I had a basis of comparison
because of Hawk. My best friend's brother. The one love of my life.
Hawk had been kind and gentle with me despite the circumstances.

Big Guy groaned. He stiffened. His fingers flexed deeper into the
flesh at my hips. He ejaculated and dropped his perspiration-soaked
face into the side of my neck. I tried not to cringe when I felt him press
his warm lips into my chilled skin.

I couldn't quite manage it.

"Let go of me." I didn't do the after-sex affection thing. Not
anymore. Not since Hawk.

I didn't give Big Guy time to get himself together. Maybe if he had
given me a climax I might have been more generous.

But then again, probably not.

"Pull out," I demanded. "Now."

"Huh?" He sounded out of it. Floating on a post-coital cloud high, no doubt, but I was done. Totally and completely done.

"Pull your cock out of my cunt," I clarified crudely. "There's a guy trying to get inside the gym, and I need to leave."

"Oh, ok. But I thought maybe we might go up to my room and get to know each other better."

Seriously? I thought.

"This was just a hookup. I told you that upfront."

I skimmed my gaze over our combined reflections in the glass. I was the pretty blue-eyed blonde, cliché unless you looked further beneath the surface. The guy, well, I knew without focusing on him why he had tempted me. Tall and darkly handsome, he physically resembled Hawk. Hawk hadn't doubted me. Hawk hadn't abandoned me in my time of need, even though he'd certainly had no obligation to me. Hawk had been a perfect man. My champion, too. I hadn't deserved him.

While my hookup had been on the treadmill, I had noted the similarity. I'd caught him checking me out as I pounded the large punching bag with my gloved hands. Boxing workouts were a coping strategy. A healthy coping strategy. I didn't have many. It was one of the few things the inpatient psych docs had recommended that I had followed through on after I had lost Hawk and then my baby.

Remembering sliced swift sudden pain straight through the center of me. Doubling over, I wrapped my arms around myself as if to hold the two severed pieces of my body together. Futile since my head and heart no longer functioned together anymore.

I sucked in a gulp of air and managed to straighten. Quickly, I straightened my clothing. I didn't linger. I didn't pause to say goodbye.

After all, I didn't know my gym hookup's name, and he certainly hadn't bothered to ask for mine.

Twisting the deadbolt, I unlocked the door. The inept guy on the other side of it raised a brow as I brushed past him. The hallway behind him was deserted.

Luckily.

My practiced mask of post-hookup indifference melting, I hurriedly retraced my steps to the elevator. Pressing the call button, I crossed my arms over my chest and tried to ignore the growing despair inside of me. Emptiness had a pain all its own. It felt like a gnawing ravenous hunger. One I had learned to accept would never be satisfied.

Don't, Marsha West, I warned myself. *Don't feel sorry for yourself. You had something real once.*

Only Hawk was gone now. The dream he represented was gone. Marriage, me, him and the baby he had been willing to pretend was his. I had buried all thoughts of a happy ending after losing him and then my unborn child.

It was just me now.

The elevator dinged. Startled into action, I swiped the back of my hand through the wetness on my cheeks as it opened. A willowy brunette I recognized tumbled out.

"Sky. Hey." I grabbed Lucky's sister, Sky, by the arm. "Where are you going?"

"I…um…" Lost in her own thoughts, it took her a moment to focus her prettily made up eyes on me. A certified cosmetologist, she did the stage makeup for the Dragons, her brother's band. She did my makeup on occasion and Raven's frequently as well. "I thought you said your workout would only last thirty minutes?" she complained, her pale pink lips pressing into a displeased line.

"I got sidetracked."

"But the gym has directions," she pointed out. "It's easy to find."

I forgot sometimes how literally she processed things. "I met a guy at the gym," I explained bluntly. "I just had sex with him."

"Oh." Over her clear blue eyes her brows rose.

I shrugged.

"That's splendid." Awe rounded her lips.

I smiled. She was likely the only person in the world who was impressed by my hookup rate rather than appalled.

"Can you perhaps help me meet someone, too?" She bounced on the tips of her toes.

"Like a hookup someone?" I cocked my head to the side.

She nodded.

"Why would you want to do that?" I motioned her onto the elevator. I didn't want the door to close. I wasn't interested in hanging around on this floor. Once I was done with a hookup, I put as much distance between them and me as I could. I knew it was settling. I knew it was sad. But it was all I had. "I mean you're beautiful." And sweet and undamaged. She was worthy of someone's love. "You could have any guy you want." I pressed the button for my floor and turned to face her.

"Not anyone I want. Not Rocky." Clouds darkened her eyes. "Since I can't have anything real, I might as well have something fanciful. Only, I don't know how to go about getting that. So, I do need your help. If I didn't, I wouldn't ask for it." A crease formed between her delicate brows.

"Ok, I guess. If you're sure that's what you want." I blew out a breath. Raven would probably kick my ass for agreeing to help her boyfriend's sister get laid. Lucky would for sure, if he found out. "Really all you need to do is find a guy you're interested in and tell him what you want."

"I'm not so sure that will work." Sky frowned.

"Trust me, coming from you it will work like a charm."

"I don't know." She shook her head. Long glossy brown tendrils skimmed her slender shoulders. "I don't think I'm explaining myself very well." She exhaled a tremulous breath. "It's not that I want to do this, but I must get on with my life. I can't sit about anymore waiting for something that's never going to happen. *Rocky* must realize I'm not sitting about waiting on him anymore."

Clarity hit me. This was about her crush on Rocky Walsh, the quick to quip Welsh drummer in her brother's band. "This is my floor," I announced as the elevator stopped. "Let's go to my room. I get where you're coming from." *Man did I ever.* "But I think this idea of yours requires more discussion."

"Ok." Sky stepped out with me, and we walked side by side together down the hall. When we reached my room, I swiped my card and pushed open the door for her to enter ahead of me. Once we were both inside, I let it close behind me and moved to the bed to clear a place for her to sit. Gathering the pile of clothing I had scattered earlier, I scooped it into my arms and transferred it all to a nearby desk chair. When I turned around Sky was perched on the edge of the bed. Her hands were in her lap, and her eyes were wide beaming beacons of trust. My heart went out to her. I didn't make friends as readily as Raven. I had too much emotional baggage. But with Sky, it wasn't just easy, it was inevitable.

"So, let me see if I have this right." Smiling gently, I moved to the bed and dropped down beside her. She swiveled to face me. "You want a guy to go out with you. You want to have sex with him, sex that doesn't mean anything. And you want to do this to prove not just to Rocky, but also to yourself, that you've moved on and that you're completely over him."

22   MICHELLE MANKIN

"Yes. That's it precisely." She bobbed her head to confirm.

"That's a pretty tall order." Pretty impossible. A stretch for Rocky, too. I knew he had feelings for her, even though he might not want to acknowledge them. I imagine he had his reasons. Complicated reasons, probably. But one thing I knew for sure. He wasn't going to accept anyone else having her. His response to the guys at the merch booth who had wanted to take her out had proven that. And in addition to Rocky, there was also Sky's brother to consider. Lucky was protective of her to the extreme. I pressed on anyway. "Do you have someone in mind? Someone you're attracted to?"

"No, only Rocky. He's all I think about." She blinked rapidly as her eyes flooded.

"I want to help you, Sky. Truly." I reached for her fluttering hands and gathered them in my own. I was a sucker for tears, likely because no one had ever cared much about my own. "But it's up to you to make this work. I mean you have to be willing to try to find someone to replace Rocky." In all the years I had been in love with Hawk I had never considered trying to get over him.

Except maybe that one time.

"But I have tried." Her gaze remained steady on my own.

"How? When?" I was skeptical. "And with whom?" We had been together nearly twenty-four seven during the filming of the first season of Rock Fuck Club. I couldn't remember ever seeing her ever go out with anyone.

"Back when I lived in the UK. Before my dad died. Before Lucky brought me on tour with the Dragons. I went out on dates. I had sex twice. The first time hurt a little. I didn't like it. The second time was nice, but it wasn't something I wanted to do again particularly. I think maybe because the guys weren't who I wanted them to be. They weren't Rocky." Her fingers quivered in my hold. "Since I've been on the tour with the band, Rocky is always there. I look at him. I think about how different it would be if he touched me the way the other guys did." She sighed and the longing in that exhalation spoke volumes about her feelings for the handsome drummer. "I keep hoping Rocky will change his mind, but I need to stop hoping...because..." Her powder pink mouth trembled. "Because it hurts too much. Because he doesn't want me that way. Because he will never want me that way." Tears gathered in her eyes.

I understood how she felt. It was how it had been for me with Hawk. My heart had fissured each time he passed me by. Those fractures had widened over the years as I had watched him date others, yet all the while I had been hoping, desperately hoping for him to have a change of heart. Until one day, he finally had.

"Rocky might come around, honey." I squeezed her hands. I had noticed the way Rocky looked at her. I think we all had. Even her brother was no longer oblivious. "If he sees you with another guy, he might be forced to admit that he has feelings for you."

"I don't think so." Her head lowering, she shook it firmly. I wondered if something had happened recently between her and the attractive Welshman that made her feel so certain. "It's time for me move on." She lifted her eyes, a difficult task to do with all the unrequited emotion weighing her down. "I must move on. And it's important Rocky sees me do it."

She was probably right. Her plan was a solid one. Though it had always been Hawk for me. Though it *would* always be Hawk for me, I hadn't lived a life of abstinence waiting for him to give me that one single chance. "Is there someone on the tour that you like? Someone you fancy? Someone who's caught your eye? A good looking someone?" Someone like that would rattle the easy-on- the-eyes drummer.

"No." She shook her head.

"C'mon, Sky. You've got to try to work with me. There are several roadies that are decent looking."

"I don't think so." She worried her lip between her teeth. "It can't be someone associated with the tour. Lucky would sack them."

"You're right." Anyway, I doubted the road crew would want to risk her brother's or Rocky's ire. "So, it has to be someone who's confident enough to stand up to both of them."

"Yes." She nodded vigorously. I got the impression she had already given the matter a great deal of thought. "One who's sexy." She withdrew her hands from mine touching her first fingers together. "One willing to sleep...have sex with me." She added her thumb to bring the count up to two. "And someone who won't care that it's not serious. I just want to feel good. I don't anyone to get the wrong idea and get their feelings hurt."

My eyes widened. It seemed like she was peeking inside my head and consulting my hookup checklist.

"You need a certain type of guy." I'd learned that important lesson early on. "One who doesn't give a fuck what anyone thinks about him. One who values his own ego above all things." The narcissistic ones never tried to fix me, and they never got attached. They were ready to move on the moment they got off. "The more terrible their reputation for your purposes the better." It would prove to Rocky that she could handle anything he could throw at her while at the same time boosting her confidence. "But before you do this," I firmed my gaze on hers, "you need to be on birth control so you don't get pregnant." My chest squeezed tight. "And you have to make sure you use a condom, too. Alright?"

"I've been on the pill for ages. I'm not going to have unprotected sex, Marsha. I'm not daft." She looked hurt.

"I know you're not, honey. I'm sorry if I insulted you. But I can't *not* caution you to be safe. I care about you. When you really care about someone you protect them and speak the truth to them, even if the truth might make them mad. And speaking of mad, you do realize your brother won't approve of this plan, to put it mildly."

"It doesn't matter." The sudden tension in her body said it did, but I didn't let on that I'd noticed it.

"Another performer then. A peer of Rocky's maybe. A guy from another band would be good. A handsome confident guy from an established band would be even better. Someone Rocky knows. Someone he would never approve of."

"Oh." Color returned to her cheeks and her troubled expression lightened.

"Did you just think of someone?"

"Well, maybe."

"A guy here?" My brows rose. "In New York?"

"Yes, I met him at WMO the other day." She nodded her head excitedly. "He's a lead singer."

"You gonna tell me who it is?"

"No." Her brow creased. "It made Rocky mad when I just mentioned speaking to him. But he was nice to me and very nice looking." The pink in her cheeks became a duskier rosier hue. "He made me laugh. He said I was pretty. He gave me his cell number."

"Then he's interested." And so was she. I could tell by the brightness in her eyes. "So, call him and ask him out. Tell him exactly what you want. Sex with no strings. If he's the type of guy we both think he is, he'll take you up on what you're offering. I guarantee it."

"AH, MARSHA. COME in." Suzanne Smith, the World Media Organization VP gave me an efficient smile and set her black and gold pen down on her desk motioning for me to enter her office. "Thank you for coming by after hours and for your punctuality."

"I can't stay long," I cautioned. "I'm supposed to meet Raven in an hour and with Midtown traffic…"

"Yes, I know. The Dragons are celebrating their upcoming tour with Noir." Her emerald eyes narrowing, the attractive redhead watched me closely as I settled into a seat on the other side of her chrome desk. The hem of my dress slid to my upper thigh. I tugged ineffectively on the leather. It was decadently short, perfect for a night at the Roxie, but way too short for a business meeting. I gave up on the dress, lifted my gaze and tried to project confidence, and not betray my surprise at the depth of the exec's knowledge regarding my plans. Raven had mentioned Suzanne seeming all-knowing. Right about now I was thinking she might be right. The VP's sharp gaze uncannily resembled my father's. Having never been the sole focus of her attention before, I found that it put me on edge just like being under the microscope of his regard did. "Since we're both under time constraints…" the exec paused, seeming to notice everything about me including my nervous swallow. "Let's get to the point right away. I brought you in to iron out a plan for the next season of Rock Fuck Club." Her eyes honed like targeting lasers on mine. "Shall we get started?"

"Alright, I guess." I had only recently agreed to be the next star of Rock Fuck Club. I had thought given my lack of experience being in front of the camera that she would have given me a little more time to get used to the idea.

"Let's go over the filming schedule."

"Yes, of course." I folded my hands together. They had started to tremble much like Sky's had earlier.

"We'll start tonight."

"What?" I squeaked. My eyes went wide, and my stomach plummeted. "I can't start tonight. I need time to prepare." Meaning I hadn't yet figured out a way to keep my father or my two brothers from finding out what I was doing. "Season one hasn't even aired yet."

"That's true. But the most important screening has already occurred in our target demographic. It has tested so well and the anticipation for the first season is already so high that I have been given the green light to proceed with the next season. And a prime opportunity has presented itself."

"What kind of opportunity?" Suspicion narrowed my gaze.

"The Gods of Rock tour."

I'd heard of it. "It's a multicity, multiple bands summer festival type of thing, isn't it?"

She nodded.

"But I thought the concept of RFC was ten rock stars and ten cities."

"Ten rock stars definitely. The number of cities isn't so important. The focus on your season will be the summer festival scene. I think it will be interesting to change that part up from season to season."

"Alright," I allowed. "But you said you wanted me to do a documentary on Raven. How am I supposed to do that if I'm doing a season of RFC here, and she's overseas with Lucky?"

"The European leg of the Noir tour is over a month away. That gives us enough time to squeeze in your ten-episode season of Rock Fuck Club while also filming the documentary portion of her season concurrently. It will save me a lot of travel expenditure."

"But I don't understand. The Dragons are on break."

"They *were* on break." Her emerald eyes brightened. "They're not anymore." She leaned forward. "I only lacked approval from their record label. Mr. Morris and I have spoken tonight, and we came to an understanding." What she considered an opportunity was not going to be viewed in the same light by Raven and the Dragons. I knew they had all been looking forward to some down time off the road. "The Gods of Rock tour organizers were delighted to add Lucky and his band to the lineup."

I just bet they were, I thought. The Dragons were a big deal now. Raven, too, and the Rock Fuck Club. If the Gods of Rock tour wasn't already sold out, it would be soon.

"The buses depart from the Greyhound station tonight. The Dragons will remain on their usual one. And I have added a rather large, comfortable one for Ignacio, his film crew, and Barbara, of course." Barbara Michaels was Suzanne's secretary, her former secretary. She was taking over PR duties for Raven. The exec tapped her power red nails together. They reminded me of talons. They glinted in the fluorescent lighting as if they had been dipped in blood. Mine and my best friend's, I mused morosely.

"If it's all the same to you…" I swallowed to moisten my dry throat. "I'll ride on the Dragons' bus with Raven." We needed to stick together. Guard each other's backs.

"As you wish." She dipped her head in agreement. "However, keep in mind that the WMO motorbus has a significant sized lounge in the back already set up with proper light and sound for filming, and that you'll have the option of the additional bunk space on board should you need it."

Why would I need it? The way she regarded me made me feel like she knew something I didn't. That thought put me more on edge. I shifted uneasily in my chair. I wondered if Raven had felt this unsettled while she had been starring in her season. Recalling the amount of heavy drinking she had done, I imagined she likely had.

"The first concert stop is the MidFlorida Credit Union Amphitheatre in Tampa." Suzanne seemed not to notice my discomfiture as she continued to rattle off logistics. "Then it's the Fairgrounds in New Orleans, and the Cynthia Woods Mitchell Pavilion in Houston. The final stop is the Napa Valley Expo."

"Napa? In California? Where they have all the wineries? For a rock tour?"

"It's the Rock the Vine Festival. All the stops on this tour are at outdoor venues."

"But Raven got to choose her cities and concerts."

"She negotiated those things upfront before she agreed to be our star. You did not."

Fucking hell.

"I choose my hookups." I sat up straighter, even though I reeled internally. *Please let her agree that I get to choose my hookups.* My criteria were very specific.

"Naturally."

I let out a caged breath. I might not be as adept at negotiating as my bestie, but I knew one thing for sure. "My season isn't going to be like Raven's."

"I would hope not." The exec's crimson lips lifted. Her version of a smile was not a happy thing. "That would be tedious. But I'm curious," she tilted her head and not one hair of her tightly wound chignon escaped its confines. It didn't seem that anything could disobey her wishes. "How do you envision it differing?"

"For one thing, I'm not doing cute little skits." I rolled my eyes. "I'm not singing, and I'm not dancing for anyone."

"Fair enough."

"It's not that I don't think what Raven did was cool. It's just that we're different. She has her distinct personality, and I have mine. Sure,

I have some decent dance moves, better ones when I'm limbered up with tequila, but I can't sing for shit."

"Duly noted."

I nodded once, gripping the unyielding armrests as if I were on an airplane during a bumpy takeoff. "Raven was tentative. She had something to prove to herself about her sexuality." Maybe even her own desirability after discovering her boyfriend Ivan Carl fucking someone else. "Her season was about experimentation. I know what I like. And I know how to get it." My recent advice to Sky came to mind.

"The basis for RFC has always been a woman's freedom to choose." Suzanne clicked her nails together peering at me over the top of her hands. "Overturning the double standard between men and women is a cause I very much believe in. I don't plan for that underlying concept to change."

"Yes. Well, good. I'm glad to hear that because I'm going to fuck whoever I want to, Miss Smith. However I want to. Whenever I want to. So, you might want to check to see how far WMO can stretch the rules with the powers that be and still maintain the show's TV-MA rating." My life was my own design. It was real. It was me. It might only make me feel good for brief moments at a time. It might violate the acceptability standards of most. It might be less than fulfilling, but I was determined to continue living it my own way doing those things that made me feel the most alive.

CHAPTER
one

"I don't believe it." Raven shook her head.

"I fucking don't, either." My eyes were as wide as hers. But there was no denying the evidence before us: Sky Spencer sweet as her favorite UK chocolate candy with Ivan Carl, Raven's ex, a rocker who rated worse than his reputation. On the upper level of the Roxie, they paused as if they were the next in-couple posing for a photo op prior to walking the red carpet.

More accurately, Ivan paused with his hand resting on the small of Sky's back, protectively like she mattered to him. Raven and I had both learned the hard way that no one mattered to Ivan but Ivan. Sky was only a prop. Arriving with her at a club he likely knew we were at, he expected to be noticed. He thrived on controversy. The lead singer of the Heavy Metal Enthusiasts enjoyed stirring things up. He was as unpredictable in his personal life as he was on stage. Acting on impulse had cost him his relationship with Raven. In retrospect, a good thing for her. I doubted he had gotten that memo.

Head tilted at an imperial angle, Ivan confidently steered Sky from the street level entrance of the Roxie to the sweeping Plexiglas staircase that connected the upper section to the velvety basement level lounge where we all were. Alec Harris, the obsessive-compulsive Dragons' bassist and Cody Charles, his partner, the carefree rhythm guitarist, were out on the pulsing dance floor not far from Raven and me. Lucky and Rocky were in the back corner by the bar signing autographs. Given the swarm of fans that surrounded them, they hadn't noticed Sky and Ivan.

Yet.

"I mean, I see them there." Raven's strident tone underscored her continued disbelief. "The two of them…Sky and Ivan. There…*together.* But I don't understand it." Her grip on my upper arm tightened. "Why?" She shifted to look at me, her golden gaze cluttered with unanswered questions. "Why is she here with him?"

"I don't know." I shrugged a shoulder, but I had a good idea. The heavy bass of the current song seemed to be synchronized to the dread that vibrated inside my chest.

"Oh, Mars." There was a crease between Raven's eyes. "We need to do something. Separate her from Ivan before Lucky sees them. He'll go nuts, and his label will go ballistic, too, if they have to defend him against another assault charge." She was right, of course. But I had a feeling that a confrontation between the two men was a foregone conclusion.

"Alright." I placed my hand over hers and squeezed her fingers firmly. Her skin was as ice-cold as the frozen margaritas we had consumed earlier. "But maybe you should let me handle it." I narrowed my gaze on her. Beneath her Navajo braids and the glamorous makeup Sky had applied, her porcelain complexion had turned ashen.

"No." Her expression reflected her resolve. "He's my past. My problem to rectify. I just hate that he's decided to drag Sky into it." She took a measured step forward, and I went along with her. Together we threaded our way through the press of people now murmuring Ivan's name.

A knot formed in my stomach. The tension wound tighter with each step we took. If only I had thought things through more carefully before giving advice to Sky.

Find a bad boy with a reputation, I had advised her. Well, she had certainly done that: she had found the worst of them. Ivan fit the criteria. Sinfully handsome. Confident to the point of obnoxiousness. A 'fuck 'em and leave 'em by the time the the tour bus pulled out of the hotel parking lot type.

Well, he had been that type with me before he and Raven had become involved.

But Sky should have removed him from consideration. Ivan Carl was Raven's ex. It broke the girlfriend code for Sky to go out with him without clearing it first with Raven.

Did Sky not get that? Or did the level of her desperation override the code?

I suspected it was the latter.

Raven stopped at the base of the stairs and lifted her gaze. I lifted mine, too. The sexy lead singer and Sky were on their way down. The staircase glowed a ruby red matching the current color of the dance floor. The brunette moved gracefully, her slinky metallic sheath swirling around her slender frame. In a scuffed pair of Harley-Davidson motorcycle boots, Ivan stomped down the steps as if laying claim to them. A dark knight on a dire crusade, he wore no plume; just his silken chestnut strands secured at his nape along with his usual heavy metal attire. A suit of armor not of woven steel but consisted of form fitting denim jeans and a dark grey muscle tee that stretched

34   MICHELLE MANKIN

tightly across the breadth of his wide shoulders. His coat of arms? The flaming wings of the 'Firebird' logo on his shirt.

"Raven," Ivan declared, his gaze on her as he disembarked the final step and assumed an arrogant stance. His abrupt stop jangled the silver wallet chain that hung over his muscular thigh.

"Ivan," Raven returned, and I noted her tension as she locked eyes with her former lover. At Ivan's side, Sky appeared to be nervous. She shifted closer to the lead singer as several fans called out his name. Breaking the connection with Raven, Ivan lifted his darkly shadowed jaw to acknowledge them.

Several squealed in return.

Idiots.

"Baby." Ivan turned back to Raven, raking his haughty gaze over her. "You look like an angel." He paused, his milk chocolate eyes lingering on her tits even though Sky was standing right beside him. "And like you missed me."

"Keep dreaming." The custom beads on Raven's chambray halter dress swayed with her agitated movements. "And I'm not your baby anymore, Ivan." Raven smoothed a self-conscious hand over her outfit.

"You could be again if you just say the word." His sculpted lips spread into a wide sanguine smile. "I'll even remind you what it is in case it's slipped your mind. It's *please.*"

Sky dropped her chin to her chest, seeming to withdraw into herself.

What an asshole. Ivan might fit the criteria I had given her, but he wasn't a safe choice—not even for a hookup.

"Please what?" Raven hissed at her ex. Where Sky had seemed to shrink in stature, my best friend seemed to grow taller. "Please go away? Please erase every single moment I wasted on you?" She put her hands on her hips. "As you can see, I'm more than willing to employ a pleasantry or two if doing so will get rid of you." Her expression was a tangle of emotion, and hers weren't the only ones where Ivan was concerned. I had a turbulent past of my own involving him that I couldn't forget.

"Why Sky?" Raven turned her troubled gaze to Ivan's companion. "Why come here with him?"

"I'm sorry, Raven." Sky lifted her head, and Ivan shifted to regard her as if suddenly remembering her presence.

"I'm sure you are, honey." Raven softened her tone. "But you've got to know Ivan is bad news and given my past with him and how your brother is…"

"I needed to choose someone Lucky couldn't intimidate." Sky twisted her hands together. "He's actually nice to me. And I didn't think you would care now that you and Lucky are together. But I can see that it was a mistake to come here." She inhaled sharply, taking a sudden step back, her widened gaze registering something disturbing over my shoulder.

"Carl!" an angry masculine voice boomed. Raven jumped. I turned. The reason for her reaction and Sky's quickly became apparent: Lucky had arrived. His blue eyes blazing cobalt, he parted the gathered crowd with that single utterance. And he didn't roll up alone. Rocky was right beside him, his Keith Richards' circa 1960 haircut frazzled as if an electrical current had passed through it. The Welshman appeared to be just as fired up as the lead singer. The vanguard of combined fury marched straight for Ivan. But did it faze him?

Hardly.

"Spencer," Ivan acknowledged the lead singer with a chin lift. "Walsh." He leaned back on his heels and crossed his arms over his chest as he regarded both men. The veins on his biceps bulged with ready awareness, but his expression remained cool, unlike the two fire-breathing Dragons across from him.

"Step away from my sister," Lucky roared, snapping his head to the side where he apparently wanted Ivan to go. Arrows of his jet-black hair sliced into the arctic blue of his eyes. "Immediately," he ordered. "Or…"

"Or what?" Ivan glanced down the length of his arrogant nose at him.

"Or I shall be forced to remove you myself."

"Seriously?" Ivan turned his gaze to Raven. "Is this Neanderthal really the guy you've chosen to replace me? Your standards have sunk to an appallingly low level."

Actually, they had risen.

"And don't talk to her." Lucky's lips drew back from his teeth. He stepped closer, the distance between the two rivals diminishing as rapidly as their tempers rose.

"I'll do as I fucking please." Ivan's insolent brown gaze clashed with Lucky's incensed blue stare, though the Heavy Metal Enthusiast's frontman stood a fraction of an inch taller.

"Not as it regards Raven or my sister you won't." Lucky's arms were straight at his sides, his hands fisted.

"I think it's up to them to decide. Sky?" Ivan slashed his gaze to her. "Baby, you want some more of what I got, I'm willing. I definitely enjoyed the sweet taste of your mouth and those tits of yours."

Sky swayed. Raven blanched. Rocky growled, and I suddenly realized how quiet the club had become. The music had stopped and so had the dancing. The drama seemed to have mesmerized everyone. The bartenders were even immobile, their shakers frozen in mid-mix.

"Only you better make a decision soon." Ivan hooked a ringed thumb over his shoulder. "I'll wait for you a bit at the bar with my fans. Just keep in mind that I've got lots of options and a limited schedule." He deliberately glanced off Lucky's shoulder as he moved away.

"Lucky," Sky pleaded, putting her hand on his arm as he bowed up and glowered at his rival. "Don't. Please don't get into a fight on my account. I just wanted…"

"No, dearest. Stay out of this." Lucky wasn't in a reasonable mood. Though he was addressing her, his razor-sharpened stare remained targeted on Ivan. "I'll handle the situation as I see fit."

"But it's not up to you." Sky's words matched her expression. She was resolute in her mission—or else Ivan had already gotten to her. "I chose to be here with him. You have no right to interfere. I'm not a child. Stop treating me like one."

"Bugger this." A visible tremor rolled through Rocky's lean frame. He also had his gaze locked on the Heavy Metal lead singer. His long fingers flexed at his sides. Maybe he imagined wrapping them around Ivan's windpipe.

He wasn't the only one.

Letting out a measured breath, Rocky turned to Sky. She lifted her chin to meet the drummer's visage. "Your brother wouldn't treat you like a child if you weren't acting like one," he said, and her bright features flared in response to his harsh words. "You're not thinking straight." He shook his head, waves of his mahogany hair shadowing his amber eyes. "I can't believe you came here with a wanker like him and…"

"Can't believe I came here with him?" she cut in, her tone shrill. "Or can't believe anyone would want me?" Her bottom lip trembled, and one of the tears that had besieged her slid down her pale cheek.

Now I had two guys I wanted to strangle.

"Don't twist my words. You know that's not what I meant, sweetling." He reached for her but grasped nothing but air as she retreated.

"Don't touch me. You have no right to touch me. No right to judge me. No rights of any sort where I'm concerned." Sky swiped away the tear that had fallen and twisted away. I watched her follow Ivan. The frontman already had a throng of adoring women encircling him.

"Ivan only thinks with his dick," Raven announced and glanced back at me.

"I'm not so sure about that," I disagreed. Considering the current havoc, it was more likely Ivan Carl was a brilliant tactician. Sky in trouble. Lucky furious. Rocky livid. My own culpability regarding the situation tying my stomach in knots. This had obviously been a calculated ploy to get Raven's attention and cause a rift between her and Lucky.

And it had succeeded.

CHAPTER Two

"I'M GOING TO KILL HIM," LUCKY DETERMINED, turning toward the bar.

"No." Raven put her hand on his forearm. "I just need to talk to him. If I can make Ivan understand..."

"Absolutely not. I don't want you anywhere near him."

"But..."

"Not happening." He cut her off, his expression as unyielding as his words.

"It's over between us." Her gaze darted across his tight features. "You know that right?"

"I do, Angel." He sighed and glanced down at her hand in his arm as if just registering her touch on his skin. He squeezed his eyes shut a brief moment and when he reopened them he seemed more gathered.

"If you'll allow it." I cleared my throat. "Maybe I can talk some sense into her."

"Someone needs to." Rocky raked a hand through his mahogany

hair. He didn't need to clarify who he meant. His loaded gaze was locked on Sky. I wondered if she could feel it where she stood beside Ivan now, his arm draped around her.

"Then I'll do it." I straightened my shoulders as everyone turned to regard me.

"Would you?" The burnished gold in my best friend's gaze shone with the light of her relief. "She might listen to you."

"I'm certainly willing to try." I would do anything for Raven. She would do anything for me. Besides, I bore the brunt of the blame for the current situation. I needed to try to fix it.

"Yo, Ivan," I said casually pretending to be unaffected by him once I reached his spot at the bar.

"Marsha," he returned, swiveling to fully face me, his lips curving upward as he gave me a slow scan. "I remember that dress." My cheeks burned hot as his grin deepened. "Actually, it would be more correct to say I mostly remember you out of it."

I shook my head in a vain attempt to ward of the memory he had invoked. Ivan and I tangled together. Both breathing hard. My skin hot. My body on fire. He had shoved me against the wall inside the elevator. He had gathered the hem of my dress, this dress, in his powerful grip. He had yanked it above my waist... I slammed a lid on the rest. Just that brief peek into the past made my respirations erratic. I darted my gaze to the side not wanting him to see anything additional inside my eyes.

"Marsha." Sky touched my arm. "Are you ok?"

"Yes." I blinked and refocused. Sky's eyes were wide. She didn't know about my history with Ivan. It wasn't common knowledge. I didn't want it to be common knowledge. For my sake, sure. But also, because I worried airing the specific details might hurt Raven, even though my encounter with the lead singer had happened before the two of them had become a couple.

"Funny." I swallowed to clear the barbs that scraped my throat, the fiery fallout from remembering the way it had been with Ivan. "I didn't find anything about that night memorable."

Ivan's gaze turned flinty "Your memory's faulty then because you were gagging for it. Clawed my back like a tigress. But lie to yourself if you need to." Dismissing me, he spun back to the bar and knocked his knuckles on the wood top. "Another shot of tequila. Make it two," he added as the bartender acknowledged him. "The pretty blonde behind me lives in denial, but she's always reliably thirsty."

"No," I managed, focusing on my task rather than Ivan's gleaming hair. It was so much longer than the last time I had seen him. The coppery-brown strands that had once only skimmed the stud piercings in his ears now kissed his broad shoulders. Another memory careened through my mind reminding me of how whisper soft his hair had been against my inner thighs and his lips... "No." Recapturing the thought, I returned it to the vault where it belonged.

"No...? How so, sidekick? I'm sorry I don't understand. Are you refusing a drink? I don't recall you ever doing that." He arched a taunting brow. "And I don't recall my offer being phrased as a question, either."

Shit. He flustered me. "I don't want a drink." I clarified quickly.

"Hmmm." Ivan cocked his head and studied me with that off-putting intensity of his. "Then why *did* you come over here? What do you really want, Martian?" He pushed away from the bar, his muscle tee stretching notably tighter across his chiseled chest.

"I don't *want anything* from you."

"I don't believe you." The bronzed skin over his biceps flexed as he crooked his hands, beckoning to the throng of bodacious babes on either side of him, Sky sadly standing among them. "Whatever it is, Miss Denial, make it quick. As you can see I'm busy at the moment.

I could add you to my *to-do* list for later. But..." He trailed off, his lids lowering as he ran his gaze over me. "I've already sampled what you have to offer." My attention diverted to his mouth and the silver hoop that pierced his firm bottom lip. "So, you'll have to up your game to tempt me a second time."

"What?" Feeling lightheaded, I lifted my gaze to discover that his eyes were a darker brown now and swirled like an ancient whirlpool in Greek mythology. Whether the dangerous depths of Charybdis or the destructive rocks of Scylla, there was something of both in Ivan. Something, if I were being honest, I had once found compelling. Something I had once considered worth the risk, but not anymore. Ivan Carl was a prince of pandemonium. A brutal vortex that drew you in and broke you on its jagged edges.

"I'm done talking to you." I gave him a dismissive wave though I suspected that the emotions rocking inside me regarding him were beyond escape. I turned to Sky, noting the narrowing of Ivan's eyes as I did and taking some satisfaction in knowing that he didn't like to be blown off any more than I did.

"Listen, honey. I think you're making a mistake. One I unfortunately have familiarity with. Ivan's fun for the short term but trust me when I tell you that the fallout's not worth the momentary sensations. Would you mind stepping away with me for just a second, so we can speak in private?"

"Ok." She nodded, and I exhaled my relief. Taking her hand, I led her toward the back hall by the ladies' restroom. I caught Raven's eye on the way past the crowded dance floor. She was on the other side of it with Lucky. The lead singer had his cell to his ear, and his dark brows were furrowed. Raven pointed to herself. I shook my head. I would have liked her company, but I had made this mess. I could clean it up.

I hope I can clean it up, I self-corrected.

ROCK *Fuck* CLUB BOOK 3   43

My best friend had enough on her plate, and I was afraid Lucky was probably just now receiving the untimely news that the Dragons were back on tour starting tonight.

"Sky," I began, turning to face her when we reached the relative privacy of the hall. "Ivan is..." I paused to tuck a strand of her brown hair behind her ear, noting how different she looked with her dramatic eye makeup and bright lipstick. Stunning, actually. "Well, he's not a good choice for you. Not even for a hookup."

"I know you're worried," she disagreed. "But it'll be ok. I know what I'm doing."

"No, I don't think you do."

"He's confident." She bobbed her head. "Cocky. Incredibly handsome. And a match for my brother. He's not afraid of him or anyone else."

"Yeah for sure all of that is true, but when we talked I had no idea who you had in mind. Ivan's not only those things, he's a whole lot of trouble. The kind of trouble that can wreck you." His sensitivity drew you in. It made you forget the danger. Like the ships that risked the Strait of Messina. "He has a past, a hurtful one. With Raven..."

"She doesn't care about him."

"She doesn't." At least, I didn't think she did. "Not in the present tense, but..."

"Who am I going to pick, Marsha? Who but someone like Ivan will stand up to Lucky? Or to Rocky?"

"I don't know, honey, but you can't go from having sex twice to messing around with someone of his caliber."

"What if I already have?"

"No way." My eyes grew wide.

She crossed her arms over her chest and glanced to the side as someone exited the restroom, murmured an excuse me and scooted past us.

"It doesn't really matter if I have or I haven't." She returned her jittery gaze to mine. "He's already served his purpose."

"To prove to yourself and Rocky that you're over him?"

"Yes." She nodded tightly.

"I'd say he did more than that. Rocky's beyond furious. Your brother, too."

"They're lads. They scream. They shout. They blow off steam, then Bob's your uncle, they're over it." She touched my arm. "But you and Ivan." She searched my features. "The things he said to you. They hurt you," she decided. "I didn't know. I'm sorry." She ducked her head to maintain my gaze. I had lowered my chin. She had seen too much.

"It's ok, Sky." I swallowed the lie. So many today. It made me feel bloated. "It's his fault, the hurt he caused. Not yours."

"I didn't mean to upset you." She softly touched my arm in apology.

"You didn't. Ivan on the other hand…it doesn't take much to set off the fireworks between us." We were as combustible together as the fuel in those vintage muscle cars he and his best friend liked to race around Texas Motor Speedway. I blew out a breath. "Obviously. I do better when I just forget he exists."

"I'll go back out and tell him it's over." Her expression was earnest and open. Two things I'd never ever be again. "And I'll make it clear that he needs to piss off."

"That would be good."

"Well, there you have it." She turned to go, but I stopped her.

"Sky, hold up."

"Yes, Mars." She glanced back at me.

"You know you really didn't need Ivan at all tonight to stand up to your brother or Rocky. You just need to believe in yourself."

CHAPTER
Three

I FOLLOWED SKY BACK INTO THE CLUB. The music pumped at a pace that seemed to match her determined march. The crowd that parted for her seemed to close on me as I tried to keep up. By the time I'd woven my way through the obstacles, she had already reached Ivan. Apparently, she had already said her piece. His handsome face hardened, and when he noticed me, the force of his displeasure rocked me backward on my platform heels.

"I'm sorry," Sky said, and his gaze returned to her. "I didn't mean to lead you on. I like you. It's just that..."

"It's just that *she* got to you." His eyes clashed with mine again. "Told you a bunch of bullshit, I'm sure. She's full of it, you know." He shifted his attention back to Sky. I started to tell him that he had the market on bullshit cornered, but he barreled on before I could. "Marsha lives in a world of make believe that revolves around one guy. The only one she considered to be worthy of her. The way I see it, she's a miserable bitch who can't stand for anyone else to be happy if she can't."

"Marsha isn't like that," Sky stated firmly, giving me a conciliatory look. My affection for her soared in that moment. The fingers I had curled inward loosened.

"She's exactly like that," Ivan refuted, and my fingers retightened. Anger and maybe more than a little hurt spilled into the toxic stew that constituted my emotions regarding him. "Ask her about the lie she told to try to bust up Raven and me when we were just starting out."

"It wasn't a lie," I whispered. A beautiful new life was not a lie. It was a miracle that had been ripped away from me. My vision tunneled. Pulling in a sharp breath, I staggered backward.

"Mars." Sky turned away from Ivan and moved toward me, stretching out her hand. The room spun. My legs wobbled. The floor started to rush up, but suddenly arms I knew well and could always rely on banded around me.

"Go away, Ivan," Raven told him.

"Now wait a motherfucking minute, Raven. You need to hear me out."

"No." I felt my bestie's arms tighten. I clung to her. I let her defend me. I gave her that play. The one I had denied her since I had chosen to keep the truth about the pregnancy from her. "There's nothing left to say that will change anything."

"What if I told you I still care about you?"

"If you cared about me you would never have fucked another woman when we were in a committed relationship."

Yay, Raven, I cheered silently. The hurt from his betrayal no longer had the upper hand, nor did he. In this moment, she ruled unopposed.

"You don't know the whole story. You never let me fully explain."

"There's no explanation that would justify that betrayal. There's no reason for me to hear another word about it. There's certainly no excuse for what you just said about Marsha. You were wrong to turn her away in the past after what she revealed to you. And you and I were *always* wrong for each other. If I hadn't been in such a fog because of my brother I would have realized it sooner. This woman right here." She wrapped her arms tighter around me. "She always has my back, and I have hers. She's family." Tears burned my eyes. I squeezed her arm to let her know my feelings were the same as hers. "Lucky and I, his sister, his bandmates, we're a family, too. That's something you and I never could have been." She drew in a deep breath and with her holding me so close I felt her chest expand to accommodate the extra air.

"Thank you, Raven." My voice was thick as I contemplated the deep bond time and our experiences has forged between us.

"For nothing, Mars. Just keeping it real."

"You're making a big mistake," Ivan declared, thunderclouds gathering in his eyes. "If you'd just let me speak to you alone..."

"You and I are in the past, Ivan. I have a new life now. A better one. A better man." She glanced over her shoulder to where I noticed Lucky stood with his arms crossed over his chest. "My present and my future are with him." Her words were a bolt that seemed to strike the center of her Ivan's chest. He absorbed the blow without flinching, but I saw it, his eyes going as inky dark as a yearning heart absent hope.

I could relate.

Maybe Ivan did still care about Raven in his own dysfunctional way. But I don't think he got until that exact moment how well and truly over it was between them.

CHAPTER
four

"Lucky is as protective of you as he is of his sister. So, you gotta tell me." In the backseat of the taxi with Sky and Raven, I bumped my bestie's shoulder as the driver steered the vehicle through the drizzle slickened streets. "How in the world did you convince him to let you talk to Ivan?"

"I have my ways." She arched a meaningful brow.

"You promised him sexual favors." I guessed immediately.

"Sure. After all, it's a promise with benefits that go both ways." Her golden eyes turned a little fallen angel tarnished as she seemed to contemplate those benefits.

"I made a shamble of things, haven't I?" Sky reached out to touch my hand and then Raven's. "I'm terribly sorry."

"It's ok, honey." Raven squeezed Sky's fingers in return just as the driver flicked on his blinker and turned onto a billboard and scaffold lined thoroughfare. The Port Authority was on Eighth Avenue where the tour buses awaited. "Ivan is good looking, persuasive and charming when he chooses to be. I understand what you were trying to do. But in the future consult Mars or me before you decide to go out with somebody we both have a history with. Ok?"

"I will." The taxi pulled in close to the curb and slowed. "But I did talk to Marsha. I just didn't…um…" She chewed on her bottom lip. "Mention exactly who I had in mind."

"Fifteen dollars." The cab driver swiveled around to inform us.

"I've got it," I said, sliding my credit card out of my wristlet and swiping it using the touch screen display to close out the fare. Thanks to my bestie and my job with WMO, I now had enough wiggle room on my credit card to afford incidentals.

"Where are the guys?" Sky asked, pressing in closer to us as a gust of cool air blew in from the Hudson.

"They should already be on the bus," Raven replied. "They're meeting with their manager." She glanced down at her cell as it chimed. "Lucky says to go in. Just past the information booth we should take the escalator up to the second floor. The bus is parked at gate 211."

We entered the building quickly, eager to get out of the wind and rain. Inside, despite the lateness of the hour there were tons of people milling around. Several turned to look at us.

"Can you lead the way, Mars?" Raven linked her arm with mine, slid a pair of shades on and ducked her chin to her chest. A recognizable celebrity, she wasn't exactly dressed to blend in at the moment.

"You bet." I glanced over at Sky. Her eyes were wide as she took in the activity around us. "Coming honey?"

"Oh, yes." She stepped closer and hooked her right arm to my left. "This place reminds me of Waterloo Station back home."

"I haven't ever been overseas," I admitted as I steered us along the recommended route, my entourage moving along with me, dodging fellow passengers and piles of luggage.

"Me, neither," Raven said. "I'm looking forward to the Noir tour."

"Which city are you most excited to visit?" Sky asked her as we separated to step onto the escalator one by one.

"Paris."

"Me, too!" Sky returned, and I caught her dreamy expression and Raven's wistful one as I rotated on the step above them. My stomach twisted, too. Now that I was filming the RFC documentary on this side of the Atlantic, I wondered if I would be welcome to tag along. Considering all the trouble Lucky had given Raven, his own girlfriend about traveling with the band, I had my doubts.

"Hey, you ok, bestie?" Raven queried as we reached the second level.

"I guess." I stepped off and turned to face her. "But I just wondered..."

"Oh no!" Sky exclaimed. I spun around. My eyes widened when I followed the direction of her gaze. Apparently, Ivan wasn't done causing trouble tonight.

CHAPTER five

"I'T'S TIME FOR YOU TO MOVE ALONG," Rocky growled, circling Ivan, his fists up in a boxer's stance.

"Remind me again why I should care what you think." His attitude and his expression belligerent, Ivan moved to keep his opponent in view. "But maybe it's better that you're using your words now instead of your fists." The frontman grinned despite his busted lip and bloody chin. "'Cause even though I can go back and forth like this all night, it looks to me like you're wearing down."

"You're not fit to even touch her." Rocky shifted. The lamp on a twenty-foot-tall pole rained light down on him. His right cheek sported a nasty cut and the eye above it was swollen. His hair was drenched. With sweat or mist I didn't know for sure. Probably a combination of both.

"What gives you that idea?" Ivan flicked his gaze our way. "I think she likes me quite a lot if the way she moaned when I touched her tits was any indication." The Welshman's arm shot out without warning.

His fist connected with the lead singer's midsection. Ivan expelled the contents of his lungs and doubled over. Rocky drew back. Turning his head, Ivan peered through his damp lashes at Raven. "Your family's got a violent streak, baby. You sure this is where you wanna be?"

"You're provoking him."

"Anger reveals the truth. Love conceals it."

"This isn't one of your songs, Ivan. It's my life, and I believe I already told you to stay out of it."

Ivan straightened, and finger combed a saturated swath of his hair back from his abused face. His usually graceful movements were notably awkward. I got the impression that he was tiring, too, and I wondered how many blows he and the Welshman had already traded.

"Why are you here, Ivan?" I stepped into the fray and the circle of light that surrounded the two men. Both turned to face me, but it was the lead singer's regard that made every cell in my body hyperaware.

"Just righting some wrongs," he answered.

"If you're trying to make up to Sky, you might want to reconsider your methods," Raven said sarcastically.

"I think that subject is at an impasse. There were other things I wanted to get out in the open once and for all."

"Such as?" Raven moved beside me.

"I know you have a bad opinion of me. I know you think I screwed over your best friend. But I don't think you know the truth about how she treated me."

"What are you talking about?" Raven gave me a worried glance.

"The night she concocted the pregnancy thing. Did she ever tell you what happened before that?"

"Nothing happened before," I countered, though that wasn't true. My stomach churned with unease.

"You having your tongue down my throat wasn't nothing. I'm pretty sure Raven would agree. Wouldn't you, baby?"

"Ok, so I kissed you," I clarified. "So, what."

"You kissed Ivan when I was dating him?" Raven asked, her eyes wide.

"Yes but…"

"Why didn't you ever tell me?" Raven's expression was confused, her gaze pinched now with hurt.

"Because you and he were just starting out and because it was just a stupid kiss. It didn't mean anything."

"If it didn't mean anything then why didn't you tell me?" Raven asked.

"Because I was afraid you might react just like this. That knowing about it might hurt you."

"Why would it hurt her if it didn't mean anything?" Ivan offered unhelpfully, his lips curved.

"Grr." I lunged for his smug face, my fingers curled. I wanted to claw his mocking eyes out.

"Uh-uh, Tigress." He captured my wrists, his much larger hands encircling them. His rings bit into my skin. The metal around his fingers was cold, but his flesh felt hot against mine. Tension crackled between us. Combustible tension. Our ignited gazes locked and held.

"I should have told you before today." Ivan released me to address her. Guilt, desire, rejection, familiar but unwanted feelings related to him assailed me. "But I know how important she is to you," he continued. "And I knew telling you *she* came onto *me* would ruin your friendship. Not to mention the whole fake pregnancy scenario."

"Marsha didn't fabricate the pregnancy." Raven's voice was thready. Something flashed in Ivan's gaze in response to her confirmation, but I didn't have time to analyze.

"I was overwhelmed. Confused. It's complicated, Raven," I insisted, but she just kept right on talking to Ivan like she couldn't hear me.

"So, you thought because Marsha came onto you, that she made up a story about a baby to coerce you to sleep with her?"

"Yes, to break us up," Ivan confirmed. "She wanted nothing to do with me until there was a 'you and a me'. It makes perfect sense. I'm sure you agree." Yet as he stepped toward Raven, his tattooed arm outstretched, he also glanced back at me. A trick of the light and the rain almost made it appear that he was conflicted.

"Then the joke's on you because Marsha's the fuck and go type. She doesn't do sleepovers."

He gave me a funny look. I shook my head quickly, my gaze beseeching. There had been extenuating circumstances the night I had been with him. His brow dipped. He turned back to Raven. "You need to listen to me." He tried to reach for her.

"Don't touch me." She backed away from him. I let out a relieved sigh and moved toward her right side, my usual supportive position beside her.

"You, either." Raven's words stopped me cold. "You betrayed me."

"I didn't betray you, Raven." I didn't recognize my voice. It was so tenuous. The bond between us suddenly felt thin and stretched. "It's not the way he's making it sound."

"It's exactly like that," Ivan confirmed, crushing years of friendship under his cavalier heel. "There's more. More that I kept from you because I knew how much you cared about her. Like the way she watched me whenever your back was turned."

"That was before..." I trailed off. I had been about to say that had been before the baby. He and Raven had dated before I had realized I was pregnant. So many times in the early days of their relationship, I had wanted to caution her about Ivan because…"Besides, if I ever gave you that type of glance." I lifted my chin. "It was only in response to the ones you gave me."

My words were a match I should not have struck. Right before my eyes I watched my friendship with Raven erupt in flames, the once indestructible connection between us set ablaze as if it were nothing more than a crepe paper ribbon.

"Raven, I'm sorry. That came out wrong." I stretched out my hands, imploring her to listen only to discover that she had retreated further than I had realized.

"Jimmy Price," she reminded me in a strangled tone.

"I was only fourteen." Ignoring the accusation in her eyes and how off center it made me feel, I tried to explain. "My mom had just left us."

"He was *my* boyfriend." Her eyes glowed. "And what about Elliott Shafer?"

My stomach clamped. I hadn't realized she had known about him. Had someone at school said something? It had only been a moment of weakness under the bleachers. It had meant less than nothing, a futile attempt to silence my father's hurtful words.

"You said you were over him," I explained.

"So many times I shared confidences with you about guys." Her expression revealed that she had retreated from me emotionally as well as physically. "I wonder how many of those you used to facilitate your next hookup."

"None, Raven. Please listen to me. Please give me a chance to speak. I can explain."

"And set myself up to be played again? By a woman who's supposed to have my back instead of screwing my boyfriends behind it?" She made a low scoffing sound. "No, Marsha. No more feeling sorry for you. No more chances." She turned her back to me.

My throat closed. My heart stumbled. Fear rose within me. By the time I managed to speak again she already had one hand on the door to the bus.

"You can't seriously believe Ivan over me." The glance she gave me over her shoulder before she entered the bus told me that she did.

I dropped to my knees.

My father's right. Nothing inside of me is right.

The rough asphalt tore open the skin over my knees, but I barely registered it. It was only flesh deep pain. It would eventually heal.

But this?

I wasn't so sure.

Raven was more than just my best friend. The bond we shared was the reason I believed my father was wrong about me. My arms banded around myself, a position my body automatically assumed after the numerous times he had laid into me.

Unlovable. Just like my mother.

"Marsha."

I looked up, my vision awash in regret, though he wasn't the one I wanted to see.

"I've opened the baggage compartment," Lucky stated flatly. His austere stance and visage reminded me of my father after he doled out the discipline he always insisted I had earned. "I've made my decision. You're off the bus. You've upset Raven. You've also proven to be a bad influence on Sky. She told me about your part in what happened tonight with Ivan. You'll keep your distance from her. You'll stay away from Raven, too. From all of us. It's for the best."

I didn't respond. His words hurt, but not as badly as hers. A sob escaped.

Miraculous that any sound could escape. My ribs felt like they were squeezing my lungs and crushing my heart. A shadow fell over me.

"Ivan," I said as an explanation for all that ailed me. Easier to blame him than myself. His form wavered through the sheen of wet filming my eyes.

"I didn't mean for this..."

"Mars," a voice called, and I turned my head toward it. Barbara Michaels crouched down in front of me. "Here." Her blond hair appeared to be dark in the rain. Had I only imagined Ivan? She stretched out her delicate hand. "C'mon. Take it." She wiggled her fingers. "You can ride on the bus with me and the crew. There's too much room. You'll be doing us a favor."

"Ok." I gave her my hand. It felt like a significant decision. Or maybe it was just that I didn't know what else to do, and I had to do something. She helped me stand, and she held me steady when I wobbled on legs that felt too weak to hold me.

"Ow." I blinked as a bright light stabbed my sensitive eyes.

"Shut them off," Barbara insisted as I swayed. "No more filming, Ignacio. Please. She's done. Can't you see she's done? I need you to help me get her inside out of the rain."

Sudden darkness descended. No, I wasn't losing consciousness. I was too fucking resilient to take that easy route. It was just the video camera light being switched off. One of the worst moments of my life had apparently just been recorded for the world to see. Everyone would get to watch me take the shit end of the stick I deserved.

Welcome to Rock Fuck Club: Season Two.

CHAPTER SIX

"Don't you think you've had enough?" Barbara asked me from her position across the small banquette table.

"No," I declared. There wasn't enough tequila on the entire planet to fill the chasm that had cracked wide open inside of me from losing Raven's affection.

"Maybe you should just call her."

"She won't listen." I had betrayed her. Truths were out that should have stayed hidden. In her mind it was a closed case. She had never talked to Ivan again after his betrayal, except for that one happenstance encounter in Kansas City. It wouldn't be any different with me. The one person I had counted on, the one I thought would never abandon me was out of my life.

My eyes burned and not just from the tequila fumes. I snagged the bottle of Cuervo. It was unsurprisingly light. I sloshed another medicinal splash in the shot glass and knocked it back. I didn't even feel its heat going down because I wasn't just empty inside anymore. I was becoming comfortably numb.

I glanced out the window. Through the tinted glass I watched a shadow of a car zip past. The WMO bus eked along at a much more lethargic pace.

"She might. You won't know if you don't try." I squinted my eyes to refocus on Barbara and the interior of the bus that was nearly an exact replica of the Dragons'. It followed a typical layout: a cab where the driver sat, a front lounge with two leather couches, a banquette and a kitchenette, a section for the stackable bunks with a tiny bathroom, and a back lounge with two smaller couches that could be brought together to form a double bed. I was slumped on one bench of the banquette. Barbara was on the other one, her spine ramrod straight. Her expression remained disapproving. We had been round and round the same circle. She kept trying to talk me out of what I planned to do, but I wasn't going to be dissuaded.

Raven's rejection triggered a core issue inside of me. When I felt cornered, hurt or in a situation where I had no control I got it back using the one thing I knew always worked for me.

Sex.

Sure, my plan was ill-advised. Dangerous even. I got that Barbara was afraid for me. Maybe deep down I was afraid for me, too. But I was low on reasons why I should give a fuck anymore.

I curled my fingers around the empty shot glass, gripping it so tight my skin blanched. Now more than ever I needed the numbness and the sense of courage the booze afforded.

"Let me have that." Her gaze imploring, Barbara reached across the table and tapped my hand. "C'mon, Marsha. Let it go."

I willed my fingers to unclasp. The instant I did she snatched the glass and the Cuervo bottle, placing them out of my reach on the bench beside her.

"You'll think better without that stuff fogging your brain," she explained, shaking her head in resignation at me. More of her blond hair escaped her messy bun as I frowned back at her. "I know. I understand some of what's going on inside your head. The need for an escape. But alcohol isn't the answer. I know. I started drinking when my parents separated. They ended up sending me to a therapist."

"I'm sorry," I told her as the bus suddenly lurched to a halt. "I'm sure that was a shitty time." I turned to glance out the window again, noting the bar and the marquee. John Got Busted was the headliner. I had googled the closest music venue on our route south. It was twisted that I chose him, but it felt wrongly right that he would be the one to inaugurate my season.

The parking lot we had pulled into was packed with vehicles. We settled for a spot in the very back of it. The film crew would have to haul the equipment a long way before they filmed my proposition. But though I was concerned for them, that was the least of my worries tonight.

"Alcohol wasn't the only problem." Barbara had more to say, and I swiveled to face her. "I had some other serious things to address, too." She dropped her gaze, and her inability to maintain eye contact made me wonder what those additional problems had been and if they continued to plague her. "I thought my parents not getting along was my fault." She lifted her gaze. "After the therapist helped me work through that, she suggested a stay at my grandmother's place to decompress and give myself some time to process." She reached across the table and squeezed my hand. "Maybe you should give yourself some time to let things sink in, too."

"I did the whole shrink thing." Twenty-eight days in-patient. I withdrew my fingers from hers. Her sharing her history was brave, and the comforting gesture was genuinely sweet. But I wasn't encouraged or comforted. I just missed Raven.

"Counseling didn't get me anywhere," I bit out bitterly. "But here and alone." Without anyone who had a real clue how messed up I was inside. "Well, fuck that shit. From now on I'm doing therapy my own way."

"I DON'T CARE who the hell you are." The stubborn-faced security guard crossed his arms over the block lettering on his chest. "No one gets backstage without a pass."

"What's going on, Marco?" A middle-aged man wearing an inquisitive expression stuck his head out the side door the security guard had propped open. He gave me and the WMO crew behind me a once over.

"I'm Marsha West," I informed him, projecting more confidence than I felt. So much more. "I'm with WMO. We're filming the second season of Rock Fuck Club."

"You want John to agree to be part of another one of those? Are you cracked?" Yet even as he said the words, I noted the calculating gleam that lit up his otherwise nondescript eyes. "Don't you know what the first girl put him through?"

"What *he* put Raven through," I corrected. I couldn't redeem myself in her eyes. But maybe I could administer some retribution and get her attention. If I were going down in flames, I might as well burn brightly. The whole idea made perfect sense or at least it did inside my tequila addled mind.

"I'm offering him a chance right here, right now to change his part of the narrative." Unlikely he could pull that off. The rapper pretended to be badass, but a badasss wouldn't force himself on a woman. I certainly wasn't going to allow him to force me to do anything I didn't want to do. I was in charge of my season. The crew was with me. They would stay with me all the way to the finale. Of course the climactic part would have to be edited out. Even TV-MA had boundaries.

"Who is it?" JGB appeared, wedging his lean body into the gap. His bleach blond hair was matted to his head. He looked like he had already been rolling around in a bed with someone. "What are you doing here?" he asked me, his tone full of suspicion. His light green eyes widened as he noted the film crew. Apparently, he didn't have much interest in me. Admittedly, I wasn't in top form tonight. His lack of interest was an arrow to my ego, but I took it without letting on. It certainly wasn't the only wound tonight. "Where's Raven?" he inquired.

"Not here."

Maybe not ever by my side again, I thought.

The tequila effect was waning. I got right to the point. "It's just me. Marsha West." I stuck out my tits. "The first season's over and done. It's my turn now. I don't do skits and shit. But I'm ready to fuck my first rock star…stars. And I choose you, Reggie and the bassist." All the guys that had mishandled Raven during her season.

"Really?" His gaze dipped to my chest. My tits overflowed the top of the black leather demi bra and the center with the crisscross laces. I'd paired it with a matching skirt, some fishnet hose, a pair of garters and spiked heels. Usual groupie attire. Nothing subtle, but then again, John Got Busted wasn't the subtle type. "Hmmm," he mused. "You're not exotic like she is, but I guess I'll have a go. I'm in a charitable mood."

Ouch.

"Alright." I lifted my chin. "But we film on *my* bus with *my* crew present. I don't want there to be any questions about consent this time around. You get me?"

"You'll get me, sweet thing, then we'll see." His eyes hardened, resembling peridots or more accurately the green of a common grass snake. "And you'll get the others, too. But just to say, if you aren't really up for it, the festivities, it'll be you who looks weak this time."

After JGB closed the door, I led the crew back through the parking lot. It hadn't thinned out much even though the show was over. JGB attracted a hardcore, dedicated crowd. Angry and sullen like their leader, they fed off his energy. He harnessed it and returned it to them from the stage. Afterward, he jazzed on the leftover adrenaline...and coke. I'd noted the signs when he had approached Raven during her filming. I noted it again tonight. Same bloodshot eyes and dilated pupils. Same darkly energetic aura. Like the vibe on the episode of *Tides of Conquest* when Rasha had been locked in the dungeon with Sir Dante, the sadistic knight who got off on torturing others.

I swallowed hard thinking about what was coming for me next or more accurately who. My eyes were large when we returned to the bus.

"Hey," Barbara greeted from the front lounge. She studied me a long beat.

"He turned you down?" Looking hopeful, she glanced around at the crew before she returned her gaze to me.

"No. He's definitely coming."

"Oh." Barbara didn't attempt to hide her dismay. I pretended not to see it like I pretended not to note it on the individual faces of the others as they filed past us to set up in the back lounge.

"Marsha, please reconsider." Barbara touched my arm. I glanced down at her warm fingers on my cool skin before dragging my gaze up to her face. Her unique seafoam green eyes brimmed with concern on my behalf, but sadly they weren't the golden ones I wanted them to be.

"JGB will be here shortly." Given the irrational mood I was in, her caution only spurred me on. "You might want to make yourself scarce." I glanced out the window as someone, a male someone, laughed loudly outside. "That's probably them."

"Them?" she questioned, her eyes rounded.

"JGB, Reggie, his drummer and his bassist." I couldn't recall the bassist's name. Not that it mattered.

"Three guys?" Her face blanched like my fingers had when I had wrapped them around my shot glass earlier. "All together? In one night?"

"Yeah." I nodded once to confirm.

"I don't think that's a good idea," she whispered.

She was right. It was a terrible idea, especially with these particular three. "But that's the point. Right?" I brazened. "To be so wicked it's good. To shock. To tantalize. It's WMO programming at its best." And me at my worst. I pictured how the cameras in the back lounge should be angled to show just enough skin. Ignacio, the director, probably already had them set up that way. After all, he had taught me what I knew about those things during season one. "I need to have Carla check my makeup." The beautiful statuesque black woman was almost as talented as Sky with low level lighting makeup.

"Alright, I guess." Barbara stepped aside so I could scoot past her in the narrow aisle between the two leather couches.

"Marsha," she called. "Hold on a minute."

"Yeah?" I turned to glance back at her.

"Give them a show if you want to, but don't give them the best of you."

"I won't," I stated firmly. I never gave any guy that part of me. Well, maybe I had given it to Hawk, but he had taken it with him. All that remained now was the dregs.

"Spread." From his position behind me, JGB kicked my legs apart.

"No." This was the same sexual setup I had been in with my gym hookup, but I was even less turned on. I rotated my head to glance at the rapper. Light shone in my eyes because of Les, the flower-power gaffer/grip. I couldn't see his long grey ponytail or his rainbow tie dyed shirt through the glare, but I knew he was there. Ernie, the audio tech, too, wearing his usual ball cap and thick glasses. He was as an unrecognizable as his counterpart. But I knew he had his sound boom mic lowered on a pole to catch every gasp and groan.

"This isn't working for me," I complained. How had Raven done it? JGB had no finesse. His fingers were grasping. I had endured about all the fumbling I could take. And there had been a lot of it before he had managed to get me naked. The process had hardly elicited a thrill. I wasn't even really self-conscious in front of everyone because of the amount of tequila I'd consumed. I remained willing if not enthusiastic. I knew I was present, but I wasn't into it. It was all I could do to continue the charade which deep down was a cry for help. But would Raven even recognize it? Would she even care? A torrent of emotions coursed through me. I restrained them, but the pressure to release them kept building.

JGB narrowed his eyes. "If you were her..."

"But I'm not her," I shut him down the way I slammed down all my emotions. "No making comparisons." I didn't need any more cuts in my psyche. Not that his were lethal ones. "But since you seem to like games where you're in charge, how about we recreate the setup you had planned for her that night?" I shielded my eyes. "Ernie?" I called.

"Yeah, Marsha. I'm here. In the right corner by the closet."

I turned my head that way. "You got any leftover zip ties?"

66   MICHELLE MANKIN

"Sure do, darlin'."

"Alright." I dropped my hand and returned my gaze to JGB. "How about I tie you up? I'll ride you if your cock is suited up, and I'll take on the other two at the same time as long as they're doing stuff I like. Sound good?"

He totally went for it. They all did. I knew they would. My ego might have taken a beating, but I knew what most guys liked. You couldn't help but learn to be adaptive when you'd lost your virginity as young as I had.

Moments later, moments that dragged on like an eternity, the logistics and positioning of bodies had been worked out to comply with Rock Fuck Club's TV-MA rating. JGB was naked, flat on his back on the foldout bed with his wrists shackled together over his head. Straddling him, I had my thighs over his narrow hips. I felt his eager cock jump beneath me.

"God's you're hot," Reggie said, his expression one of stark hunger. His rough ropy Rastafarian dreads scraped my breasts. Reggie straddled the rapper also, only higher up. Facing me, he began to stroke my tits and dropped his head to suck on my neck.

"That feels good," I praised, arching into his caresses. I felt my cunt softening. Now. Finally. We were getting somewhere interesting.

"Kiss her," the bassist ordered. His ball cap was off now along with all of his clothes. He had a lean body like JGB, but he had dark red hair. "I wanna suck on her tits. They're fucking phenomenal." My inner thighs became slick. Why didn't guys get how much of a turn on it was to be praised?

Firm lips pressed to mine. Others latched onto my nipples. Light on the suction at first, then stronger pulls with erratic flicks of a warm wet tongue.

"Yes." I affirmed against Reggie's mouth. "More. I like it." His face wedged in between Reggie's body and mine, the bassist complied. Reggie twisted his torso to grab the bottle of Cuervo from the nightstand. He offered me a swig straight from the bottle. He tipped it up to my lips. I chugged an unhealthy amount. And then things got really interesting. Reggie poured tequila on my tits. The bassist lapped at it, licking every rivulet and following every drop. Then Reggie refastened his mouth to mine. No subtlety. No soft build up. He thrust his tongue between my lips while the bassist...well the bassist went low...on me. Laps. Circles. And lots of tongue.

"Yes." I moaned as it built. "Yes. Don't stop."

"Baby, I don't want to stop," the bassist groaned. "You taste so good." More wet heat soaked his fingers as he swiped through my swollen folds. "But let JGB slide in your pussy now. I like to watch, and you can watch me if you like. We can all come together. All three of us. Yeah?" His heavy red hair shadowed his features and his eyes were so dark now they were black.

"Yes." I kept my gaze on him. JGB might be the leader of the band, but the bassist knew what he was doing in this set up, or he certainly did with me. I pulled in an anticipatory breath when he repositioned on the side of the bed. He stroked the underside of my breasts while Reggie sucked hard on the tips. I shut my eyes, threw back my head and gave into the decadence of it all, barely noting the lights lowering and the intense spots shutting down. Nor did I care about the shuffling of retreating feet. I just surrendered to the sensations. Being lifted beneath my ribs by a strong grip. A hard sheathed cock sliding inside me. Sucking, delicious and warm. Firm long laps and pulls at one tit and then the other. Bucking from beneath me when my languid riding rhythm was too slow.

Heavy breathing filled the air.

"Fuck her faster."

I opened my eyes.

Reggie released my right tit, leaving it wet and throbbing like my core. Lifting onto his knees, he quickly positioned his cock between my breasts. He pressed them together. I arched into his hands, willingly. Oh, so willingly. This was so wrong, but it felt so good to be the focus of not just one but three very wicked men.

"I love your tits." Reggie began pumping his cock between my breasts and thrumming the tips with his thumbs at the same relentless pace JGB was hammering me.

"So good. Yes." I cracked open my heavy lids. Reggie's pelvis was in front of me. The head of his engorged cock was purple and glistened with precum. I wet my lips.

"Fuck," the bassist groaned. I turned to look at him. On his knees beside the bed, he was jacking off into his hands.

"So sexy." I closed my eyes again. JGB's thrust were violent. I took them, each hard unrelenting thrust. "Yes. Oh, fuck, yes. Harder," I begged, feeling it. The tightening of my nipples. Each brush of Reggie's thumbs. I panted each time JGB thrust into me. My pussy tightened around his cock. Each time I heard the slick, slippery sound of the bassist's hand gliding over his shaft, the hot heat inside of me rose. Swish. Thrust. Glide. Repeat.

"Fuck," Reggie said.

"Ahh," JGB groaned.

"Yes, shit, yes," the bassist moaned.

My moan melded to his. I thrashed on JGB's cock as it hit me.

Wave after wave of hot pleasure.

Wrong, it was wrong. I knew it was wrong.

But for a brief fleeting moment, it felt right.

CHAPTER
seven

THE DAWN ROSE AS WE CONTINUED speeding along interstate 95 on our way south. I clicked off the episode of *Tides of Conquest* and turned away from my laptop. Out the bus window, the pink and violet hued sunrise was beautiful, but I didn't find much joy in witnessing it alone. They say burdens are halved by sharing them. Well, beauty was diminished by at least that much, too.

I picked up my phone and checked to see if the connection remained good. Five bars, yet no calls or texts from Raven. I sighed.

Every hour dragged. Re-watching episodes I had already seen didn't make them go by faster. And the more time that passed without hearing from her the more I feared I never would.

As far as the emptiness inside me that never went away?

It was still there. And I feared it might be expanding.

What would be left of me if it didn't stop?

And would I even care?

Would anyone?

70   MICHELLE MANKIN

A sleep deprived, panicked laugh escaped that sounded a lot more like a sob. Regret lodged inside my burning throat like a hot coal. *Keep it together, Marsha*, I told myself. The things I knew I shouldn't do, but did anyway, they took away the pain at least for a while. So what if deep down they were cries for help?

Enacting a moratorium inside my head regarding any further bullshit psychoanalysis, I clicked onto the Rock Fuck Club Facebook page and busied myself tweaking a few unflattering descriptions on my post ranking the controversial rapper. Where Raven had written about what she had learned from each of her hookups, I planned to review them. In JGB's case the message was clear: do not go there.

My convoluted attempt to send Raven a message saying that I had gotten the upper hand on JGB on her behalf, that I was making him pay for what he did to her, had obviously failed to register.

She no longer saw me.

She no longer heard me.

More than likely she no longer cared.

"Morning," Barbara mumbled, shuffling into the front lounge wearing a faded robe and powder pink slippers. She went straight for the carafe of coffee I had brewed.

"Morning," I returned, noting her tangled mane of blonde hair. Apparently, I hadn't been the only one tossing and turning inside my bunk. "Did you get any rest?"

"Some. It's hard to get used to a new space." She lowered her delicate frame onto the bench seat opposite me "You sleep?"

"Nope." I shook my head, wrapped my hands around the mug that had long ago grown cold and dropped my gaze from her eyes that I suspected read too much in mine.

"Regretting last night?" she asked, scoring a direct bullseye on the center of my thoughts.

I snapped my head up.

"No bullshit, ok?" She looked me straight in the eyes now, pressing me with the full weight of her concern. "What's the point of pretending a lie is the truth? Unless you prefer self-deception and don't want a true friend. I mean, as for myself I've had enough people in my life who were just feigning interest in me because of who my father is. You're likely to attract plenty of those types now that your season of RFC has officially kicked off. I understand if you would prefer to be alone. I get that I'm not her and that no one can ever replace her."

My throat closed in on itself. The throb of the burning knot forming inside of it made it impossible to speak. Replace? That implied she thought I'd lost Raven completely. She was Raven's PR rep after all. Had she been in contact with her? Losing my best friend forever? It was what I most feared.

"You ok?" Barbara reached across the table and covered the hands I had wrapped around the cup with her own.

I shook my head. A fresh batch of tears leapt into my eyes. "I don't know if I'll ever be," I admitted, surprising myself. Raven had understood that. She had accepted me, damage and all. Probably because the pain she carried around from being a disappointment to her father had been so similar to my own. But I couldn't go there. My past was pockmarked with broken dreams, pitiable failures and too many losses. I had to refocus on the here and now. The alternative was something very dark indeed. Something always lurking in the shadows. Something Raven's light had prevented me from ever seriously considering.

And now I had to stand alone.

With being strong on my own in my thoughts, I withdrew my hands from Barbara's. I pretended I didn't see the flash of hurt in her sea glass green eyes. I couldn't manage being real with myself let alone someone I barely knew, even if that someone was as well-meaning as she seemed to be.

"What's on the agenda today?" I asked, my tone overly bright. I had to say something to fill the uncomfortable silence.

"Well for one I think you had better prepare for a phone call from Suzanne Smith." Her tone indicated an emotional retreat as well.

"Why's that?" My brows dipped together.

"I read the post you put up on the Rock Fuck Club Facebook page last night. She starts her day pretty early. I bet she has, too."

"Oh."

"There's thousands of comments already."

My eyes rounded.

"John Got Busted is going to be pissed." She tapped her fingers on the table. I glanced down, noting the appealing rhythm. "He's got legions of loyal fans." I lifted my gaze. She was shaking her head at me sadly. "Prepare for a backlash from them. He might even sue you for slander.

Shit. "I hadn't really thought about that," I confessed.

"On the positive side, he signed the contract. And WMO is lawyered up."

"That's good." Relief stemmed the rising panic within me.

"But Suzanne's still going to be furious. There wasn't any ambiguity about your encounter with him."

"No," I agreed. Tequila had taken away any desire I might have had to filter.

"Are you planning to use the same ranking system going forward?"

"Yeah, I want to keep it simple. Recommend. Not recommend." And for those guys who turned out to be like JGB, I wanted to drape them in yellow and black caution tape like a crime scene to warn other women away.

"Simple is best," she agreed. "It removes the possibility of confusion."

I nodded. That had been my reasoning.

"Might cause some difficulty going forward in recruiting other rock stars for the show, though."

The crease in my brow returned. Another thing I hadn't thought through. She seemed to consider things from lots of different angles. I wasn't as global in my reasoning.

"But then again…" She trailed off, her gaze dipping to my chest. I remained in the same scanty clothing from the previous night. "Looking the way you do I'd guess a lot of them will be willing to take the risk of disappointing you."

"I don't know about that." I was hourglass shaped. Most guys liked my curves. I knew how to accentuate what I had, but I thought my attributes were pretty average.

"So, is JGB really that bad?"

"Oh, yeah. He has zero skills." He had just laid beneath me and thrust a few times. "His ineptitude flashed me back to when I was thirteen and had sex for the first time." I'd had no experience and neither had my partner. It had been memorably amateurish.

"You were only thirteen when you had sex the first time?"

"Yes."

"That's pretty young."

I was aware. The start of my quest for significance through sex. The shrinks at Sheltered Valley had been particularly focused on that milestone. They had decided that I was trying to find approval from my sexual partners since I had never received it from my father.

I never bought it.

"JGB's full of himself." I swallowed the dry dust of the past that often clogged my throat. "He thinks because he's a big rock star he can do whatever the hell he wants without any consequences." My lips curved slightly. "Well guess what? Now he's got some."

"For sure." She nodded. "But there are going to be consequences for you, too. The fan backlash I mentioned. His lawyers. Suzanne."

"What's going to be her problem? Won't the notoriety be good for the show?" That old adage that any publicity was good publicity came to mind.

"She's a control freak. You went off the prescribed path without consulting her."

"Oh."

"And Raven will wonder..."

"Let's avoid the subject of Raven." My heart slammed around inside my chest just from speaking her name. "At this point, it seems she's unlikely to understand or give me a chance to explain anyway. Besides, it doesn't matter what she thinks."

Liar, my inner narrating voice corrected.

Shut it, I parried. I had some experience silencing my 'let's be real side'.

"Let's change the subject." I rapped on the banquette tabletop with my knuckles. My pattern wasn't near as appealing as hers had been. But then again Rayne Michaels was her father. She had to have been genetically blessed with rhythm. "Can you get me the bios for all the bands on the Gods of Rock tour?"

"I can."

"Great. I'd like to see who I have to choose from. Strategize. I think you probably have an exaggerated idea of my appeal."

A ring tone like an end to a boxing round sounded.

"Oh shit. That's my phone." Barbara lowered her head and drew her cell out of her pocket. I wondered if the robe and slippers had been hand-me-downs from her grandmother like her overly large handbag. They certainly appeared to be old enough to be vintage.

Wincing, she placed her cell on the table and spun it around so I could see the caller ID.

Suzanne Smith...

I sighed.

The sun was barely up.

I hadn't even had a shower or a second cup of coffee.

But I should have known that the exec didn't bow to social niceties any more than JGB did.

The first of my consequences had officially arrived.

CHAPTER
eight

"YOU WILL NEVER COERCE THE PRODUCTION crew into an impromptu filming without my express consent again." Suzanne Smith didn't raise her voice, and yet the ear I had pressed to Barbara's cell burned. "Are we clear?"

"Yes." Fucking shit. The exec had laid into me for the past half hour. "And you were clear thirty minutes ago." I had a post-tequila binging, post-exec reaming, post-JGB pounding headache.

"Is that sarcasm I detect in your voice? "

Oh shit. "No, absolutely not."

"Good. Because I'm not quite sure I'm finished with the lecture. Did I not mention how very fortunate you are that the slander charge has been dropped?"

"Yes, you did. I..."

"It's a good thing Barbara is with you. At least there is one level head on that bus, at least there is one person I can count on." Suzanne might not be yelling, but she spoke loud enough that Barbara could overhear her. Across from me the blonde dropped her chin. I didn't think Raven's PR rep wanted to be viewed as Smith's surrogate.

I empathized with her. I was sure she felt like an outsider. I felt like hanging my head, too. And I wanted to end the call already. But unfortunately, the exec kept going.

"Raven called me this morning."

"She did?" I asked, eager for any news about her status though my stomach cinched as though it were locked in a steel vice.

"She's threatened to back out of the behind the scenes interviews with you."

"Oh." Tears pricked my eyes. Another consequence to weather.

"She was adamant, but she doesn't have a legal leg to stand on. I had to remind her of the terms she agreed to." There was a clacking sound over the line that I couldn't quite identify. The exec rolling her expensive pen back and forth between her hands over a ring?

"She will complete the interviews. However, they will be conducted by Ignacio rather than you."

"Ok," I managed in a barely audible voice. Could Raven not even look me in the eyes anymore?

"And since he will have his hands full, I'm delegating interviewing Raven's hookups from Season One to you."

"Oh no." That list included the one that had sparked Raven's journey.

"Do you have a problem with that, Marsha?

"Yes. No. Oh, I don't know." It wouldn't be easy. If my best friend had shut me out, the Dragons likely would, too. There were three of them to interview. Plus, Ivan. If Raven didn't already hate me, she certainly would afterward. She would blame me for anything they said that wasn't favorable.

"Well I suggest you figure it out. If you can't set aside your personal challenges and focus on the business, you might as well go back to being a transcriptionist, typing what others dictate to you."

I couldn't go back to that. A world absent color, creativity or emotion, it had nearly stifled me.

"I can do what you need me to," I decided with more confidence than I felt.

"Good. I'll forward a contact spreadsheet to your email."

After she hung up I stared out the window some more. I wasn't alone in the front lounge. Ignacio came in from the bunk area, poured himself a cup of coffee and moved to one of the couches. A few minutes later Carla, Les and Ernie joined him. I listened with a dispassionate ear as they discussed the episode they had recorded last night, but I had never felt more alone. It was like I was an observer inside my own life.

Totally surreal.

I popped in my ear buds, selected Two Rows Back and pressed play. After the first couple of songs, the tightness inside of me loosened. Because of the music I wasn't completely alone anymore.

By the time the team finished editing, my stomach was grumbling. Nearly noon and I still hadn't moved from my spot at the banquette. Trees and concrete highway barriers whizzed by. The roofs of other vehicles crept along, keeping pace with us or falling behind. We crossed a state line, but I couldn't recall which one or whether there had been more before it.

Suddenly, I felt a tug on my earbud cord. "Hey," Barbara said, looking concerned. "You awake in there?"

I nodded, noting that the bus had slowed down. I blinked at her. I had been on a circuitous path inside my head for a while flipping back and forth between songs and the memories they evoked. Two Rows Back was the soundtrack of my friendship with Raven. I found myself second guessing everything that had happened with us. Everything I had said and done in the past twenty-four hours. "We're stopping to eat, and you might want to go grab your shower stuff."

"Why?" I couldn't think of any reason to move away from my spot. Despite my stomach grumbling, I didn't feel like eating, and I certainly didn't relish bathing in the tiny bus shower stall.

"Because..." She frowned. "You've been sitting there like a lump all day, ignoring everyone, and you haven't even changed out of last night's clothes."

"I don't see why it matters."

"Well, it does. Withdrawing from your life doesn't solve anything, and you need to eat. You didn't touch any of the food I put next to you. You're going in with me." She gave me a firm look. "There's a sit-down restaurant with fried chicken that Yelp says isn't too bad, and there are nice, clean, hot showers. You'll feel better after you get cleaned up and have something in your stomach."

"I doubt it," I mumbled.

"You will," she insisted. "And don't bother trying to put me off. I know you don't want me to get in trouble with Suzanne. And anyway, I won't take no for an answer. So, you might as well agree. The sooner you do the things I'm asking, the sooner you can go back to wallowing in your misery if that's what you're determined to do."

I decided it would take more energy to argue than to comply. Plus, I truly didn't want Barbara to get in trouble with the exec on my account. I went to the back. I stuffed my toiletries and a change of clothes into a drawstring bag. When I reemerged in the front lounge Barbara was waiting. We got off the bus together and worked our way through the rows and rows of semi-tractor trailer trucks. Our goal was the bustling oasis ahead. A bell jingled as we entered the convenience store section of the truck stop. A clerk at a desk framed by liquor bottles and cigarette boxes greeted us. Barbara waved, returning the greeting. I trudged along beside her. A sidekick once more, in tow rather than steering my own destiny. I frowned at myself and was just about to open my mouth to protest to Barbara when I heard a familiar voice breathe my name.

"Mars." It was soft, but one I would recognize anywhere.

"Raven." Swallowing hard, I turned and feasted my eyes on her. Her black hair looked messy and dull like she hadn't washed it, and her gold eyes were red rimmed. Had she been crying? For me? Or about something else entirely?

"Are you ok?" My first instinct was always her well-being. It was so closely tied to my own

Glancing around as if expecting a reprimand, she took an abrupt step back and. bumped a display of snack cakes.

"Don't leave," I begged, my voice thick while wondering offhandedly if Barbara had orchestrated this chance encounter. "We need to talk."

"What's there to say?"

"Years of stuff. Year of friendship to remind you of if all it takes is a couple of words from Ivan Carl to come between us like this."

"But what he said…what you did…" Her eyes glassed up. "You knew how I felt about him. How serious we got in such a short amount of time."

"Raven." Lucky suddenly appeared, his arms loaded with the usual array of convenience shop purchases including Raven's favorite Zapp's potato chip flavor and Sky's Maltesers. "Mars," he acknowledged me with a deep frown. "Everyone's waiting, Angel." He moved toward her, placing himself between us. "Are you ready?"

"Can you give me a minute with her?" Raven asked.

"Do you think that's wise? After Sky? After Ivan? And what she did last night with JGB? She's a mess and a wrecking ball to anyone in her path."

"Marsha. What's going on with you?" Raven shook her head sadly. Her disapproval cut through me like a blade. "Why did you steer Sky toward Ivan? Why go with JGB? I don't understand you. I thought I did at one time. But now I'm questioning if I ever really knew you at all."

"If you really wanted to know what was going on inside my head all you ever had to do was ask." The pressure of tears built behind my eyes. I clenched my fingers into my palms willing them to stay away. "Go on back to your family. Your new family. Enjoy their support while you have it. You and I both know how fickle life is, and how quickly those you think love you can turn on you."

I heard her gasp as I spun away. I brushed past Barbara, her mouth hung wide open in shock. I blazed by and knocked over the display Raven had only wobbled. But then that was one of the many differences between the two of us. Her pattern was to right her missteps. I more often than not made bigger wrongs of them.

CHAPTER
nine

Tears blurred my eyes. Finding the shower stalls, I entered one, slammed the door and bolted it shut. Sliding to the floor within the small cubicle that contained a shower head, dressing bench and sink, I dropped my chin to my chest, my hair providing a curtain. Even in private I found it uncomfortable to be exposed. From an early age, I had been trained by my father to be mentally and physically tough. I invited more severe discipline when I had revealed anything he perceived to be a weakness such as softer emotions. I might not have become as stoic as my two older brothers, but I had learned the lessons well that my father had taught me.

I remembered all the times I had escaped to Raven's house after one of those lessons. I recalled how sweetly she had comforted me without ever asking me to explain. Well, that was over now.

I started to cry harder. I let it go, the hurt that ran so deep I had never fully verbalized it even to my best friend. Now without her, I wrapped my arms around myself. Big shuddering sobs wracked my body.

Time passed. Time that eventually slowed the flow of tears. My chest ached, and my butt became numb from sitting on the cold tile floor. But tears wouldn't change anything. As I well knew.

Feeling more alone than ever, cold, achy and shivery, I stripped off my clothes, laying them on the half-bench along with my bag. I got in the shower wearing only my flip flops. I cranked the heat to scalding hot. I washed my body, scrubbing away the evidence of my tears. I composed myself under the pelting spray.

It took a while.

After that while, I emerged, dried off and put on a new set of clothes. Frayed jean shorts and a navy handkerchief top, that had sleeves that tied above my elbows. I didn't feel better, but at least my clothing was fashionable, and I wasn't cold anymore.

As I ran a brush through my wet hair, someone knocked on the door. Assuming it was Barbara checking on me, I pasted on a pulled together expression and unbolted the lock. My eyes went wide and so did the two sets of eyes on the other side of the door when they saw me.

"What's wrong?" Ivan asked, after taking one single look at me. Apparently my pulled together expression sucked.

"Tyler," I ignored Ivan and acknowledged the drummer of the Heavy Metal Enthusiasts standing beside him. Tyler Vaughn was his own brand of devastating sexy with thoughtful caramel hued eyes, a thick mustache and a beard that was almost as long and unruly as his brown hair. I had no quarrel with him. His best friend on the other hand was an entirely different matter.

"Go away," I told Ivan without glancing at him. "I have nothing to say to you."

"I disagree."

"I don't fucking care whether you agree or not. I don't care about your fake concern. I don't care about you at all."

"Mars, I never knew the baby was real." My knees wobbled from his unexpected admission. "If I had known, I never would have reacted the way I did when you came to me. I'm sorry." Ivan took a step toward me. His eyes were dark melted chocolate pools. They swirled with sincerity.

"Don't." I shook my head. I couldn't deal with his regret on top of all my own. But as was usual with him, he just did whatever the hell he wanted to do. Reaching out as if sensing a need I couldn't, wouldn't verbalize, he pulled me into him. Shocked, I was unable to speak. His strong arms banding around me, he crushed me into his hard chest. It felt incredible to be there, and it was every bit as tempting as it had been the night we had spent together. What the hell was I thinking? I truly was a terrible friend. I had enough guilt without adding to it by letting him console me again. My stupid eyes began to fill, my frayed emotions unraveling in his sheltering arms.

"Ivan," Tyler began in a cautionary tone, though I couldn't see him anymore. My head was lifted, but I was held hostage by the compelling sight of Ivan's empathy. "Do you think this is a good idea considering..."

"Go back to the bus," Ivan cut in. "I'll catch up to you later."

"No," I protested. "Catch up to him now. Let me go, Ivan." Yet, my body betraying me, I burrowed closer. His sweet sandalwood, comforting leather and hint of motor oil scent made me want to stay right where I was. My knees went as mushy in his embrace as my emotions. "I can't do this." I couldn't do this. I couldn't dwell on the details of our night together. There had been so much more there than I could ever let on to myself or to Raven. Least of all to him.

ROCK *Fuck* CLUB BOOK 3   85

He's the enemy, I reminded myself. He turned you away.

"Stay." I heard the voice of my best friend insisting sarcastically. "Don't separate from him on my account."

"Raven," we both said, responding at the same time. I pushed Ivan away, and he twisted toward her.

The pattern of the past, repeated, I thought bitterly.

Apparently, Ivan had noticed her before I had. Had his comforting me been yet another calculated ploy to set me up to fail in her eyes?

"How long?" she asked me, her eyes accusing daggers. "How many times did you fuck him behind my back?" The sting in her gaze sliced through me.

"Raven never. Only that one time before you started dating him."

"I don't know why I even asked." She waved me away when I tried to move toward her, and I realized I had only thought she had cut me before. "It doesn't matter, Marsha. It just doesn't matter. It's my bad really. Us remaining friends for as long as we did. So many people warned me about you. How you enabled me. How you encouraged my destructive behavior. How you were drowning and how afraid they were that you would pull me under with you."

"Who, Raven?" I asked, though deep down I was afraid I knew. "Who said those things?" New tears pricked eyes.

"My parents." She paused to deal the deadliest of blows. "Hawk."

My mouth gaped open as that truth lodged in the target at the center of my chest.

"I should've listened to them." She turned and walked away from me.

This time I didn't fall to my knees. I stood where I was and watched Ivan pursue her. No surprise there. Raven ran back through the convenience store. He jogged after her while I processed what remained of my heart breaking.

Barbara blanched when she found me. "What happened?" she whispered.

"Nothing. Nothing at all. Nothing that matters." I forced my feet to move.

"I don't understand." She fell into step beside me. Through the glass window, I saw Raven. Out in the parking lot, she had her arms wrapped around herself like I had earlier. Ivan was talking to her looking as upset as she did.

"It doesn't seem like nothing," Barbara observed. She had noticed the direction of my gaze.

"Trust me. It's nothing." There had to be some love left inside your heart to register the loss of it. "Let's get something to eat." My tone was wooden, but from now on I would be pulling my own strings. "Then I'm going to have some fun." No agenda. No apologies. No more giving a fuck. Not needed anymore by my best friend? No problem. Not searching for significance? No worries. I had been aiming too low with my hookups. I was going for notoriety now. Shooting for the stars. Rock stars. Paving the road to hell with the most infamous of intensions, I planned to have the type of fun that would make even my recent threesome seem pedestrian.

CHAPTER
Ten

"Y OU LOOK..." BARBARA TRAILED OFF, pressing her lips flat.

"Like a hooker," I completed her sentence, my eyes meeting hers in the motel mirror.

"Yeah," she agreed.

"Good." I spun around to face her. "That's exactly what I was going for."

"You don't think maybe you should leave a little more of you to the imagination?"

"Nah." I cocked a hip, the micro leather dress lifting to show a hint of my panties. "It's a thrash metal venue. I'd be laughed out on my ass if I went for subtle sexuality like you."

"I thought I looked sultry." Beneath her fanciful arrangement of blonde curls, her brow creased.

"You do. That's what I meant." I touched her arm. The lace that made up her sleeve and a lot of her black dress reminded me of a spider's web. Well, she might be dressed like the web, but I planned to be the spider weaving a snare for my next victim slash rock star.

Von Arnold. The Beast. The six-foot-four jacked up lead guitarist of the Monsters, a band that was joining the Gods of Rock tour. We might not have made our first stop yet, but I had already set up fuck number four. The crew had gone ahead to film background stuff and to secure the appropriate release signatures.

I was taking this season to the next level my way for sure, only this time I was doing it with Suzanne's stamp of approval.

"Ready?" I asked Barbara, scooping my black and silver studded clutch from the bed.

"Yeah," she answered. "I already activated Uber. Our ride's arriving now." She grabbed her own bag, and we stepped out of the motel room together. In the parking lot, the tour bus sat alone and empty. The driver had checked into a room to decompress. He had to have eight hours of rest before we could continue our journey.

"Have you been to a thrash metal show before?" Barbara asked after we were settled into the back seat of the sedan that pulled up.

"Sure. Lots of times. You?" I queried.

"No." She shook her head. "Brutal Strength is about as heavy on the rock as I go. Anything I should know etiquette wise?"

"Do's and don'ts, you mean?"

She nodded.

I thought about that a moment. "The most important thing is to be polite."

"At a heavy metal concert?" She arched a disbelieving brow.

"Yeah, for sure. The fans might seem a little intimidating with their studs, devil horn gestures and head banging, but they're actually very respectful of each other and extremely loyal to their bands."

"That actually sounds nice."

"It is," I confirmed. "And refreshing. There's no holding back. The fans are there to have a good time. The audiences really get into the shows. It's a lot of fun and by the end you usually make a lot of friends. Raven and I..." I trailed off remembering all that I had lost. For a moment I had been able to almost forget. The couple of liberal swigs of tequila I'd had while Barbara had showered and changed had certainly helped. But it all came back to me in a rush. Raven and me. The dancing, the laughter, the silliness and the camaraderie. The love we had for each other and our love for the music. My chest got so tight I suddenly couldn't breathe.

"It'll be ok, Mars." Barbara softly touched my hand. My fingers curled around my clutch so tightly that the sharp studs bit into my flesh. "She'll remember. She'll forgive you."

"Unlikely."

"In time."

"No," I said firmly. Time needed hope to sustain it. It didn't heal all wounds. It just led to more heartbreak. I didn't have it in me to expect anything good to come my way anymore. Maybe before my mother had left me and my brothers when she knew how our father was. Maybe before I had lost Hawk and the baby. Maybe before Raven had turned on me. But not now. No more wasted hope. No more wasted time. And no more wasted love.

I HAD BEEN A little worried that the metal fans in North Carolina might be different than the ones back home in Texas, but I shouldn't have been. The Fillmore, a replica of the one in San Francisco, was packed wall to wall with two thousand eager standing room only fans. Beneath the blue chandeliers that glowed moodily, we all pressed toward the stage as the concert time drew near. We were ready to rock, and Ignacio and the crew were ready to film. They hovered in the periphery, discreet and barely noticeable.

"Don't they usually have a couple of opening bands before the headliners?" Barbara asked me while bringing her drink glass with the thin bar straw to her lips.

"Usually, but the bartender told me the scheduled ones withdrew at the last minute. The Monsters are apparently bringing in a special guest band. They reimbursed the ones that got bumped. It must be somebody big."

As the lights inside the venue lowered, I brought the double shot of Cuervo to my mouth. I refocused on the stage, ignoring the film crew... mostly...and so did everyone else as far as I could tell. I was glad for the anonymity I currently enjoyed. I didn't much care for everything I did being recorded. I preferred being behind the camera. In control, rather than subject to the whims and expectations of others.

"Hey, Charlotte!" Speaking into the mic he carried, Von Arnold stepped onto the stage, wearing only a pair of black jeans. He was so massive I imagined I could hear the floorboards groaning beneath his feet. "There's been a change in plans for tonight."

"I want to have your babies tonight." A woman behind me shouted.

Von Arnold smiled. His teeth gleamed. They were whiter than the white makeup that covered his entire face. His ebony hair was a sharp contrast to it as were the black kohl circles around his piercing blue eyes. "I have other plans tonight." The dual silver studs on his thick black leather collar flashed within his spotlight. "But I'll keep your offer in mind." He placed the mic in the center pole and spoke into it again. "For future consumption." His smile deepened, and his boulder biceps bulged. I think he flexed them on purpose. "For now, prepare yourselves, metal hearts to get ready." He leaned into the mic.

The eight pack on his stomach tightened, and I went a little fluttery inside imagining him focusing all that floorboard bending strength solely on me. "If you're hyped as hell, get your hands and horns in the air and give my brother Ivan Carl and the incomparable Heavy Metal Enthusiasts a big Carolina welcome!"

A roar swept through the crowd. Arms shot up all around us. The sound of a lone guitar split the air, and Ivan materialized in a spotlight that followed him as he laid claim to the stage.

My stomach didn't just flutter, it completely flipped over. And though I wished I could look away, I couldn't because Ivan wasn't one of those performers who asked for your attention. He demanded and got it.

Dark chocolate eyes aglow, he aimed the headstock of his ebony Les Paul at the audience as if it were the barrel of a rifle, and the crowd went crazy. Hands over their heads in surrender, they pumped their arms as they chanted his name.

"Fuck!" he growl-shouted when he reached the center mic Von Arnold had abdicated.

"Fuck me!" a woman close to me yelled before swooning backward into the waiting arms of her boyfriend. It didn't seem like Ivan heard her. In his own realm, the Enthusiasts' frontman leaned back on his booted heels and let his silver ringed fingers do their thing. A churning rhythm emerged. It looped and repeated at a faster pace as his bandmates appeared. The lights flashed on them as they filled their appropriate places. Jagger 'Jag' Anderson, a swath of black bangs hanging over his cool green eyes went to the right of Ivan with his bass. Nicholas 'Arrow' Winslow, a blond with dancing hazel eyes and rhythm duties on his ESP guitar went to the left. Tyler 'Ty' Vaughn jumped on his riser. Ivan's best friend immediately fell onto his seat, lifted his arms and sticks into the air and brought them down with a crash. He attacked his drums, his beat the lightning to Ivan's thundering chords. The two of them were the indisputable eye of the storm. The energy they generated radiated outward, a sonic hurricane.

"My brothers," Ivan introduced them simply as he spoke into the mic. His lips curving his pleasure, he shifted his body. A back and forth shuffle, he danced as he moved, at one with the music and in sync with his band. Adjusting his stance to accommodate his guitar, he pressed his sculpted lips to the mic. "It ain't no mystery my woman disrespected me." His voice was different now. Smooth. Devastating. Melodic. Earnest like his expression. "She broke my heart, cut her feet on the pieces as she walked away." Leaning back, his fingers conjured more magic from his guitar, only this time to unleash a flurry of pain. I felt it in the ragged riff. Uneven like a sharp-edged hunk of shattered glass, it pierced my skin, fileted it. Bleeding from his wounds, I staggered. His pain and anger vibrated through me. I recognized them. They had been close companions nearly all my life.

"Fuck her. Fuck me. Fuck it all." His voice turned guttural again. It scraped my nerve endings raw leaving me exposed. And he took advantage. He was a dark knight after all. He wasn't up on that stage to influence the hearts and minds of the masses. He was there to conquer them.

To take them hostage.

To force them to their knees.

Well mainly one.

"Get ready," he said, my eyes the target his seemed to find. 'It's you, Mars. I'm coming for you.'

CHAPTER
eleven

"No," I protested as if Ivan had spoken directly to me, which of course he hadn't. That would've been impossible. A piercing bright light in my eyes, I swayed and lost my equilibrium. Sudden, staccato gunfire popped, rending the air. My heart seized in my chest. My body jerked.

Then Ivan sang again. My vision returned. My heart resumed beating. I came back to myself. Ivan hadn't really been speaking to me, and I hadn't actually heard gunfire. It had just been Tyler duplicating the pattern of machine gun fire on his drums.

I locked my limbs refusing to let Ivan get to me. Always wary where he was concerned, I should've been more in tune with what a potent force he was on the stage.

Folly to forget. Dangerous to discount anything when it came to him.

Unsettled by him and the unresolved feelings he stirred without even really trying, I tried to plant my feet only to get uprooted by two overly enthusiastic guys 'hell yeah'ing' and body slamming each other beside me. Moving away from them, I slipped backward through the crowd. Finding a place to deposit my drink and a pocket of relative safety on the sidelines, I watched Barbara and the rest of the audience head-banging and chanting right along with Ivan and his band to the easy to follow 'fuck the world' chorus.

Up on stage, the strobes splattered Ivan and his brothers in blue and violet camo. The song reached its climax. The stage plunged into darkness. The disorientating silence that descended felt suffocating. I felt like I could barely breathe. The roar of approval from the crowd jarred me. I backed further away from it all, rocked by the sudden realization of why Ivan's music resonated with me. The rage against everything and everyone. I identified with it. Not only identified, I was ready to fully embrace that mentality.

Permanently.

But dare I take the self-awareness further? Was he...had Ivan always been less a nemesis and more a comrade with similar sentiments?

I knew why I was so angry.

But why was he?

"Go away." I spoke the words to Ivan. He had suddenly appeared. Shaken by the way he seemed to materialize from my thoughts, I backed away from him.

"Mars," he stated, giving me a once over that made my body flash with awareness as the house lights came back on. "I wasn't finished talking with you earlier." He uncrossed his arms.

"It's just Marsha to you." I lost his eyes for a moment as I fixated on his sculpted and sleek-with-sweat chest. I regained them as he moved closer to me.

"I don't like being ambushed." I licked my dry lips, stopping as I found my backward progress halted by the leaning rail.

ROCK *Fuck* CLUB BOOK 3   95

"Mars," he insisted. "No formalities. Not with me. Not after I've had my mouth on your sweet pussy."

Heat flared in the very spot he mentioned.

"I don't like being turned away." He closed the space between us. "Shut down. Ignored."

I didn't like those things, either. I'd had my fill of them. He was only inches away now. His scent washed over me. My heart thundered. My pulse pounded. My eyes grew wide as he reached for me. The crowd cut off any possibility I had of a successful escape.

"There you are." Her eyes narrowing, Barbara slipped into the minuscule gap between Ivan and me. "Ignacio called me on my cell when he couldn't reach you on yours. "Von's ready for you." The lead singer frowned. "He wants you to come backstage."

"Alright," I replied, turning to Barbara and feeling like I had skirted certain disaster as I fell into place behind her leaving Ivan behind. He had not seemed pleased, though the fans that had quickly surrounded him in my absence had mostly been underdressed women.

"Thanks," I told my rescuer as she led the way to a door beside the stage.

"Ignacio did truly call me, but you're welcome." She lifted the badge from her lanyard to show the security guard. He dipped his gaze to mine, or maybe he just wanted to check out my boobs. They were rising and falling with each breath. A post Ivan after-effect.

On the other side of the door, we traversed a short hall lined with disinterested people staring at their phones. We made a right and climbed a set of steps, emerging just to the right of the stage. There were tons of people here, too. But they were all busy. Crew. Techs. Venue personnel. Groupies dressed like me. And then I noticed the band. Breaking from a huddle, the lead singer, who wore makeup that resembled a skeletal mask, brushed past me taking the cordless mic someone thrust at him. The bassist looked like Dracula, cape and all, and the drummer looked like some macabre dungeon master. They hardly paid any attention to me as they moved to take the stage. But Von Arnold did.

"Marsha?" He queried from a foot above me.

"Yes." I nodded and craned my neck backward to regard him.

"Fuck, you're pretty." His black rimmed eyes burned bright with definite approval.

"Well, you're pretty something, too." I stamped a hand to one hip and gave him the side view. His gaze slid down the two-inch peekaboo seam on the side of my dress.

"Arnold!" A middle-aged man wearing a headset hissed. "Put it back in your pants and get on stage."

"Alright." The Beast tromped closer. The ground seemed to quake with each of his footfalls or maybe that was just me. I'd gotten a peek of my own at what he had in his pants. A beast, indeed. I flushed with heat.

"Ryan has a drum solo in 'Wasteland'." Arnold trailed his thick tatted forefinger down my arm. "Get ready. I'm coming for you then," he growled as if he really were a wild beast. "By that wall right there." He gestured with his thumb. "I'm gonna rip those seams. I'm gonna fuck you hard, and I'm gonna fuck you fast." Heat rose to paint both of my cheeks. Unable to speak, I was practically climaxing on the spot, I stared at him slack jawed as he stomped off.

"Holy shit!" Barbara exclaimed.

Eyes wide, I refocused on her and nodded.

"Whoa," another feminine voice said, and I noticed Carla. She moved forward. "Great scene." She circled a hand over her shoulder. I noted the rest of the crew. Brown curls in his eyes, Ignacio was hunched over his viewfinder looking over the playback. Les was in the corner his boom somewhere above us. Ernie was cranking up the lights.

"Nice job Marsha." Ignacio gave me a thumbs up.

I acknowledged him by dipping my chin.

"Let me touch up your makeup," Carla said with a smile. "You look a little melty."

I felt a lot melty. Finding an empty folding chair, I sank into it. She fluffed my hair, swept on some powder on my dewy cheeks and by the time she applied a thick layer of red gloss to my lips the Monsters were on their second song. My heart started pounding inside my chest. It pounded harder when Von Arnold reappeared. I forgot about everything as he fastened his hungry gaze on me. I rose from the chair. He stomped straight toward me.

"Wall," he barked, kicking the chair I had been sitting in aside. The metal clattered and so did my thoughts as he eliminated the distance separating us. He grabbed me with his large hands just under my ribcage, lifted me and pressed me into the wall.

"I..."

"No talking." He lowered his head, his mouth finding mine. His lips were warm, his hands were hot brands and his tongue as he thrust it into my mouth was as relentless as he was. I was a little frightened and a lot overwhelmed, but he was exactly what I needed. He told me not to talk, and I could respect that. So, I didn't tell him how much I liked what he was doing. I showed him. I mewed in his mouth. I clawed at his thick leather collar, and I climbed his huge body with my stilettoed heels. He sucked on my tongue. He ground his cock against me to a rhythm that matched his tongue. I latched my limbs tighter around him. I writhed. He grabbed and ripped the seams of my outfit apart on both sides. The torn pieces slid away from my body. He lifted his head to take me in. His heated approval was all I saw.

And then I felt it.

Everywhere.

His hot hands sliding gliding, shaping, lifting. My frantic fingers finding a condom packet in his front pocket, I undid the front laces of his pants, and he took over to apply it. His tongue distracted me from the show that sheathing his cock was.

"Yes." I breathed my approval as his wet tongue pierced my lips. He swallowed my breath, gulped it down his cavernous throat and aligned and glided his monstrous member inside me.

Pinned to the wall, the cinderblocks were cool, the surface rough against my naked skin, but Von Arnold was rougher, and I reveled in it. Thrust after hard thrust he fucked me. And he didn't stop until we both came undone.

My cell rang as I regrouped in the woman's restroom. Unclipping and sliding my phone out of my clutch, I put it to my ear without looking at the display.

"Hey, Buttercup." *Shit.* My heart sunk. It wasn't Raven. It was my younger brother.

"Hey, Lars."

"You ok?"

I cast my gaze to the ceiling. I was in the stall in a public restroom. I'd shuffled in clutching the remaining tatters of my outfit in front of the important parts. I had no clothes to speak of. I guess the answer would depend on your definition of 'ok'.

"Sure," I lied. "What's up? You made Captain yet?" Lars never called just to chat. Robert, either. Both my brothers were logical and matter of fact. Any sign of gentler emotions had been drilled out of them at an early age. Everything, even a simple phone call, had to have a purpose.

"No. Dad's still the only Captain in the family." He sighed loudly. I could almost see him running a hand over his blond shorn to the scalp hair. "Well, I just wanted to call to make sure you're alright. A reporter from the Dallas Morning News called Dad. He knows what you're doing Mars. He knows you're starring in the second season of RFC. He saw some pictures of you with that rapper. He's upset."

I just bet he was.

"I mean really upset." Lars paused, and I could imagine in that span of time just what my father's version of really upset entailed. I hoped Lars hadn't been around to bear the brunt of it.

"And I don't think that will be the end of it." Another sigh. "Don't come home, Marsha. Don't come anywhere near home."

"Alright." I swallowed another poisonous dose of my father's rejection. As always, it left a bitter taste in my mouth.

"ARE YOU SURE you should go away alone?" Barbara trailed off, glancing at Von over my shoulder. "I mean..." She swallowed, set down her Solo cup on a nearby side table and lowered her voice. "You hardly know him, Mars."

"I know enough." My eyes met Von's across the room. He was talking with his tech, one of the few remaining people inside the only-a-little-bit-larger-than-the-front-lounge-of-the-tour-bus-after-party space. Deep inside myself, after my conversation with my brother and after everything else that had happened, I was feeling more than a little lost. Struggling. What was my place in the world? My offering of revenge Raven hadn't even noticed let alone understood. If no longer a best friend, what was I? I wanted so desperately to believe I wasn't who my father envisioned me to be.

Von thought I was beautiful. Couldn't I start there? He had given me what I had needed. Afterward he had dedicated a guitar solo to me. He'd also thoughtfully procured a change of clothes for me to wear from his merch booth girl since he'd shredded my outfit.

He was a little odd with the whole Frankenstein regalia, but then again that was the theme of his band.

I liked him.

"Mars?" Von inquired, crooking his tatted finger.

"Coming," I tugged down on the borrowed slightly undersized Monsters' shirt that kept riding up. I touched Barbara's arm. "You got someone to ride back to the motel with you?"

"Yeah. Carla's waiting out in the hall."

"Good. Girlfriends stick together." Raven and I had a rule at clubs or concerts. Never leave a girlfriend to fend for herself. We didn't even go to the restroom alone. Too many dark corners. Too many opportunities for something to go wrong without anybody to intervene.

And didn't that about sum up my life right now without my best friend?

"They *should* stick together." Barbara gave me a penetrating glance. Yeah, yeah, I got it. She was talking about right here, right now. Me.

"No one's gonna mess with me when I'm with…" I paused to do air quotes, "'the Beast.'"

"But…"

"I won't be able to sleep, and I can't knock around in that motel room all night." I'd slide into the morass of what ifs and self-pity. "I have my cell. I'll call if something doesn't feel right. Ok?"

"Ok, I guess." Her words were the ones I wanted to hear. The uncertainty in her eyes I pretended not to see. I pretended not to see other things, too. The typical after the show debauchery, for instance. Everyone had piled into the small room after the encore. The guys from the Monsters had all picked out a babe or two and wandered off somewhere to get some action. The Heavy Metal Enthusiasts' crew had done the same. Except for Tyler. For some reason he had stuck around. Maybe because his best friend was here. Did guys have a rule to stick together, too?

Yes, Ivan was inside the room. A presence I couldn't ignore, but not alone like Tyler. Not that it mattered that I could recall only a handful of times when I'd seen Ivan without a babe on his arm. A random thought surfaced. Gratification. Validation. Was it possible that his hookups served the same purposes as mine? It was just something to note, like when I had realized earlier how much I identified with his music. Currently, he had his arm around a woman with long black hair, blue eyes and bigger tits than mine.

"Babe." Von recaptured my attention as he slid his arm around my shoulders. "Let's get out of here and go somewhere else." He squeezed me into his rock solid, immoveable side.

"Sure. Let's." I smiled up at him, widening it when I noticed Ivan staring.

"Mind if we stop at my bus first?"

"Well, I don't know." My stomach swirled with the ice of sudden unease.

"Just so I can wash off the stage makeup. Grab a change of clothes. You can wait outside. You don't have to come in. I'm not trying to take advantage of you."

I exhaled my relief. "That's probably best."

"Then that's the way it'll be."

"Thanks." I touched his arm and gave him a genuine smile.

"She's playing you, Arnold," Ivan commented from where he stood by the door, his current babe leaning into him, casually twirling a stand of his hair.

"You're seriously warning me about players?" Von's brow rose. "I guess you think being one makes you some kind of expert. But I'm curious why you think you have any say in the matter."

"It's just that Marsha and I, we go back a ways. We know each other."

"You fucked her you mean?"

Ivan nodded once to confirm.

"He doesn't like me." It was time for me to speak up for myself. I was so done being there for someone else, being tossed aside, being forgotten. "The feeling is mutual."

Did Ivan actually wince? Was my disdain for him really a surprise? I returned my gaze to Von. "But if his opinion matters to you..." I let that hang for a moment before I started to pull away.

"It does. He's a bud from before anyone would even give our music a listen. When I wanna know if a riff is any good I ask him. If I want somebody to shoot the shit with and he's in town he's my guy." Von reeled me back to his side. "But when I've got a hot chick on my arm, and he says shit about her that I don't like, my response is, 'shut the fuck up, asshole.' You getting me, Ivan?"

"Yeah, dude. Have at it." Ivan's dark brown eyes blazed as he attempted to bore holes into me.

"I will if she grants me that honor again. But I'm guessing by the way you've been watching her all night that you might be thinking along those same lines."

"Not, Marsha. I don't...

"You might wanna think before you say something that's not retractable."

"Love ya, like one of my own bandmates, bro," Ivan returned. "But just reconsider if you're thinking you're going to try for something real with a chick who makes fucking rock stars her claim to fame."

CHAPTER
Twelve

"I GOTTA GO IN. IT'S LATE."

"But I wanna talk to you some more."

"You wanna feel me up some more."

"Don't do that." The teasing lilt disappeared from Von's voice. "I mean sure I'm gonna touch if you're giving me that option, but when I said talk that's what I meant. I told you about my social anxiety disorder. How hard it is for me when I'm not in character behind the makeup and shit. Stuff I wouldn't admit to just anyone." He traced a strand of my hair from the shell of my ear to my shoulder. "But you're easy to talk to and a good listener. Really, Marsha when we get to Tampa, I need to see you again."

"I like you, Von. But I don't think that's a good idea." I knew him as a person now. There was no going back to a hookup and no going forward, either. Not with the plans I had. "I've got lots of RFC left to do. My life's not really open to anything beyond the feel good kind of fun we had tonight."

104 MICHELLE MANKIN

"Say you'll at least think about it." His huge forearm resting on the wall above my head he leaned closer and touched my cheek. "Isn't there anything I can do to change your mind?" His gaze dipped to my mouth. He leaned in. I side stepped away.

"No. I'm sorry. There isn't. Goodnight, Von." I didn't do the relationship thing, even before RFC. I lowered my head, unclipped my clutch and withdrew my keycard.

Aligning it to the reader, I heard the car door shut hard behind me. Von had gotten back in the Lyft that had brought us back to my hotel after we'd had a couple of drinks together. He was leaving and probably mad, but it was for the best. I was alone in the hush before the dawn.

"Hey there, Martian."

"Ivan." I gasped. My spine snapping straight, I spun around. My breath caught. On him. Leaning against his hunter green 1969 Firebird, like an ad in *Car and Driver*. A very sexy ad.

He took me in, his intent gaze traveling the length of my form wrapped in the borrowed too tight shirt and ass baring shorts. Admittedly, my gaze took a similar trip in return. His jeans fit him like a coat of paint and his muscle tank, a charcoal grey one hugged his chiseled chest. Something flared in his eyes as he caught me staring at him. I used the key card as an excuse to drop my gaze. I wasn't backing down from the challenge he represented. I wasn't afraid of him. No way. I just, you know, needed my card so I could go in and take a shower while I still had time to get one. Morning was coming fast, and the bus would be leaving soon.

Bending over, I scooped the wayward card off the pavement. I heard a low hiss as I straightened with the key in my hand.

"Always a tease." Ivan mumbled.

"What?" I narrowed my eyes.

"I said you've got an amazing ass, and you don't mind showing it off."

My brows rose in surprise. "Was that a compliment or a dig?"

He ignored my question. "Don't pretend you don't know what you're doing. You know how good you look. You're always working it. Like the first time I ever saw you, down in the pit, in front of the stage, angling your body just so. Every guy around you was trying to get the view down your dress that I had. You were doing it again tonight, practically begging me to chase you. And backstage that pose you struck for Von. There's no way any guy could resist you." Pinning me in place with his gaze, he stalked closer. He stopped less than a foot away. My eyes widened. My heart hammered. My throat went dry.

"Don't." I took in a gulp of his tantalizing scent. The sandalwood had taken a backseat to the motor oil tonight. Had he been working on his car?

"Don't what, Mars?" he questioned in in a throaty seductive whisper.

"Don't flirt with me." I put a hand on my hip and glared at him. "Don't compliment me and put me down in the same breath."

"I'll stop when you do." As if choreographed, a sudden gust tossed my hair into my eyes. He stepped forward. The tips of his boots touching my sandals, he reached out and smoothed one strand and then another away. His touch affected me the way it usually did. My skin tingled. My already racing heartbeat accelerated. My lips parted to intake additional air. Stunned, I blinked up at him. He stared down at me, his large soulful brown eyes arresting me. Just like that first time. What if…the thought arose before I could brush it aside…what if I had taken him up on his invitation that night? Not to take his cock. That had been a foregone conclusion. What if I had taken him up on his other offer? What if I had stayed after he had fucked me? What if

I had called? Would he have looked at me in the daytime the way he had looked at me that night?

"No." Of course not. I brushed that daydream aside. The sex had been hot, but rock gods like Ivan didn't really want anything more than sex from the women they picked up. Unless that woman was someone like Raven, someone who possessed inner worthiness that could make him want more. On the thought of my best friend, the key card fell through my fingers.

"Mars, what's going on?" Ivan seemed to have lost his train of thought. Mine had certainly been derailed. A common malady where he was concerned. Reframing my face, he resumed staring deeply into my eyes. He stroked my cheeks. "Are you ok?" The pads of his calloused thumbs felt rough against my smooth skin, yet his touch was hypnotically soothing.

"People keep asking me that," I muttered.

"Probably because they're worried about you."

"You? Worried about me?" I clucked in disbelief and reached up to pry his hands away from my face.

"Yes…"

"Please," I cut him off. "How stupid do you think I am?

"I don't think you're stupid at all." His brows dipped together over his narrowed eyes.

"Good" I crouched down and scraped my key card off the pavement. Again. "And it's not me who's a player. It's you. I *played* right into your hands when you offered your insincere comfort at the truck stop. Don't think I didn't figure out what you were really trying to do. Thanks to you, Raven thinks we've been fucking each other behind her back all along. She hates me now, maybe as much as she hates you. We have that in common. You've made a mess of my life from the day you stepped into it. That ends tonight. I have a job to do. I don't need any distractions. So, I want you to stay away from me."

"Was that Ivan Carl you were talking to?" Barbara asked as I stomped onto the bus.

"Unfortunately."

"He didn't look too happy."

"I told him to stay away from me."

"Hmm. I'm not sure he got the message. He's still out there."

I moved next to her on the couch. Ignacio and the crew were crammed into the banquette that had become our usual spot. I casually glanced out the window. Barbara was right. Ivan remained. Leaning against the driver's side of his Firebird again, he had his arms crossed and his brows lowered.

My breath caught. He definitely saw me. Even across the motel parking lot, even through the thick noise canceling glass, I felt the pull of his gaze. For one beat, then another, it held me. He seemed to be sending a message. A challenge. His typical type. Withdrawing a pair of shades from the collar of his shirt, he unfolded them and slipped them on. Tipping his chin down, he regarded me over the aviator shaped lenses before he finally turned slowly away, releasing me. I turned away, too, but not until he opened the door of his Pontiac and folded his lean frame into it. Miss watching the show that was Ivan Carl from the backside in those jeans of his? Um, no. I wanted him at a distance, sure. I needed him at a safe distance away from me. But that didn't mean I was going to deprive myself of the view.

"It's going to be hard to avoid him if that's your intention," Barbara said. "His band is one of the co-headliners on this tour."

I swiveled to face her. "I thought the Dragons were the top draw."

"Well, Lucky's band might be bigger in overall sales right now with their latest album, but the Gods of Rock is mostly a metal show. The

Enthusiasts have been in the lineup ever since the first one. They're a definite crowd favorite."

"How come you know so much?"

"I read the dossiers on all the bands the research department sent over." She arched a golden brow. "Haven't you read any of your emails?"

I shook my head. "I've been kinda busy...processing."

"I get it." She touched my hand softly. "Processing is a good place to start. Though your type of processing scares me a bit, Mars. I gotta tell you."

"Yeah?"

She nodded. "You're pretty reactionary." She gave me a long, searching look. "Don't you think maybe you might want to take a little more time considering before you choose the next guy?"

"How do you mean?"

"Well, like, what do you want? The show's about you and your right to choose. So what kind of message are you wanting to send to the viewers? The guys you select should reflect that message, right?"

"Whoa. Why are you only Raven's PR rep? You'd make a great executive producer."

"Suzanne would never let me have that much power."

"Why not?"

"Too little experience."

"Experience isn't everything. Passion. Intelligence. Vision. Those should count for something. And anyway, isn't Suzanne the youngest exec at WMO?"

"Yeah."

"So, someone had to give her a first shot. If you're interested in more responsibility, maybe you should ask for it."

"You're right." She nodded firmly. "Maybe I will."

"You should. You would kick ass at it. I'll tell her I think so the next time I talk to her."

"Thanks."

"For nothing. I could actually use a little help out here as you've probably noticed."

"Yeah, I have, and that's what I've been trying to give you," she pointed out. "But you haven't been all that receptive to it."

"I'm sorry, Barbara. Truly. My life's kind of in the shitter. I went from being the supportive best friend to flying solo rather abruptly. I wasn't really in a receptive mode."

"And you are now?"

"I still have a lot of clutter in my head that needs clearing. I'm trying to figure things out. My life going forward without Raven in it, for one. And other stuff."

Like the miscarriage. Like my love for Raven's brother. My unrequited love. Had I ever even had his genuine regard? Barbara's blue-green eyes brimmed with empathy, but she didn't press me. She had been around to hear a lot. But she didn't know the half of it.

"You seem to be a little out of control." She dipped her head, holding my gaze for a meaningful moment letting that observation sink in. "I think you know what I'm saying. I read the transcript of your conversation with Smith. You had a plan before you and Raven had your falling out."

"A falling out? Is that what she's calling it? She carved me out of her life without even giving me a chance to explain."

Barbara's brows rose from the violence of my response.

Yeah, I had a lot of anger to work out.

"I hear you, Barb. I get what you're saying. Raven's season was about her sexual awakening. What she liked and who she chose in the end. I need an overall theme for my season."

But I had absolutely no clue what it would be.

CHAPTER Thirteen

I RETIRED TO THE BACK LOUNGE while the crew and Barbara watched a movie up front. Trying not to think too much about what had gone on the last time I'd been in the back, I sank onto one of the couches and cracked open my laptop. I logged onto the bus Wi-Fi and gasped when I saw the number of unread emails in my personal account.

The relative anonymity I had enjoyed in Charlotte? Well, that was over. No wonder my brother and my father knew about JGB. My private account had become as public as my sex life. And by public I meant everyone who had logged onto the internet in the past forty-eight hours likely knew all about it.

I had messages from the major networks wanting to interview me. The top talk shows. And I had tons of product endorsement opportunities. I skimmed them. The amount of money they were offering made my head spin. Many of the messages had been forwarded from Suzanne Smith's new secretary. I realized by the time I got through the last of them that being the next star of the Rock

Fuck Club wasn't just a job. And it wasn't just a foot in the door to the film career I had always wanted, either. It could be whatever I wanted it to be.

Hours later, I was leaning back and staring blankly at the screen filled with details about the tour: the venues, the bands and the guys in them when Barbara knocked on the door frame to get my attention.

"You started on your emails," she guessed.

"Uh- huh." I nodded. "And googled my name."

"It's a lot to take in." Apparently, she had, too.

"Holy shit, there are so many photos and videos of me." Most from the first season. I had been at Raven's side then and those had probably been easy to find. But the ones from high school? The last spring break Raven and I had taken to Cancun? That had required some digging. Plus, the interviews with former hookups, including the guy from the gym just a couple of days ago that seemed like a lifetime.

"How the hell did they find them all?"

"Privacy laws are lax and barely enforceable. Besides, WMO's fanning the flames of interest wherever they spark."

"Yeah," I guess.

"Start writing your own narrative is my advice. The sooner the better."

"I think I got your point about that earlier."

"Good." She gave me a commiserative look. "I don't envy you your position."

"I imagine you don't." No one who was sane would.

"With my dad being who he is I had a front row seat to see what fame can do to life, love...and friendships," she ended in a whisper.

I swallowed hard and nodded.

"Does she..." My voice cracked, and my eyes registered the tightness in my throat. "Does she ever ask you about me?"

"Yes. But..."

"But what?" I prompted when an uncomfortable moment of silence stretched out.

"Give it some time, Mars. Give her some time. And don't do any other things like that bit with JGB or being alone with Ivan if you don't want her to see you in an unfavorable light. You make Lucky's case for him when you do, and you set her off as well."

"Alright. I guess I can do that." JGB was out of the picture. Avoiding Ivan wouldn't be too hard. I'd become an expert at keeping my distance from him the year he had dated Raven. But deep down, it wasn't only that I had no hope in my heart that Raven would change her mind. I was afraid if she had too much time to reflect, her heart would harden against me for good.

WE STOPPED FOR fuel again at midday. There was a Taco Bell inside the convenience store, and I was in the mood for a salad. But since I'd missed a shower at the motel earlier, I went there first. I had my wet hair wrapped up in a towel and was shuffling along in my squishy flip-flops when I heard a familiar voice. Two actually. I stopped in my tracks. Peering through a break in the candy aisle, I saw them. Rocky and Sky. My eyes widened as he grabbed her arm and spun her to him.

"You will listen."

"I won't. I will shag whoever I want to Rocky Walsh. You do."

"I do not." He was facing me but looking at her. His golden eyes blazed. "If I could be with whoever I wanted to it would be you."

"Then why aren't you?" she whispered.

"I can't, sweetling. You don't understand. The way I am. The way you are. It wouldn't be right."

"It would be just fine. I think you're afraid."

"I'm not, little one. But you should be," he growled. "Let me show you what I mean." And then he kissed her. Really kissed her. I was so shocked I gasped and dropped my toiletry bag. He released her, throwing his arm to the side to move her behind him. Fingers on his flexed bicep her lips red and swollen, she peered over him at me.

"Mars!" She took a step toward me. He grabbed her arm and pulled her back.

"You're not to speak to her."

"I will," she refuted. "She's my friend."

"IF you want me to kiss you again then you will obey me. If you want to be in my bed, you'll come to it on my terms or not at all."

Whoa. My gaze traveled from his stern face to her conflicted one.

"Don't throw away what you've always wanted on my account, honey."

"I don't know." She gnawed her lip

"I do," I stated firmly. "Sex is my game, not yours. It's about getting some, not giving something away. If you want more than that, if you trust him to keep the best parts of you safe, then give them to him. Give all you have to give and don't fucking hold back." I had done that with Hawk. Even though I knew what Raven said was true, and he had never thought of me the way I'd thought of him, I had loved him. The best I knew how. And I had the memory of it, and our one night together to hold onto.

I walked away as Sky turned back to Rocky. I hoped for her sake he was the man she thought he was. I hoped he was worthy of her.

On the way back to the bus, I had both my hands full, a plastic takeaway sack with my salad in one and my toiletry bag in the other when my cell rang.

"Dammit," I muttered, recognizing the Darth Vadar ringtone. It was my boss.

"Need some help, Martian?"

"Oh fuck." I threw my gaze to the sky. *Why me?* I asked the puffy white clouds that dotted it. They didn't respond. So, I reluctantly did.

"Go away, Ivan. I told you to stay away from me." My phone stopped ringing. I sidestepped around the lead singer, who incidentally looked like he had just rolled out of bed. His coppery brown hair snarled around his wide shoulders and smushed to his face on one side, he wore only a pair of basketball length exercise shorts and tennis shoes with the laces all undone.

"Already here. Might as well let me help you. Oops." He caught my towel as it took that inopportune moment to unravel from my hair. "Almost lost your turban in the dust." He extended it to me, but of course I couldn't accept it because my hands were full. He grinned. "Looks like you might have to accept my help after all."

"Fine." I sighed. "But don't get any ideas."

"I've got lots of ideas where you're concerned, Tigress. But don't get all huffy with me, and I'll table them for now." I didn't bother speaking to him again. It only seemed to encourage him. He followed alongside me as I practically sprinted to the bus. "I heard what you said to Sky."

I glanced his way to find him staring at me.

"Interesting insights into your views on sex."

Oh joy.

"Can we *not* have this conversation?"

"Too late. It's already out there. So, as you eloquently described it. You got some from me, a lot of some..." He paused to emphasize.

"I did. You were great. You're a fantastic fuck. You're also a first-rate jerk. Now give me my towel back." I stretched out my hand, but he shook his head.

"Uh-uh, not until you answer something for me. Did you trust

ROCK *fuck* CLUB BOOK 3   115

Hawk? Was he the one you gave that part you wouldn't even consider giving anyone else?"

"On second thought." I spun and walked away. "Keep the towel."

He didn't follow me. I stomped onto the bus and gave Les my taco salad. I didn't feel like eating anymore.

Later, much later, I emerged from my bunk and found the towel folded on the floor beside it.

CHAPTER
fourteen

I SNAPPED AT LES FOR LETTING IVAN in and then had to apologize to him afterward for being an ass. The gaffer/grip wasn't to blame for my irritation. I knew how effortlessly disarming the lead singer of the Enthusiasts could be. After all, hadn't he used kindness to set me up and put me on the spot?

Listening to my voicemail message from Suzanne after eating a protein bar for lunch didn't improve my mood. She was vexed that I hadn't started the interviews on the guys Raven had fucked.

Oh, yay me. I was just raring to get on that job. Don't do anything to make Lucky's case against me or solidify Raven's low opinion, Barbara had cautioned. Well, I don't think she factored in the interviews.

Yet, wouldn't it be better to get all the potential pain over with it as soon as possible? We still had four more hours on the bus until we got to Tampa. I decided I might as well get started. I mean what the hell else did I have to do?

"Hello," he answered on the first ring. Suzanne's secretary had scrupulously obtained direct private cell numbers.

"Hi Mr. Michaels. It's Marsha West calling from WMO."

"It's just Rayne. Is Raven with you?"

"Um, no. But I wanted to ask you some questions about the night you spent with her on the record if you don't mind?"

"I'd rather talk to her."

"I'm sorry but it's only me for now. And I just have a few things to ask."

"Alright, shoot."

"Well for starters. Why did you agree to be Raven's first fuck?"

"Isn't it obvious? She's a gorgeous woman. And intriguing."

"You were attracted to her. So, that's it? That's the only reason you agreed to be on the show?"

"Well." A pause. "That, plus, my agent advised me it would be good publicity for me with the younger demographic Raven represented."

It always came down to that, I imagined. All these guys cared about was their careers. No wonder he'd approached her in New York. His interest had less to do about her as a person than as a marketing tool. Something I should keep in mind going forward, not that I had truly bought into Von's attentiveness. But if deep down I had, I would be wise to remember my role and keep in mind that the desire the rock stars showed me was likely even less honest than my usual hookups.

"I only have one more question. If it were Raven talking to you right now instead of me what would you say to her?"

"I would say I've never been with a more beautiful woman. I would say let's get together again. I would tell her to return my calls."

I said goodbye to Rayne after emphasizing that I had absolutely no sway with Raven where he was concerned. I jotted down a few notes, mostly about what video footage that I wanted to include with his segment. Then I went to the next name on my list.

"John speaking."

"Hi. It's Marsha West from...

"Hello cunt. Goodbye cunt." He hung up.

I rolled my eyes. Jotted down one word: asshole. I had plenty of things to say about him. Tons of footage. Stuff that had been cut from the other night. He had been so high his close-ups had been truly unflattering. I smiled. I looked forward to including them.

Onto the next. Juaquin 'King' Acenado. I circled his name. The hot sexy Latino drummer for Tempest. His band would be making a guest appearance in Tampa. I typed up a brief email listing a few questions, copied Barbara in on it and dialed my boss' personal number.

"Hello Marsha. I tried to call you earlier."

"I got your message. I've started the phone interviews and copied you in on my proposed questions for Acenado, but I phoned because I wanted to talk to you about Barbara. I think you should consider her as an executive producer for my season.

"I thought you wanted that credit for yourself."

I did. At least before I had lost my support network. "Not anymore. Barbara's been looking out for me, functioning in the role of a producer without getting proper credit or reimbursement. She's really the best woman for the job."

"Fine. I'll call her right now and offer her the position." There was a short pause as if she were typing. When she didn't continue, I started to say goodbye.

"There's another thing. The JGB segment didn't test favorably."

"I know. Barbara told me. I'm working on a theme for my season."

"Branding is paramount in this industry. If viewers can't empathize with your decisions, then they won't identify with you and your season will be a failure."

"I get it."

"Choose who you want to Marsha, but you're going to have to let the audience have a glimpse into your mindset and motivations."

"I understand." My conversation with Rayne had driven that point home. "Is there anything else?"

"Yes. I wanted to be sure you didn't leave off Ivan Carl when you're doing the interviews. He's the reason Raven started the RFC. And his band is headlining the tour."

"Co-headlining," I corrected in a grumble, not liking the reminder of the unpleasant task ahead.

"As you wish. I cannot overemphasize the importance of sitting down with him. There are always two sides to every story. A good interviewer never lets bias and preconceived notions enter into the equation."

"Be objective. I hear you. Well, if that's it, I'd better get back to work." Surely, she had other stuff to do besides hassling me.

"Marsha, one more thing."

Ok, maybe not.

"I'm not oblivious to what you've been going through on a personal level."

I squeezed my eyes tightly shut.

"I want you to take some time for yourself today. The Grand Hyatt is close to the venue and near some excellent shopping. Buy yourself a few things. You've been wearing outfits that don't seem to be in line with the way you dressed in the first season. Don't change who you are to reflect who you're with. Change who you're with by being who you truly are. Go to the spa today, too. Haircut and style, massage, the works. You're looking subpar. Sleep deprived and wan. Hang out by the pool. Get some sun. And drink less tequila. Don't drown your feelings. That never works. And don't give up on Raven. She sacrificed a lot for you. She just might come around."

I stared at my cell for a few moments, wondering what had gotten into the normally reserved exec. Then, I set my phone beside me and got back to work. I still had a couple of hours trapped on the bus. After that I had a WMO credit card and carte blanche from my boss. Which meant...

I had some serious shopping to do.

CHAPTER fifteen

I DON'T KNOW WHAT IT WAS ABOUT getting a mani-pedi that made me feel like a brand-new person. I know. I know. So, I had added in a few extra services at the spa that hadn't exactly been preauthorized, but they had fallen within the spirit of Smith's suggestion.

As I sat in a lounge chair beside the infinity pool, I held my hand out in front of me and admired the polish. The deep sapphire shade complimented the baby blue shine of my eyes or at least that was what the technician had said. It might have been a line, but it looked good, and more importantly...it felt good.

"Another piña colada, Miss West?" the young waitress asked.

"No, thank you," I shaded my gaze with my hand over my sunglasses to see her. The setting sun was in my eyes. "But some ice water would be nice. One for me and one for my companion."

"Yes, please." In the chaise beside me, Barbara lifted her hand an inch, rotated it slightly and stuck her thumb in the air to show her approval. No doubt, she was exhausted. I had drug her along with me shopping and then to the spa. She had been so liquified after the massage that she had practically melted into her lounger.

"Maybe we should think about going in soon." She peered at me over the rim of one of her new purchases, a cute pair of Cat-Woman shaped Revo sunglasses.

"Nah. Give me a few more minutes, Mother Hen." I fake-whined. "Please."

"Alright." She huffed a lock of golden hair out her eyes. "But that's executive producer to you."

"Yeah. Yeah. Executive task master is more like it. Do I really have to meet with Juaquin tonight?"

She nodded. "He's got three interviews for his rap album before you, so it won't last long. Then, we'll go over the band bios one more time. Then, you'll need to pick your fuck number five. I'll take care of the logistics. Then, and only then, we'll both call it an early night. Tomorrow's going to be a long day. Don't forget you have to interview Ivan in the morning, so no tequila. I know you'll want to be sharp for that.

I would want a sharp object handy, I thought but tabled the quip. Movement across the pool deck had caught my eye.

Ivan and Tyler, both looking sexy as shit in board shorts and nothing else. My gaze stalled as they stopped by the railing to watch the sunset over the bay. Of course I tried to pretend I didn't see them. The young waitress, who had been heading toward me and Barbara with our two glasses of ice water, u-turned for them. No pretense with her, she smiled widely, her flip-flops snapping her eager willingness to serve and obey. She didn't seem deterred by the entourage that went along with them. Each guy had two girls, one on either side. Model types. The confidence I felt in the white crochet bikini I had just bought diminished greatly when I compared the way I looked in mine with the way they looked in theirs. Younger. Prettier. Curvier.

Even my pleasure in my manicure seemed chipped as I watched a pretty redhead trail her hand down the rigid contours of Ivan's chest. I glanced away when she reached the waistband of his light blue swim trunks. They were slung low. They couldn't go much lower without revealing secrets I already knew. Not that I wanted to see any of him again. And not that I cared how he looked, or who he was with. I was just irritated because I was thirsty and hot.

I threw my legs over the side of the chaise arching my back and stretching. My muscles were tight. So what if my itty bitty top rode a little higher exposing some serious under boob.

"Where you going?" Barbara asked, her gaze where mine had been a moment before. Male laughter and fake feminine giggles drifted our way.

"To the bar to get us something to drink."

"Mars," she cautioned.

"Just water. I'm hot, and our waitress got waylaid." Ivan and Tyler—the bastards—were currently drinking our waters. "I'll be right back."

I slipped my glittery toes into white wedge sandals that matched my bikini. My hips swayed as I glided to the bar. In my peripheral vision it gave me some satisfaction to see Ivan's head turning to mark my movement. Once I reached the round rattan topped Tiki hut, I located an empty stool and bent over to straighten —unnecessarily— the fastening on my ankle bracelet.

Suddenly there were large hands bracketing my hips. "Stay like that. I want to savor this." A burst of hot breath gusted my ear. Turning, I found Ivan grinning unrepentantly.

"Uh-uh," he tutted at me. "Sheath the claws, Tigress. You got my attention."

"I wasn't trying to get your attention," I sputtered. "I was just making a point."

"And your point is?" His eyes flashed with challenge, and my body flashed with heat in response. His long fingers were spread wide on the skin above my barely there bikini bottom. His strong thighs were pressed to my softer tapered ones. Every part of me was immensely aware of every part of him. The need I desperately wanted to deny was telegraphed throughout my body originating from those points where we were connected.

"I'm hot." I flicked a lock of damp hair over my shoulder.

Yes." He lowered his gaze to my tits and the rest of me, taking me in and looking like he wanted to devour me that very moment. "You most certainly are."

"Those two waters you and Tyler drank," I said out loud while my lowered lids and parted lips said, 'Yes, look, take, lick, suck and swallow.' It couldn't be as good as I remembered it, being with him. It was just his proximity, his sexy body, his compelling heat and the woodsy masculine scent of him that demanded, that coaxed, that urged me to give in and have him again. "Those drinks were mine," I complained.

"I'll buy you other ones."

"You ruin everything."

"You assume I ruin everything." His voice gravelly, his dark brows lowered over his even darker eyes. "Because when we're alone, you never give me a fucking chance to react, let alone fix anything."

"I..." I lost my train of thought as his eyes blazed into mine.

"You know what I mean." I felt his fingers at my hips digging deeper into my flesh. "I know you do. You decide, you determine how it is, you and you alone. Don't deny it." His gaze intense beams like truth seeking lasers, he held me, my body and my mind captive.

"No. Not me. You. You can't turn this around." The past was set. Yet, here he was attempting to recast his role in it. Like a fire, he was dangerous. So dangerous. He incinerated my willpower and burnt up my better intentions, but I couldn't allow him to put a torch to history.

"Well, well, well, what do we have here?"

Ivan snapped his head to the side to regard the devilishly grinning guy who had just spoken. I took advantage of the interruption. Stepping backward, I breathed in and out, my nerves sizzling and my chest heaving for air.

"Seems they'll let any old loser on this tour."

"Apparently," Ivan returned.

"Touché, asshole."

They thumped each other on the back like good friends who hadn't seen each other in a while. "Let me buy you a beer." The devilish grin widened. "And one for your lady friend. She can have whatever she wants, including me."

"I don't," I huffed, and his booming laughter drowned out the rest of my denial.

Oh great, I thought. *Now I've got two arrogant men to deal with.*

"What's your name, sweet thing?" the newcomer asked giving me a head to toe leisurely scan.

"Cage it, Mike. She's not on the menu."

"Oh fuck!" I exclaimed as recognition dawned. "You're Mike Shocks from Rage Element." The ball cap and the shades he wore were a good disguise. "I love your music."

"I love that you love it, darlin'," he drawled. He was a southerner like Ivan and me, only his accent had been tempered by years of living in England. "What's your poison of preference?" He smoothly inserted himself between Ivan and me.

"She likes tequila," Ivan answered, frowning as Mike shifted closer to me and placed one of his hands low on my back.

"She one of yours?" Ivan's friend queried.

"I'm not one of anybody's. I'm Marsha West."

Both of Mike's blond brows rose above the rim of his sunglasses. "The Rock Fuck Club chick?"

I nodded. "My reputation precedes me."

"Your pictures hardly do you justice." He lowered his voice while Ivan noticeably bristled. "What'll it be?" He gave me another 'I'm imagining you naked' look. "And how soon before I can get it…I mean you up to my room? Or on your bus? Or against the wall? Or preferably all three?"

CHAPTER
sixteen

U P IN MIKE'S ROOM, A PENTHOUSE SUITE much larger than the room Barbara and I shared, I held a shot glass between my hands while the lead singer of Rage Element stood behind me trapping me in his arms.

"Nice view," he commented, shifting to brush a length of my hair aside and pressing his warm lips into the sensitive skin beneath my ear.

"Yes," I agreed absently. Feeling hardly anything from his affection, I feigned a smile for Ignacio's video camera lens. Carla shifted nearby, waiting in case any part of me got smudged unbecomingly.

"I meant you." His hands moving to my upper arms, Mike turned me away from the view of the harbor out the window directly in front of us. More pointedly, he turned me away from the reflection of the interior of the large living slash dining space behind us occupied by twenty or more others and featuring Ivan and the redhead. Those two had been making out the entire time the crew had been filming.

"Hey, why the sad eyes?" Mike ran the back of his knuckles down my cheek. "You're a million miles away."

"I love that song." My flattened lips lifted.

"There's my girl." He searched my gaze a beat. We had barely spoken beyond some flirty words at the bar and a few pleasantries as the crew had set up. But I didn't correct him that I wasn't his or anyone else's. I was my own. My thoughts were my own. My life was my own. Being self-contained used to bring me comfort. But right now, with the camera on and everyone watching my every move, I wasn't comfortable at all.

Mike was contributing to that unease. He had morphed from hard press come-ons to waxing poetic as soon as Ignacio had started filming. My guess was that he had a directive from his label to soften his appeal with women. Well, fine. If he wanted to pretend in front of the lens I could, too. Though that wasn't what I had done with Von. So far my fuck with the Monsters' guitarist had been the most like the hookups that had been my norm before the RFC.

"You want another shot?" Mike's gaze dipped to my empty glass, then lifted, the question remaining in his light grey eyes.

"No. Not right now."

"Whatever you need, babe. Whatever you desire. I'll fulfill all your wishes tonight."

Ugh, another song reference. I started to frown but noticed Ivan watching us closely. "I have a lot of fantasies involving you. What woman doesn't?"

Focus on that, Marsha. There's truth in that. I had watched him, stared into his half-lidded eyes in his music videos and wondered what it would be like to be with him.

I swiveled to deposit my shot glass on a nearby table, so I could place both my hands on Mike's solid chest instead. A real rock star was better than the seductive image of one on the screen.

Wasn't it?

A couple feet away, Ivan's gaze met mine. Sometimes it was even b…I shut down that stray thought as the frontman of the Enthusiasts frowned at me. He was eyeing me closely despite the fact that the redhead was suctioning the side of his neck with the focused intensity of a vampire searching for a carotid artery.

"Fantasies, huh?" Mikes lids lowered. The video rock star and the live one next to me morphed into one. "What's the first one on your list?"

"I don't know if I should tell you." I batted my lashes. "It's very naughty."

Obviously listening, Ivan came forward onto the edge of his seat. Undeterred, the parasite on his throat moved with him.

"Naughty is my specialty." Mike informed me.

"Yeah?" I purred.

"Try me."

"How about your brother?" I glanced across the room at the blond who resembled his younger sibling only with shorter hair and sand rather than grey eyes.

"Daniel?"

I nodded, deeply pleased to note Ivan's scowl.

"Does he like it naughty, too?"

"You wanting to do both of us darlin'?" Mike's grey eyes flared.

"I've heard about your naked parties for three."

"You have, huh?" It suddenly didn't seem as though he was playing a part anymore. He gave me a long measuring glance, then turned, grabbing me by my upper arm. "I'm in," he said. "But let's go check with my brother." On the way across the room, I noticed the camera tracking us and Ivan as well. His frown had deepened.

Good.

Put me on the spot? Play me? Make me doubt myself with his revisionist history? Two could play that game. It was my turn to ruin something for him.

As Mike introduced me and explained what I had proposed to his sibling, I felt Ivan's laser gaze trained on us.

"Count me in," Daniel decided, after looking me over. Exchanging a glance with his brother that seemed to communicate something additional, he relinquished his hold on a brunette and pulled me into him instead. "You start on the top half of her bro. I'll work on the bottom." As Mike reached for and then yanked loose the top bow on my bikini top, his brother tugged on the scrap of fabric at my hips. The outside door to the suite suddenly rattled as it slammed. A glance over at the couch revealed Ivan and the redhead had exited the scene.

That didn't bother me in the least. He had his fuck, I had mine. He might have left with his. He might fuck her real good like he had done me once upon a time. But I would bet he would do her tonight thinking about me.

"OH, YES," I MOANED my approval.

"You like that, babe?" Mike queried.

"Yes. Do it again. The plucking thing, but harder."

"This?" Mike rolled my nipple between his finger and thumb.

"Yes," I moaned as he pinched the elongated tip. "Again, please," I begged.

Mike complied, and at my other tit his brother did the same. Both twisting and pulling my nipples as if they were plucking their guitar strings. Pleasure resonated from my breasts to my pussy. Wet heat rushed to my core.

"Mouths, too."

I didn't have to say more. Warm lips latched onto each of my breasts. Wet tongues licked and circled. When they both sucked and lapped my nipples in concert, yet in different rhythms, my knees suddenly went weak.

"I can't stand," I warned.

Mike released my nipple with a pop. "I've got you, babe." He swept me up into his arms. Daniel gave me one last leisurely lick, then lifted his blond head and gave me a devilish look like his brother had when I had first met him.

"This naked party is moving to the bedroom," Daniel decided.

An anticipatory shiver rolled through me. A couple of determined strides later we were in the bedroom. Aquatic blue and ocean foam white decor greeted us. The door clicked closed. Mike deposited me in the center of the bed someone had already turned back. Both men stared at me. Only in my crochet cover up—the bikini top and bottom having been left behind in the other room along with the film crew—I felt exposed but didn't attempt to cover my nudity. This was a naked party after all.

"Take off your shorts." I dipped my head and followed my own hand as I trailed it down the center of my body all the way to my pussy. I drew in a sharp breath as pleasure pierced my core. Because of what we had already done in the other room, I was ready. I heard two groans that told me I wasn't the only one.

"She's hot as fuck."

"I get her first."

"No, you were first with the last one."

I glanced up to see both men were naked. About the same height, both were in excellent shape. Slabs of hard muscle. Even harder cocks jutted out from between their tensed thighs. But the arguing that continued over apparently a specific woman other than me diminished my desire greatly. So did the sudden thought that their arguing reminded me of my own brothers.

"Hey guys." I wiggled my fingers. "I'm still here. Alone."

Both turned to me, the surprised looks on their faces cooling any lingering desire.

They had forgotten me.

"I'm leaving." I pulled the edges of my cover up together and scooted to the edge of the bed.

"Whoa." Mike put a hand on my thigh.

"Yeah, hold up." Daniel placed his hand on my other thigh.

"You're perfect."

"Sexy as hell."

"I remind you of someone else?"

"Yes," they replied in unison.

Oh, joy.

"Someone who wasn't open to the idea of the two of us sharing her." Mike frowned.

"It's tricky." Daniel's dark blond brows dipped. "We don't have a thing for each other. We just both love her. It feels right when we're together. We tried to explain that to her."

"But she didn't go for it." Mike's frown deepened, as did the dip in his sibling's brows.

"You don't have to stay of course," Daniel said, stroking my knee.

"Even though we are both very much interested in having a turn with you." Mike slid his hand up an inch and squeezed my thigh. Warmth flared at the point of contact. Not the heat of a moment before but something more.

"We can pretend," I offered.

Two sets of eyes widened.

"I mean, you can close your eyes if you need and pretend I'm her. I have someone I loved and lost, too. This can be total make believe for me, too. Or we can call it off. Keep each other's secrets. WMO doesn't have to know everything that happens once the cameras go off and the bedroom door closes."

There was a moment of consideration. Both siblings exchanged a long glance. Then they turned back to me, their intent obvious, their motions and desires in sync once more. They each put a hand on my shoulders and slowly slid the other ones up my thighs.

"Let us love you, baby," Mike said with so much emotion that I felt it in the center of my chest. Daniel didn't speak but wore a look that mirrored the longing in his brother's words.

"Yes," I agreed.

How had this woman refused them?

I certainly didn't. I surrendered to their affection. It felt as though I were being worshipped. Each guy stroking my skin. My feet, my calves, my thighs. Then they separated, Mike up at the top, he seemed to be a breast man, or it certainly seemed that way by the amount of attention he gave my tits. Shaping and lifting each with his hands. Showering the surface of my skin with warm kisses. Then circling and sucking one taut tip and then the other before I could catch my breath. Daniel wasn't idle. But his focus was between my legs. He teased at first, caressing my thighs and stroking my mound but didn't spread me open until his brother's wet lips fastened on my nipple. At that very same moment, Daniel put his lips on me.

On my clit.

I moaned.

Daniel groaned.

I felt the vibration of his need. Already swollen and wet, I began to throb. The rhythm of my pleasure matched theirs. Mike started to lick my nipples faster. Daniel tongued my clit harder. Mike sucked one aching tip and pinched the other. Daniel circled.

It built.

Fast.

"So good," I panted, arching my back off the cool sheets beneath me. It was a sharp contrast to all the heat.

"Let it go." Between my legs, Daniel breathed a burst of warm breath onto my clit.

"Explode for us, pretty girl." Daniel's blond head lifted, his hot gaze meeting my equally hot gaze.

I let it go.

I closed my eyes.

A wet mouth sucked my nipple. A firm tongue lapped at my clit. I reached deep into the vault for a memory. Emotion pricked my heart as I held a snapshot of one in my mind. His caring golden eyes. His gorgeous smile. My body started to quiver like a bow getting ready to release an arrow. I felt the fine edge of sharp teeth, a bite and a sting at my nipple. I felt hard suction at my clit, the pleasure rising and intensifying inside of me to the point where pleasure almost became pain. I cried out as it hit me. I did explode. I shattered. I lost it. I lost him. I couldn't see his face anymore. Caring eyes became mocking ones. A safe smile a dangerous one. And as my spent psyche plummeted downward from the stars like a dying dream, it wasn't Hawk anymore in my mind's eye.

CHAPTER seventeen

"Hey. You ok?" Barbara asked, skirting the couch and coming toward me as soon as I entered our room.

No, was on the tip of my tongue after my tête à tête with the brothers, but then I noticed the guy on the couch who had turned to regard me. I pulled the edges of my cover up together as he swept his dark gaze over me.

"Do I need to reschedule King?" Barbara asked, a worried crease marring her delicate brow.

"No, of course not." I frowned. "Might as well get his interview over with." And did I really want to be interrogated by my roommate or worse be left alone to examine my own thoughts?

Why the fucking hell had I been thinking of Ivan Carl while being worshipped by two gorgeous men?

I didn't want to know. I truly didn't. I rubbed my upper arms trying to remove the chill from my skin.

136   MICHELLE MANKIN

"So where should we do this *bonita?*" King asked, raising an inky black brow. "Your crew's room?"

"I sent Ignacio and the crew away," Barbara explained. "You were late. I assumed you were..." She blushed. "You know having a good time."

"I was, until I wasn't anymore," I stated cryptically. I was staunchly opposed to breaking down what had occurred any further.

"Whatever you say," she decided.

"It's probably for the best." Ignacio was too good at what he did. With me feeling this unsettled his camera might catch something I didn't want preserved on film.

"How so?" The crease in Barbara's brow deepened.

"Just that it would take too long to reassemble them." I set down my room key on the entryway table. "I'm tired, and I'm sure King has better things to do. Why don't you just record us on your cell."

"Me?" Barbara asked. "The film quality won't be very high."

"I'll splice it together with some footage from the concert tomorrow." I moved to take a seat in the easy chair beside King. "It'll be fine."

"Alright," Barbara agreed. "Just pretend I'm not here."

"Ok, I will." I could do that. I was good at faking. Or was I? I mean I'd done alright at the beginning with Mike and Daniel. It was the ending I had flubbed. But was it a flub? I hated Ivan, didn't I? Had thinking about him as I climaxed meant something? What were my true feelings toward my best friend's ex?

"Did you want to ask me a question?" I started as King's voice cut through my thoughts.

"Yes, of course." I cleared my throat. "Um, I only have a few." I planned to ask all the guys the same thing, so I could put the replies together to compare and contrast them. "Why did you agree to be Raven's fuck number three?"

"I was her third?"

I nodded.

"Surprising. I thought I was her last. Most women don't want anyone else after me." He grinned, his teeth a flash of white against his bronzed skin.

"No." There had been the rap duo after him, after she thought Lucky had moved on.

"Guess I didn't make the impression I thought I had." He shrugged shoulders that were as massively wide as Von's.

"You made an impression. But you haven't answered my initial question. Why did you agree to be Raven's fuck?"

"I was at a crossroads in my life. She was an attempt to try to see if I could move on, forget someone else who meant a great deal to me." He let out a breath. "No that's not right. Someone who meant everything to me."

I leaned forward. "Did it work?" His answer was suddenly very important to me. Hawk meant everything. Every guy, every hookup was an attempt to move on, to forget.

"No," he replied.

I sagged.

"And yes."

I sat up straighter.

He tapped rhythmically on his arm rest. "I'm an Acenado man. Once we give our heart away, they're gone. We don't ask for it back." He drummed some more on the upholstery, formulating his thoughts.

I suddenly remembered his pattern with the strippers. How they all had looked alike.

"Did..." I swallowed as my throat went dry. "Did the one who took your heart, is she...did she..." I wanted to ask if he had stood beside her coffin with his hand on the gleaming ebony box wishing he could touch her living breathing warm body one more time.

"Are you ok, *bonita?*"

"Why does everyone keep asking me that?"

"Because you're crying, Mars." Barbara set down her phone on a side table, snapped a tissue from the box beside it, then half-sat on the wide armrest of my chair.

"We'll do this another time," King decided as I dabbed at my cheeks with the Kleenex. "You're upset."

"I am, but I just have to know, how do you do it? How do you live without it?"

"Without what?"

"Without your heart?"

"I have my heart, *bonita*"

"But you said you gave it away. I just thought..."

"I gave it to her, but she kept it safe. At the right time, the best time, she gave me hers in return." He thumped his chest with his fist. "Even when she's at home and I'm away from her she's always with me."

"Oh." I scooted back into my chair, my hand fisted, too, but at my side. I didn't thump my chest with it. The corresponding empty echo would be too harsh. My heart wasn't a home. It was a wasteland. Hawk had never given me his love to keep safe. He had given me his body. He had offered me his name for the baby. But though I had offered him my love he had never, not once, spoken the words in return.

Hawk had been wise to reject me.

I was as untrustworthy as my mother. She had left my father, left all of us, for another man and never looked back.

Raven's parents were right to warn her about me.

It was probably for the best that our friendship was over.

CHAPTER
eighteen

IN THE LOUNGER ON THE SAND, I HUGGED the empty tequila bottle to my chest and watched the sunrise peek over the horizon.

It had been a long night.

I had tried to doze off but given up and gone to the bar instead. The waitress had given me the bottle as a souvenir. She said I'd earned it given the fact that I'd still been able to walk out of the bar after draining it. Well, I'd made it out of the bar and across the pool deck, but I hadn't gotten much further. The ocean had called to me, or maybe I just couldn't stand for my roommate or anyone else to see me in my current condition.

As I expected, the beach was deserted this early in the morning. There was only a private *casita* on stilts on one side of me and a fishing pier on the other, plus a small opening in the dense underbrush leading to a jogging path along the waterfront. I had plenty of space to contemplate. The problem? I was never a big fan of the exercise. It meant thinking too deeply. It meant pondering my life. My motives.

My mistakes. The disaster I'd made of everything and the likelihood that my father had been right all along about me.

I closed my eyes and scrubbed at my closed lids seeing stars behind them. The stars I'd been catapulted into earlier and imagined not the man of my dreams, but the one troubling my slumber.

I groaned and cracked open my bleary eyes. I just couldn't do this introspective shit anymore.

I suddenly heard a door sliding open on a metal track, footsteps on the wooden deck above me accompanied by voices. Panic sliced through my tequila haze. I didn't want anybody to see me so vulnerable like this.

"What good can come of it? She's not going to change, Raven."

I tripped over the leg of the lounger I'd been trying to rise from. The tequila bottle I'd clutched to my chest fell. It hit the metal side table, clattering loudly while I stood there mesmerized by it. Simultaneously footsteps rushed to the railing. Because I couldn't make myself invisible and because my life sucked, Lucky and Raven looked down at me.

I glanced up, wobbled and waved. "Hey, how 'ya doing? Sorry to interrupt. I thought I was alone out here. I'll just go now."

My getaway skills sucked, too, I only made it a couple of steps.

"Mars." Raven hurried down the stairs and stopped in front of me. Her long black hair loose, she wore a white hotel robe along with an appalled expression. "You look terrible. You're still in the swimsuit you had on yesterday." How did she know that? I narrowed my eyes and she did, too. "Have you been drinking?"

I didn't respond. I would think the answer was obvious given my appearance, the empty bottle and the tequila fumes leaching out of every pickled pore. Plus, my ploddingly processing mind had slowed even further hearing her use the diminutive form of my name.

"Raven," I managed though I had to lock my muscles to keep

from throwing myself into her arms. "I miss you." My eyes flashed with wet. I stared at her, and she stared back.

"I'm sorry I'm such a fuck up. That I fucked up." I slurred my words, and my stomach sloshed as I waved my arms.

"You are who you are," she allowed. Her eyes were soft for a moment, but the moment passed. Warm gold like a new sunrise became the tarnished bronze of some long-forgotten memento.

"Yes, I guess. But I can change. I'm trying to do better."

"Better meaning fucking around with Ivan."

"I'm not. We're not."

"Oh, please. I saw you at the truck stop. Both truck stops. And then here at the pool."

"Oh. Well. It's not what you think." My words sounded hollow and false, even to my own ears.

"It doesn't matter. You can fuck whoever you want, Mars. You usually do." The way she said my nickname this time didn't make me feel all warm, fuzzy and nostalgic. She sighed, and the pitying look she gave me made my eyes burn and my lips tremble. I glanced away so she wouldn't see.

"Alright." I lifted my chin to the water. "I guess I will. And I guess we're through being friends." I tensed, curling my fingers into fists at my sides, not even breathing hoping she would deny it.

"I guess we are." The empty cavern that was my chest collapsed in on itself, my held breath expelled. "Lucky doesn't want me around you when you're being so destructive. And Ivan and me, well you know how I feel about that. After what he did to you I don't know how you can even tolerate him." She exhaled again. "I just don't understand you. And I wonder if you even understand yourself. I thought you loved my brother."

"I did. Then I didn't, I guess. Back when we were friends you might have understood. I understood you while you figured things out with Lucky." A shadow crossed her gaze.

"You did. I remember. I remember a lot of things."

"Not well enough," I snapped unkindly. "Not all the times I was there for you. Not all the promises we made about being there for each other no matter what. I've always honored those promises. Even after I checked myself into the psychiatric hospital, I called you every day. It was so easy to fool you about where I was, and what I was going through. You were so wrapped up in your cocoon you didn't even notice."

"I'd lost my brother, Marsha. And my mother before that."

"At least you had a mother. I lost a lover and a baby. Do you really want to compare lives and losses?" My eyes blazed accusation. I pressed on when maybe I should have shut my stupid mouth. "Didn't you ever wonder why I always wanted to be at your house? Why I always envied you? Why I went for the guys you rejected? Maybe I wished I could have some small portion of the good life you had."

"No, Mars." Her gaze hardened. "I didn't because you never shared. You always shut down when I dug too deep."

"Maybe because I knew we'd always end up right here. With you being disappointed with me. With you judging me like my father does."

"Marsha." She stepped closer. "No." That's when I saw that I wasn't the only one with tears in my eyes.

"I don't want your pity. I don't need it or your friendship. Go on back to Lucky. Don't worry about me anymore. I'm ok. I'm fine. I have Barbara looking after me. I have lots of rock stars to fuck. There's so much fun to have, I really don't have any time for you anyway."

"Go away, Barbara." Rising up on one elbow in the bed, I lifted my other arm and shielded my eyes with my hand to ward off the arrow of light from the open door.

"It's not Barbara," a deep male voice replied.

Fuck. I collapsed back on the sheets and yanked the comforter over my head. "Go away, Ivan."

"No way." I heard a jingle that sounded like his wallet chain as he crossed the room. "Guess you forgot my interview. "But this is much more fun." He dropped down on the bed. The mattress dipped from his weight jostling me. His scent, more sandalwood than anything else as if he had just showered in a stream of his cologne, rolled over me. My stomach roiled.

"I'm gonna be sick," I warned.

He got up as quickly as he had taken a seat. I jumped out of the bed and sprinted to the attached bathroom, making it to the toilet just in time. Heave after heave of surplus tequila came up. My sides were aching by the time I was through. I reached for the hand towel above my head, but he beat me to it.

"Here."

"Thanks."

"Don't mention it."

"Don't you ever mention seeing me like this," I croaked. Dabbing my mouth with the towel, I started to stand. My head jerked back. "Let go of my hair, Ivan."

"Just trying to help out."

"I don't need any help."

"I don't believe that's true."

"I don't care whether you do or don't."

"I get that. But I'm already here, and I have some experience with your current state, though it's been a while for me. Trust me when I tell you it's best not to get agitated."

"Ok." I was in too much agony to argue. I let him help me to my feet. I avoided his gaze and my own reflection in the mirror as I brushed my teeth, then finished with a gargle of Listerine. "Step aside." I glared at him after I turned around. The room spun with me. But I got that he looked good. Really good. Button down shirt in olive that brought out the copper in his brown hair and deepened the rich chocolate ganache of his eyes. Except, he appeared to be vibrating as he casually leaned against the door frame. Vibrating I noted to the same beat as the incessant drumming inside my head. "I need...

"Some Advil," he filled in, turning sideways so I could brush past him. I could feel him watching me as I returned to the bed. "Yikes, babe. You're tiptoeing like the carpets made of broken glass."

"No, just my skull."

"Gotcha. I'll get three caplets."

I carefully climbed into the bed, propped up a few pillows and laid back on the mattress with my arm over my eyes again like a compress. It didn't help. Just the diffused light that leaked through stirred another wave of nausea.

"Sit up." I felt his hand slide along my back. I didn't protest his help. I needed it. "Here." Still holding me steady with one hand, he offered me the ibuprofen.

"Water?" I asked.

"Oops." He withdrew his hand from my spine. I immediately mourned the loss of his warmth on my skin.

"Here." This time he held a glass of water in one hand and the caplets in the other.

"Thanks," I mumbled taking the pills, my fingertips brushing the skin of his palm, and my stomach summersaulting before I even popped the Advil in my mouth. Touching him felt more like a caress.

ROCK *Fuck* CLUB BOOK 3   145

After I swallowed the painkillers gingerly with a few sips of the water, I handed him the glass and collapsed back into the pillows.

"You think they'll stay down?"

"Fifty-fifty," I mumbled with my eyes squeezed closed.

"You'd probably up the odds if you could tolerate some dry toast."

"I can't."

"Alright."

I cracked open an eye. "You never agree with me."

"That's not true."

"See," I pointed out.

He grinned. The brilliance of him with that smile directed at me was too much. He saw it. The result on my face. Then the sudden pallor. He jumped out of the way. I leapt from the bed. I repeated the ick in the bathroom, rinsed, brushed and gargled, and he assisted, helping me back to the bed afterward. I didn't just collapse into the bed the second time. I passed out cold.

CHAPTER
nineteen

"**H**AVE YOU SEEN MY BLACK BRA WITH the purple lace?"

"No." Barbara sighed. Turning away from the dressing mirror she'd been using to put on her makeup, she frowned at the sight of me still in my robe. "You need to get dressed. We're already late. Ignacio has texted me twenty times asking when we're going to arrive."

"We'll get there when we get there." I didn't like to be rushed, especially when I was irritated or trying to work something out in my head. Something was different inside me. Something had changed. Something that made me feel lighter. I went back to sorting through the pile of clothes on the bed while also running through the events of the night before. The bar. The beach. Raven. How could I possibly feel lighter after that?

"Give it up." Coming closer, Barbara put her hands on her hips. "You're not going to find it. Pick another bra. You have at least three that color."

"Four," I corrected, giving her an imperious look. Didn't she know you could never have enough black bra variants? "I don't like giving up." I wasn't a quitter. I had a host of readily apparent faults, only that wasn't one of them. "A-ha! Here it is!" I drew the bra to my chest but stopped when I saw what had been lying underneath it in the bed. "Um, Barbara." I shifted to regard her. "Why is Ivan's wallet chain on my bed?"

Her brow scrunched. "I guess it came off while he was sleeping with you."

My eyes rounded. "I didn't sleep with Ivan Carl." I wouldn't forget that.

"Whatever you want to call it, Mars. When I came in her to check on you, you were both pressed together in this bed with lights out and eyes closed."

"With clothes or without?" I gulped.

"You don't remember?"

"Uh-uh." I rubbed my temples. I'd woken up without any headache, and I had felt surprisingly well-rested, but suddenly, my headache was trying to make a comeback.

"Wow. Well." She tapped her chin. "I could only see your top half. You were in the bikini top." I let out a relieved breath. That's what I had woken up in along with the matching bottom. "He had his arms around you, Mars."

"Shit." I squeezed my eyes shut. I didn't want to hear more, but she kept talking.

"You looked very comfortable with him. You had your head on his chest. He had his hand over yours beside it. You were smiling."

"Blah. Blah. Blah." I quickly covered my ears. "Don't say anymore," I begged. "Please."

She nodded. I dropped my hands. "You wanna tell me what's really going on with you two?"

"Nothing's going on," I insisted. But was that the truth? Was it possible that the lightness I felt was somehow related to him? My cell dinged with a text.

Yay, I thought, letting out a relieved sigh. A timely interruption slash distraction. I scooped my cell off the nightstand and glanced at the display.

Lying, cheating, arrogant prick: Hey Martian.

I had renamed Ivan in my phone contact list after he had cheated on Raven.

Lying, cheating, arrogant prick: I can't find my wallet chain. Have you seen it?

I threw my eyes to the ceiling. Not a distraction just a continuation of my headache.

Marsha: I'll have someone bring it to you at the venue.

I dropped down on the bed after I typed the reply.

"That Ivan?" Barbara guessed.

"Yeah," I nodded numbly.

Lying, cheating, arrogant prick: Thx. When u getting here? I thought u were a rock chick.

Marsha: I AM a rock chick.

Lying, cheating, arrogant prick: Hmm. Doubtful. A rock chick's top priority is the music. And the first band's already been on. You missed them.

Marsha: I know. I'm trying to get there before I miss any more.

Lying, cheating, arrogant prick: Then get your sexy ass here already.

Marsha: If you would leave me the hell alone I could get dressed and do just that.

Lying, cheating, arrogant prick: You're not dressed??? (A tongue hanging out emoticon). Are you naked?

"Sleeping together? Lightning texting back and forth afterward? Nothing to tell, huh?" Barbara shook her head at me as I stared at her blankly. Then she snorted. "Yeah, right."

OVER THE COURSE OF the ten-mile chauffeured drive over to the Midflorida Amphitheatre, I went over my plan for the evening with Barbara.

"So, Gale LaFleur from Anthem is your guy?"

I nodded.

"Kinda tame after the ones you've had so far."

"Yeah." He probably was, but I wasn't in the mood for naughty again tonight. I had that something I needed to figure out. I had decided that the lightness I currently felt must be because I had gotten some things off my chest with Raven. The flirty stuff by the pool, the unexpected consideration when I had gotten sick, the sleeping together, the cute texting after? The sexy lead singer on the other side of all those things? He didn't factor. He couldn't factor. I wouldn't allow it. "This is my season. I hold the cards. I choose. And I choose nice tonight."

At the venue we were greeted by an onsite event coordinator who seemed to have been waiting for us. All efficiency in a blue blazer with the amphitheater logo pinned to his lapel, he escorted us straight to a VIP area. We were frowned at by the masses as we bypassed the long lines for general admission and entered a roped off area with lounge type seating directly in front of the stage. Barbara took a seat in one oversized upholstered chair, and I took the one next to her. The chairs faced the stage. We were close enough that we could easily see everything that went on up there, but far enough away that we didn't

150   MICHELLE MANKIN

have to crane our necks to see it. A waitress in a short skirt about the same length as mine suddenly appeared with a tray and two glasses of champagne and two red roses.

"Marsha West?" she queried looking at me.

"Yes, that's me." I nodded.

"These are for you and your friend. Compliments of your favorite rock star."

"Oh. How...nice." I didn't know where Gale LaFleur was or when his band was scheduled to take the stage, but I saw Ignacio and the crew. They were in position and already recording.

Smiling softly, I thanked the waitress and took one of the roses and one of the flutes. I laid the rose on the cushion of my chair and lifted my flute up in the air as if to toast my invisible benefactor then clinked my glass with Barbara's before taking a sip. It was dry, bubbly and cold. A good choice for a humid Tampa evening. The VIP seats, the flowers and champagne for me and Barbara? So far Mr. Nice was racking up a lot of style points.

"Eminence is rocking it," Barbara commented, pointing at the stage with her glass.

"Yeah," I agreed. "I've always liked them." Eminence had been around a while. They had hit it big with their first album, but then had mostly drifted into mediocrity with the ones that followed. However right now they were playing some new stuff I hadn't heard before. It was loud and raucous, a good fit with the Gods of Rock lineup.

"Who's next," I asked Barbara after Eminence finished their set and exited the stage. I had noticed she had somehow gotten possession of a printed program.

She lifted her head. "Your guy."

"Oh." My mouth rounded. "So soon?" A band as big as his? They hadn't played live in eighteen months. It was surprising that they weren't scheduled more strategically toward the end of the show.

"Not that soon," she explained. "We missed most of the opening bands. All that's left are Anthem, the Dragons and then Heavy Metal Enthusiasts.

The roadies scrambled around setting up as she spoke. I smoothed the hem of my mini dress, hoping Gale would like it. Deep purple, it featured a retro-inspired silhouette with a double exposed front zip closure and bustier-inspired bodice. The purple lace of the lost-and-then-found bra complemented it. I imagined the bodice to hem zipper of my dress would come in handy as would the front clasp of my bra.

"You look nice." Barbara captured the hand I had been using to fluff my hair.

"You sure?" I grimaced. I hadn't had time for Carla to do my makeup or my hair.

"Yeah. I don't know what product you sprayed on your hair to get it to shine like that, but it's pretty. You look like you just had a blowout."

"Thank you." I captured her hand, squeezed it and pulled in a deep breath. "I'm sorry I've been so hard on you. I've been hurting because of Raven and some other stuff. But you've been nothing but kind and supportive of me. I don't know what I would have done without you."

"Apology accepted, but not necessary. You're under a tremendous amount of stress. It's understandable the way you've reacted. I'm here for you. I'll continue to be here however long you need me. Ok?"

I tilted my head back for another sip of champagne to disguise the way my eyes had watered from her words. If only my former best friend could be as magnanimous.

CHAPTER
Twenty

THE STAGE WAS SET. THE ANTHEM roadies had faded away. The lights across the venue lowered. I scooted forward in my seat.

"I've got goosebumps," Barbara whispered.

"Me, too."

"Have you ever seen them live?"

"No. By the time I got clued into how awesome they were Gale lost..." I trailed off. The lead singer of Anthem had weathered a tragedy that had cut him to the bone much as mine had.

"His wife and son," Barbara completed my thought and touched my hand softly. "And he got on his motorcycle for a year and a half. No one, not even his bandmates heard from him."

"It takes a while to come to terms with something like that," I admitted.

"I don't think you ever come to terms with it," she said gently. "It's more that you come to eventually accept the way things you never wanted to happen end up shaping you."

"Yeah, that's about right," I agreed, but didn't really get a chance for her weighty summation to sink in because moody bass notes suddenly filled the air. Everyone rose to their feet and the band took the stage to thunderous applause. LaFleur came out first followed by the two men who had supported him while he had taken that eighteen-month sabbatical. They all took their customary places on the stage. Gale with his bass guitar slung low, headed to his keyboard. Noah Pearl went to his massive cage like set of drums and Arthur Levine with his gleaming cherry red Les Paul took the left. Beams of lavender and ruby downbursts rained down on the band, a three-man group, a rarity in rock, let alone heavy metal. But then Anthem wasn't a usual band.

Complex compositions, meaningful lyrics, synthesized rock, they were a throwback to the prog rock era and at the same a futuristic stone's throw ahead of everyone else. By the end of their set they proved to any doubters that the trail they had already blazed before Gale's break was only the beginning. The music of Anthem was far from over.

"Wow!" Smiling widely, Barbara fell back into her seat and then scooted forward to bounce on the edge of it. "They were incredible."

"Hell, yeah," I agreed, returning her smile. "Now I'm even more excited to go backstage and meet them."

"Gale doesn't do meet and greets anymore. I thought you saw that in his bio."

"I must have missed it." I frowned. "Shit. I kind of wanted to go to the after-party and meet all the bands."

"You should. We need as much b-roll footage as we can get for your season of RFC."

"But I already agreed to meet Gale right after the show."

"I'll contact him for you. Explain. Tell him you'll be a little late."

154 MICHELLE MANKIN

I gnawed on my bottom lip like Sky did when she was nervous. "But what if he changes his mind?"

"Then he does. You've got a whole slew of bands and lots of guys to choose from."

"Sure," I agreed. "But none as nice as him." And nice seemed important tonight.

"Ivan was pretty nice this morning."

"Yeah, I guess," I allowed. "But I really don't want to think about Ivan right now." And I especially didn't want him anywhere in my mind when I had my seventh RFC fuck later tonight.

A scintillating guitar chord blasted through my thoughts and practically raised the half-roof over the venue. Turning my attention back to the stage, my jaw dropped as I watched Ivan Carl swagger onto the stage with his guitar. A heavy staccato assault heralded his appearance. Tyler was already on his riser, his beard seeming to conduct electricity to his blurring arms as he beat the ever-loving hell out of his kit. Once again, the two best friends were in complete harmony, the rhythm of one complementing the other.

Jagger and Nicholas materialized together. The bassist wore shades and peered over the top of them at the crowd, his green eyes and his manner projecting his cool personality. At the middle of the stage, the two men split off from each other, Jagger going to the far right and Nicholas to the left. Ivan dominated the entire center portion. Only in jeans, his guitar slung low over his narrow hips, Ivan spun as he played. He flirted with the crowd as he worked his way back and forth across the stage. Intimate club or packed venue, front and center was where Ivan Carl belonged. Not that I would ever share that revelation with him. He didn't need more fuel for his inflated ego.

"Why are the Enthusiasts performing now?" Barbara had to shout for her question to be heard over the screeching guitars and thumping drums.

Keeping my eyes on the stage, I shrugged. I had no idea why they weren't owning the honor of headlining. And I didn't want to look away from Ivan. Actually, I wasn't sure I could look away from him, and that was before he started singing.

One number. Two. Whether the actual man himself or the several stories tall projection of him on the seventy-foot LED concert screen, Ivan was power, energy and action. Back to back with his golden-haired rhythm man, grooving with his jet cool bassist or out front with a booted foot balanced on one of the speakers, he jammed on his guitar as if nothing else mattered but that moment in time and his music. It always seemed that way with him. But there was a difference tonight. Tonight, it seemed as though he performed each song for me. His gaze kept returning to the spot where I sat. I tried to play it cool. I didn't stand. I didn't head-bang like everyone around me. I tried to tell myself that I was only imagining his interest and that there was no way he knew where I was in a crowd this large with the spotlight in his eyes.

But he did know I was out there. Without a doubt he knew because he basically addressed me after the final Enthusiasts' song.

"The Dragons are next," Ivan said after thanking the audience for their support. He grinned his sexy half-smile as they cheered louder and raked a thick swath of his sweat drenched chestnut-brown hair out of his glistening chocolate eyes. "There was some dispute with our labels and the tour operators about who rocked harder. But you and me, the guys in my band and a certain rock chick out there." He paused and stared right at me. I sat up straighter. "We all know that Heavy Metal Enthusiasts rock motherfucking harder than anyone else!"

"Whoa. Is it just my imagination?" Barbara flopped back in her seat and gave me a narrowed look as the Enthusiasts took their bows and exited the stage. "Or did Ivan Carl serenade you up there the entire time he was performing?"

"I think he was just trying to get my attention." Why? I had no idea. But then why did Ivan do anything he did? The man's motivations were as difficult to decipher as my own.

"You think?" She snorted. "You mean, you know he was." She shook her head. "You wanna go backstage and see him now?"

"No."

"That was an invitation for you to dis the Dragons, the way they've all been dissing you lately."

"I got the memo." It was a meaningful gesture on Ivan's part. He seemed to be thinking of me even though he had to be fuming mad at his label for letting the Dragons have the top billing tonight. "But if I take him up on it," I reasoned out loud. "Then every single step of my walk backstage is going to be recorded." That would be fine if I was determined to completely torch any chance of reconciling with Raven. But despite all my reckless behavior and bold talk, I wasn't really ready to end things with her for good. If I publicly sided with Ivan, that's for sure what I would be saying to her. Did Ivan want me to align with him? If so, then why? Could it be that the sparks between us were real? What about the concern he had been showing me lately? Was that real as well?

No, Mars... I snuffed out any further reasoning along those lines. The answer was no. The answer was always no with him. We had nothing. We would never have anything. For him it was Raven. Always her. Never me. On the heels of that I had another thought. Maybe Ivan wasn't trying to get Raven back as his girlfriend. Maybe he was trying to get back *at* her—to hurt her—by using me.

IN THE CROWDED after-party room, I spotted Ivan right away. He was surrounded by throngs of groupies. He and Tyler.

"Turn back this way," Ignacio said. "Yes, that's it. Tilt your chin toward me, too. The lighting is good back here and I've never seen that look in your eyes before." Before I could worry about what his lens had captured, large hands, hands I knew all too well, grasped my hips firmly.

"Hey there, Martian." His deep voice rumbled into my ear. My breath caught. I remembered him saying other things while holding me in a similar position. Only it had been a long time ago, and we had both been naked. And it had been so good, so hot when he slid inside and groaned...

"Don't." I swallowed. The heat of his fingers singed my thoughts and the thin cotton of my dress. "Don't touch me."

"Why not?" Ivan released me, but only to grab me by my shoulders to turn me around to face him. "You didn't mind me touching you in your bed earlier." His eyes narrowed on mine.

"I passed out." I glanced over at Ignacio and shook my head at him begging him without words to stop filming.

"I touched you plenty before that."

"That was different." I refocused on the way too handsome frontman trying to ignore how devastating he looked in his slim fitting shirt and sinfully sexy jeans. "If I'm conscious then the answer for you is always no."

"Bullshit." His cajoling expression turned hard. "It wasn't no the first time I ever laid eyes on you. Or the second. Or anytime I'm around, and it's just the two of us. Your pretty blue eyes get sapphire dark. You shiver whenever I touch you. Your pulse flies."

"That's just chemistry. I can't control it."

"You want me." He walked me backward. My back hit the wall. He lifted his arms and caged me in with them.

"I want dick. You have one. You are one. I settled for what I could get, or I used to. Now I have lots of other options. Better ones."

That seemed to really make him mad. "Not like mine." He rolled his hips. His cock—and I remembered it well—was thick and steely-hard. "Not like the party your cunt and my cock have together."

"Maybe not. You have *some* skills." His eyes flared. "But the fallout with you is so not worth it."

"Maybe if you would stop to consider..."

"Oh, please," I cut him off. "You expect me to believe that your sudden interest in me is real?"

"It *is* real. It was real from the very beginning if you would remember correctly. Why are you in denial?"

"I know what you really want."

"Oh, do tell me. I'm just dying to know the tangles in your twisted head."

"You want to fuck me to hurt Raven. You had your eye on Sky first but when that didn't go the way you planned, and you saw how easily you could manipulate me to hurt her..."

"Motherfucking hell!" He threw his arms up in the air and took a big step away from me. "I'm a rocker not some soap opera actor, Mars. I can't believe you think I'm capable of convoluted crap like that." He gave me a hooded look. "You don't know shit."

"I do know. Don't deny it."

"Tyler warned me." He blew out a breath and raked damp hair that seemed freshly washed back from his face. "'Not her,' he told me, "'not again'. But would I listen? Oh no, not me. I thought this time would be different. You're free. I'm free. She's with someone else. And after you two argued I thought I might have a shot without her in the middle between us. But thinking," a guttural self-deprecating sound emanated from deep in his throat, "well, that's obviously a big mistake where you're concerned. So, you wanna know what?"

I nodded, though given the hard way he was regarding me now I was pretty sure I actually didn't want to know.

"Sure. Yeah, I wanna fuck you. I just don't want anything to do with that fucked-up thing inside your chest that substitutes for a heart." He gave me a cutting look. "No one who knows anything about you wants any part of that."

CHAPTER
twenty-one

I MIXED AND MINGLED. I posed for promo shots with all the bands and even the tour promoters, but I worried if any of it would be worth a damn.

Tonight's B roll might all end up on the cutting room floor.

I was too distracted. I couldn't focus after the things Ivan had said. Definitely not after he had stormed out of the party grabbing a blonde wearing too much makeup and a brunette wearing barely enough clothing to cover the important parts along his way.

I wanna fuck you.

Not that badly apparently.

You're free. I'm free.

Um, what the hell did that mean?

Then that last parting jab.

That fucked-up thing inside your chest.

Yeah, ok, that part I got, and it stung, because deep down I agreed with him.

On that unsettling note, I went straight to the bow tied bartender and ordered a double shot. I noticed Ignacio's worried look and his camera lens on me. Barbara frowned but I knocked the shot back anyway. As I blinked through the burn, Von appeared.

"Hey," I said giving him a soft, but genuine smile. "I'm sorry I missed the Monsters' set."

"We were a little off our game tonight." He raked his gaze over me. "Well, I was. Couldn't find you in the audience. And I've been wondering if you gave my idea any more consideration?"

"I'm not free to date anyone right now," I reiterated, my sentiments incongruent to Ivan's. "And you deserve better than me."

"I don't buy that at all." He gave me a firm look. "I think I get to make that determination anyway, not you."

"Don't wait around on me," I insisted, reaching for and squeezing his hand. I hadn't given him the specifics about my life, but I had hinted about a love found and then lost.

"I hear you." He captured my hand before I could withdraw it. Holding it, he peered down at me with his kohl circled, piercing blue eyes. "But I'm still going to leave the door open for you. I like you, Mars. I want you to call me if you need someone, and I'll come. No questions asked. No strings attached."

I should have been comforted by Von's words, and the fact that I had his support, but I was too discombobulated. The anger that had propelled me forward into my season well before tonight's first official tour stop was AWOL. The fuck the world and any sexy rock star I wanted and gain notoriety mentality had fizzled out. Naughty had taken an unexpected turn with the two brothers last night that I hadn't liked.

And now I was here. Not at the venue, but back at the hotel. In the hallway outside Gale LaFleur's penthouse door. Rattled. Majorly. My thoughts in constant rewind with Ivan in the recurrent role.

162 MICHELLE MANKIN

"Ready?" Barbara gave me a searching look with her finger hovering above the ringer to the penthouse.

"Absolutely." I lifted my chin.

"Alright, then." She pressed the button while exchanging worried glances with the crew that I continued to pretend not to notice.

I heard a muffled, "Coming". Then the door popped open.

"Hi," I said as Gale stared at me through his tinted half-moon glasses without speaking a single word. "I'm Marsha."

"Marsha West. The RFC girl." He blinked slowly. "Yes, of course. Pardon my terrible manners." I could hear a Canadian accent in the formal way he pronounced his words. "Come inside." He stepped back and swept his arm wide. "You and your crew."

"Thank you." Balancing in my spiked heels on the plush carpet was difficult, but I somehow navigated to the aqua and cream-colored seating area by the floor to ceiling windows without tripping. It helped to know I had Barbara beside me. A sidekick was important to have along and for nearly the hundredth time I thought about Raven. I wondered if she missed me as much as I missed her. Probably not possible. I gave Barbara a grateful smile wanting her to know I appreciated her before I turned around to face Anthem's lead singer.

"Can I get you anything?" he asked, his gaze pointed just slightly lower than mine. He seemed nervous. In his dark indigo jeans and a t-shirt featuring a complicated physics equation that I'm sure was some kind of geeky inside joke t-shirt, he shifted his slender frame from one navy converse sneaker to the other. "I have sodas, sparkling water, juice perhaps."

"A shot of tequila would be good," I muttered. I needed something to calm my nerves and numb my thoughts. He wasn't the only one who was nervous.

"I'm sorry." A troubled crease marred his sensitive brow. "I don't have any alcoholic beverages. And I won't allow any filming in which it might appear that I condone drinking. I thought I made that clear when I conversed with your producer." He swung a questioning glance to Barbara.

"You did," she said. "You absolutely did. But we've been running behind schedule all evening. I didn't get a chance to brief Marsha. I'm sorry."

"I'm sorry, too," I interjected, feeling bad I hadn't remembered that his wife and infant son had been killed by a drunk driver.

"It's ok." He ran a hand through his hair, pulling the heavy tumbled brown layers out of his silver eyes, but not the sadness. That was a weight I knew from experience never lessened.

Only hadn't my own eased somewhat just recently?

"If you don't want anything to drink, would you care to sit?" Gale gestured to the large u-shaped sectional.

"Yes, of course." I moved to the left taking a seat on the end near an ottoman. "Thank you." I glanced up at him through my lashes.

"You're welcome." He lowered himself onto the ottoman sitting so close to me that his knees touched mine. "You're quite pretty."

I felt warmth hit my cheeks. He noticed it and smiled. He had a dimple in his right cheek.

"You're cute yourself," I returned.

His grin widened.

"So, how does this work, pretty girl? You tell me. I'm out of practice with all this." He crooked his fingers at me. I leaned forward, and so did he. I noticed his gaze dip to my cleavage. A nice, sweet guy, sure, but I think he had more than a little bit of a devilish streak. He cupped his hands around his mouth. "The cameras are making this awkward," he whispered. "And I want to kiss those petal soft looking lips of yours."

"Then why don't you?" I challenged.

"Because a kiss is very intimate, and with the cameras on, this is all pretend. I want something more honest the first time I put my mouth on yours." He stared deeply into my eyes a moment holding me captive before he dipped his gaze again watching his own movement as he reached for and traced a long length of my hair. His warm fingers skimmed the shell of my ear, my neck and eventually my chest. I shivered.

"For a guy who's supposed to be out of practice you're pretty good at this." My heart hammered as he leaned back on the ottoman but continued to stare at me. His analytical gaze was unnerving. He was intense. This suddenly didn't feel like a hookup at all, but a dress rehearsal to something much more serious.

"Tell me something about yourself. Where you're from. What your family's like. Why's a nice girl like you doing something like this."

Alarm bells went off inside my head. "I'm not nice. I've never been nice." Or at least I hadn't been after my mother left, and my father had focused his resentment toward her onto me. "And there's nothing much to tell." Not to a nice guy like him who would run away fast if he knew how fucked up I *really* was. "I'm a Texas girl. My father's a cop." A cop who treated me as if I were a perp instead of a daughter. Sure, he had never actually physically abused me, but his style of discipline had left marks on my body, my mind and my soul.

"Are you ok, Marsha?"

"Huh?" I blinked, refocusing on the atypical rock star across from me. "Sure." I tossed the lock of hair he had traced over my shoulder. "I'm ok. I'm fine." A self-deprecating laugh escaped as I realized how often I had been saying that lately.

"I'm not so sure." Gale frowned, then turned his head to the side. "Everyone out. You can leave the equipment. But I want to talk to

Marsha alone. Determine if she truly wishes to continue with all this."

The crew murmured their acquiescence, each giving me a questioning glance as they filed past me on the way out. I don't think they had been close enough to see within my troubled gaze what Gale probably had.

"You ok being alone with him?" Barbara touched my arm.

"Yeah." I covered her hand with my own, pressing her fingers into my skin for a moment.

"If you're sure." She searched my gaze for a moment, her scrutiny almost as intense as the lead singer's.

"I am." I removed her hand from my arm squeezing her fingers firmly.

"Alright." She turned and moved toward the door, her footsteps silent on the thick carpet.

"You have a good friend there," Gale commented.

There was enough of a question in his tone that I answered what might have been only a casual statement.

"Yes. I'm short on those lately. But she definitely is."

He nodded thoughtfully. "So, who calls the shots on this show?" he asked as the door clicked closed after Barbara. "Someone back at corporate? The crew? Or you?"

"I do."

"Hmm. I wonder." He placed his hands on my knees and stroked his thumbs back and forth over my skin. "If you run the show how come your producer contacted me instead of you?"

"I was busy." Busy binge drinking to escape my problems, then busy sleeping it off later with Ivan.

"What kind of busy?" He seemed to zero in on everything I said in addition to the omissions. "Busy with Von?" My brows rose. "Or one of the others?" My body went tense. His eyes narrowed. His

166   MICHELLE MANKIN

thumbs stopped stroking. He cocked his head to the side. "Seems as though they're all quite territorial when it comes to you. Now that I've met you, I think I get it. You're more than just a shapely body and a lovely face, pretty girl. You've got that look of vulnerability in your eyes. That's a siren call to guys like us who jam hard, live harder and sing out our catharsis when our hearts get ripped from our chests." My jaw dropped, but he wasn't done. "While you and your team researched me, I did a little digging of my own. Plus, I had some interesting conversations that came off more like warnings from those other interested parties."

"Huh? I'm not following."

"Von and Ivan," he clarified.

"Ivan's not an interested party. He hates me. I hate him."

"Hate's a strong emotion. But animus doesn't preclude interest."

He had a point. A very good one.

I got up, skirted around him and his disturbing insightfulness and moved to the windows. Staring out into the black starless night, the half-circle bay of darker ebony offered little distraction from my thoughts. A sudden flurry of movement drew my attention to the lit-up pool area directly below. At the same time Gale came behind me, placing his hands on my shoulders.

I barely registered the warmth of his fingers on my skin. There was a fight. A crowd circled it. And the two men pummeling the shit out of each other like prize fighters vying for points in the deciding round were Ivan and Von.

"Now why does this not surprise me?" Gale muttered.

"It surprises me." I clasped my hands to my chest, my breath catching as Ivan turned, glanced up and looked right at me. A mistake. A costly one. Von's fist smashed into Ivan's midsection.

"No," I gasped. The force of the blow lifted the Enthusiasts' front man completely off his feet. Too close to the pool, Ivan fell in. His body hit the water and released a huge splash.

"Shit," Gale commented drolly. "That's going to play hell on his favorite pair of boots."

"How well do you know Ivan?" I asked absently. My hand on the glass, my fingers traced Ivan's movement as he broke the surface of the water and swam to the side of the pool. The crowd drew in closer behind Von. The Beast said something. Ivan grinned in response and lifted his arm. Throwing back his head, Von laughed, then crouched down, clasped Ivan's outstretched hand and pulled him from the water. Clothes glued to his lean body and his hair plastered to his skull, Ivan glanced up at me once again.

"I know him rather well. We frontmen usually stick together." Gale turned me around to face him. "I think the better question is how well do *you* know him?" He was gentle, but he had to forcefully grip my chin to redirect my head away from the drama.

"What?" I was trying to work out in my mind what I had just seen. Why were Ivan and Von fighting?

And why were they now laughing together like they were best friends?

"Never mind, it's not important. What is important is that you're here with me right now. And I have another question I want the answer to."

"What's that?" I slowly blinked at him. He moved his hands to my upper arms and drew me closer. We were silhouetted in the glass, but I didn't realize it or anything else because all of a sudden Gale's mouth was on mine, and he was kissing me. And his lips demanded a response. Moments went by, moments where I didn't notice anything but him. His urgent passion. His tongue in my mouth. His groan. My corresponding moan. His frantic fingers on the toggle of my dress.

The zipper lowering. The cool rush of air on my skin as the two sides of the dress separated.

"Fuck this shit," a deeply masculine voice I knew very well uttered.

"What the..." Gale broke the kiss just before he was ripped from my arms and pressed backward into the window.

"Why him?" Ivan glared at me as if I had somehow wronged him while holding Gale at bay. His forearm pinned the other man's neck into the plate glass.

"Why not him?" I put my hands on my hips.

"He give you VIP tickets that cost him a shitload? He send you roses? He hold your hair back from your face while you puked your guts out? He hold you tight while you whimpered in your sleep?"

"Um..." Dumbfounded, I just stared at Ivan. He stared back. A long moment passed. Rivulets of pool water ran into the carpeting faster than my brain processed the information Ivan's questions had just revealed.

"You?" I concluded, my eyes widening.

"Yes, me." He released Gale who grinned goofily as if he had gotten just what he wanted instead of a furious frontman in his face and a forearm shiver to his windpipe.

"I don't understand." I shook my head at both men. That's when I realized there weren't just three of us in the room. The crew had returned. Ignacio's camera was on. Les' light. Ernie's sound pole. Barbara and Carla gaping.

Who was in charge of this show indeed?

Gale had been right to wonder.

At the moment, it certainly wasn't me.

"What the hell are you doing? I stared down at Ivan's wet head.

"Refastening this thing."

"But..." I protested.

"But nothing. 'I'm done with you calling all the shots. You're coming with me." My zipper drawn up, I suddenly found myself lifted into the air and unceremoniously thrown over Ivan's shoulder. He strode toward the door with his hand on my ass to hold me still.

"Stop kicking," he growled.

"Hey," Barbara said, stepping in Ivan's way. "You aren't going anywhere with her unless she gives her consent."

"Tell her its ok," Ivan insisted, cupping my ass more firmly. "Or she and everyone else in this room is going to know things I can guaran-damn-tee you will wish had been kept private."

"It's ok," I said quickly.

"Alright then." Barbara opened the door, frowning at me as she stepped aside. Once we were out in the hall Ivan started moving faster.

"Where are we going?"

"To my room."

"But I thought you said this was going to be a private conversation?"

"I did, and it will be." He stopped at a door at the far end of the hall. He nearly dropped me as he withdrew his keycard.

"You can put me down, caveman."

"No fucking way." He got the door opened, entered the room and strode toward the huge king-sized bed that dominated it.

"Hey," I protested, but it was too late. He tossed me expertly on it.

"You said talking." I bounced on my back on the hard mattress then came up to a seated position, rumpling the aqua and cream comforter in my agitation. "And you got me all wet," I sputtered, scooting to the end of the bed with the intention of getting right off it.

"I've gotten you wet before." A wide grin split his handsome face, making it even more appealing. "You didn't seem to mind."

"Ass," I huffed.

"Bitch," he returned.

"Grr." I tried to stand.

"You stay." He put his hands on my shoulders. "I like you in my bed."

My eyes rounded. I was so shocked by his words that the rest of me went completely still.

"I thought that might shut you up." He squeezed my shoulders firmly as if to emphasize his point, then released me. I found myself missing the warmth of his hands as I watched him run one over his face.

"I thought you had something to say," I prodded cattily. The longer he stared at me the more self-conscious I felt.

"I do."

"So, say it already."

His jaw tightened. "I don't want you sleeping with anyone else."

"I don't plan to."

His eyes widened. Not for the first time I noticed how beautiful they were. How beautiful he was. His features were so perfect. Aquiline nose. Full lips. Sensitive brows and thickly lashed chocolate brown orbs with glittery gold sparkles.

I tried to shake off the magic dust effect he had on me. "I only slept with you. It was an accident. One I don't plan to repeat."

"You know what I mean. No fucking anyone else, Tigress."

"Are you kidding me?"

"Do I seem like I'm kidding?" He shook his head. The movement seemed stilted. His shirt and jeans were so wet they were restricting his motion.

"Well, I'm the Rock Fuck Club chick. If you haven't clued in that means I'm in charge, and I still have more fucks to go."

"You've got *no* more fucks to go. Film can be manipulated. Gale, that grabby asshat can count, but he's your last one. The rest are going to be me, me and me."

"Um, no." I stamped my hands on my hips, "You've got no right to say who I choose. No rights whatsoever."

"I have every right." His expression darkened. He came closer. My breath caught as he slid his hands into my arm pits and lifted me up.

"What do you think you're doing?"

"'I'm going to prove something to you."

"Oh no, you most certainly are not."

"You want it. Your lips are parted. You're breathing fast. You can't wait for me to put my mouth on you."

"Don't." I put my hand on his chest. His shirt was cold, the fabric wet, but the skin beneath my palm felt like it was on fire.

"Do, you mean." He came even closer, trapping my hand between our bodies. His water-logged jeans saturated the bottom half of my dress. His dripping wet shirt drenched the bodice. I started to shiver not from cold but in anticipation as he stared down at me.

"No." I shook my head as he lowered his.

"Yes," he breathed. "Say it," he whispered as he framed my face in his capable hands.

Maybe it was the warm plea in his eyes. Maybe it was how carefully he cradled my jaw.

Maybe it was the coaxing back and forth motion of his rough thumbs on my soft skin.

Maybe it was just him.

Maybe it had always been him.

My free hand came up, not to refuse him but to cover one of his hands with my own, I pressed it more firmly into my skin. "We shouldn't."

172   MICHELLE MANKIN

"We should," he insisted and brought his mouth closer to mine. I felt his breath. I inhaled his scent. Sandalwood. Leather. Motor Oil. A little chlorine. A lot of arousal.

"Yes. Ivan," I surrendered and all of him washed over all of me. His earnest expression. His mesmerizing eyes. His potency filled my mind. I closed my eyes. "Yes."

"Fuck yes," he groaned. Then his mouth was on mine.

His ravenous lips.

His rapacious tongue.

His hunger and my own.

And his need.

So much need.

Need that he felt for me. Need that I returned. Need that when I was with him like this became everything.

"No." I somehow ripped my mouth from his.

"Yes," he insisted. "Get on the bed." He rained a spine tingling barrage of kisses down the side of my neck.

"No. Stop." Wedging my hands between our bodies, I pressed my palms to his rock-hard chest, resisting the compelling contours and the intriguing warmth, though nearly every single part of me wanted to conform to every single part of him.

"Fucking hell. I want you. You want me." He stepped back so abruptly I swayed. "What the fuck is the problem?" He snarled the question, his expression as dark as his eyes.

"We can't." My breaths were ragged.

"Why the hell can't we?"

"Because..." I trailed off. My eyes filled with tears of frustration. "Because she's my best friend, Ivan. I told you that the last time I made you stop." I held the sides of my dress that had somehow come undone again together and ducked around him.

ROCK *Fuck* CLUB BOOK 3   173

"No." He grabbed my arm and swung me back to face him. "Not this time. It was a mistake to let you go."

"What?" Dazed, I blinked up at him.

"Put the pieces together, Mars. I let you go that night because I thought you were playing me." He wrapped his long fingers around my upper arms and pulled me into him. "I didn't believe you." He stared down at me. "Why would I? You refused me at every turn, yet just when things got serious with Raven? Boom." He squeezed me tighter. "You come to me in the middle of the night, come onto me and tell me you're pregnant."

"You didn't want the baby."

"You assumed I wouldn't want a baby because I didn't believe one really existed, Marsha." His eyes were active and full of emotion. "That's on me, the lack of faith." I could feel the tension in his body. "Do not take that on as more guilt. I won't allow it. Do you hear me?" The fierceness of his commands imprinted in my skin from his grip and delved even deeper than that the longer he stared at me. "You've been grieving a long time. I just started the process. So, you need to be patient. I don't have a fucking clue how to make this right."

"There's no making it right." My eyes burned.

"Then let it go. Let some of the burden go. Let me help you carry it."

"I can't. I have to keep it. It shouldn't be a burden. It's all I have left of her." I had never shared a truth so telling with anyone, not even Raven.

"She was a girl, Mars?" His voice was thick.

"In my heart she was. But the doctors said it was too early to tell."

"Oh, babe." He lifted his hands and framed my face with them. "I'm so sorry you went through all that on your own."

"Why are you being so nice to me?" I whispered as he tenderly swiped through the wetness on my cheeks. Wetness he shared. It shone in the brilliance in his eyes. "You don't even like me."

"Well, that's crazy. I like you a lot. Too much. It messed with my head and made being fully emotionally invested in Raven nearly impossible when you were around."

I searched his eyes finding nothing but sincerity blazing back at me. "You cheated on her with that groupie," I reminded him.

"That was a misguided attempt to wake her up. She had drifted so far away from me after Hawk died. It was like making love to a ghost."

"You should have told her." His bringing up Hawk made more guilt rise in me.

"I tried to make her understand. Over, and over, and over again."

"She never told me."

"She was so insulated inside her grief she probably doesn't even remember."

"Why didn't you just say all this in the first place?"

"She wouldn't listen to me. Neither would you."

"I don't understand you."

"Welcome to the fucking club, Mars. I don't understand you all the time, either. But I've been listening and watching closely lately, and I think I get you a lot better than anyone. We are a lot alike. If you'd give me a chance, if you listened, if you watched, if you cared enough to do those things, you might reach the same conclusion about me that I've reached about you."

"And that is?"

"That I want to try for something with you."

"You said my heart is too fucked-up."

"It is, babe. It's a motherfucking mess. But then so the hell is mine."

CHAPTER
twenty-two

"I HAVE TO GO," I TOLD HIM. "I have a job to do. You shouldn't have interfered."

"You won't even think about it?" His strong jaw firmed as if he were clenching his teeth. "Is that it?"

"Yes." I avoided his eyes and the treasure trove those flecks of gold and the concern within them might represent. "I appreciate all you've told me. I understand you a lot better than I did before." I drew the toggle of my zipper up and smoothed my dress, preparing to leave because I was way too tempted to stay. My brain barely functioned when he touched me, hell when he even looked at me a certain way. "But you and me equals disaster. We've already proven that." He flinched. "We were irresponsible. We drank too heavily that night and didn't use protection." I didn't mean her. I would have cherished a baby. I would have loved her. I would never have abandoned her the way my mother had abandoned me.

"I don't drink to excess anymore."

176   MICHELLE MANKIN

"I noticed that." A responsible choice I would be wise to make myself. But tequila was the only thing that temporarily numbed the pain and helped me sleep at night. I discounted the one recent time with him. An anomaly, or was it?

"But the past and its consequences will always be there between us. Raven will always be there. Those are immutable truths. They will never change."

"Wounds eventually heal. Burdens can be shared. Truth is relative. Things *can* change." He seemed so certain. I had never seen him this way. Well, actually I had. Recently. When he had seemed so hellbent on pursuing Raven.

"In New York..."

"This isn't about Raven," he cut me off. "She has moved on. I'm moving on." He said her name without inflection or emotion. Maybe it truly was over for him. "This is about Hawk."

"Don't bring up Hawk," I whispered, my mind suddenly reeling, but he went on.

"Someone needs to. You've built him up in your mind to be this ideal man."

"Hawk was perfect."

"Perfect for someone else maybe. Not for you." This time I flinched at that sting of truth. "He never gave you the time of day until you went to him pregnant with our baby."

"How do you know that?"

"I followed you that night. You were upset. I was worried about you getting home safely. You went straight from my place to his. Another reason at the time that made me doubt you."

"Oh." His actions showed a level of concern that softened him further. But I stubbornly stuck to my narrative. I had to. My world was all I had, even if it was only a fragile construct. "Hawk was a wonderful man," I persisted. "Caring and compassionate. Gentle. Even tempered. Wise. A doctor in training."

"Don't forget, boring. Dull. A motherfucking idiot if you ask me. So not right for you if he knew you were into him, and he didn't care."

"That wasn't Hawk at all." I shook my head, refusing to let Ivan crumble my world.

"Relative truth, babe."

He was right.

Dammit, Ivan was right.

It scared me to think that I might have been wrong all along.

"I can't do this."

"You won't, you mean."

"The answer's no however you want to spin it," I stated firmly, and his open expression completely closed off before I even left his room.

"WHAT THE HELL happened to you?" Barbara asked when I stomped into the bedroom of our suite moments later.

"Ivan," I stated drily. "Ivan happened to me."

"Well." She gave me measured glance as I stripped out of my dress and padded toward the shower in my black bra and panties. "I think that happening has been a long time coming."

"How do you mean?" Did everyone know how insanely attracted to him I was? I paused halfway to the shower and turned to look at her.

"Chemistry. From hate to hot sex. It happens. Don't beat yourself up about it."

"We didn't have sex."

"You didn't?" Her tone was incredulous.

"Uh-uh. Almost." I shrugged as if that weren't significant. "I put the brakes on. He wasn't too happy about it."

"Oh my. I bet he wasn't." She gave me a head to toe scan. "But you look like you've been..."

"Ridden hard and put up wet?"

Her eyes widened.

"I wish." And I did wish. With Ivan sex wasn't the problem. But going there again with him? Premeditated? And trying for something more? "But he and I are two wrongs that will never make a right."

"Hey, sleepyhead." Barbara stood over me holding a large pot of coffee.

"Thank you." I muttered, throwing back the tangled covers, glancing at the bedside clock and cringing. "Is it already morning?"

"Yeah. Bus is pulling out in thirty minutes," she informed me. "I let you sleep in as long as I could."

Sleep was a relative term. Thanks to Ivan's insights, I had mostly tossed and turned with my eyes closed.

"Alright. Just give me a few minutes to get going." I sat up in bed and pushed my hair out of my eyes while she poured me a cup.

"Cream or sugar?" she queried.

"Black." I stretched out my hand to take it from her. "Thanks." I closed my fingers around the cup gratefully.

"'You're welcome." She continued to study me as I took a careful sip. I peered back at her through the cloud of steam.

"What is it? What's going on that you don't want to tell me?"

"Drink your coffee." She glanced away.

"I am. But I get the idea that caffeine isn't going to make it easier whatever you have to say. So why don't you just go ahead and spit it out."

"I ran into Ivan at the buffet."

"He was up early," I commented evenly.

"He runs in the morning. Did you know that?"

I shook my head.

There's lots you don't know, I told myself. *Maybe lots that would change your view of him.*

And you're afraid.

Hell yeah, I was afraid. For a lot of good reasons.

"You're frowning."

"My inner monologue. In regards to him, it's kind of a split personality thing."

"Whoa."

I nodded. Whoa was right.

"Anyway, I don't think he got the message about the two wrongs. Are you sure you were clear about that?"

"Yes." I narrowed my gaze. "Why? What did he say?"

"He just asked about you. He wanted to know if you slept ok."

Fuck. "What did you tell him?"

"The truth."

"And that is?"

"You didn't sleep at all. You haven't since we left New York. No, don't shake your head at me. You've only nodded off a time or two except for that time with him. You were out like a light then."

"Did you tell him all that?"

"Yes," she confirmed.

Double fuck. "Ok." I set the empty cup on the nightstand and threw back the covers. As I put my feet on the floor I noticed she was still watching me. "Is there something else?"

"Yeah."

"Great."

"Suzanne called."

Just what I wanted to hear. Not. I squeezed my eyes shut. When I reopened them Barbara was still there. She took my hands. "She wants you to interview Ivan. She insists that you do it today. She says the footage they filmed when he was in New York was compromised."

"What does that mean?"

"Someone forgot to get the proper authorization from him. They can't use any of it, and they want something right away for the lead in to Raven's season."

"That's soon."

"It airs day after tomorrow," she informed me.

"What do I have to do?" I asked dully though I was pretty sure I knew.

"You have to talk to him today, Mars."

So. I was screwed and not in the I'm-in-charge-and-I-say-what-where-and-when type of way.

CHAPTER
twenty-three

"Hi, Mars. Long time no talk."

"Yeah. Alright. Stow the sarcasm, Ivan. You're on speaker, and I know Barbara's already talked to you about the interview." I glanced at the other bed where she sat across from me wearing a pretty lemon colored sundress. She gave me a thumbs up. "So, are you going to sign the disclosure form or what?"

"'Or what' sounds about right."

"Ok. Fine." I started to hang up the phone.

"Unless..." I paused with my finger hovering over the end the call button.

"Unless what? Don't yank my chain. You're holding everybody up. The rest of my crew's on the bus ready to roll out."

"I know. I saw them packing up." I heard a metallic sound like blinds being dropped back into place over a window.

"You stalking my bus?"

"I'm stuck on mine fucking bored with nothing else to do. Why don't you come join me? I can think of lots of ways you can ...entertain me...I mean interview me on the drive."

"I'll ask questions. You'll answer them. Nothing else." I dropped my head in my hands, cursing Ivan and Suzanne under my breath.

"I heard that, Tigress."

"I meant for you to."

"Oh well, in that case I might need to add on the extra stipulation that you have to be naked when you interview me."

"Ivan," I complained. "Are you going to do it or not?"

"Ok, alright, babe. You got your interview. And I'll even let you keep your clothes on."

"Hey, what took you so long?" Ivan opened the door as soon as I knocked. "Let me take that." He slid my backpack from my shoulder. "Fuck, this is heavy. What's in this thing?"

"Just a few bricks to hit you over the head with if you piss me off." He grinned at me over his shoulder, and I tried to pretend my heart rate hadn't accelerated from his smooth lean in and from being on the receiving end of one of his I'm-the-lead-singer-in a rock band throw-me-your-panties smile. "Actually, it's video and audio equipment. Since you won't let the crew on board, it's going to be me doing the recording and the interviewing."

"Sounds good." He tapped the driver on the shoulder. "Let's hit the road, Jeeves. And floor it. Before she changes her mind." In the front lounge, Ivan set my backpack on the left couch beside a guitar case and turned to face me.

"Babe." He grinned. He had caught me staring at his ass. An asset. One of many. His voice. His eyes. His sculpted muscular body and the way he moved it. All had caught my attention the first time I had seen him perform on stage.

"Your driver's name is Jeeves?" I asked.

"No, it's Peter. But he prefers the nickname. And I know what you're doing." He came close again, so close his body nearly touched mine. His heat and his scent washed over me making my heart race faster. "You're trying to redirect me." He put his hands on my shoulders and squeezed. "I won't be redirected." He peered at me through the thick fringe of his lashes. "I want you. I remember how it was. I know you do, too. Addictive and so fucking hot I thought we would set the world on fire."

I gulped. That was exactly how I remembered it, too.

"We'll be doing it again. My body over yours. Yours underneath mine. Both of us coming. Over and over again. It's not if. It's a matter of when."

"No, we won't," I insisted, following him with my eyes as he circled me. "That's not why I'm here. No more naked times with me and you. Not once. Not again. Never."

"Yo, Mars." I turned my head as Ivan's best friend appeared.

"Hey, Tyler."

"Ty," he insisted, raking a long swath of tangled brown hair out of his slightly unfocused caramel eyes. He yawned and stretched, his motion lifting his too small shirt above the waistband of his boxers. At the kitchenette, he bent at the waist and opened an under the counter refrigerator. "Don't stop the debate on my account. I've already heard the key points. Ivan's been like a broken record about you since the truck stop. You might as well give in. It's not if." He lowered his voice to mimic his friends. "It's when." He winked at me.

Heat hit my cheeks as if his teasing had stamped it there. "Where are Jagger and Nicholas?"

"Sleeping. They had a long night. The blonde and brunette Ivan snagged at the venue and dropped off here were insatiable."

My stomach twisted remembering Ivan leaving the after-party with them. Had he only dropped them off? Or had them himself then returned for a second go round after I had refused him?

"Grab me a beer while you're at it," Ivan told his best friend before shifting to face me. "You wanna sit down here on the couch?" Was it my imagination or was he the one who now seemed eager to do the redirecting?

"Yes, that's fine."

"Would you like a beer?" he asked, watching me closely as he twisted off the top on his bottle of Shiner.

"Yeah, sure." It was early, but my throat was dry.

"Corona?" he queried as I unzipped my bag.

"Yes." I stopped digging around for my GoPro and gave him a surprised look over my shoulder. "You have Corona?"

"Just got some. I know what you like, Mars." He took the bottle Tyler passed to him, then he moved close to me. "I remember lots of things." I sucked in a breath laden with sandalwood. "Things I plan to repeat."

"I'm getting my camera out." He didn't put his hands on me, but he pressed his hard body into my back. "I'll sit on one couch. I want you to sit on the other." My breath hitched as I felt his cock against my ass. It was long, hard and thick.

"Where's the fun in that?" His hot humid breath misted the fine hairs on my nape. A shiver rolled down my spine. I regretted tying my hair back.

"This isn't fun, Ivan. It's work. We can't all do whatever the hell we feel like doing twenty-four-seven."

"I don't do whatever I want, Mars." He stepped back. Cooled air replaced his tempting heat. "This band isn't a dictatorship."

"Nearly," Tyler grumbled, and his bowl clattered against the linoleum top of the banquette.

"Fuck you," Ivan said without malice.

His best friend shot him the finger, then shoved a huge spoonful of breakfast cereal into his mouth.

"As I was saying before I was rudely interrupted...." Ivan trailed off, gesturing for me to take a seat on one couch. I had my GoPro on and dipped my head to encourage him to continue. He waited for me to get situated before he took a seat of his own beside the guitar on the opposite couch. This wasn't the first time he had demonstrated good manners. Someone had likely taught those to him at a young age. I wondered not for the first time who that someone had been. If he had told Raven, she had never shared, and there was very little information about Ivan's upbringing on the internet to fill in the gaps in my knowledge.

"You're from the Dallas area like me. Why don't you tell me a little about that? What was Ivan Carl like as a child?" The lead singer noticeably tensed. He had gotten his guitar out. An acoustic with a light natural wood finish. His fingers paused over the strings.

"Yes. Corsicana. A little town just south of the metroplex. It's a quaint little place, if a bit boring." He peered at me across the aisle. His expression was as closed off as it had become when I had turned him down. He either didn't like being interviewed or he didn't care for questions about his childhood. "Next question."

Hmm, I thought. *Maybe both.* I tried again.

"Tell me about your father." I'd never heard Ivan mention him. "Your mother? Do you have any siblings?"

Ivan dipped his chin. I couldn't see his eyes anymore, but he gripped the headstock on his guitar so tightly I was afraid the wood might splinter.

"I told you this was a bad idea." Tyler's spoon clattered into his bowl. I glanced over at him. "He doesn't talk about his childhood. Ever. Delete that question. Move onto stuff that's relevant. The start of the band. His musical influences. Past relationships. That kind of thing. Understand?" His expression was hard, his grip on his spoon bending the metal.

"Alright." I agreed. Tyler gave me a curt nod. I glanced over at Ivan. Music emanated from his instrument. I zoomed in on his face as he played. The tension in his expression relaxed as he strummed the strings. I listened. He played. The mood lightened. Eventually, Ivan looked at me again. His gaze was hooded.

"Ty and I met when we were sixteen. I was bussing tables. He was a dishwasher. It was just him and me with guitars writing songs together for a while. We brought Jag and Arrow in later and formed the group. We worked our asses off. Now we're here. Any other questions?" His tone was terse. He was angry. But I didn't get the idea that it was directed at me.

"Musical influences?" I asked, hoping to further lighten the mood by following the script his friend had given me.

"Led Zeppelin. Black Sabbath. Motley Crue. Metallica. The usual suspects."

I blew out a breath. I didn't think anything about Ivan Carl was usual. I tried to dig a little deeper.

"Favorite guitarist?"

"Me."

"Aw, come on." I smiled even though he was giving me a hard time because his lip had curled, and the devilish gleam I was more accustomed to seeing when he was looking at me had returned. "Not Eric Clapton or Slash?" I pressed.

"Nope. Just me." He carefully lifted the guitar, his biceps in his muscle tee flexing as he returned it to the case. "And before you ask, no serious girlfriends. Not one, until Raven. That's over and done. Blah, blah, blah. This interview is over."

CHAPTER
twenty-four

I STARED OUT THE WINDOW. PASSING THE LINE of pine trees along I-75 held my attention when I was actually straining my ears to listen to the conversation Tyler and Ivan were conducting in low voices on the couch directly behind me.

"Mary Timmons will have our asses if we're late to another show."

"I know, but I can't hack nine hours straight trapped on this bus. I need a breather man."

"I hear you, bro. I'm in. Jag and Arrow will agree, too, but they probably won't even wake up to vote until we get there. Alright. Let's do it, but..."

I stilled, willing even my heart beats to slow to quiet thumps as I heard Tyler whisper my name.

"She's cool," Ivan said.

"She is, but for some other dude to tangle with. Not you. Von's into her. Gale now, too. Let them have a go."

"Hell fucking no," Ivan hissed.

ROCK *Fuck* CLUB BOOK 3   189

"It's too late to go back to the start and do this over. This isn't fixable. If you'd think with your brain instead of your cock you'd realize it. She's Ravens best friend, Ivan. That's some fucked up shit even for you."

"Was her best friend."

"So that's all that I said that got through to you? They're like sisters, bro. They might be mad now, but they'll eventually get over it."

"I have a shot, I'm taking it."

"Shut it, man. I think she's listening."

"Yo, Marsha." I jumped as Tyler suddenly sank down onto the cushion beside me. "How much of that convo did you just hear?"

I went for a vague response. "I zoned out when you started talking about the sales stuff. Facts and figures are not my thing."

"Ty's determined to make this band a tremendous success," Ivan said at my other side. Though there was plenty of space on the couch, he slid in right beside me, the length of his solid body gliding along the softer curved edges of mine. "But making the record label a shit ton of money's not my gig, either, babe."

"What is your thing?" I asked, reaching for my camera. What I had recorded so far sucked. And right now, he seemed to be in a more talkative mood.

"Rocking hard. Fucking harder."

Ok now we're getting somewhere, I thought and switched on my GoPro. He frowned as he noticed the light.

"And if you had to describe your music in one word what would that be?"

"Fucking awesome." He grinned and fist bumped his best friend's outstretched arm across me. The polished metal of his rings flashed as brightly as his smile.

"That's two words, for the record. What's your favorite thing to do besides performing?"

"Writing music. Fucking. Driving fast."

"I think the first two are self-explanatory." It was interesting to note the order. "Why do guys get off driving fast?"

"Rolling down the windows, music blasting, feeling the wind in your hair. It helps me get things straight in my head."

"Like meditation?"

"Works for me."

"Do you ever drive the speed limit?"

"Why would I?"

"More of that the rules don't apply to me Ivan Carl attitude?"

"When the rules don't make sense, then I don't feel compelled to follow them."

"Do you feel like you have something to prove?"

"Only to myself. Fuck anyone else who doesn't get me."

"Rebel without a cause?"

"That's fucking rock 'n' roll, baby."

"Tyler implied you run this band with an iron fist. Is that true?"

"This band is a beast. Someone's got to control it."

"So, being in control of your music is important?"

"I guess. There's not a lot artists really control in this business. Mostly, I just want be left alone to write and play my music."

"You can't deny that you enjoy being on stage, Ivan. Playing in front of thousands of people. That's hardly alone."

Both his brows dipped as he gave that some consideration. "When I'm up on stage with a guitar in my hand everything makes sense."

"It's your Zen place."

"It's the only place where everything clicks. Up there with the mic in my hand with my brothers beside me, it all feels right. I don't think about what all the other bands are doing or the dollars and cents. It's just about the music. And my music isn't just a part of me, it is me."

"That's pretty heavy." I licked my dry lips. This was cream I was sure WMO was going to lap up. And even more than that it was insight into him. Music was as important to him as it was to me. "So, you were 'born to rock' like it says on your tat?

"Yeah." His gaze had dipped to my mouth. "I think you're the same way, rock chick. I've seen you with your headphones on. Your lips parted. Your eyes iced over. Your expression blissed out. You go to an otherworldly place. Music is your personal Valhalla."

"I'm sure I look like a dork."

"You're enchanting." His gaze rose to meet mine. His eyes were dark brown and so compelling. I was ensnared by their warmth the way the Vikings he alluded to were drawn from their land of the ice and snow to new horizons. "The only other time I've ever seen you so peaceful is when you're asleep."

"Music's always reliably there," I admitted, forgetting the camera was on, and how revealing my words were to someone who paid such close attention to me the way he seemed to. "It never lets me down. When I'm sad, it's my companion. When I'm angry, it's my megaphone. When I'm happy, it gives me an excuse to dance."

"That sounds about right. In the end, we're all fans and it's all about the music." He nodded thoughtfully and then grinned inexplicably as the bus suddenly slammed to a stop. "Speaking of music, it's time to crank some up." Unfolding his frame, he stood and held out his hand. "I'm taking the Firebird out for a spin. You're coming with me, and I'm going to drive motherfucking fast."

CHAPTER
twenty-five

"Can't we listen to something else?"

"My car, my rules, babe." He dipped his head. The wind from his open window carded through the silky chestnut strands of his shoulder length hair the way my fingers once had and ached to do again, if I were being truthful. "You're having a good time, aren't you?" The gold flecks in his chocolate brown eyes glowed as brightly as the sun as he peered at me over the rim of his vintage aviator shades.

"The best," I admitted. "Your car's awesome. And I'm always up for a good road trip." I thought of my old and now retired Accord and how many times I had hopped in it and headed away from the metroplex. My destination had often been a concert. A quick escape into the therapeutic world of music helped me reboot, and I had nearly always returned to my life refocused and recharged. But that was over. My companion for those jaunts was lost to me. My lightened heart started to sink, but I reached for the life preserver I had. This moment. This now. It had turned out to be a great day. I refused to think about

ROCK *fuck* CLUB BOOK 3   193

tomorrow. Ivan's enthusiasm wouldn't allow any negativity. It was potent. Contagious. His body had practically vibrated with it since he had backed his Firebird off the trailer. Sure, the wide-open road, the abundant sunshine and the blue skies contributed to his buoyant mood and my own. But I knew deep down that it was mostly just him. Being right here. Right now. With him.

"You're good company, Mars. I enjoyed our conversation about music. But if you truly want to understand the mythos behind the legend that is me you need to try a little harder to get into my favorite bands."

"Hmm, I think I'm tried out. We've looped through your heavy on the metal playlist twice now. It's time to switch things up. If you won't consider Two Rows Back..." I let that hang knowing his answer before he gave it.

"Nope. There's too much southern comfort in that rock." He grimaced.

"Ok, so we compromise. I vote for a little less screamo and a lot more singing. We need a proper soundtrack for when you and I quote open up the throttle unquote for the four-mile-long St. George Island Bridge."

"What do you have in mind...friend?"

We had agreed to spend the day as friends and as such, I had made a pact not to work anymore today. I had left both my GoPro and my cell behind. We had been joking back and forth ever since. I liked it. A lot. I couldn't remember kidding around with any guy. I certainly had never ridden shotgun beside one as sexy and intriguing as Ivan Carl.

"Marsha, you still with me?"

"Yes, of course. But when I'm contemplating an appropriate playlist for a momentous occasion, I prefer to be addressed as music guru."

194   MICHELLE MANKIN

"How about just rock chick?"

"That works, too." I smiled, and his gaze dipped to my mouth. He stared a beat longer than was probably safe... for his driving or my willpower.

You have a gorgeous smile, Mars."

"Thanks," I said, and felt my smile widening from his compliment.

"You don't do it often enough, especially lately." He returned his attention to the road, slowed the vehicle and put his blinker on. His thigh muscles in his jeans flexed as he applied the brakes, and his biceps bunched as he turned the wheel. My cheeks flushed remembering our night together. I turned my face into the cooling wind out my open window. He wasn't the only one battling distractions.

"We're almost there," I announced as we passed the large green directional sign for the island. I got excited. It had been a long time since I had hung out all day at the beach, and that was just what we planned to do. The band, too, as soon as they arrived. But that would be a while. The bus needed to refuel, and Jeeves slash Peter drove it a lot slower than Ivan drove his vintage Pontiac.

"Thanks for coming with me and agreeing to leave work and everything else behind for a while."

I glanced at him. He was staring at me again. The words were on the tip of my tongue. Telling ones about how it wasn't any hardship to be with him. He was sexy and smart. Thoughtful when he wanted to be. When I wasn't arguing with him, I enjoyed his company. Hell, I even liked arguing with him. It was stimulating. But I swallowed those thoughts. This was an escape. A moment in time. One day away from everything. It wasn't real.

"I've got it," I decided softly. I had something alright. An ill-advised attraction to my best friend's former boyfriend.

"What's that?" he asked in a low rumble. The question was an innocent one, but his tone and the smoldering glance he sent me over the tops of his smoky lenses was far from innocent. My favorite kimono slipped off my shoulders. My navy tank followed. My faded cutoff shorts. My bra and panties. Everything stripped away in the wake of his regard. I might as well have not been wearing anything. My body responded to him as if he had shaped and molded it with his hands. "I'm answering for you. Me is what you mean. You've got me. You considered my proposal." He raked another heated glance over me. "You want to test out this chemistry between us. You've changed your mind."

"I've got the set list," I said, shaking my head at him. "Well, the album anyway." I looked away. I pretended I didn't see the promise in his eyes. I ignored his words and the corresponding sigh from him that had followed my most recent ones. "Can I use your phone to play it? We're almost to the bridge." Through the front windshield, I saw the ramp up ahead.

"Sure, babe. You can have anything of mine you want. Anytime. Anyplace. Anyway. You don't even need to ask. Though the longer you keep putting off what's inevitable between us the more I plan to make you beg for it."

Imagining an anytime, anyplace, anyway scenario with Ivan, I fumbled as I reached for his cell. Feeling him watching me, my fingers trembled as I opened his music app. My nerves were jangled by the feelings I held back but wanted to share with him. My stomach fluttered like a moth with its wings on fire from drifting too close to the flame.

And because music revealed the things my heart was too cautious to put into words, I really wanted him to like the song I had chosen.

"Hell fucking yes, rock chick! Good choice!" He slammed his palm against his steering wheel as the synthesized chords of 'Foreplay' the prelude to 'Long Time' filled the air. "I haven't listened to Boston in forever. Classic."

I couldn't suppress my pleased smile, and he couldn't let it go when he saw it.

"I see that grin, Tigress. Is your seat belt buckled?"

"Yes." I checked the fastening and turned to regard him. His shades slid to the tip of his nose.

"You're safe with me." He trailed his gaze over me before he used his middle finger to glide his sunglasses back into place over his eyes.

"Mostly." He grinned at the road. I stared at him, imagining tracing the curved edges of his lips. I imagined feeling the firmness of his mouth on mine. I remembered the inferno his kiss had been. My heart kicked up. My respirations increased. My lips parted. He punched the accelerator. The car lurched. My body was pressed backward into my seat. "You're safe in this car while I'm driving it. But one day, one day soon, Mars, I'm getting you naked, and I'm laying you out across the hood while it's still popping, and then nothing's gonna stop me."

CHAPTER
twenty-six

Seated in the sand right at the water's edge, the wind whipped stray strands of blonde back from my face, ones that had escaped the tie on the drive. My emotions had nearly escaped their confines as well. Not a good plan lowering my guard around Ivan. Foolish to pretend to be friends even for the day with a guy I was so ridiculously attracted to.

As soon as he had set the brake, I had popped open my door and sprinted for the ocean. And on the shore I remained, my eyes filled with the expanse of the sea and my ears with its roar. But what I couldn't do was put out of my mind the compelling man behind me.

A quick glance over my shoulder confirmed he was still there... watching me. I had known. I had felt his gaze. He was taking a moment of his own. Bringing a cigarette to his mouth, he took a drag and leaned into the driver's side of his Firebird.

Get a handle on it, I told myself. *It's chemistry.*

It's more. It's the way you feel with him, the other half of my personality argued. That nearly silent part that usually only made its presence known when he was around. It was the me I used to be before my mother left. The little girl who had dressed up in sparkly princess gowns and plastic heels. The me who had once believed in happy endings and that she was worthy of being loved.

"Hey, Martian." Two long legs attached to a lean body appeared at my side. A half-smoked cigarette hit the ground by my knee. He used his foot to cover it over with sand.

"That's littering."

"It's biodegradable."

"I'm not so sure. Besides, there's a trashcan right behind us."

"You're such a pain in the ass." He sighed as I uncovered the cigarette and handed it to him. But he took it and threw it away.

"Thanks."

He nodded. "Mind some company?"

"No. Only no more smoking. I'm enjoying the fresh sea breeze." He dropped down behind me, pulling me backward between his parted legs.

"Ivan," I began. "Don't."

"Shut it, Mars. You agreed to friends for the day. What's got you frowning and wanting to renege on our agreement?"

"I'm not frowning."

"You are." He swiped his thumb across my downturned lips, and I felt the motion of his caress at a location much further south. "And I don't smoke. Not anymore."

"But…"

"I gave it up over a year ago along with the drugs and heavy partying. I had to dig deep in the glove box to find an old pack."

"Why'd you want one if you quit already."

"You rattle me, Mars. I want to do bad things with you, and I want to do good things that make you smile. I like looking at you. I like having you around. I like the way I feel when you're around. You make me think about things I don't normally consider. And you've been having that crazy jumbled up effect on me from the moment I first laid eyes on you. But I think you get that. I think you get it because you feel the same way I do."

"Yeah," I admitted. "Only..."

"Liked your playlist. Your song about a love left behind. About time rolling on. In some cases, as you and I both know, it can slip away completely."

I went very still. He meant Hawk. Had he stopped smoking and drugs because of Hawk? I had never considered how Hawk's passing might have changed Ivan, too.

"It's about not waiting," he continued. "About taking what you want today because tomorrow it might be gone. Some thought went into that song choice even if it was only subliminal. Makes me want to add one more stipulation to our agreement for the day."

"I'm not letting you fuck me on your car, Ivan."

"There won't be any letting involved, Tigress." He smiled. "You'll beg for it. You'll shake and shiver while I do you. You'll scream my name when you come. But that wasn't the proviso I was thinking of."

"Then what is it?" I narrowed my eyes on him.

"Turn back around," he ordered. Throwing his strong arms around my shoulders, he pulled me into him. His sandalwood scent and his warmth rolled over me as he rested his chin on the top of my head. I felt protected and cared for. Yet my heart thumped madly like a caged thing inside my chest. "Let's agree to give our turbulent past a rest today. I want you to relax. I want to see you smile again. I want to know what the thoughts were that took away the fun we were having earlier and put a frown on your pretty face."

"I was thinking that you rattle me, too. I was thinking about regrets. Choices I shouldn't have made. Things that I lost because of those choices. Love I'll never get back. And how little control I have over any of it. It would be easier to try to stop the sea right here from coming to the shore."

"Raven still loves you if that's what this is about."

"She doesn't. You're wrong. And she doesn't care about you, anymore, either."

"Ouch. Sheath the claws. She doesn't care, but she does. She and I were together a while. You two have been friends even longer than that. Those feelings may have evolved, but they won't ever go away."

"She'll never completely trust me. We'll never be best friends again," I clarified. My voice was strained, the pronouncement ripped from the place inside where I'd buried it.

"What does love mean to you, Mars?"

"Staying. Never leaving. Protecting and defending those you care about no matter the cost."

"Wow. You didn't even need to think about your explanation. That's the way you are with Raven. Your devotion to her is a remarkable thing." His lips moved to my ear. "So, who left you when they should have stayed?" he whispered gently. "Who didn't protect you, and what didn't they protect you from?"

"Let me go." My spine snapped straight. I tried to twist out of his arms, but he held me. He held me so tight.

"I won't tell anyone."

"No. You have your secrets. Things you won't talk about. Places you won't go. I have mine."

"I wasn't about to spill my ugly truths on camera. I'm not asking you to spill your guts while someone records you. I'm just asking you to share with me."

"Why?"

"Because I want to know. Because I think you need to get some things out. I've put together bits and pieces. From that time your old man called you. And from the conversation I overheard."

"What conversation?"

"In Tampa. I was coming in from running around the bay. I heard you and Raven arguing. I heard you talk about a lot of things, but the part about you never wanting to be at your own home resonated with me."

"Oh."

"I can wonder and form certain conclusions based on my own experience, but I'd rather have you tell me."

"This is not going to make me smile," I grumbled. "Or relax."

"Maybe there's a better smile on the other side of the frown. Maybe you just need to get those things off your chest so you can genuinely relax."

"What makes you think you're so wise?"

"I'm not. But I know what you've been through. Not just in my head. Inside my own heart. I think our backgrounds are similar."

I stared at the water considering. Maybe I could share with him. Maybe it would help. Who else was I going to tell? It wasn't like his knowing would change anything. This was one day. One moment in time. It wasn't going anywhere.

I pulled in a breath. I exhaled. "My mother left us when I was fourteen. We never heard from her again. She probably left because of my dad. No, that's not right," I sighed. "She definitely left because of my dad. He was abusive and controlling."

"Was he abusive with you?"

"I wasn't a well-behaved child. He had to discipline me a lot. He strung me up in the doorframe for hours at a time. If I goaded him, he made me run on the driveway rocks barefoot. And after my mother left it got worse. If there was trouble to be found, I found it. I could never meet his expectations. So, I quit trying."

"Did he hurt you, Mars?"

"Yes."

"I'm sorry." His arms tightened around me. "I understand, and it's not your fault. No parent should hurt their child. No parent should abandon them. It breaks a sacred trust. It's wrong."

"Did your father hurt you?"

"No. I never had one in the first place."

"How do you mean?"

"The douche who got my mother pregnant wasn't interested in being involved with the raising of a child. Being a sperm donor doesn't make you a father. I wouldn't have been that type of father to our girl," he stated fiercely.

"I believe you. I wish things had been different. For you growing up." *Between us, too*, I thought. Bringing my hands up to his forearms, I curled my fingers around as much of them as I could grasp and held on. "I'm sorry."

"Don't be. It was probably better that he wasn't around if he didn't want to be there."

Yet, it was still a rejection, and it hurt.

"And your mother?" I swallowed to clear the tightness of emotion from my throat. "Where is she now?" Surely, she loved him and was proud of him.

"Corsicana. With her new family. The man she's married to now and his two kids from a previous marriage." I could feel the sudden tension in his frame as he shared. "The trouble you think you were as a child? I was worse. I made it an art form to piss her off because it pissed me off that she preferred her new, improved family to me."

"How old were you when she got married?"

"Thirteen."

So young. Younger than I had been when my mother had abandoned me. My heart ached for him. Rejected before he was born. Rejected as an adolescent. "What did you do to get her attention?"

"I stole. I flunked classes. Got into fights. Too many of them. She couldn't control me, so she put me up for adoption."

I sucked in a restricted breath. "That's horrible."

"Foster care was pretty awful. No one adopted me of course." More rejection. "But it was better than all the fake bullshit with her."

I tightened my grip on his arms. I didn't say I was sorry again. I didn't think he would appreciate the words. With wounds as deep as his were, I knew it was better to be shown empathy. Actions were more believable than tired platitudes.

"She tells people who ask that I was ruining her marriage and her family with my behavior. I don't hear from her unless she wants money. Ty says it's good that she's out of my life."

"Oh." I certainly agreed with him. "That's terrible of her."

"It's fucked. But it's behind me. I have a new family of my own now."

"The guys in the band?"

"Yeah. Common experiences. Shared burdens. Never turning your back on someone no matter what, even when they inevitably screw up. That's a family. That's real love."

CHAPTER
twenty-seven

THE BUS PULLED IN TO THE PARKING LOT behind us as I was considering how nearly indistinguishable Ivan's definition of love was from my own.

"They're here, babe." Ivan squeezed my shoulders and stood. "Let me help you up." He offered me his hand. I took it without hesitation. His rings were cold, and his fingers were so long my hand was completely engulfed by his. I didn't lift my head to look at him, but I felt something shift inside of me, something that originated from his touch, something significant and undeniably real.

"I know." I forced levity into my tone. "It's kinda impossible to ignore a huge tour bus in an empty parking lot." Impossible to ignore the huge ball of emotional weight that I suddenly wasn't dragging, either. "Can we please rewind and forget all I said?" I whispered while staring at our joined hands. A moment in time that wasn't supposed to have gone anywhere impossibly had.

"Why would you want to do that?"

"Because it's embarrassing." Because I had never told anyone. Sharing lightened the burden. He was right. But knowing those secrets, all my secrets, made me feel vulnerable and gave him power over me.

"Did what I share about me embarrass you?" he asked carefully.

"No, of course not." Was he feeling vulnerable, too? I glanced up at him. His eyes were narrowed behind his tinted lenses. His fingers tensed over mine. He might very well have power over me, but apparently, I had quite a bit of leverage on him now, too. "I actually feel privileged that you trusted me enough to share something so personal."

"Just so." He covered our joined hands with his free one. "That's exactly how I feel."

"This isn't supposed to be like this."

"Like how?"

"You and me together and so serious."

"It can be anything you want, Mars. Anything *we* want. Can't you give us that possibility?"

"I don't know," I answered truthfully. "I don't do possibilities, Ivan. I do hookups. And right now, I do them with a camera and crew in tow recording it all."

"Yeah." He dipped his head. "Kinda difficult to forget. But they're not here today. Today it's just you and me. Two friends getting to know each other. Can we focus on that?"

"Yes."

"Good." He agreed so readily to the temporary arrangement. Maybe I should have been warier of his motives. Maybe deep down I was. Maybe deeper down I recognized the risk but didn't care.

"Yo, guys." Tyler shouted, and Ivan shifted us toward his best friend, lifting one hand and waving it to acknowledge him. What he didn't do was release his hold on me. Tyler wore a pair of black boxers,

206   MICHELLE MANKIN

and an H.M.E. ball cap with a flaming guitar logo that matched Ivan's tat. He dipped his shaded gaze to our joined hands as he moved toward us. Ivan and me being together seemed to displease him. "What've y'all been up to?"

"Nothing much," Ivan returned. "Drove here. Fast. Like I told you I would."

"Seems like more than just the Firebird's been moving fast."

"Ty." There was a warning in Ivan's voice.

"You sure you know what you're doing?" Apparently, Ty planned to ignore the warning.

"We're just spending the day together," I offered wanting to dispel the sudden tension between them. I tried to tug my hand free of Ivan's. He didn't allow it.

"I'm holding your hand while we spend the day together, Mars. I'm going to touch you. Lots. Friendly touching," he clarified, and I swallowed my protest. "Get over it. Smile. Relax. Let's enjoy this motherfucking day."

"Sounds awesome." Jagger stepped down from the bus. The offshore breeze blew his black bangs back from his wide forehead. In a pair of dark navy boxers and nothing else, he loped over to us. "Arrow's making sandwiches and putting a bunch of beers in the ice chest." He tossed the football he held up into the air and caught it as it fell. "Once we get out of the cage, we don't plan to go back inside it again unless it's for a damn good reason." He swept his sunglasses shaded gaze around the group. "Hey, Marsha." He greeted me casually. We had met before. I liked the bassist with his meandering style of communicating and his counterpart who was more straight to the point.

"Hey Jag," I returned. "How long you think your buddy's going to be?"

"A bit longer. He's mixing up some of that protein glop he likes to drink. He thinks he's going to get as big as the Beast. That then you might consider him as fuck number eight. Can't believe you gave Gale a go. The guy's got absolutely no moves whatsoever."

"How do you know all that?" I asked when he paused in his rambling to take a breath.

"Your cell's been going off all fucking morning. Tons of texts from Barbara. Keeping you in the loop, I guess. Links to posts on the RFC Facebook page."

"Oh, great."

"Don't go there, Martian." Ivan squeezed my hand reminding me he was there, right beside me. "She's not the Rock Fuck Club chick today," Ivan announced, sending a gaze around the group. "Today, she's just Marsha. You got that Jag?"

Jagger nodded.

"Ty?"

"Processed."

"Arrow?" Ivan lifted his chin to the rhythm man who had stepped off the bus, dressed as all the guys were in only his boxers. Bright red ones. His blond hair was an unkempt every which way disaster, and he wore a white protein shake mustache above his full lips.

"Roger that, boss." Nicholas tapped two fingers to his temple. He had an unlit cigarette wedged between them.

"Good. And no smoking. She doesn't like it. Messes with the Feng Shui of the ocean and shit."

"Alright. She's a VIP. I get it." Arrow swept an interested gaze over me. "Never had actual royalty on the bus before." There was a hint of sarcasm in his tone. "Not sure I know how you want us to act."

"Never allowed any chicks on one of our band outings." Jagger lifted his Wayfarer Ray-Bans onto his ebony hair while squinting at me. "Not even Raven."

"Only after show fucks inside the bus before it pulls away from the venue." Ty gave his best friend a questioning glance.

"Yeah, you're breaking a lot of your own rules here, boss," Arrow pointed out.

"Yeah, well. Mars is different."

"Different how?" Ty asked.

"No one makes a move on her. No one looks at her a certain way. No one touches her."

"You saying we should treat her like a sister or something?" Jagger asked.

"That's exactly what I'm saying," Ivan answered. "Starting today I want each of you to treat her like family."

CHAPTER
twenty-eight

THE BUS HAD BEEN PARKED ON the horizontal across several empty spaces, so the door faced the ocean. After taking a few commemorative photos of the beach, me and the guys, and videos of the guys goofing around on it, they had moved off while I sat on one of the beach chairs under the tarp they had rigged to extend outward like an awning from the bus.

In the shade, I watched them throwing the football around. Well, I mostly watched Ivan. In his jeans and a muscle tee, he had certainly been a compelling spectacle. But barefoot and stripped of his rings and wearing only his boxers, he was another level of enticing entirely. How was I supposed to drag my gaze away? His entire body was a decadent dream, wide shoulders, tapered waist, narrow hips, long legs. A sinful fantasyland of sinew and muscle. His face was a portrait of male beauty, too, whether he was screaming a metal manifesto, crooning a love song or bullshitting with his bandmates. Catching my eyes on him, he crooked his fingers at me.

Again.

I gestured to myself. I'd taken off my kimono and draped it over the back of the chair, but my tank and cutoffs were all I had brought to wear, and they weren't a swimsuit. I had already explained that, but I shook my head anyway and pointed to the buds in my ears. His buds. I gave him a thumbs up to let him know I was good. I had music. I forced my gaze to another section of the beach. There were other guys in the surf, but none unsurprisingly that I found remotely interesting.

As the current song ended, a Dirt Dogs' tune about finding the perfect wave, I leaned back in my chair and scrolled through the music on Ivan's phone. He had lent it to me. He didn't want me on mine. I didn't want to be on mine. Finding another album I liked, Tempest's latest, I tapped my toes on the sand, sucked in a deep draught of salt saturated air and noted the other people on the beach: families with coolers, fishermen with poles and others simply walking along shaded from the sun's rays with their floppy hats.

I tipped my head further back to follow a seagull as it soared into the sky. It likely felt as serene in this setting as I did. Smiling softly, floating on the familiar currents of songs I knew so well they felt like old friends, I closed my eyes and drifted further into my thoughts.

In other words, I mused about Ivan and all he had shared.

What we had shared with each other.

What it all might mean.

Suddenly, wet drops one after another in rapid succession landed on my sun warmed legs.

"What the hell?" I cracked open my eyes to discover Ivan standing over me. And ok, so you know the fantasyland he was from a distance? Well, up close he looked even better. Thrill inducing, spine chilling, stomach plummeting, roller-coaster ride better.

He grabbed one of the strings attached to the bud in my ears and tugged, popping it out. "C'mon, Mars. Quit stalling. Come on out and swim with me."

"I don't have a swimsuit," I reminded him.

"I don't either," he volleyed back.

"You're a guy, Ivan."

"So, your bra and panties will work as well as my boxers."

"Not really. For guys it's entirely different. You can blur the lines and get away with stuff like that. If I strip down to my lingerie and go out there someone's gonna call the cops, and I'm gonna get arrested."

"Unlikely." His voice had dropped an octave. "But anyway, it's worth the risk." His eyes dipped to my chest.

Underneath my tank and bra my nipples preened to points for him. "No, it's not," I insisted.

"Trust me. You haven't tried it. The water's wonderful." His gaze lifted. My eyes stalled on his. They were dark chocolate indulgence. "You really afraid of a little trouble or a stare or two?"

"No, of course not."

"Glad to hear it." He nodded once. More water dripped onto me from the ends of his slicked back hair. Saturated, it shone a rich sable brown. "You don't strike me as a stickler for rules."

"I'm not." I laughed. His gaze went to my mouth. My lips tingled.

"Then come."

"I don't know."

"Quit sitting there watching the world go by and join in for a change. Be a part of something."

"I *am* a part of something."

"What? The RFC? That's not participation. Not the way you're doing it. It's more like a kamikaze mission."

My lips flattened, but I didn't argue. It was a valid point. He had made more than one today. He watched me a beat, his expression softening and so did his voice. "There's a time for listening to the music and a time to get off your ass and dance. Right, rock chick?"

"Yeah." I smiled. I took the hand he extended to me, and he pulled me into him. I rested my hands on the hard slabs of his shoulders. His went to my hips. I gave myself and him a moment to appreciate the differences in our two bodies. Rigid steel to yielding flesh. My curves to his contours. Breasts to chest. Thighs to thighs. My hips cradling the promise of his... I stepped back.

"You got me all wet again," I complained. He blinked through the sensual daze and grinned his sexy half-smile in response.

"That I did. Again."

"Guess I'll have to go in after all." I grabbed the hem of my tank and yanked it over my head. His gaze dropped to my tits and the satin demi-bra that barely contained them. His lips parted. I unbuttoned my shorts, lowered my zipper and shimmied out of my shorts. He went as still as a statue, only his eyes moving, all along the length of my body.

He groaned. "Maybe you should put the clothes back on, Mars."

"No." I moved toward the water. He tried to catch me, but I dodged his attempt. I didn't feel vulnerable anymore, serene or relaxed. I felt empowered because of the way he looked at me.

"C'mon, baby." I curved my fingers at him and laughed as I turned to give him the back view. My panties were satin, too, and Brazilian cut. They showed a lot of cheek. "Let's dance."

CHAPTER
twenty-nine

"Stop splashing me, you ass."

"You splashed me first, Tigress. Don't start something you aren't prepared to finish."

A couple of feet away from me, Ivan shook water from his hair, and I watched him transfixed. The setting sun made the droplets that cascaded from him look like a waterfall of fiery diamonds.

"Yo." Ty tossed the football to Ivan. It almost hit him in the head. Ivan hadn't been paying attention to the game. While I had been watching him, he'd had his eyes on me, too.

Coming out to the ocean with Ivan was like foreplay. If I still had a best friend looking out for me, she would no doubt have advised me against my current course. Barbara might have, too. Because after the truths Ivan and I had both revealed, every touch we exchanged was an invitation. Every word was a prelude to seduction. Every move was a sensual dance that led to only one destination.

"Enough! I'm waving the white flag. I surrender."

"That's a football, not a flag. Besides, I see it more as a temporary truce."

"That works for me." Grinning, he put his sunglasses up on his head and waded through the water that came to his waist, stopping when he was less than a foot away.

"So, you glad you came out?"

"Maybe."

"You've smiled so many times I stopped counting them. You even laughed at me when that asshole Jagger dunked me under the wave for absolutely no reason at all."

"Yanking down his boxers isn't a reason?" I reminded him.

"Oh yeah. I guess it is." His grin widened, his eyes twinkling more brilliantly than the crystalline surface of the ocean.

"Smiles *and* laughter." He moved close. So close. "You *are* glad you came out." He grabbed me by the upper arms and pulled me through the water into him. Close became slow dancing close. "Admit it, babe."

"Why should I?"

"You're stubborn as shit." His eyes searched mine.

"I've been told that once or twice."

"You're also sexy as hell, and I've had a hard-on since you did your little striptease."

"You provoked me into it."

"You like being naughty."

"Sometimes."

"You also like nice."

I nodded.

"I can give you both. Anything. Anyplace. Any way you want it, Mars." His gaze dipped to my mouth. Mine fell to his and the piercing in his lower lip glinted in the sun. Releasing my arm, he framed one side of my face with it, swiping across my satiny bottom lip with the rough pad of his thumb. "I want to kiss you." A shiver rolled through me. I wanted that, too. His caress. His heated gaze. His words. All sparks to blaze an ever-smoldering fire.

"Friends till the sun goes down," I reminded him, my tone breathy. "In case you didn't notice, it's setting right now."

"So it is."

"And this temporary truce?"

"Yeah, what about it?

"It's over."

"What?"

"I'm not asking anymore." He stared deeply into my eyes. "I'm taking what I want, when I want, how I want. And, babe," he framed my face in his hands, "I'm claiming you." He held me captive, though his hold was unnecessary. I wanted what he wanted. I knew I shouldn't. There were so many reasons why I shouldn't. Only one why I should. Acting on that one, I went up on my toes in the sand bringing my lips to his mouth. His mouth curved as he pressed his firm lips against my soft ones. I felt his pleasure. I reveled in pleasing him. In being claimed by him, by his potent kiss, the seal between our mouths so sure his hoop imprinted my lip. I didn't think about how very likely it was that the man himself was imprinted on me somewhere deeper. This kiss, his kiss, like all the others he gave me drew me inescapably to him and became everything. The tide that brought us together. The push and pull of his will against mine. Before the eventual surrender.

I moaned approvingly and willingly parted my lips. I yielded to his rapacious tongue and his ravenous hunger. Then I shared my own. His need fed my need. My own fueled his. Our mutual appetites merged into one.

"Ivan," I breathed against his mouth as he adjusted his angle to deepen the kiss. "We can't." Reason tried to surface. The RFC. Raven. The havoc this all might wreak.

"We will." I felt his hands flex demandingly on my hips. His fingers gliding and finding the waistband of my panties, he yanked them off my legs easily without having to bend over because of the water.

"Don't lose those," I said sassily, my feet floating back to the sand. "They're my favorite."

"They're my favorite now, too." He grinned a wicked grin. He knew I was giving in. He threaded my panties around my wrist. "Arms around my neck, babe." As I complied, my panties a watery corsage, I pressed my aching breasts to his deliciously hard chest. I felt his hand glide between my legs. He found and circled the pad of his thumb around my swollen needy clit. That felt so good, I moaned, and my lids fluttered only a breath later as he slid one long finger inside of me.

"You're so wet."

"Yes." I panted my agreement.

"Hot."

"Yes."

"Hold on to me," he ordered, and I did, losing his hands for a minute. My bottom half floated in the surf as he made an adjustment under the water. Then his hands were back. "Love your sexy ass." His voice a rasp, he grabbed my cheeks, squeezed them hard, lifted me and thrust his steely length deep, so deep inside of me.

"How did you..."

"I'm always prepared, babe."

"But..."

"Except for that one time." He read my mind.

"Stop talking. I need you to move." I clawed at his shoulders.

"Fuck yes." He fastened his mouth back on mine. He thrust his tongue between my lips. He glided his cock, in and out of me, again, and again. His Prince Albert piercing increased the intensity of his climax, but I had forgotten how much it heightened my own pleasure.

I ripped my mouth from his. I grabbed his face. I rained appreciative kisses on his forehead, his nose, his cheeks. The skin along his strong jaw was covered in a shadow of stubble, rough and salty against my seeking lips. While I worshipped his face, I also moved with him, meeting each thrust and grinding when he was deepest inside me.

"Mars, so good," he praised loudly, and I glanced around. The guys knew what we were doing beneath the waves, given the motion of our bodies it was obvious. They had formed a protective circle blocking us *mostly* from being viewed by the others out in the surf.

"You feel so good," I returned. And yet we were so bad to fuck dirty like this in public. The risk of being seen didn't dampen my enthusiasm, nor did the ocean. The water lapped at my skin. Waves nudged our already rocking bodies like an additional lover. My nipples tightened to points inside my bra. My clit throbbed. My desperation grew, and it built higher each time his piercing raked over me. "You're so big. So thick. So hard inside me."

He groaned in reply, his rhythm becoming more forceful and erratic. His tight grip on the sensitive skin over my cheeks stung my ass. I squeezed tight while he plunged deep, decadently deep inside me.

"Yes, Ivan," I praised. "Oh yes. Don't stop."

"Not. Going. To. Can't." He punctuated each word with a purposeful thrust.

I'm going to...." I warned, feeling the yearning explosion, the fiery heat, the blinding intense heat reaching the crescendo.

"Come, babe," he demanded. "Come now." He refastened his lips to mine, swallowing my cries and giving me a deep groan that made all of me tighten before my climax detonated inside me. His shoulders bunched beneath my clawing nails. His cock stiffened as his release struck him as well. A bolt of intensity radiated within me pools and pools of pleasure. I clenched around his length, repeatedly, absorbing each and every one of his shudders.

CHAPTER
thirty

Mᴙ ʜᴀɴᴅs ᴏɴ Iᴠᴀɴ's sʜᴏᴜʟᴅᴇʀs, I softly glided my fingertips across the crescents my nails had left in them. I savored the velvety warm texture of his skin and the remaining connection to him while he slid my water-logged panties up my legs. We'd just fucked, yet here I remained giving him more after-sex time than I gave any guy.

It's not just sex with him, Mars.

Yeah, I knew. It had been the same way that first time, too. So, there was no need to point out to myself that Ivan Carl wasn't just any guy, either.

I had forgotten how good it had been with him. No, that wasn't quite right. It was more that I had purposefully blocked it out, so it wouldn't feel like settling with the guys who had followed him.

Even Hawk.

On that note, I silenced any further reverie.

"Ivan," I began as he lifted his gaze. "Maybe we should talk."

"About what, babe?" His expression was casually enigmatic, his eyes nonchalantly hooded.

"About what just happened," I clarified carefully, hating to potentially ruin his languid mood.

"If this talk is going to be like the one we had the last time I had my cock in you…" His gripped on my hips tightened, and his shoulder muscles turned to steel beneath his skin. "…then I'm going to decline."

"But…"

"You said you would consider. Do you remember that?" His eyes wide now, he hit mine with the full force of his displeasure. "You let me fuck you. Several times. Then, I held you after your father called. I got a glimpse of the power and the vulnerability in you that night. More than enough to hook me, but not enough for you apparently."

"I did consider," I protested. I had considered him a lot. I had turned that piece of hotel stationery with his phone number on it over and over in my hand until his masculine scrawl had become barely legible.

"I went out with your best friend, hoping maybe in the beginning that you would get jealous. But I saw pretty quickly that I didn't measure up, that no guy could break through the impossible filter of Hawk Winters."

"Oh." My lips rounded in surprise.

"So, no on the talking. We did things your way once. I already explained how it's going to be from now on."

"You mean that 'what you want whenever you want it' speech?"

"Yeah." He shrugged, dislodging my hands. They slid off his shoulders and dropped to the crook in his arms. "That sums it up."

"Funny. Because that's my gig. I have a show to do that revolves around the same premise. And two more guys left to fuck now that I've done you." Truthfully, I hadn't even considered counting him as an

RFC fuck until he had pulled this high-handed shit on me. I cocked my head to the side, pushing his buttons because he had pushed mine. "Your 'what you want whenever' schedule gonna be able to accommodate me if I decide to have another go at you?"

"No." His eyes flared. "You know it's not." His hands leaving my hips, he grabbed my upper arms. He had me. I had him. Subconsciously maybe we were both reluctant to let the other go. But we needed to figure it out because neither of us had the first clue what to do next. That problem remained the same as it had first time we were together.

"Ivan," I tried again, gentling my tone. "We're just two damaged people who comforted each other and had a good time. A completion of sorts. Closure. But that's all it was, and it's over now." I removed my hands from his shoulders, reluctantly sure. I wasn't totally un-self-aware.

"Completion? Closure? What a bunch of motherfucking bullshit." He blocked me as I tried to wade past him, his expression fierce as he stared down at me. "That's not what this was, and you know it."

"It was sex. Sex is about getting. We both *got* off. Don't tell me you really believe it was anything more, or that you want it to be. Because I'm not buying it." I started to say something additional, only to be struck senseless by the intensity in his glare.

"I already told you I wanted more multiple times." His jaw locked tight as he studied me. "What's it going to take for you to make that leap, Mars?" he gritted out.

He was pissed off, and he was being confrontational. I got why now. So much made sense regarding him. Rejection was his trigger. Raven had pulled it when she had walked away without even giving him a chance to explain. So had I by refusing him just now. I needed to find a way to end this with the least amount of pain. I needed to be honest, as honest as I could without leaving myself too open. "I'm not capable of taking that leap with anyone." I decided on the brutal truth.

"The woman who sat in my arms on this beach and told me about her shitty childhood is. The one who stubbornly goes toe to toe with me at every turn is. The one who clawed me up and got what she wanted just now, she's capable. Hell, she'd jump first and drag me along with her for the plunge...if she weren't so afraid."

He had hit the center of the target. "I'm not afraid," I lied and lifted my chin.

"You are, babe. And that's ok because to tell you the truth I am, too. But if you feel strongly enough to be afraid then that's how you know it matters. That's how you know it's real."

"Yo, asshole."

Ivan shifted to face his friend while I reeled from the significance of that statement. "Go away, Ty," he growled.

"I would, bro. I totally would." Ty waded toward us. He gave Ivan then me a narrowed look that told me he had seen and heard everything and that he very much disapproved. "But the sun's practically gone. And Jeeves just texted me." He waved his cell in the air as proof. Where had he kept it while he'd been out in the surf? His hat? "He just woke up. He's rested. He'll be ready to pull out soon, and we all need to get cleaned up and get some food before then. You said if we took this time off we had to drive straight through to make all the morning preconcert shit."

"You're right, and I hear you." Ivan raked a hand through his hair, dislodging his sunglasses. I caught them before they hit the water and held them out to him.

"Thanks, babe." He took them from me and our hands brushed together.

"You're welcome." My skin zinged from the connection with his.

222   MICHELLE MANKIN

Our gazes remained locked together for a long meaningful beat and as they did something out of phase shifted into focus inside me.

"Life's taken bites out of both of us." Ivan's tone was reflectively soft. "Done its damage. Left us with a lot of ragged edges most people wouldn't understand. But I understand, Mars, and I think maybe if we stop cutting into each other for a change we would discover that we actually piece together very well."

Chapter Thirty-one

I THREW THE STRIPED TOWEL I HAD BORROWED over the cinderblock half-wall in the public shower facility. The graffiti of the St. George Island lighthouse spray-painted on it kept my thoughts from Ivan and his words and the wonder of what the hell had I gotten myself into…for a few miraculous moments. The mirror with its wide-eyed reflection of me brought me right back to the issue at hand.

I'd fucked Ivan Carl, and I'd done it right out in the open. Literally and figuratively.

Ok, Mars. So, it was not my brightest idea. More like a moment of weakness brought on by soul to soul baring and the idyllic beachside setting. Still, besides his bandmates, a few swimmers in the ocean and maybe a couple of other stealthy eyed ones on the shore, who really knew? I could get back on the bus, behave myself and rejoin the tour with no one the wiser. That was the bullshit I fed my reflection as I contorted my shoulders to unhook and remove my sopping wet navy bra. My reflection wasn't having any of it.

Face the reality, she fired back as I tossed the likely ruined undergarment beside the towel. *What reality?* I played the dumb blonde card and shimmied out of my Brazilian cut panties tossing them next to everything else. I was just too crazy for his hot cock and those rich chocolate eyes of his. I would succumb again and again if I couldn't figure out a strategy to resist him.

Yeah, right. What strategy would work short of placing me on one side of the planet and him on another?

Shaking my head at myself, my dueling personalities and my utter lack of willpower regarding Ivan Carl, I moved to the row of nozzles. I chose the one on the far right. Turning the crank to hot, I waited until I saw steam rising, then ducked underneath it to warm my chilled skin. I began to scrub the salt from my body.

"Need some help?" A deep familiar voice questioned, interrupting my efforts and making me utterly aware I was completely naked.

"Ivan," I complained, pretending I wasn't aware of my body's reaction to him. "This is the women's side." I blinked water from my eyes, shifted slightly and turned my head to glance at him over my shoulder. Yeah, I knew that was a seductive pose. Turns out it was overkill. His eyes were already glazed with desire.

He stood just outside of the tile step-over into the shower. He looked as though he'd already bathed. He had a white towel tucked around his waist. My eyes did some glazing over of their own. Ivan in only a towel, his skin taut and bronzed from the sun and his hair soaked sable and slicked back, he exuded sex appeal.

"You can't come in here." My words were trembly.

"Can't I? The guys are standing outside to keep anyone from intruding."

"Your sentinels," I muttered.

"What?"

"Nothing." I shifted so the hot spray hit my cupped hands and arced over my shoulder. Unfortunately, my attempt to splash him and wash away the pheromones that seemed to saturate the air fell short.

"Missed." His sculpted lips formed his sexy half-smile. "I brought you some soap and shampoo." He stepped over the ledge that was no more of a barrier than my willpower. He sauntered over almost touching me as he placed a bar of soap in the dish along with a travel sized bottle of shampoo. "I thought you might need them."

"I do. Thanks."

"You're welcome." His gaze dipped to take in all of me. And being the vixen I was I didn't shy away as he stared appreciatively at me. Did he want another round? I suddenly couldn't remember why I should say no. I was wet. I was willing.

"Want some help soaping off the...you know...important parts?" His voice rumbled, and the acoustics in the shower magnified it so it vibrated through my body like it did through the speakers when he was on stage.

"Important as in my tits, pussy and ass?" I had chill bumps all over my skin from the shiver that had rolled through me.

"Those would be the ones." His eyes lowered to have another look at those parts. Those parts liked his attention. They reveled in it.

"I could use some help actually." I managed a saucy smile. "It's been a while since I had a bikini wax. You got a razor with you?"

"No." He shook his head slowly.

"Oh, too bad."

"I can get one. Hold on." He turned and retraced his steps. I watched him of course.

I was lathering my hair when he returned. Eyes closed, I didn't see him. But I felt him. His hard body sliding behind mine. His completely naked hard body. I drew in a breath. I held it as he pressed even closer his pecs, hips and thighs against my shoulders, spine and ass. Reaching around me, he covered my breasts with his hands.

"That feels so good." I arched into his fingers as he lifted and shaped my tits.

"Give me your mouth babe." He pressed a hot kiss into the side of my neck. "I love your sexy lips."

"I love that you love them," I muttered inanely. It was difficult to think straight with him plucking and twisting my tight nipples. He knew just the right pressure to apply to build the ache and make me burn.

"Mouth babe," he reminded me.

"Mmm," I replied incoherently, leaning my wet head back onto his strong shoulder. I tipped my head up at him, peering at his handsome face through my lashes.

"Beautiful." His dark brown eyes were melted chocolate hot. He lowered his head and stamped his lips to mine. Firm to soft. I had a moment to savor, to feel the metal bite of his piercing before he repositioned and swiped his eager tongue through the droplets of water that had gathered between my lips. My body melted as he licked them away. I moaned when he penetrated my mouth with his tongue. I felt it in my clit when he rubbed his tongue against my own.

Throbbing now, I shifted my legs restlessly and ripped my mouth from his. "I want..."

"I know what you want," he growled against my lips. Leaving one hand at my tit, flexing his fingers possessively as if to remind me it was there, he dove his other hand lower. He skimmed it fast through the slick sudsy trail my borrowed shampoo had left on my skin. He went straight to my mound and covered my pussy with his hand.

I moaned, loving the feel of being pinned into place against his body. My tit in one of his capable hands and my pussy in the other.

ROCK *Fuck* CLUB BOOK 3   227

I rocked into each, needing more, always wanting more with him. "You're hot as fuck, Tigress. Your perfect ass, your fucking phenomenal tits, your greedy cunt." He found my entrance and stroked his long finger inside. So slippery wet. Always so eager and wet for me." He swirled his thumb slowly, achingly slowly around my swollen clit.

"Ivan," I moaned. "More. Please."

"I'll give you more in a minute. First, move your head to the left for me," he demanded. As soon as I complied he ran his hot open mouth along the taut line of the tendon that connected my neck and shoulder. I felt a corresponding rush of heat in my core. Before I could fully process how great that felt, he retraced his previous line with the blunt edge of his tongue.

"Ivan. Fuck." My entire body shook and my cunt spasmed around his finger. "I'm going to come. Tell me you have protection," I panted.

"I do." He released me abruptly. My cunt protested the loss of his finger. My breasts were heavy and ached for his touch. My body swayed as he reached for a foil packet I hadn't noticed him placing in the dish earlier. "Put your hands on the wall," he ordered, his voice gruff. I moved. I turned quickly, slamming my palms flat to the tile, noticing my movement in the mirror on my right but not fully because his body covered mine from behind. And Ivan's body demanded all my attention. "Good girl." He bit down on the sensitive skin between my neck and shoulder.

I hissed and my empty cunt spasmed. It didn't stay empty long. His fingers swiping through my wetness, the shower spray now pelting us from the side, he aligned the blunt head of his cock and plunged it inside of me. "So good," I praised.

"Babe," he groaned. "You're so hot...so tight around me." His large hands on my hips, he withdrew. My cunt clamped wanting to keep him there.

"No," I whimpered.

"Shh," he soothed. He didn't pull all the way out, just until only the engorged head of his cock remained. Then he slid back inside, his piercing stroking hot friction inside of me.

"Yes," I approved.

"Marsha," he whispered my name. No one had ever whispered my name so adoringly. His hands at my hips, his grip firm, he pulled out and he stroked back in again. And I turned my head to watch him do it. The lines of his face were drawn. His neck taut, his head thrown back. Heat shivered over my skin. It was so incredibly hot to watch myself being fucked by him.

My lips were red and parted, my breasts heavy and full, and my eyes drifted halfway closed as he stroked in and out again, faster, his hard cock sliding readily. I was so wet, so turned on, so close. I started to tell him, but he knew. Increasing the pace, his grip was so tight it stung my skin. His thrusts were so hard the flesh at his hips smacked my ass. The stinging pain and the hot pleasure melded to become one.

I closed my eyes. I tipped my hips. I took his cock deeper. He fucked me, and he fucked me. My breasts bounced. He lifted me off my feet. My cunt spasmed around him. The entire world became me and him. The two of us and this insatiable need. Until we were there. At the pinnacle. Both at the same time. I cried out his name as it hit me. He gripped my hips with a bruising intensity and marked me so deeply I knew I would never be the same.

CHAPTER thirty-two

I VAN GOT DRESSED BEFORE ME AND GAVE me a sound kiss on the lips like we were true lovers, instead of only transient ones.

"Take your time, babe. I'll see you in a bit," he said, waved a hand over his shoulder and disappeared from sight.

I stared at the spot where I had last seen him for a few moments before I shook myself out of my daze.

It was time to face reality. I cast my gaze around looking for something to ground me. My eyes snagged on my favorite satin navy bra and the matching panties. I picked them up and tossed them in the trash. They were ruined, and if I thought too deeply about it, I would know I was, too.

Ruined over him.

So not thinking about it.

I pulled my tank top over my wet head then shimmied into my cutoffs. I avoided the mirrors. The blue-eyed blonde? A cliché. The former sidekick, now the front and center star? A farce. Laughably

230   MICHELLE MANKIN

pathetic. Tangoed with the bad boy. Again. Got her head screwed up by screwing around with him. Not once but twice. You would think she would learn.

Apparently not.

She seemed to be an Ivanaholic.

"Hey, sis?" A masculine voice queried as I exited the shower facility.

"What?" My hand went to my throat.

"Sorry to scare you. It's just me." A shadow separated from the outer wall. Discombobulated, I took a step backward before I realized it was only Arrow.

"We're just looking out for our adopted sibling," Jag said from the other side of his companion. "Since we're family now, though of course we're not really related. But those are the guidelines Ivan put down, and he's the boss." He stepped more into the light. His black hair was slicked back like Ivan's had been and his earnest face appeared to be freshly shaven. His gaze dipped to my chest as I moved closer, his green eyes widening. "Um." He took a big step backward, rubbing the back of his neck and suddenly looking uncomfortable.

"What's wrong? I glanced down and realized the problem right away. With my hair wet and dripping, and no bra, my navy tank left little to the imagination. "Oops, my bad. Awkward sibling moment." I smiled and pulled the sides of my kimono together. "I'll be less like a wet t-shirt contestant once my hair dries. There wasn't a blow-drier." I shrugged. "And I didn't have a brush or a comb, anyway."

"You can borrow one of ours," Jag offered.

"Thanks, bro." My smile widened. "I appreciate the offer. But I have a toiletry bag on the bus. I think I'll just go find my own."

"Uh-no, I can't let you." Jag stepped in front of me and hooked a thumb over his shoulder. A ringed thumb. A silver flag one with stripes and stars that looked like one of Ivan's. Did they share accessories?

"And why not?" I glanced at the bus where my stuff awaited, along with the potential to find a quiet refuge from a certain soulful eyed lead singer who had my head spinning and my insides all knotted up.

"We've got our orders," Arrow informed me.

"Boss man said guard the front entrance," Jag elaborated. "Intercept her when she comes out and escort her to the snack shack."

"It's time to eat." Arrow nodded. Slices of air dried blond hair settled like, well, like arrows arcing into his hazel eyes. His hair was cut a lot like Lucky's. "We got jack to feed you on the bus."

"Ahh." Understanding dawned. "Well then let's get to the food. I'm starving."

"Us, too." Arrow linked his arm to mine. Before I could protest about him dislodging my grip on my kimono, his companion hooked my other one.

"Come along now, sis." Jag grinned down at me. I realized how tall he was when he was this close to me. Arrow, too.

"You always do what Ivan tells you to do?" I grumbled. The frontman of the Enthusiasts tended to be pushy and high-handed with more than just me. A character trait. One that grated. Mostly. Sometimes, it felt like he was looking out for me. Maybe that he even cared.

Um, not going there.

"Not always," Arrow informed me. "Just when it's necessary to keep the peace." His gaze swept over me, and his nostrils flared. "I volunteered us to get you. And should the sister thing fall through, I want you to know I'm an interested party."

"Nicholas," Jag warned. "She only used your soap on account of it's the only one that doesn't smell like men's cologne. The thing with her and Ivan ain't falling through. You know how he is. And he made himself pretty clear how she was off-limits after the Southside Ballroom show."

My eyes widened. That was the Dallas show where I had first seen the band...Ivan...live.

"That was then," Arrow disagreed. "This is now."

"Now ain't no fucking different." Jag shook his head.

It's a lot different." My escorts set the brakes on our walk, bringing all three of us to an abrupt stop a couple of feet from a lit-up clapboard building. Leaning, with a huge hole in the roof, it bore a sign that identified it as the Snack Shack, as if it could have been called anything else.

"Why did we..." I trailed off as I heard them...saw them.

"Marsha's not Raven, Ivan." Ty had his hands on his hips. Standing under the eaves, his frame appeared to be just as tense as his best friend's.

"No, she's not." Ivan returned. "Thank God. She actually responds when I touch her."

"She's a slut."

"Shut your fucking mouth, Ty." Ivan threw his arms out and shoved the unprepared drummer into the side of the building. The rotting wood siding shuttered and dusty fragments rained down.

"Fuck you." Tyler knocked Ivan's hands away.

"Told you to lay off, man. You don't know the shit she's been through. She's not Priscilla."

I know that." His caramel eyes flashed reflecting the porch light. "She is what she is. Messed up like the rest of us. But you can't fix her."

"I don't need to. Maybe I need her to fix me. Did you ever think about that?"

"Fuck, this is worse than I thought. You can't bring her into the family if she doesn't want to be here, man. If you didn't have your head so far up her ass you'd clue in how this is going to go down." He shook his head. "You're gonna get screwed just like when you went for

ROCK *Fuck* CLUB BOOK 3   233

her best friend. And we'll all get to witness the fucking spiral again. I mean, Ivan, you've just starting to write again. Don't..."

"Hey, um." Arrow cleared his throat, released my arm and stepped forward into the crescent of light from the porch. "We're here." He hooked his thumb over his shoulder. "She's here."

I tried to pull my arm free from Jag, but he wouldn't let me.

"Don't," he whispered, placing his hand over my own on his forearm. "Arrow's just got a crush on you. Ivan's interest is legit." He patted my hand. "You feeling me?"

I nodded. I got what he was saying for sure. I just wasn't sure I believed it. My perception of reality had taken a complete turn since I had stepped onto the Enthusiasts' bus.

"Babe." Ivan closed the distance separating us. My skittering heart thumped faster, then settled into a more sedate rhythm when he stopped right in front of me. I felt his body heat. His gaze hit mine. My cheeks warmed from the intensity of it. "I'll take her from here." He didn't take his eyes off me as Jagger carefully removed my hand from his arm and placed it on Ivan's. "Thanks, man."

"No problem."

"Order's up. Can you put a lid on ours or something while I talk to Mars?"

"Sure." Jag confirmed, uncharacteristically succinct. "Hey, Arrow. Let's get those burgers." His voice and the others faded into the background as Ivan drew me into his arms.

"You hear all that?" He peered down at me. We stood in a circle of light. Darkness all around. The noise of the crickets seemed to pause as if they were holding their breath. It suddenly seemed as though Ivan and I were the only two people in the world. That nothing else mattered. That nothing could touch us in this moment with him holding me and staring at me so intently.

"Yes," I heard it, I admitted. "I just don't know..."

"You know, Mars. You fucking know. Ok?"

"Yes." My throat constricted, and my eyes burned. "I do now, I guess."

"Give me some time, then. Ok? Meet me halfway. Give me a little fucking opening to work with. Stop shutting the door in my face, alright? Can you do that?"

"But all those things Tyler said." I swallowed. Tears stung my eyes. I knew my role. If I stepped outside it was when I got crushed. "They're true. I'm not wor...I'm not the type..." I sighed. "I'm not her. I'm not..."

"Stop it, alright. Stop telling me the things you're not. It's not up to you how I see you. It's not up to Tyler. It's not up to your old man or fucking anyone else. Just me and you. Don't you get that?"

Could it be that easy? Could he simply erase the past? Not just our personal past but the deeper stuff? The damage wrought to my psyche and his own by our twisted upbringings? Were desire and declarations all it took to redefine our roles?

I couldn't believe it was possible.

But I wanted it to be. For once in my life, I wanted to be the reason someone stayed.

CHAPTER thirty-three

"SO, THIS NEW MUSIC?" I QUESTIONED, going for a diversion, one I hoped would get some attention off me. Well, off the idea of Ivan with me. Like *really* with me. On our side of the picnic bench across the table from his three bandmates, he had one arm looped around my neck and the other on the half-full bottle of beer in front of him. They were all pretending not to be as thrown off by the dramatic Ivan plus me turn of events as I was.

"The new tunes are fan-fucking-tastic." Arrow helped me out with my flailing attempt at redirection. I gave him a grateful nod. Not too much encouragement. He was an interested party, after all. His gaze kept dipping to my tits. Explaining why Ivan's propriety arm kept ratcheting tighter and tighter around me.

"So, you say. But how come I haven't heard any of them? Charlotte. Tampa. All you guys played was..."

"Old, tried and true stuff," Jag interjected. "The new material is a departure from the strict heavy metal sound we've been doing since the beginning."

"Really?" That sounded interesting. I sat up straighter. My inner rock chick was engaged. "How big of a departure? Even a little could be a risky move. Your fan base is pretty hardcore."

"A pretty big shift. We're going for the middle ground between metal and rock. Message wise a few less songs raging against the injustice in the world and a couple more about how if we work together we can change some shit." Arrow shook his blond head and lifted his beer. His second. He chugged back a healthy swig like the risk the band was taking made him nervous.

"We all know it's chancy." Ty met my gaze for the first time since I had overheard his argument with Ivan. "But our fans are incredibly loyal, and we believe in what we're doing. Plus, the stuff's that good." His gaze shifted to the man who held me. "After not writing at all, Ivan suddenly got fucking inspired."

"Why?" I angled my head and tipped it back to study the man in question, the primary songwriter in the group. More evidence of his sensitive soul. I'd seen it the first night we had spent together. He had comforted me after my dad had gone on a typical tirade about how I was such a disappointment as a daughter. An entire night, I had spent in Ivan's arms before the tour bus had pulled out. Then that space he had given me that I hadn't repaid by choosing him. So, he'd chosen my best friend instead. I'd seen him with her at their most destructive. Parties, drinking, heavy shit. Until Hawk died. Then Raven had stopped the drugs. So had he. Apparently, he had even taken it a step further and given up the heavy drinking, too. Still he had remained loyal, by her side at the funeral and well after when she had retreated into her walled off world. And then he had screwed up, and here we were again, him comforting me as if none of that had ever happened.

ROCK *Fuck* CLUB BOOK 3   237

Surprisingly, at the ready each time I crumbled. Ivan wasn't the man I had painted him to be in my mind. I knew that. Nevertheless, I still denied acknowledging all that he might be, because just like before I knew deep down I couldn't keep him.

"What?" He raised a brow at me. "Why are you staring at me like that?"

"Like what?"

"Like maybe I'm not the bad guy to you anymore?"

"Oh. Well, maybe you aren't. Maybe I got it wrong. Maybe I got a lot of things wrong."

Typical for me.

"Whoa. "His pierced lip tilted up on one side. "Run with those maybes. Gives me some solid ground to stand on with you for a change. I'll take those maybes and forge them into certainties." He crooked his arm tighter, added his other hand to tilt my head and kissed me. Soundly. Thoroughly. With lots of tongue.

I was breathless and more than a little dazed by the time he ended it.

Transient lovers?

Maybe not.

Maybe this could be lasting. That's how good his everything kisses were. That's how certain I felt in his arms. Plus, the fact that he claimed and kissed me in front of his family. It felt momentous to be validated at all but especially to the people that mattered most to him.

"So." I stroked a finger down Ivan's arm, back and forth across the bronzed skin his Firebird muscle tee left exposed. Decked out in board length shorts and flip flops, it seemed he wasn't ready to resume his full-on rock star persona. That was part of him, for sure. But this casual beach guy was him, too. Out here, he didn't have to maintain pretenses. He could be whoever he wanted to be. Maybe even a true forever away from the bright lights and screaming fans.

238   MICHELLE MANKIN

"So, what, babe?" Ivan queried, his tone deep. His gaze dipped as he followed the movement of my fingers on his skin. Stroking him was like petting a lion, a leopard or a tiger. No chance to tame him, I could at least soothe him for a time.

"When do I get to hear a demo of the band's new sound?"

"We've got amps in the back lounge," Arrow offered. "We could demo it live."

"I don't have a full kit, but I guess I could pull out a snare from the luggage compartment," Tyler offered, surprising me. I cocked my head at him. He didn't like me. He'd made his feelings crystal clear. I didn't understand why he would facilitate something I wanted.

"Mic's barely decent." Ivan's lip went between his teeth as if he were undecided.

"Oh, please," I said. "As if you need a mic to project in a space that small with your voice."

"Like my voice, huh?" He zeroed in on that statement and me.

"Oh yeah," I admitted. "The gravelly angry screamo, for sure. And the softer baritone stuff most definitely. I...ahhh!" I jumped up and scrambled off the bench.

"What's wrong?" Ivan boomed. Standing faster than I had, he moved into a protective stance in front of me.

"Something just climbed up my leg!" My hands on his waist, I curled my fingers around his belt-loops and peered around him. "It's under there." I saw a shadow of movement. "Under the table. What is it?"

A soft meow answered my question. A tabby cat materialized, a half-starved one with big forlorn golden eyes.

"Oh my." I felt a pang in my chest. The poor thing was so skinny. I abandoned my knight's protection and held out my hand. The cat peered at it suspiciously. "C'mon baby," I coaxed, wiggling my fingers. "I just want to pet you."

"Hey, that's my line," Ivan deadpanned. The guys laughed, and as I laughed softly, too, the cat came closer, dipping its head to let me scratch behind its pointed ears.

"It's adorable," I decided as it arched its back under my hand and purred loudly.

"It's a stray," Ivan countered carefully. "You probably shouldn't touch it. I doubt it's been vaccinated. It might have rabies or something."

"Nonsense. It just needs a home and something to eat," I argued.

"It's a pain in my ass." The old guy with a Snack Shack paper chef hat and a ketchup splattered apron stuck his head through the pass through serving window.

"You know this one?" I asked.

"Do I ever. I fell for its woe-as-me-I'm-starving-routine. Got it checked out. Shots and all. You think it would be grateful. But, oh no. Is it happy? Will it eat the cat food I buy?"

"Uh, no," I guessed.

"Damn straight. It only wants to get on the counter to eat the hamburgers and lap up the shakes that are for the paying customers. Health inspector gave me another warning today. Spoiled thing's going to the animal shelter first chance I get."

Oh no, I thought, and as if he sensed his impending death sentence, the cat leapt up into my arms. "It's so soft," I marveled and smiled as it burrowed closer.

"It likes you," Arrow said.

"More than likes. It's taken to you like a dolphin to water, a bird to the sky, a..."

"Like a conman to his next sucker." The old guy interrupted Jag's soliloquy.

"What's its name?" Ivan asked.

"Mine," I announced as its tongue darted out, licking the vanilla shake residue from my fingertips. The sandpapery texture on my skin made me giggle. I stroked its head as it purred louder, and my heart decided right then and there. Unequivocally. "It's Mine."

"We'll take him." Ivan's gaze met mine. He grinned as the tabby climbed my chest and dove under the tangle of my uncombed hair. "Add Mine to my tab."

CHAPTER
thirty-four

"W"E CAN'T KEEP A CAT ON THE TOUR BUS, Ivan," Ty complained as we worked our way through the packed grocery store parking lot laden with purchases.

"Why the fuck not?" Ivan questioned. "It seems low maintenance. It likes to eat what we like to eat. And we certainly bought enough shit for it tonight."

Everything Walmart had on the shelves for cats for sure, I thought, but stayed out of the debate. After all, Mine and I were guests on the tour bus. Once we got to Nola, I'd be back on the WMO bus with Barbara. I hoped she wasn't allergic to cats.

"Including a place to shit." Jag slapped his knee. "Ha-ha. The litter box. Get it?" He laughed at his own joke. I got the idea he amused himself a lot. He scrubbed Mine's head. The bassist had grown up around cats. He loved them. He and Ivan approved of Mine. Two more Enthusiasts to win over. I was pretty sure Arrow was teetering on the brink of being a Mine-fan. He'd insisted on the deluxe kitty play-tower. Ty was going to be as much of a hard sell about the cat as he was of me.

Ivan bumped the bus door with his shoulder when we reached it. He was carrying two huge plastic tubs full of kitty litter. The door yielded.

"Holy shit," Jeeves said when he saw us. Everyone had two plastic bags. I just had Mine.

"Yeah, shit." Jag's pealing laughter followed me as I climbed the stairs behind Ivan. I almost missed the last step. Watching Ivan's muscles flex with his heavy load had distracted me.

In the lounge, everyone dropped their bags and flopped on the couches. It was hot away from the sea breeze at the beach, and we were all tired. Ivan threw his arm around me and pulled me close. Mine hopped out of my hold, meowed plaintively and went off to explore.

"He's making himself at home," Ivan mused, watching Mine sniff around the trash drawer.

"Yeah." I nodded, laid my weary head on the rock-hard pillow that was Ivan's chest and tunneled my hands under his back, so I could get my arms around him. "You think he's ok?" My brow creased as Mine ducked under the banquette table. "What if he's hungry?"

"He ate an entire hamburger, Mars." Ivan's voice rumbled through his chest into my ear.

"Oh, yeah," I remembered. And he'd lapped up the last quarter of my shake. "But what if he puts something in his mouth and chokes on it?"

"He's a full-grown cat. He's not a toddler," Jag informed me.

"But what if he needs me?" I started to sit up.

"Stay. I like you here." Ivan pulled me back down. "Also how you didn't even hesitate to relax on top of me."

"I'm not in top of you," I protested, propping myself on my arm to look at him. "I just, you know..."

"Sat right next to me." He wore a bemused expression as he stared at me. "Laid your head on my chest and draped your sexy body over me."

My jaw dropped.

"Yeah, babe. You fit really well there, too. Seems significant to point out."

"I..."

"Relax." He smoothed his hand up my spine to my shoulders while applying pressure to draw me back into his side. His stroking felt so good I arched into it like my newfound feline friend.

"Fine." Complying, I laid my head back down, inhaled Ivan's sweet sandalwood, part-ocean scent and yawned. "Maybe I'll just close my eyes for a bit."

"You do that, babe." Ivan's deep voice rumbled again. He stroked my back from the base of my spine to my shoulders again. My skin tingled with the crackle of attraction along with a warm contented pleasure. "Rest a while. I'm not going anywhere."

I woke after what seemed like only moments. However, there was a tellingly large damp spot under my cheek. I tried to sit up, but a heavy weight pinned me down. Ivan's arm, I realized as I became more aware of my surroundings. The lights were low. It was quiet. The guys weren't around. I shifted carefully as I heard a soft sound. Two soft sounds, actually. One underneath me snoring softly. The other behind my back. The purr identified the latter as Mine. I tilted my heat to look at Ivan. His sexy lips were parted. I tucked my fingers under my chin and watched him sleep. He was fascinating. His serene expression framed by his medium length tousled chestnut hair. His eyes closed, the whirlpools behind his lids at rest. He looked so young.

I thought back to the basic details I'd been able to look up about him on the internet. He was only twenty-four. Barely older than I was.

"You ok?" His eyes cracked open, his chocolate gaze and those swirling depths drawing me toward him again.

"Yeah." My brow creased. It had been a while since anyone had asked me that. "I got your shirt wet. Sorry." I grimaced.

"I've gotten you wet a time or two." His lips curved.

"Yeah." My cheeks heated. Why was I embarrassed? Ridiculous after all I had done with him.

"Wanna get wet for me again?"

"Huh?" My heartrate sped up.

"Your hair babe. It's dried all tangled."

I sat up, careful of Mine, reached up, touched my head and felt the clumps of tangles. "Oh no," I muttered my dismay. "It always does that if I don't comb it out before it dries."

"I can see that."

"I bet you can," I huffed. "Why didn't you say anything? Like: here's a comb, your hair's doing some bride of Frankenstein thing."

"I didn't say anything because you didn't seem to care. I certainly don't. The enjoyment I find spending time with you doesn't just have to do with how great you look. It has everything to do with who you are."

I just blinked at him.

"Sweet, sexy, sassy, smart," he explained. "Those things don't change just 'cause you're your hair is messed up, babe. What is it?" he asked when I continued to stare at him.

"I wish..." I truncated that statement. I wished I had called his number that night, wished he had never gone out with Raven, wished I could rewind time and go back to the start. But I knew time marched in only one direction.

You're frowning again. I don't like when you frown."

"Me, either."

Let it go, Marsha. You've got tonight on this bus with him. That's certain. Don't worry about tomorrow. And don't waste right now on impossible wishes.

"So, getting wet? I batted my eyelashes at him. "That sounds interesting if it's me and you without any clothes on. Is that what you had in mind?"

"Wait, what are you doing?" I questioned when I saw the brand new disposable razor he held in his hands

"I'm looking after you." I gave him a blank look. "You mentioned needing a Brazilian. How about a handsome lead singer from Texas who's willing to go down low and get very personal with your pussy instead?"

"Um, no." My heart went haywire thinking of Ivan with a razor focused on that part of me. "That's ok."

"C'mon, babe. I've got the razor, and I've got the time. We'll shower together after." I just stared at him. He was only inches from me. His heat and his scent intoxicated in the tiny, for function only bathroom. My elbows touched the wall behind me. His backside hit the sink. "Let me do this." His expression was earnest. "I think you might like it." He grinned. "I know I will."

"Alright. But..."

He kissed the protest from my lips and all reason from my mind.

"First, I'm going to shave your pretty pussy." He gave me a slow wicked smile. "Then I'm going to eat you. Then we're going to fuck in the shower."

"Ambitious agenda." My eyes twinkled as devilishly as he smiled. "I like it."

"Great." He leaned close, grabbed the hem of my tank and yanked it over my head.

"Amazing." His tone reverential, his gaze dropped to follow his hands as he cupped my breasts. "Your tits are fucking phenomenal." He flicked the already peaked nipples with practiced thrums. The fiery sensation shot straight to my pussy.

"Hurry," I breathed.

"Patience, babe." He unbuttoned my shorts and slowly glided down the zipper.

"No panties, either," he hissed when the two sides separated. "Sitting next to me for hours. Access just a button and a zipper away."

"You like the commando thing?"

"Babe." He lifted his gaze and gave me a look. "I'm a guy. I appreciate sexy lingerie sure, but I much prefer you out of it."

"Then let me help." I wiggled, then shimmied the shorts over my hips and down my thighs and calves. He watched me with rapt attention. "I'm wet already," I admitted.

"I'm hard already," he returned.

I grinned. He smiled.

"Your turn then." I reached under the hem of his muscle tee. I placed my hands on his warm skin. I glided my fingers upward over the smooth sculpted ridges of his abdomen. My mouth parted as I spread my palms wide. His pecs were defined slabs of muscle. His male nipples were dark brown, the tips hard. He drew in a breath as I skimmed my hands over them. Desire pooled between my legs. My heart raced, and it raced even faster after I drew his shirt off and peered into his eyes. The brown was black now, and the black flickered with fire. "Ivan...." I swallowed. "I don't think I can do this. I'm throbbing already. If you only touch me, I'm going to come."

"Then come, babe. And I'll watch. It'll be a hell of a show."

"Alright." I licked my lips. His gaze dipped to my mouth. I reached for his zipper, but he stopped me.

"No." He grabbed my wrist. "Once my cock comes out, its going in you. We clear?" He gave me an imperious look, his eyes intense, his hunger ruggedly displayed in stark lines on his handsome face. "Let's lather you up first." He turned on the water, placed his hands under the stream, pumped liquid soap into them and rubbed them together. Then he reached for me with his soapy hands. His lips curved. "Thank you for standing still. I can't wait to touch you."

"I'm not sure you're the more eager one."

"We'll see." His eyes twinkled. "Put your hands on my shoulders so I can take care of you." As I complied, he touched me. I gasped. With only one warm wet hand he completely covered my mound. I moaned as he began to apply the lather. Very slowly and deliberately, he rubbed working it in. Warm shimmery sensations spread outward from my pussy, to my legs and all the way down to my toes. My nipples tightened. My breaths shortened and inexplicably my scalp tingled. While I trembled and stared at him like a bewitched woman, he ran his hands under the water and grabbed the razor. Then he crouched down and knelt on the floor in front of me. Transfixed, I watched Ivan Carl. The lead singer of the Enthusiasts. My once nemesis on his knees and by his own admission poised to take care of me.

"Babe, you ok?" He glanced up at me through his long lashes.

So, fucking irresistibly handsome.

Sex is supposed to be about getting, I had told him. But here he was turning everything around and making it about giving instead. He knew what he was doing, too. I saw it in his gaze, more than just sexual need. His desire to be something more to me. And I feared if he looked too deeply he would see that same desire in mine.

"Ivan...I..." I glanced away. "Maybe you shouldn't. I mean, have you ever done this before? It's a very delicate procedure."

"No. Never. But I want to, Mars. And I'll be very careful. I have a vested interest in this area. Trust me."

Was that what this was? About trust? Was I ready for that? I gulped as I stared at him, on his knees in front of me. Yet why did it seem like he had all the power?

"Ok," I agreed, my heart thrumming from more than just desire now.

He didn't speak. He grabbed me firmly by the hips and pulled me closer. I felt his hot breath gust on the very center of me. I let everything in my mind go as he began the process. Everything but him and me and this intimate moment.

I drew in a shuddery breath as he stroked the razor over me. I exhaled as he rinsed. There wasn't much hair. I got a Brazilian regularly. I kept that region tidy.

"That's good, babe," he groaned. He was turned on. I was turned on, too. Letting my hips go, he stretched my skin taut with one hand, making a frame using his long first finger and his thumb and with his other hand he shaved me. Another slow purposeful steady stroke accompanied by my broken breathing. Then another deep exhalation as he rinsed. Then he repeated the procedure. Stretch. Stroke. Rinse. Repeat. I was totally under his control. The significance wasn't lost on me. My entire body drew taut. Shaky and shivery, my breaths came shallowly. My skin felt as if it were stretched too tight to contain the sensations that expanded inside of me.

All focused on him.

"Ivan," I warned.

"Done," he announced thickly, throwing the plastic razor in the sink. Cold air rushed over my smooth as silk pussy. Then warmth so much warmth. His hot mouth and his wet tongue as he ravenously feasted on me. It was too much.

"Ivan. Oh, Ivan." I praised. Just one stroke of his wet tongue over my swollen clit, and all that tension inside of me unwound and I came undone. Before I stopped shaking from my release, he had his shorts off. He grabbed me, lifted me and slammed me back into the wall.

"Open your legs," he demanded gruffly.

I opened them. I would do anything for him in that moment. His cock sheathed, he positioned and then slid inside me. His entire length. He captured my mouth, covered it with his own and then he started to move. I tasted myself on his tongue as I sucked on it. I felt his hot cock filling my cunt. It was glorious. Possessed by him. Connected to him. In and out, he stroked. His tongue gliding in my mouth. His cock in my cunt. The wall behind me was cool against my back but everywhere else was liquid fire.

He ripped his mouth from mine and shoved it into the side of my neck. I felt his hot breath on my skin, his firm lips stamping his desire into it. I clawed at his tense shoulders. He slammed his cock inside me, again and again lifting me and squeezing my ass cheeks with each deep decadent thrust. The pleasure built. Each thrust fiery ecstasy. Desire spooling throughout my body. Higher and hotter I went the harder he fucked me until he groaned, and I felt him stiffen inside me. Then I was flying. Flying from the highest heights, and I wasn't alone. He was up there floating with me.

CHAPTER thirty-five

THE SHOWERING TOGETHER AFTERWARD seemed more significant than before. There was no ambivalence. No hesitancy. No mad rush. Just a kind of deep awe and savoring of each other.

I washed his satiny hair and soaped his sleek body. Every sculpted muscle. Each chiseled contour. Every single masculine inch.

He washed my hair. His massage of my scalp made it tingle. His large hands and rough fingertips soaping my skin raked it with heat. Every curve received his attention. Each silky-smooth swipe and warm sluicing rinse turned me on at the same time it made feel like each part of me was a new discovery to him.

He took me again against the shower wall. Slowly. Oh, so incredibly slowly. The culmination was achingly sweet.

Did he fear what tomorrow might bring?

The night raced toward the morning. The bus kept rattling down the road.

Since time marched only one direction, this little pocket of it would soon be behind us and gone.

It seemed we each wanted to wring as much from every fleeting moment that we could.

While avoiding the big question.

What was happening between us?

Under the warm spray in the small shower stall we pressed together. Massively large feet to dainty feminine ones. Hard thighs to creamy soft. His pierced cock already hard again, a formidable and tempting presence against my belly.

Each time my skin brushed against him, it leapt eagerly. My clit throbbed for him, my cunt ached, and a burning longing seared every single cell in my body. All of me longed to be fully connected to him.

Again, and again, and again.

I reached up and framed his handsome face in my hands. I brushed my fingers along the honed edge of his jaw, determined strength covered by a rough sandpapery layer of stubble. His nose proudly commanded the center of his face. His eyes represented dark brown portals to his sensitive soul.

His mouth... I skimmed the tips of my fingers over his firm upper lip, a rosewood hue like his nipples. I traced the full bottom one, flicked his piercing and dipped my thumb into the seam of his mouth. I felt the heat of his groan right before he licked me with his wet tongue. My legs quivered.

"Ivan." I infused his name with everything I felt but wouldn't say, as if each syllable was a beloved note in my favorite song. I lifted my hands higher, spread my fingers wider and filled my fingers with greedy fistfuls of his thick satiny hair. "I need your mouth. For you to kiss me. You," I whispered with a telling moan.

"I need you too, babe." His hands on my shoulders merged

together at the apex of my spine and he arrowed them straight down to my ass. He grabbed a rounded cheek in each hand, lowered his head and fastened his mouth to mine. Bliss. To have his lips on mine again. All the emotions coursing through me: the passion, the yearning, a trickle of concern, and the inkling of what this might be between us. It all coalesced in that kiss. My mouth trembled as he covered it with heat and doused it with flame. His tongue dipped inside the fire and stoked it. Everything flared hotter.

Him. All that he already was. All that he stood on the brink of being to me if I would allow it. I felt it all. I wanted it all. I wanted it so much, but I knew even as I acknowledged it what would happen next. If I reached for it, if I attempted to hold or keep it for my own, I would lose it. Him. This. Me. Everything. Just like I always did.

The trickle of concern became a torrent of fear. I ripped my lips from his. I turned my head to the side.

I retreated.

"Babe, what is it?"

I shrugged his grip away as I got out of the shower. I heard him call my name. I mumbled an excuse about the water temperature, grabbed a towel, exited the room and backed away from the shining lure of it all.

It wasn't meant for me.

"Hey." Ivan appeared a few moments later. Just as I was pulling my clothes back on. "What just happened in there?"

"Nothing. I mean, lots did. It was so good, Ivan," I admitted without making eye contact. "But I'm tired and anyway the water was getting cold."

"You're getting cold feet, you mean," he said, and moved toward me. I watched his capable hands hooking the white towel around his narrow hips. "Let's go get in my bunk."

I lifted my head and shook it.

His gaze swept over me and took in the contents of my backpack spread all over the couch next to me. "It's too late to work."

"I napped earlier. I'm not sleepy. I'll just edit the stuff I filmed earlier and send it off."

"You just said you're tired. I want you with me. I like having you with me. I think you like it, too." His eyes narrowed. "I won't be able to sleep with you here and me back there."

"I'm sorry." I dipped my head and busied my fingers with bullshit tasks, so he wouldn't see things I didn't want him to see. "I don't sleep anyway," I admitted.

"You do sleep. What the hell do you call what you did earlier?"

"I nap." I shrugged. "Here and there." Rarely as long or as soundly as I did with him, but I didn't admit that.

"Why?" He came and sat down beside me. "Why can't you sleep?"

"I don't know." I sighed. He was always trying to delve deeper. Too deep. "My mind races, I guess."

"Races about what, Mars?"

"Stuff."

"Talk to me." He grabbed my hands, stilling them. "Stop shutting me out." He peered down at me, intensity radiating from his gaze every bit as compelling as the rest of him. "This is happening between us. There's no denying it."

He was probably right. It had probably already happened for me. It had probably started the first time my eyes had connected to his. But he was wrong about one thing. I was going to deny it. I had to fight it.

"I don't sleep in a bed all through the night, ok?" I withdrew my hands from his. I grabbed my cell. I hadn't turned it on yet. I knew…I could practically feel it ready to explode with unread messages, a ticking time bomb like the ugly things inside me that I never shared.

Only with him staring at me so expectantly, I found myself doing it. "My father got rough with my mother at night. The walls between my room and theirs would shake. The yelling. The crying. The begging. I'd hear it, flesh against flesh. The crack of worse if he hit her with something. And then the silence. The terrible silence. I would try to muffle my own tears in my pillow. But I think my mom could sense them. Some kind of instinct to comfort, to protect..." I trailed off, lowered my head and placed my hand low on my abdomen. I understood her better now. Terrible. It felt so terrible to fail your child.

"What happened then?" he asked gently, covering the hand on my stomach with his own.

"She would come to my room once he went to sleep. She would climb in my bed with me. She would wipe my tears away. She would hold me. We would share a set of headphones and listen to music. She would talk to me and for a while I would be able to forget what I had heard...at least until the morning came."

"What did she talk to you about?"

"Her favorite songs. The words. The people who wrote them. What she thought the music was saying to her. About how much she loved me." Tears pricked my eyes. "How special she thought I was. Her hopes for my future. Dreams that never came true."

"Did your father ever hurt you the way he hurt her?" Ivan whispered.

"Once." I had to swallow to loosen the memory of harsh hands wrapped tightly around my throat.

Ivan's fingers softly stroked mine. I focused on them. On him.

"Only once. I was eighteen. It wasn't sexual. He only choked me. My brothers pulled him off me. Then I left," I recited the details dully, separating the event from the emotion so I could talk about it. "I never went back home after that. I'm never alone with him anymore, either."

"Good plan." I glanced at him. His voice was so strange. And I saw why. He was angry. Furious about something that had happened to me.

"It was a long time ago, Ivan."

"Doesn't matter. Hurt like that doesn't go away."

I nodded. "You just learn to deal with it."

"But you don't discount it." He took my hand and placed it on his knee and covered it. "You don't downplay it. You don't take the blame." He stroked my knuckles with his thumb. The pad was calloused from his guitar playing and rough on my skin, but I didn't mind. His touch was soothing, and his words were wise.

"Neglect, rejection, abuse, whatever form it takes, it twists you up inside and keeps you from seeing the truth." He shifted to more fully face me. "And the truth you need to clue into is that you're an incredibly beautiful woman. Strong. The best lover I've ever had the pleasure of holding in my arms. You're gifted. You're a caring and loyal friend. You're brimming with potential, and there's no dream that is out of your reach"

CHAPTER
thirty-six

"I THINK YOU MIGHT BE A LITTLE BIT DELUSIONAL." My eyes had gone misty from his praise. No one outside Raven had ever said such affirming words. "But thanks." As if sensing my current jumbled state, Mine appeared. He rubbed against my ankle then jumped in my lap. Staring at me, he blinked his golden feline eyes. "He wants to be petted," I decided. "Now that the novelty's worn off, he's feeling awkward and displaced." I slowly separated my hand from Ivan's and proceeded to give Mine the reassurance he obviously needed.

Ivan searched my gaze for a long moment. "You think maybe you might be feeling that way, too."

"A little," I admitted, always telling him more than I should.

"I wish you didn't. I wish you felt comfortable here and that you would accept that the things I tell you are true." Staring at me, probably seeing way more than I wanted him to, he raked his wet hair back from his face. "I guess it's just going to take more time for you to believe me."

ROCK *fuck* CLUB BOOK 3   257

Time we don't have, I thought. Maybe time he also sensed running out.

He sighed, and his gaze lifted to my head. "I'm going to grab you one of my shirts. I think it might be more comfortable than what you have on. And we're going to need to tackle your hair."

"Oh." I had forgotten about it. Apparently, a big sign of being an Ivanaholic was cognitive dysfunction.

"I'll be right back," he said and returned before I had managed to do more than open my laptop. He had replaced his towel with a tight-fitting pair of dark grey boxers. A tossup in my mind which look was sexier. He had a shirt wadded in one hand and a bottle of detangler and a brush in the other. "Set that computer aside. You don't want it to get wet from this spray."

"Yeah. I guess you're right." I placed it on the couch.

"You say that like you think my being right is a rare happenstance."

My lips twitched. "I think *you* think you're *always* right."

"Aren't I?" His brown eyes twinkled like the sand back on the beach as the sun had set. A beach and a day that I would never forget.

"Um, hmmm. Well, maybe in the kingdom ruled by your ego inside your own mind."

He laughed. I froze. It was an amazing look on him. And to know I prompted it? Well, it made the moment seem nearly as intimate as it had been when he had shaved me.

His expression turned serious as he took in mine. I think he might have been processing similar feelings. "Not a lot of people giving me pushback. Not when they need me to keep doing what I'm doing, to get on stage night after night, to sell more records, tickets and merch. To rock and repeat." He came closer, dropped his bounty on the couch and then eliminated the space between us. Since I was frozen as well as being an idiot, I didn't try to dodge him. He framed my face while

258   MICHELLE MANKIN

I just stood there, arms loose at my sides, completely entranced. "Yet another thing I like about you." His eyes traveled across my features and softened. "You're not afraid to call bullshit on me."

My eyes rounded.

He cocked his head. "Sexy and adorable. Less femme fatale Marsha with your hair like that. More romantic comedy Mars." His tone lowered. "Get naked."

"I don't think...I mean, it's late and I..."

"I'm tired too, babe. But with you around I won't make any hands-off type promises. You just look at me a certain way with those baby blue eyes of yours, and I get hard." He lips lifted. "And there's that look." He chuckled, a deep dark rumbly sound that made me shiver. "I'll turn around. You get out of those clothes and put my shirt on. Then we'll finally untangle your hair. Yeah?"

"Ok."

"Agreeable Marsha. That one rarely makes an appearance." Chuckling again, he turned. I ripped my tank off, unbuttoned my shorts and snagged his shirt. He peeked over his shoulder as it settled into place around me. His gaze went dark and possessive as it swept over me. My legs got trembly from his stare and the scent that clung to his shirt. I was in Ivan sensory overload.

"You look good in my t-shirt, babe."

"It's soft. It smells good. But it's a muscle tee, Ivan. It's not PG with these wide arm holes."

"Yeah, I get that. But it's just you and me right now. And anyway, PG is not my thing or yours. That would be boring."

His words pleased me. I was far from the prim and proper southern lady my father had always wanted me to be. It wasn't who I wanted to be. But maybe deep down I had wondered if there was something wrong with me. Well, even if there was, Ivan didn't seem to mind. And his opinion meant something to me.

"Gonna have to use a lot of this stuff." My thoughts cleared as wet spray misted the air around me. "You're gonna smell like Arrow. This is his spray, but I'll just have to deal." He circled his finger. "Turn around. I'll start at the back."

"I can do it myself," I protested.

"I know you can, babe. It's been established that you're capable, or at least I've shared my opinion with you. Whether you take my words at face value is up to you."

"I hear you." I frowned.

"Don't get all closed off on me. I'm just going to keep chipping away at that armor you hide behind until you start saying thanks when I compliment you instead of deflecting me. Understand?"

I nodded, and the words slipped through an Ivan shaped chink in my defenses. "Thanks," I whispered.

"You're welcome. Turn around, babe," he ordered, and this time I did. And then his hands, Ivan Carl's talented hands —attached to one of the best frontman guitarists around, don't tell him I thought that, he would need another tour bus just for his ego—started very carefully brushing the tangles from my hair.

It felt divine. He started at the bottom. His fingers brushed the top of my shoulders, lots. My skin zinged with awareness every single time.

"How come..." I trailed off, my voice husky. "How'd you learn to do that so well?" Had he combed out Raven's hair? The thought made me feel a little queasy.

"I helped my grandma when she was in the nursing home. My mother's mom." His tone turning reflective, he continued to separate long strands of my hair as he detangled it. "She and my grandfather raised me more than my own mother did. My grandfather was the one who taught me how to fix old cars. He passed before I went into the foster system, and my grandmother had a stroke shortly after that from the stress. She went into assisted living, then full care. She died before I turned eighteen."

"I'm sorry." I could hear the pain in his voice. I turned around and saw it, too, in his eyes, before he glanced away. I lifted my hands and framed his face. He had such a handsome face. Such a strong jaw. But he allowed me to gently turn his head. "I'm truly sorry, Ivan." I blinked back the emotion that seeing his sadness caused. "I understand how it feels to lose someone who believes in you." I swallowed thinking of my own mother. "But I'm glad you had both of them for the time you did." I was grateful for my mother. Talking to him about her reminded me about the good she had granted before it had all been ripped away. "I bet your good manners came from your grandmother."

"Yeah. She was a stickler for all that stuff. Opening doors. Yes, ma'am. No, ma'am." He covered my hands, removed them from his face and lowered his head to press a soft kiss to the back of each one. I felt more than a shiver. I felt something monumental lock into place inside of me as I stared at his bowed head. He wasn't mine. I would never be able to keep him, but I would protect him and defend him however I could if anyone tried to hurt him again. He had been through enough.

"What is it?" He had caught me staring at him. "Why are you crying?"

"I'm not." Only I was. For him. For what he had been through. I hadn't realized. I swiped them away. "Just you know feeling sad about your grandmother losing your grandfather."

About your loss, too, I thought. But I wouldn't let him know I felt sorry for him. He had shared something very personal. I wouldn't make him regret it. I would protect him from feeling vulnerable about it, the way I would want someone to protect me. He certainly hadn't made me feel awkward about anything I had revealed.

"Oh, no," I said as a reminder alert went off on my computer. "That's the deadline for your interview." I scooted around him, and the fundamental change he represented within my world. I would just have to figure it all out later. Detangle the threads that wanted to tie tighter to him rather than loosen like they would have to once we reached New Orleans. "I'm up against it. I need to slap something together and send it to Smith right now."

"Smith?" he parroted.

"The WMO exec who oversees the production of Rock Fuck Club," I explained. "She's a real hardass. She takes everything about the show from concept to execution very seriously."

"Oh," he frowned. "I remember her." I could tell by his tone that he wasn't happy to be reminded of her or the show. I wasn't thrilled, either. My part in all of it was a means to an end, but it felt more like a trap now.

"Yeah. I can see that you found her to be about as problematic to deal with as we all have."

"But it's so late, Marsha."

"I know." It was too late in a lot of ways. "I shouldn't have put it off." I shrugged. I had put it off to spend time with him. "Luckily, I had that nap, right? No need to stay up on my account."

"I won't be able to sleep if you're not with me." His eyes blazed that truth at me.

"Um, I don't sleep anyway, remember." I curled my fingers into a fist to resist caving. "I'll get this done." I sat down and picked up my computer. My recently detangled wet hair swished around my shoulders. "I'll see you in the morning." Trepidation crawled up my spine at the thought of what the bright light of day and the return to the tour would certainly bring. His shadow fell over me. His opposing will eclipsed those trepidations.

"I'll get my guitar. I have some ideas buzzing in my head. I'll stay up with you."

He bolted before I could work up a protest. Getting right to work, I plugged in my memory card and downloaded the raw footage I had recorded to my computer. Once I had the files transferred to the editing program, the real fun started. I enjoyed manipulating film to make it cohesive and compelling. Given that it was Ivan, that task wasn't going to be very hard. I had just started the playback when Mr. Compelling reappeared. I lifted my chin, pausing to glance at the 3D vison. He had the neck of his guitar in one hand and a yellow steno in the other. Compelling, indeed. I had to force my gaze away as he took a seat on the couch right next to me. His voice playing in my ears from my headphones, I smiled at the snappy answers he had given me about himself and his music. It was awesome stuff. Well, Ivan was awesome. Handsome and cocky as hell, his vibrant no holds barred personality practically leapt off my computer screen. But it could be tweaked a little. Something with the transition points between the questions needed to change.

I felt a tap on my shoulder. I glanced at the strong hand then followed the muscular arm to the man himself. Ivan lifted a brow and pointed to his ears.

"Oops, sorry," I said over-loudly, removing my over the ear headphones and dropping them into a comfortable position around my neck. "Did you say something?"

"Yeah." He wore a chagrined expression. "You've been at that awhile. You doing all right?"

"Yeah." My lips framed my satisfaction. "It's good. I'm almost finished." My gaze drifted downward as a soft pelt rubbed against my calf. "Aw, Mine," I cooed. "I'm sorry. I've been neglecting you, haven't I?" Golden eyes blinked up at me as if in agreement.

ROCK *fuck* CLUB BOOK 3   263

"What's left to do?" Ivan asked, and I returned my gaze to him. My heart stumbled a bit...ok a lot. He had an acoustic guitar in his lap. A guy with a guitar was always cool. But Ivan with one was Ivantastic.

"Um, sorry. I suddenly couldn't remember the question. "What did you say?"

He grinned. I think maybe he knew what effect he had on me. "How much longer you need with that?"

"I dunno." I dropped my gaze to the screen and gnawed on my lip. What did it need? "A-ha. I got it." I turned to Ivan. "Think I could get some video with the guys after they wake up?"

"What kind of video?" He narrowed his eyes.

"I wanna ask them some of the same things I asked you. Intersperse their answers with yours. You know, for a contrast between what you said and how they see it."

"That sounds pretty cool. I'm sure they'd love to bag on me. You're really good at the interview stuff. But we've got radio promo spots to do pretty early when we get to New Orleans. You sure you're up for it? I mean that's only a couple of hours from now."

"Sure," I said, though my enthusiasm over improving the interview waned at the reminder that our time was nearly spent.

"I want you in my bed with me for those few hours, Mars." The way he phrased those words it didn't sound optional. A tiny bunk? Ivan's bunk? Lying down together? Likely with his arms around me? I wanted that, too, even if it wasn't wise. Even though I probably wouldn't sleep.

"Just let me type a note and send what I have to Smith, and I'll come with you." No argument. I was totally compliant Marsha, because honestly there was nowhere else that I wanted to be more than with him.

CHAPTER
thirty-seven

Cognitive dysfunction? I thought the next morning. *Nope more like total insanity.*

I hadn't slept. Not even a little.

How could that have even been possible?

I had laid on sheets saturated with his scent wrapped in his strong arms, and I had felt...well, more than just desired, more than just safe and more than just validated.

But as soon as the bus had lurched to a stop, I had slipped from his bed. No glance back at him. He wasn't mine to keep. I had stolen a day and a night of something infinitely beautiful.

It was time to go.

Take that, world that gave and then snatched away from me anything that ever mattered. This time I was letting go before it could pull the rug out one last time.

I gathered my things and set them near the door. Mine meowed at me as if to protest. I had fed him. He would have to settle for having a tummy full of food. Being cared for? Being with someone who understood us? Being part of Ivan's family? Uh-uh, those things weren't for us. We weren't staying.

We couldn't stay.

On the way out the door, I said good morning to Jeeves. From the driver's seat, he smiled. I think he had liked that I had used his nickname. I told him where I was headed and that I would be right back.

This time.

I didn't want there to be any misunderstandings. I wasn't abandoning anybody in the middle of the night without a word and without a trace.

The line and the takeout window under the green and white awning was nearly nonexistent. I had figured it might be with the sun not even above the horizon. After I got my order, I dodged the truck spraying detergent on the streets to erase the indulgences of partygoers from the night before. There would be no erasing the impact of my night with him, indulgence though it had been.

As soon as I entered the front lounge, I knew something was wrong. Everyone was up for one thing. They all were frozen in place and staring at me as if I had done something terribly wrong. It was Ivan whose feet came unglued from the floor. He stormed straight to me and grabbed me by my upper arms.

"Whoa." I let out an uneasy laugh, glancing around him avoiding his eyes. There was something in them that reminded me of the way I had felt when my mother had left me. "I guess you guys are ready for breakfast." I tried to make light of the situation. No one budged. Ty maintained his position at the kitchenette with his arms crossed frowning. Jag and Arrow stood side by side leaning against the banquette table. They appeared to be more worried than anything.

"I brought beignets from Cafe Du Monde." I jiggled the white bags, a difficult maneuver to pull off with Ivan's fingers banded so tightly around them. "You can let go of me Ivan," I whispered.

He didn't respond. No one said anything for another long uncomfortable moment.

"Hey, yeah, thanks, Marsha." Arrow bailed me out. "That was, uh, nice of you." He came forward and snatched the sacks from my hands. Ivan released my arms and stepped back from me. That's when I got a close view of his expression. He wasn't feeling vulnerable. I had been mistaken. He was angry, seriously pissed. I rocked back on my chunky heels.

"What's wrong?"

"What's wrong?" he roared, and my eyes rounded as my hair practically blew off my head. "Let's start with number one. Do you know what time it is?"

"Um, yes."

"And yet you thought it was a good idea to go traipsing about the French Quarter with no bra on and no panties, by yourself, without anyone along with you for protection?"

"I um, didn't traipse. I walked fast. And I brought breakfast." I pasted on a smile.

"You could have been raped or killed, Marsha." His volume was lower now. His speech pattern slower, but no less intense.

"I can take care of myself." I put my hands on my hips and lifted my chin.

"I'm not so sure." His gaze dipped to my bag and all of Mine's things by the door. Ah, he'd noticed those. I got the impression that there was more than just my early morning excursion he was upset about.

"Ivan." I put my hand on his arm. His muscles were so tensed

ROCK *fuck* CLUB BOOK 3   267

my fingers nearly bounced off his skin. He glanced down at my hand. That's when it hit me that he was dressed. No more casual outing Ivan. He was in full rocker regalia. Muscle tee, the one I'd worn to sleep in last night and left folded on his bed. My heart skipped on that. Tight faded jeans. Silver rings. A cool black leather cuff with embedded coins around his strong wrist. "I know my way around New Orleans. I've been here before. I stuck to the well-trafficked areas. I know what I'm doing," I offered those additional details gently. He lifted his gaze to mine. His brown eyes swirled this morning like that treacherous whirlpool from the Odyssey. Only the danger I used to see in them had given way to pain and conflict so very similar to my own. "I can't stay." I gave it to him straight. The way I had planned to since I had woken from the dream our time together represented.

I removed my hand from his skin, feeling an immediate ripping, rending pain in the center of my chest from the loss. I injected an overdose of cheeriness into my tone to cover it up. "I'm on my way out. Can't stay of course. This is your bus. I have mine. Me and Mine, have ours." I fake laughed at my own joke. No one bailed me out, not even Arrow. "Well, back to work and all, just like you guys." I hit Ivan with a look. One that pleaded for him not to make this more difficult. He read me so well most of the time. Couldn't he see this was the way it had to be, and how hard it was for me to leave when I had never been anywhere that had ever felt so right?

"You're leaving?"

"Um-yeah. Of course," I replied. "One thing first, though."

Ivan's eyes narrowed to slits. His jaw clenched.

I looked away, casting my gaze to the others. "Ivan said I could interview you guys before you leave for your radio spot. Just a real brief set of questions like I asked him. How about I start with Arrow?" I turned to him. His expression was no longer worried just terribly inexplicably sad. "We can sit at the banquette," I offered. "You can eat your beignet while I set up. Shouldn't take but a few minutes. I..." I pulled up short as Ivan grabbed me by my upper arm and pulled my moving feet to a halt. His grip wasn't tight enough to hurt me, but it wasn't gentle, either.

"Don't do this," he gritted out through his clenched teeth.

"Do what?" I asked.

"Leave," he replied, his voice raw, his expression matching it. Corresponding serrated emotion sawed through the center of my chest. "I thought maybe we could talk. About how I might convince you to stay." Oh, what a bright and beautiful shining castle in the clouds offer that was. Totally unrealistic of course. He knew as well as I did that it would never work.

"I can't stay, Ivan," I explained, my voice soft. My eyes darted across his. "It was great." I swallowed and powered through the fettered feeling inside my chest. "I'll still be around. You'll still be around, too. We're on the same tour after all. We've been at odds a lot of it so far. I'd really like it, I mean I think it would be nice if we aren't adversaries anymore. Maybe we could even try to be friends."

"Seriously? You're seriously telling me that's all you want us to be? Just friends?" His eyes blazed emotion at mine. I willed all the telling ones in my own gaze far to the back of my mind where he couldn't see them.

Nothing. This meant nothing. *Make that lie believable, Mars. Sell it.* I gave him a wobbly smile. "Yes, of course. If we both try I'm sure we can manage it."

My cell suddenly rang. It sounded overly loud in the tense silence that had followed my words. I sighed. "Sorry, I switched the ringer and everything back on this morning. I better get this." I glanced away and stepped aside to slide my phone from my pocket. And yes,

I took the call to avoid being dashed to pieces on the jagged edges of disappointment in Ivan's eyes.

"Hello," I answered cautiously. I hadn't bother glancing at the caller ID.

"Mars, it's Barbara."

"Hey, what's up? I pretended my stomach wasn't clenched as tightly as Ivan's jaw.

"Well, a whole lot of stuff that I will table for later. But there's one big one that can't wait."

"Oh yeah?" I blew out a caged breath. "What's that?"

"Raven wants to talk to you."

I was so surprised, I stumbled backward and dropped down onto the couch. Sensing my distress, Mine hoped up in my lap. Ivan even took a step toward me, too. "Raven wants to talk? To me?" I semi-repeated in my daze. "Why?"

Why now? I wondered. *Did she know about Ivan and me?*

Ivan stopped right in front of me. I lifted my head. Our gazes met. I think his thoughts about what she might or might not know were similar.

"About you and her," Barbara replied. "About Ivan."

Shit. Shit. Fucking shit. I glanced away from the man in question.

"She didn't give a lot of specifics. Just that she's worried about you."

She should be. The guilt about everything I felt for the Enthusiast frontman but had to deny fell on me at once, as though the castle in the clouds were made of real masonry and all that weight had rained down on me.

"Oh, well that's good, I guess," I managed to speak somehow. "I mean of course it's good." I stroked Mine's soft fur, trying to convince myself to settle. "I'm right in the middle of something work related right now. Did she say when she wanted to talk to me and where?"

Barbara didn't immediately reply. I heard muffled voices in the background on her side of the connection. Lucky's, I recognized. Raven's, too, of course I recognized hers. "She says for you to come to the Dragons' suite. Everyone on the tour is booked at the Omni on Royal Street. Lucky says make it soon, so he can be around, too. Definitely before the band's scheduled to go to the Fairgrounds for soundcheck."

"So..." I TRAILED OFF, trying to get my train of thought back on track after Ivan had stormed off the bus. He hadn't said another word to me after Raven's call. I hadn't said anymore to him, either. What could I say? But his thundercloud expression spoke booming volumes. He felt like I was choosing her over him, I supposed. That I was betraying him somehow. But there was nothing to betray. Nothing I could do if there had been something. Nothing between us was always the dead end where he and I were destined to find each other.

"So..." Arrow stroked my arm with his fingertips just as calloused as Ivan's. "You were gonna ask me a question, I think."

"Oh yeah." I refocused on the blond across the banquette table from me. "Um, you might want to, you know," I gestured to my mouth. "Wipe off the powdered sugar on your face." That stuff left an impossibly wide debris field of white when you ate a beignet. And didn't I have as big a mess on a personal level to deal with after the day and the night I had spent with Ivan?

I sighed. *Give it a rest, Mars. Onward. One foot in front of the other. Step by step toward your next mistake.* But was Ivan a mistake? I glanced back at the spot where I had last seen him. He didn't feel like one. He felt like an affirmation. Like something positive. Something vital.

Something maybe that I had always needed.

Hey," Arrow said with another friendly arm touch that would probably have made Ivan growl if he had seen it. "Why don't we do this interview another time?"

"No, no. Let's do it now. Get it done." I needed to put some distance between me and the Enthusiasts' crew. Between me and *him*. Surely that would make doing what was best for everyone easier.

"Ok, Mars. Shoot."

I flipped on my GoPro and did just that, asking about his musical influences, the band and what he liked about music.

"I'm more of an eclectic listener than Ivan. I'm a big fan of Two Rows Back just like you." He grinned, and his hazel eyes crinkled.

Trouble, I thought. This guy was trouble.

"I joined the band after I got injured playing football."

"Quarterback with a full scholarship to Penn State." Jag slid into the booth beside his friend, completing his thought, only with more details as seemed to be their way. "But they withdrew it after he blew his ACL."

"I lost a lot of things," Arrow mumbled, a faraway expression glazing his eyes.

"She wasn't who you thought she was, or she would've stuck by you." Jag's electric green eyes flashed beneath his ebony bangs.

"Yeah," Arrow agreed. "Like you did. Gave up your own scholarship to Notre Dame. Got me through a really rough time."

"Damn right, I did," Jag returned. "Can't get rid of me that easily. You're stuck with me like a piece of gum on your shoe." The bassist turned to me. "Can you imagine a cool guy like me finding anything worthy of my time in South Bend, Indiana, anyway?" He shook his head, answering his own question. "Hell, no. Would've missed all of this luxury." He twirled his finger up in the air to encompass the bus lounge.

"You like all the touring?" I asked.

"Hell, yeah. If you got the right people beside you, you got a home with you wherever you go. We're all just a bunch of damn gypsies anyway."

"More like strays." Arrow interjected getting more to the point. "Like that cat. We were just wandering around doing jack shit. Feeling sorry for ourselves mainly. Until Ivan. He had this vision for a band. We'd been messing around at a few clubs with our sound. We all got together. Jammed. He liked what he heard. And the rest is history."

I thought there might've been more to tell, but I also got the feeling that maybe the more intimate details were ones they preferred to keep private. Like Ivan had held back in his interview.

"Alright guys," I told Jag and Arrow and switched off the camera. "That's good." I turned to Ty. "You're next."

"Yeah?" He glanced up from his phone. His caramel gaze wasn't melted on a sundae, it was glacier hard and icy. "Sure. Only it might be best if Jag and Arrow get going. Ivan just texted. He's gone off in the 'Bird. We're gonna need to get some bodies over to 104.1. Stall them till he gets his head clear. Alright?"

They murmured their agreement to him and then their goodbyes to me. After they scooted out of the hot seat Ty slid in. But why did I suddenly feel uncomfortable?

He spread arms as toned as Ivan's across the back of the bench. The sound of his bandmates' departure faded as the drummer made himself comfortable. "Switch the camera on, Marsha. Let's get your shit done, and you the fuck out of here." I went statue-still as he glanced down the length of his nose at me. "Newsflash. Don't like you tooling Ivan around. Warned him off you once. After his last overnight run in with you, he didn't write a single lick of new music for months. Almost torpedoed the band. Missed a fucking lot of deadlines with the label. He keeps insisting that he sees something in you that I have told him repeatedly isn't the fuck there."

"Um..."

"Um, nothing. I know your type." His eyes narrowed to slits. "You think you're all that. Think your pussy's fucking pure gold. It ain't. Move the fuck on. Ivan got the message just now. You were clear. Thanks for that. Now go back to that buddy of yours who's cut from the same cloth. And don't come back here. Don't even think about giving him any more mixed up signals. You waver, I'll send Raven the video of you and Ivan fucking dirty right in the ocean where anybody could see you. You getting me?"

CHAPTER thirty-eight

"Hey," I greeted Barbara dully as she opened the door. The walk over by myself —sans bra or panties or protector— had been a one foot in front of another daze. Ivan might have seen something worthwhile in me, but Tyler certainly did not.

"You look awful," my producer-friend whispered, closing the door after me. "Maybe you should..."

"Mars!" Sky came skipping over to me, her pretty face aglow and awash with pleasure.

"Sweetling," Rocky called in a cautioning tone from the seating group where the rest of the band was gathered.

Her expression fell. "Hi Marsha." Her bottom lip twisted beneath her teeth. "I've missed you."

"I missed you, too, honey." I reached for her and stole a hug. When I let her go, I noticed her sky-blue eyes were as watery as my own.

"It'll be ok." She found and squeezed my hand. "We're going to make things better. Promise." As she ducked past me, Raven appeared.

The tears balanced in my eyes spilled down my cheeks as I took her in. Long black hair framing her beautiful face, she wore jeans and a Dragons' t-shirt along with a worried expression.

"Aw fuck," I said, trying to swipe the evidence of emotion away, but it was a futile effort. More just kept replacing it. "Shit. Seems the dam has burst. I had in mind how to do this, but I can't even say goodbye to my best friend properly."

"Why are you saying goodbye? Are you going somewhere?"

"Um, no. But I just assumed this was some kind of intervention. Like I'm screwing up your life and my own hanging out with Ivan and the band. Stay away from you. A repeat of where we've been, only a more permanent definitive type of parting."

"Oh, no, honey. No." She held up her hands, and even dumfounded I nevertheless knew the drill and the significance of the gesture. I lifted my own hand and pressed my palm and each fingertip to hers.

"Yá'át'ééh," I greeted.

"Yá'át'ééh," she returned and smiled softly. "There's been a lot of misunderstanding between us. Come sit with me. Let's talk and figure things out together like we used to. Alright?"

"Ok." I put one foot in front of another. In a daze for the second time today. But this time I wasn't alone. Raven held my hand. She led me to a large sectional. She sat on the far end away from everyone else and pulled me down beside her.

"Would you all give me and Mars a little breathing room?" she aimed her question at the others, but her eyes went directly to the end of the sectional where the lead singer of the Dragons roosted.

"Angel," Lucky said in a cautioning tone almost identical to the one Rocky had employed with Sky. "I don't think that's wise. We decided to..."

"No, babe." Her fingers flexed on mine. "You decided. You've been deciding a lot of things, and I've let you because of the way things went down and because Sky's your sister, and this is your band. But we have new information..."

"What new information?"

"Ivan called."

"What do you mean? When?"

"Just after I had Barbara call you to come over."

"After?" I had crushed him after. Crushed myself. Crushed the unattainable dream. He assumed I had chosen Raven over him. I hadn't, not really. She might have been an obstacle, the RFC another. But the real barrier was the one inside me.

"Yes, afterward. Are you ok, Mars? Have you been drinking?" Her golden eyes narrowed, reminding me of Mine's. Hopefully that cat was behaving himself downstairs with the concierge.

I shook my head. No, I wasn't ok, and no I hadn't been drinking.

"Well, that's good. It's not good to drink as much as you've been doing lately. It muddles your thinking. I get that. You know I do. Before Hawk died I..."

"You're right, I remember." I helped her out. Because of her depression over her mother's death and issues with her father, she had partied harder than I ever had. Until her brother's death. Then she had swung the entire opposite direction.

"Drugs and alcohol," she continued, hitchhiking on my lead in. "They just mask the symptoms while the underlying issues remain."

"Sure," I allowed, "but sometimes they're the only thing that dulls the pain."

"A temporary fix, at best."

"Yeah, I guess," I trailed off, noticing everyone was watching us very closely.

"Lucky." Raven lifted her chin. "Please."

"Right." He stood. "Lads, you heard Raven. Wind your necks in." Rocky unfolded his tall frame from the ottoman. Cody and Alec rose from the dining chairs they'd been sitting on. They were holding hands. It was encouraging to see them no longer hiding how they felt about each other.

"Hey, Mars." Cody's gunmetal eyes were gentle, and his sandy curls fell into their usual disarray as he touched my arm.

"Hey." Alec parroted, touching me, too, though his eyes were a warm jade and the oak hued layers of his hair stayed in place, precisely controlled like his personality.

Rocky gave me no touches or soft looks as he exited the room trailing behind Alec and Cody. Whatever, Ivan had said, it hadn't smoothed things over between Rocky and me. Likely because it involved Sky, and where she was concerned he was as unreasonable as her brother.

"We'll be just down the hall in Rocky's suite." Lucky bent to kiss the lips Raven lifted to offer him. Afterward, his eyes that nearly matched the shade of Sky's met mine. I was surprised to see an apology in them. "I was quite hard on you, Mars. Your priority has always been Raven. I'll admit I'm a bit protective of her. It sometimes clouds my judgement. I'm sorry."

"It's ok," I muttered to his back as he departed. I turned my attention back to Raven. "What did Ivan tell you?" It must have been significant to have the frontman of the Dragons apologizing to me.

"Everything, Mars."

"Everything's a pretty broad term." Nervous chill bumps erupted on my skin. "How about you break it down for me"?

"About your father. What he did to you. To your mom. He pointed out how that all affected you. I can't believe I didn't put the clues together."

"He had no right," I gritted through my clenched teeth. Was this a way to get back at me? Or an attempt to help? "I told him those things in confidence." Betrayal sliced through me. Betrayal maybe he had felt, wanting me to stay when he had to realize I had no choice but to leave. Before I got more attached. Before he realized his mistake in asking me to stay. Before he reached the same conclusion about me that Tyler had.

"You should have told me." Raven looked hurt.

"I probably should have," I decided, reaching deep down to make that admission. I took her hands. Anchored myself to her. She was my friend. My best friend. The only one I trusted to protect and defend me after my mother's departure. Yes, Raven had left me for a time, but she was here right now. She hadn't completely abandoned me. "But some wounds are too deep to put into words."

"I understand that."

"I know you do, honey, but the things you went through in your life, and the things I went through in mine, they're not the same." Her mom had died. Her dad had blamed her for Hawk's death. Those were shitty things. Awful events, undeniably. But I had endured an entire lifetime of abuse and heartache.

Just like Ivan.

AFTER TALKING TO Raven, I retreated to my hotel, flopped on the bed face first and crashed.

Totally and completely wiped out.

Spent.

After what felt like only moments later, soft pads tiptoed over my back.

I registered them but rolled over on my side and fell deeper into sleep.

My cell rang. I shifted to the other side, groped for it without opening my eyes and switched the ringer off.

More blessed sleep. And then not.

"Fuck!" I jumped up from the bed, wobbled and glanced down at myself in disbelief. I was completely drenched in water. "You threw ice water on me." I blinked through the rivulets running into my eyes to look at the three women responsible. "You suck!"

"It was her idea." Blue eyes wide, Sky pointed to Barbara. Expression sheepish, Barbara pointed to Sky. Raven just stood beside them looking amused and shaking her head.

"Get up." Sky demanded.

"Concert's about to start and you're not dressed," Barbara complained.

"What kind of festival would it be without the coolest rock chick in attendance?" Raven slapped the mattress near me to emphasize her point. I ducked my chin, dropping my gaze to hide the way it hurt to be called an affectionate term he had used.

A furtive meow sounded from somewhere under the bed.

"What the hell is that?" Raven asked.

A timely distraction, I thought.

"It's a pussy!" Sky exclaimed. She'd dropped to her knees and had the comforter peeled back to peer under the bed.

"Aww, come here, kitty," Barbara cooed, taking a seat on her ass beside Sky. Not allergic apparently and liked cats. Yay, me.

"Have a look Raven." Sky crooked her fingers and pointed as a tabby head peeked out from the darkness. "Isn't it cute?"

"Yeah." Raven glanced at my feline friend then at me. Her brows were raised. "Is this thing yours?"

280   MICHELLE MANKIN

I nodded.

"Where did you find a cat? I thought you were on the Enthusiasts' bus rolling down the highway."

"Uh, well. We kinda detoured to St. George Island for a day."

"That explains your tan." Barbara nodded and tapped her cheek like a detective solving a mystery.

"But it doesn't explain why you're so knocked out." Sky shook her head. "We couldn't wake you without that trick with the water."

"You're not doing drugs are you?" Raven asked, looking genuinely concerned.

"Hell, no." I'd seen what those had done to her life. Plus, stuff like she had fallen into was illegal. My shoplifting incident in high school was my one brush with crime. My father had left me to rot in a jail cell all night. I still had flashbacks about it. They were right what they said. Crime doesn't pay.

"Why are you so sleepy then?" Raven queried.

"Being out in the sun's draining. So's swimming," I hedged. I couldn't admit what I'd been doing with Ivan, how much it had meant and how letting it go had been so difficult.

"You and he, um, you know, have it off then?" Sky queried.

I shook my head. It hadn't been just sex. But as for the way he viewed it, well, I didn't know. Not for sure. Not knowing why he had called Raven left me feeling even more uncertain about everything. Bottom line: whatever it had been with Ivan, it was over. I had ended it. So, it sure as hell wouldn't happen again.

Plus, if I even thought of wavering, Ty had the sex video he would show Raven. I couldn't hurt her that way. Not again. Life would go on. It always did. Absent Ivan. An absence I felt keenly. Only as I glanced around the room at the three women who were each trying to coax Mine to come to them, I realized I wasn't alone. For now, I had Raven, plus two. The sisterhood might be newly reformed, but at least it was back.

Having them with me made all the difference in the world, and I had a feeling I was going to need their strength.

CHAPTER
thirty-nine

"YOU LOOK GORGEOUS AS USUAL," Raven commented, peeking around me. We were both standing in front of the full-length mirror in my room. She remained in her jeans and t-shirt. Meanwhile, I had glammed up. Smoky eye makeup. Rich plum shaded lipstick. A deep indigo silky slip dress. High heels. And a shimmery translucent shawl around my shoulders. Sky had applied my makeup then scurried off to answer a mysterious summons from Rocky. Barbara was at the desk in the other room of the suite talking to Smith and coordinating logistics with the film crew for the show tonight.

I so didn't analyze why I took such care with my appearance. It certainly wasn't to facilitate my next RFC hookup.

"Are you really ok about what happened between you and me?" Raven's uncertain golden eyes met my resolved –mostly resolved--blue ones in the mirror.

"Sure, I'm sure."

"You haven't really let me apologize for the way I acted. The things I said. I'm not sure I deserve such carte blanche forgiveness." Her expression turned more troubled.

"Friendship isn't about getting what we deserve. It's about caring. It's about all the time we've spent together and having each other's backs when no one else did. It's about love growing from those shared experiences." I pulled in a breath and kept on going to get it all out. "It's maturing and making allowances. It's about forgiving each other when we mess up."

I trembled on my stilettos as it hit me how much my definition of friendship sounded a whole lot like Ivan's definition of family and love.

"I messed up, for sure. I knew something bad was going on in your house. I should have pressed you harder to share." She gnawed on her lip. "Ivan apparently did," she muttered.

"I'm glad you didn't push me. I probably would have pushed you away if you had. I wasn't ready to talk about it back then."

"I missed the pregnancy."

"I *hid* the pregnancy from you. I also didn't tell you about the kiss with Ivan. That was a mistake."

"Then my brother died."

"Yeah." Tears sheened my eyes like hers. "Then we were both reeling."

"I'd prefer if we did our reeling and processing together from now on." She placed her hands on my shoulders right on my skin. I felt a lot of the unease from our separation evaporate. But not all of it. I still needed to figure out a way to tell her about the beach and Ivan.

"I've missed you. Talking to you. Being close to you." Her ready affection made up for my reserved version. "I love you." Vowing to try harder to be more like her, I reached up and touched her hands. "I need you around, you know."

"Ditto for me. Forever and always."

"From now on always." Our eyes met in the mirror. Tears blurred the reflection of the two women in it. We didn't share the same genes, but love stitched us together and made us true sisters in all the ways that counted. But my feelings for Ivan, even though I had ended it, remained a secret between us. How was I going to explain those feelings to her when I wasn't even ready to categorize them for myself?

I turned away from the mirror and Raven. Her hands slipped back to her sides.

"Are you certain there isn't anything else we need to talk about?" Raven asked. Could she read my mind? Did she already know? I froze, watching her tip her head to the side. Waves of ebony cascaded over her graceful shoulder as she studied me. "Other than how you got the short end of the stick friendship-wise."

"Um, actually, that's how I feel," I retorted to dispute the erroneous notion that I was a better friend.

"How do you figure, Mars? You're loyal and protective, a sacrificial friend. And a beautiful and confident woman."

"You're describing yourself. Not me." I rolled my eyes. "And by confident, do you mean with men?"

She nodded.

"Other people might call me a slut, Raven. Most actually."

"But they don't matter right? It's just you and me."

Again, I thought of Ivan. His words were so similar. It had been nothing between us, I reminded myself, denying the longing inside of me.

Raven studied me another long beat. "You're confident about who you are and what you want. I admire that Mars, truly. But knowing about your father, and well…" She trailed off as I tensed. "I just wonder if you should continue with the show."

"I'm fine." I lifted my chin. So, I had some daddy issues. I needed to move on and finish the season. Only three to go. The best way to get over one lead singer was to move onto the next one, right?

"Would you at least consider taking the night off from filming? I'd love for you to come sit with me and talk some more. I have VIP passes. Being with you at a concert will be like old times."

"I don't think Smith would go for that."

"Push her a bit. I did."

"Yeah, that's easy for you to say because you're not under her thumb anymore."

"I'll stand right by you if you want to call her. C'mon." She bumped my shoulder. "The RFC can wait until you get things straight inside your head."

"What things——" I began.

"Actually, it can't wait." Barbara rapped on the doorframe, her expression ominous. "Ok for me to come in?"

"Of course," I answered, but a surge of anxiety made my stomach churn. I regretted the room service burger I'd recently scarfed down. On the bed, Mine was licking the remnants of his portion of my dinner from his paws. "So, what can't wait?"

"You have to interview Ivan again."

"No," I rasped, dropping to the bed. "Why?"

"Suzanne liked everything you sent her. I especially liked the background stuff on Ivan and his band. It's really, *really* good."

"Get on with it Barbara. I don't need the buildup before the bad news. Just give it to me in one fell swoop."

"Well, the series debuts tomorrow night. The first episode of Raven's season. And you didn't ask Ivan any questions about them."

Oh, fucking shit.

I dropped my head into my hands.

"Hey." I stumbled on my greeting. It didn't seem like I was expected.

"Oh, hey, Marsha." The look on Jag's face wasn't welcoming. I smelled alcohol on his breath. He leaned heavily on the dressing room door.

"Can I come in? We called ahead."

"I dunno." Jag squinted skeptically at the film crew behind me.

"Ty said it was ok," I explained.

"Oh, in that case." He stepped aside while holding open the door. "Come in." His black hair was styled just so. He wore nice jeans and a pressed olive shirt that buttoned down the middle. He appeared ready to take the stage. But he was the only one. I realized it as I stepped further into the Enthusiasts' dressing room. It should have been called the undressing room. What I encountered slammed me back on my heels. This wasn't the cohesive group of guys I'd hung out with at the beach. The beast had slipped the leader's leash. This was the band in degenerative disarray. A full-on orgy. Ty with two naked women over by the cinderblock wall. Arrow on the leather couch with two more straddling him. I should have turned away and left the room. But no, not me. Like a car wreck waiting to happen my gaze swept to the other side of the space, seeking and finding the one I sought. Pain lanced through the center of my chest when I did. Bile rose to coat the back of my throat. The beautiful thing we had shared together was defiled. No, not defiled. To acknowledge that would imply it had been real.

"Hi, Ivan." I feigned nonchalance, admirably trained as I had been by a lifetime of disappointments. I waved my hand in front of my face to dispel the lingering skunky fumes and blinked through the threatening tears behind my eyes. "You might wanna let that poor girl have a chance to come up for some air."

He had ripped his lips from the brunette the moment I had spoken his name. He swept her aside. She tumbled from his lap. That's when I realized, unlike the others, he still had his pants on. Thank, God. Not that it mattered. Just that...at least this wasn't quite as bad and as deja vu as what had happened to Raven.

Oh, stop, I told myself. *Please.* This is not like what happened to Raven because you had nothing with him.

If it had truly been nothing the way I wanted my heart to believe, it sure hurt an awful lot.

"If I can just have a moment to ask you those few extra questions you ok'd with my boss, I'll let you continue, you know..." I trailed off, licked my dry lips and glanced away from his eyes. That hurt the worst, looking into those soulful brown eyes of his, and seeing...seeing nothing but a fog within them.

Note and remember, Mars, I told myself. *This is confirmation. You did the right thing this morning. He wasn't hurt. He wasn't feeling rejected. He didn't really want you to stay. He was probably relieved you left.*

"Which of you ashhole's approved her coming in here?" Ivan slurred the words terribly. I narrowed my eyes and stepped closer to him noting all the obvious all too familiar signs. Bloodshot eyes. Blinkless gaze. He stood and swayed unsteadily. "Get out. You left. Turned your back on me. I don't need you. I have a replacement. Becky, come back here." He waved his arm wide and the whisky bottle he held tipped upside down, spilling the remaining quarter of the liquid in it onto the carpeted floor.

"It's Brenda," the brunette huffed. "Not Becky and not Mars. That one wasn't even close. You're too drunk to even *try* to remember my name." She grabbed a t-shirt dress from the floor and yanked it over her head. Tossing back a long length of her hair, she stomped over the detritus of beer cans and snack wrappers on the floor between us. "You part of the Rock Fuck Club?" she inquired.

"Um, I guess you could say that."

"Well, do me a solid as a sister." She hooked a thumb at Ivan. "Besides the one sloppy kiss I had to initiate, all he wants to do is drink away his sorrows and talk about some chick who did him wrong. I'm gonna put up a post on him, an all caps 'do not go there'. Can you like the post, maybe even comment on it?"

"Sure." I nodded tightly. "I can do that."

"Way to go." She gave me an affirming head bob. "You're cool."

"Not so sure about that," I told her retreating form. If I had been cool, I wouldn't have succumbed to his dubious charms and gotten myself in this predicament in the first place. I was working on it. I was fixing to get my fuck-you-Ivan-Carl groove back on. I drew my shawl around my shoulders as he sprawled backward into his chair.

"What?" he asked as I continued to stare at him. "I don't remember that look."

"You haven't seen this one yet. But strap yourself in tight to that chair before you slide out of it. I'm about to give it to you good."

"Oh." He gave me a slovenly version of his sexy half-smile. "Sounds like you want to play."

"Not tonight, Ivan. Not any night."

"Huh?" His eyes narrowed as if I were being cryptic. I wasn't of course.

"Start the film." I circled a finger in the air.

"Wait a second." Ty rose from the wall he had been propped up against, hitching up his pants. If it were possible he looked worse than Ivan. "I didn't authorize this."

"You so did." I shook my head at him. "How the fuck do you think this is looking out for him? You're supposed to be his friend. You're supposed to be all concerned about his well-being, the band and his career. Wasn't that how it went down when you threatened to show

Raven the sex tape of Ivan and me if I didn't stay away from him? Or did you just make that shit up? He's drunk off his ass. He goes on tonight like this he's gonna be heckled off the stage. Worse, he could fall and get hurt."

"If *you* care so much what are you doing here?" He exhaled sharply and pointed. "With a camera crew?"

I did care. I cared too much.

"I'm doing my job, Tyler. And when I'm done, I suggest you do yours as his wingman and get him sobered up fast."

"Ivan, hey." I moved closer to him. His head had lolled back, his silky red-brown hair a tangled lion's mane. "Wake up, big boy. Talk to me."

"Mom?" He peered at me through the slits in his gaze.

Oh, no. Was that what she had nicknamed him?

"Don't..." His Adams apple moved as he swallowed, and a pleading look came over his face that twisted my stomach. "Don't do this. I'll do better. No more fights at school. Honest."

Shit. I'd have to get that part edited out.

"Get him some fucking coffee, Ty. Now!"

"Right." Buckling his jeans, the drummer staggered toward the door using the table and the chairs he passed as if they were the only things bolted down on a listing ship.

"Ivan. Hey. Listen." I squatted down in front of him and pulled his hands away from his face. "It's me, Marsha."

"Mars?" He blinked at me slowly.

"Yeah," I confirmed.

"I didn't think you'd come back. Ty said you wouldn't."

"Fucking Ty," I mumbled.

"What?"

"Nothing. Listen. I just need to ask a few questions about you and Raven."

"Never a me and Raven."

"Um, yeah, Ivan. There sure was. You were with her a year. Think carefully about what you say, I'm filming you for the show."

"I already answered questions about Raven."

Probably in New York. "Well, could you answer them again? Just a few? For me?"

"Sure. Anytime. Anyplace. Anyway for you, Mars. Told you."

"Ok." My throat closed. I had to swallow to loosen it. Now I felt like the room was slanted and not in my favor because I wanted to take his words, clasp them to my heartsore chest and believe them.

"Why'd you get into a relationship with Raven if you weren't going to be faithful to her?" That was the ten million dollars question. Why did any guy step out on any woman? "It made you look like a dick, Ivan."

"I was a dick. Shouldn't have dated her to start out with. Wanted you. You wanted Hawk. Then... Then I didn't believe you about the baby. Hawk died. And then I couldn't leave her. You don't leave when someone's hurting, Mars. You don't."

Oh, fuck. Because I was as fucked-up in the head as he was I followed that logic.

"Cut." I levered up using his knees.

"Mars, stay." He grabbed for me, but he missed. He must have been cross eyed drunk. No way in hell he would have been so transparent answering my questions if he hadn't been so completely trashed.

Ignacio gave me a sad look over the rim of his glasses. "You use that footage, Marsha, he's going to hate you forever."

"Yeah, well. He told my secrets. He already hates me anyway. I hate him. It's the circle of fucking life, isn't it?"

"You don't hate him, Mars." Carla shook her head of tight black curls at me.

"I do," I insisted on sticking to that lie and continued toward the door before Ernie and Les could chime in. "Send the video to Suzanne," I paused and glanced over my shoulder before exiting into the hall. "Include everything but the stuff where he thought I was his mother."

CHAPTER forty

I found Raven, Barbara and Sky rocking it out to the side of the stage while the Monsters played for a crowd of tens of thousands.

"You look frazzled," Raven decided after scanning me. She was all glammed now. She peered at me through subtle eye makeup that enhanced her golden eyes. "Where've you been?" She had to shout to be heard over Von's guitar solo.

"I just saw Ivan," I shouted back.

"Oh." Her mouth rounded, but her eyes narrowed more. Again, I had the feeling Ivan might have said more to her besides the details of my fucked-up childhood. "How did that go?"

"Not so well." I fidgeted with my Gods of Rock Tour VIP lanyard. We were all wearing one. It featured a flaming guitar that reminded me of Ivan's Born to Rock tat. Everything seemed to remind me of Ivan Carl lately. I tumbled the laminated card portion of the lanyard end over end, twisting the cord into a tangled knot like I felt inside.

Seeing Ivan kissing Brenda?

ROCK *fuck* CLUB BOOK 3   293

I had barely been able to breathe. But I needed to remember I had called the shots. I had stayed emotionless. Life might keep knocking me on my ass, but I wouldn't stay down.

But though I'd drawn from that practiced defiance with Ivan tonight, I didn't feel any better. I was confused, sad, angry and disappointed. And if I were being completely honest with myself I would acknowledge that I'd felt that way since I had ended things, and he had stormed off the Enthusiasts' bus. But why? The reason for the way I felt was right there burrowed under the surface of my skin like he seemed to be. But I was afraid it was going to take precision surgery by someone who really knew me to get to it. And I wasn't sure I was quite ready to have that truth out in the open yet.

"Hey." I touched Barbara's arm. The blonde had on another cool black dress heavy on the lace that revealed very little but was super sexy in spite of that. She had her soft green eyes locked on Von. Yeah, I got it. He was sexy as hell with his guitar. But I knew, though of course I hated him, that Ivan with his guitar was even sexier.

"Hey, what's up?" Barbara shifted to regard me. Her pupils were tellingly dilated.

"Um." The Monsters' song suddenly segued into an uncharacteristically quieter segment. Luckily, so I no longer had to shout. "I need a fuck for tonight, but I didn't get a chance to look at the bios. Is it basically the same lineup of bands as Tampa?"

"Yeah." She nodded, and I noticed Raven and Sky shifting closer to me. Protectively? I certainly liked the idea that might be the case.

"Shoot. I'm pretty familiar with the roster." And the type of guy I needed wasn't on it.

Maybe because you just left the one who fits the bill for all you really need back in his dressing room.

Um, so not acknowledging that thought.

294   MICHELLE MANKIN

"I need someone super-hot. Edgy. Dangerous. Tall. Arrogant as hell...." Longish chestnut hair that feels like silk in my hands. Long eyelashes and soulful brown eyes that seem to see into my soul. Gives out wicked everything kisses.

Oh fucking hell.

"Anybody like that been added for tonight?" My voice had a false enthusiastic ring to it.

"You thinking who I'm thinking? Barbara queried the others. They all looked at each other, nodded, then looked at me.

"Cush Diamond. The lead singer of No Holds Barred. Short blonde hair. Tall. Piercing blue eyes. Tatted up his neck and everywhere else. Gauged ears."

"He looks like a fallen angel," Sky's eyes were appreciatively wide.

"I heard he kisses like the devil." Raven fanned herself. She raised a brow when we all stared at her. "Hey, I'm totally not interested. I've got the only guy I want. But I've read the posts on the RFC page. If super-hot is what you're going for, and you're sure you don't want to take the night off to get things straight in your head..." She left that hanging.

Again.

"No. I'm so not taking the night off." That something I didn't want to acknowledge buzzing under my skin practically yelling to be heard? I was going to try very hard tonight to silence it.

"Alright honey." Raven's black brows dipped together. She seemed less certain than I pretended to be.

"Then he's the one," Barbara decided. "I'll find him. Get him signed up and send him over. Unless you want to approach him yourself?"

"Send him." My lips curled, and I felt my eyes taking on an ill-advised anticipatory glow. "Send him right here by the stage." The Enthusiasts were scheduled to perform soon.

"Um, honey," Raven said. "A word of caution about Cush."

"Yeah?"

"His band beat out the Enthusiasts at the Grammys in the metal category. He kinda dissed the competition. Ivan hates him."

"Then he's perfect." I smiled.

I sensed someone staring at me and turned. Expecting to see my next fuck striding toward me, instead I saw a brooding figure leaning against a stack of amps by the far back wall. My heart stopped, then restarted beating faster. No longer appearing inebriated, Ivan ensnared me with his intense gaze.

Unmindful of anyone else in the crowded backstage area, I watched him bring a cigarette to his lips. Through the white cloud of his exhale, I noted that his coppery brown hair remained mussed, not that it detracted from his looks. His jeans hung low. He wore no shirt. But it made sense not to have one. It was sultry hot at the outdoor fairgrounds. However, Ivan was arguably hotter.

As the cloud around him dissipated, he took another drag. His gaze narrowing, he exhaled to the side, pushed away from the amps and ground out the cigarette with his booted heel. My breath caught as he moved. He was coming straight toward me, his chocolate eyes glowing with an inner fire brighter than the end of his cigarette before he had snuffed it. I thought about trying to avoid him, but I already had a scheduled meeting set up for right here, and I had a feeling I wouldn't get far if Ivan was determined to talk to me, especially in my heels. And anyway, why should I abandon my spot? What did I have to fear? He was the one who had shown his true colors tonight, not me. That vulnerable part of myself I had shown him at the beach? She was under wraps again. The opening I had given him? It was slammed shut. He no longer had access. He had no power over me. And yet my heart hammered as I watched him dodge a roadie with a cart. He had almost closed the gap between us when a flurry of movement had him turning his windblown head and me shifting my attention in that direction. It was Barbara and the crew alongside an impressive blond.

Cush Diamond came striding toward me. His gaze locked with mine, it might have sizzled. He was hotter than hot. Edgier than edgy. Taller than tall and undeniably arrogant as hell. But I felt nothing but trepidation when he passed within inches of Ivan and the two rivals took each other's measure. Narrowed glances. No chin lifts of respect. Ivan's entire body tensed. His biceps snapped taut. The two lead singers were the same height, nearly nose to nose as they prolonged the silent exchange.

Wow. Definitely no love there.

"Hey, Marsha." Cush stopped in front of me raking his sharp blue eyes over me. "Your producer said you wanted to *see* me." The girlfriends had undersold the fallen angel thing. His hair dipped to a v between his brows. His ears were pointed, his chin, too. His aura radiated a dark intensity of the sinful sort. Only it wasn't him I was tempted by. Cush and the crew had come between me and Ivan, blocking my view of him, but I knew without the visual verification that the Enthusiasts' frontman lingered.

"Hey, back." I moved directly to the No Holds Barred lead singer, rolling my hips. Cush's devilish gaze dipped to watch the show.

"It's a…" He lifted his gaze and paused, his sexy lips curling, "pleasure to meet you."

"We haven't gotten to the pleasure part yet." I placed my palms on his chest, directly on the skin the unsnapped military style shirt he wore left bare. "But we might get there tonight if you pass the test."

"Test, huh?" He moved his hands to my upper arms. His grip was strong. His fingers were long, but not the ones my body wanted. My flesh didn't even tingle.

"You think I'm not up to your standards?" One of Cush's slashed dark blond brows lifted. I was afraid he wasn't, but I only shrugged a shoulder in response. His eyes followed the movement that I knew drew attention to my tits. "I guarantee I'll surpass 'em."

"Actions speak louder than cocky words, Cush."

"I'm up to the challenge." A smile creased his stark cheeks. He drew me closer. His belt buckle cut into my pelvis. I didn't register any other attributes as he lowered his head, and I went up on my toes in my heels to meet him. His nondescript male scent washed over me as his mouth pressed to my own. It was all wrong. There was no spark. No anything, just firm lips moving across mine. I grabbed the edges of his shirt. I pressed closer, trying harder to feel something. I opened my mouth for his prodding tongue. I sucked on it. He moaned. I fisted my fingers into the cotton of his shirt. I gave it a good effort. But I felt absolutely nothing.

And then that nothing was ripped away. Losing my balance, I staggered backward and grabbed for a nearby mic pole. Rocking on my heels, I watched with rounded eyes and a slackened jaw as Ivan lifted Cush off his feet and slammed him into the closest wall.

"Whoa, dude." Cush's piercing gaze was no longer piercing. Ivan had his rival pinned like an insect to a display board. "What's your problem?"

"You're my problem." Ivan shoved the hard edge of his elbow deeper into Cush's throat.

"Ivan, don't," I begged.

"Don't what?" He slowly turned his head toward me. The inner flicker? Ignited. His eyes were a complete inferno, incinerating me to ashes on the spot. I had never seen him so pissed. I took a step back. "Don't fucking beat the shit out of him for touching you? For putting his mouth on you?"

"My choice, Ivan. Like you with Brenda earlier."

"Was that her name?" His eyes narrowed on me even as he shoved Cush further into the wall. "I couldn't remember. All I could think about was you."

"I'm supposed to believe that?" I shook my head.

"No denying it. I already told you." He turned away from me and focused on Cush. Removing his elbow, he lifted the man as if he weighed nothing, then dropped him a measured foot away. Before Cush could get his bearings, Ivan shoved him in the chest. "Get gone." He hooked his chin in the opposite direction. "You ever touch her again or even look at her in a way I don't like, and I'll finish this in a way she won't approve of, but that I will thoroughly enjoy. You getting me?"

"Fuck you," Cush said with bravado that seemed to be an attempt to save face. The crew continued to roll film as a crowd had gathered. The rival frontman rolled his shoulders and straightened his shirt, but I didn't think it was my imagination that his hands were shaking.

"Don't try me asshole," Ivan warned, his voice lethal low. "Unless you're anxious to find out just how badly I can fuck you up."

The two stared at one another. One beat passed, two. I started to say something, but Ivan threw his arm out to me, hand up, the shut-it message clear. I pressed my lips together, silent until Cush conceded to Ivan with a final glare, turned on his heel and walked away.

"I can't believe you!" I screeched, my arms as rigid at my sides as his were.

"And I can't believe you let that piece of shit put his hands on you," Ivan returned, his menacing expression now focused on me. I took another step back.

"Uh-uh, Tigress." He stalked toward me. "This isn't over. You wanted a reaction from me? You got one."

"I didn't...I wasn't..."

"You did. I let you go one time too many. Should have tied you to the fucking bus this morning. Get the message and get it clear. You're mine, and this is me right the fuck now making my stand." He was so visibly tense I saw the shudder that rippled through him. "RFC? Fucking rock stars?" He moved so we were eye to blazing eye, toe to incensed toe. "You think you're gonna keep this little game up?"

"Um yeah, Ivan." I put my hands on my hips and leaned toward him. "I do."

"Wrong. You played enough already. You're done. Choosing time's over. It was over for you the first time you took my cock. It sure as shit was over after the last time. Stop running from the truth."

"Ivan, man." Arrow called, suddenly appearing. He had Ivan's electric guitar in one hand and his own strapped to his chest. I clued into the world outside the capsule that seemed to contain just Ivan and me. People still milled around watching our drama around it. The crew was still filming. Fans on the other side of the stage were clapping loudly and chanting the lead singer's name.

"Ivan, dude. C'mon. It's time to get out there." Arrow looked nervous.

Ivan turned back at me. Behind us, the crowd's fervor rose in volume, yet the frontman remained with me looking conflicted.

"Go, Ivan. Your fans are calling. But just so you know, up on that stage you might rule them all, but you don't control me."

"I know that, Mars." Eyes remaining on mine, he stretched out his hand to his bandmate. His silver rings flashed in the lights as he took his guitar from Arrow.

"I don't think you really do. You want what you want, and you think the sheer force of your determination is all that it takes to have it. You can't ignore all the obstacles between us. You might not think they matter, but they do."

"The debate is over, babe. We can keep on doing this back and forth dance if we have to, but you and I both already know the outcome's been decided."

CHAPTER forty-one

Ivan's thunderous expression when he had left the bus this morning? That was nothing compared to the darkness that drew down over his visage like a visor after he exited the stage. His hair swirled agitatedly around his tensed shoulders. The lighter reddish strands seemed to crackle with electricity. The soles of his black boots struck the floor so forcefully I imagined the ground quaked beneath him.

Ok, maybe that was just me.

"Mars." Oh, the thrill that shot through me just from hearing him speak my name.

"Ivan." I affected an exaggerated sigh. "I'm expected at the afterparty. What do you need?"

"That's a loaded question. I need a lot of things, and I want them all from you." He studied my face, and his lips curved. The sexy halfsmile made every single feminine part of me preen.

"You don't get anything from me anymore, Ivan. We're over and done. I told you back in the dressing room if you recall."

"That part's a little hazy. But I'm crystal clear about what I want from you, Mars,"

"Wanting's not having. If you have cravings get someone else to satisfy them. I certainly plan to."

His eyes narrowed to slits. "It's just you for me, Mars."

"It wasn't just me in your dressing room."

"It was as far as I was concerned. You left me. You ended us this morning."

"Yes, I did. That's a good point."

"I think you just need a reminder how it is."

"No, I don't. You and I don't work in the real-world, Ivan."

"We work very well. I'll demonstrate."

"No, you will not." I took a step back as he reached for me.

"Are you afraid of me?"

"No." I lifted my chin. "Of course not."

"Then go for a ride with me in the 'Bird."

"I can't."

"I'll let you drive."

Oh, shit. "Truly?"

"Sure. I've given you the keys to everything else. My music. My family. My body. Why not my car?"

He turned, and I followed him, shooting off a quick text to Barbara as I did. She fired one right back.

Barbara: Why aren't you coming to the after-party?

Marsha: um

Barbara: You with Ivan?

Marsha: Yeah

Barbara: Be careful

ROCK *Fuck* CLUB BOOK 3   303

Marsha: If I were careful I wouldn't be going with him. But get the bus ready to go and if you don't hear from me in an hour send out the NOPD.

Barbara: I will. Don't test me.

"I don't have much time." I had to jog to catch up with Ivan and his long strides. In the parking lot, the tour buses walled us in on either side.

"Don't need much," he replied without turning to look back at me. "Here we are." The Firebird was off the trailer, parked behind the Enthusiasts' bus. He stopped in front of it and tossed me a set of keys. "Be careful with her. She's my baby. Took me two years to get her restored to her present condition."

"I'll be careful." I met his gaze across the hood.

"I trust you, babe, or you wouldn't have those keys." He lifted his chin. "Get in and pop the locks. I'll navigate. With my blood alcohol level, I'm in no condition to drive her anyway."

I got in and stretched over the narrow center console to let him in. As he put on his safety belt, I adjusted my seat, pretending his scent and having his gaze on me in such a confined space didn't get to me.

"Quit stalling and fire her up."

"I'm not stalling." I put the key in the ignition and cranked it on. The rumble of the engine made me smile. I turned that smile to him, an automatic response to share the pleasure it gave me to be behind the wheel of such a cool automobile. He didn't smile back, but his gaze dipped to my mouth. "She's beautiful." He lifted his gaze to mine. "Like you. There's a lot to admire. I didn't realize how much when I saw her the first time. Well, the rusted frame of her. She was busted to hell, but she had a lot of potential. I bet you can understand that."

I swallowed and nodded, knowing he was talking about more than just the car.

"Back her out." He leaned forward to look in the rearview mirror. "It's clear behind you." I felt his heat. It washed sensation over me. Every cell in my body seemed to shimmer with awareness when he was near.

Lip between my teeth, I shifted into reverse and threw an arm over the back of his seat taking the car out of the slot nice and slow.

"Good job," he commented. "Take her straight out. There's a freeway entrance just outside the gate."

"Alright." I gripped the steering wheel tight and caught his grin as I carefully inched the 'Bird toward the exit.

"You can give her more gas than that. She can take it. She's a lot tougher than you think." His smile in profile was almost as good as a full frontal.

"I can't go anywhere far, Ivan." I warned him as I pressed on the pedal and turned the car toward the ramp.

"I know. But let's pick up some momentum. See how it feels. I think you'll like it...being behind the wheel."

I gave the car more gas finding myself pressed backward in the seat, my hair whooshed back as we hit highway speed. My smile widened.

"Knew you would like it."

"It's awesome. She handles really well. But where are we going?"

"It's kind of unsettling driving someplace you've never been. Right?"

I glanced at him. Was I reading another hidden meaning in that statement, too?

"Just take the second exit up ahead. There's a parking lot by the river. It's a nice secluded spot. There's a view of the bridge."

"How do you know?"

"I found it on my drive this morning."

ROCK *Fuck* CLUB BOOK 3 305

"Ok." I put on my blinker and exited where he showed me. A quick right took us along a narrow road that sloped toward the water. I pulled us into a spot. There were only eight spaces, and there were shrubs on either side.

"This place would be impossible to find if you didn't know it was here."

"Yeah, like a lot of things. You gotta know what you're looking for to find it."

"Ivan." I knew what he was trying to say. I switched off the engine and swiveled to face him. "We haven't found anything. We can't be anything."

"We can. We will. Once you stop running."

I shook my head, thinking about Raven, the RFC and how deeply it had cut me seeing him kissing someone else tonight.

"Put the keys in your pocket, babe. Come see the view with me. You might change your mind if you change your perspective." We each unfolded out of our sides. I moved in front of the hood and froze. The bridge was lit up. The girders sparkled beautifully as did the sphere of the moon behind it.

"It's lovely."

"You're a better view."

"Ivan," I cautioned. "Don't."

"They say you can wish on a new moon."

"Do they?" I turned my head to look at him. The sultry breeze lifted his hair and the reflection of the bridge lights sparkled in his eyes. He was the best view.

"Yeah. I just made mine." He glanced at me. "What would you wish for, Mars? To bring your mother back? To bring Hawk back? Our baby?"

Tears pricked my eyes. "Yes."

"I would wish those for you if they were possible. But we both know they're not. But I'm here. And I just have one wish.

"What's that?"

"For you to see yourself the way I do. But while we wait for that one to come true, I'm going to show you how it is between us."

I gulped as he suddenly grabbed and tugged my wrist. I was off balance in my heels and in the knowledge that he didn't need to show me. I remembered. And because I did, I didn't protest as he pulled me into his arms. Even in this deserted place, there was no place I felt safer. No one I would rather be with.

He yanked me into him. My palms went to his chest. His went to my waist, his fingers encompassed my hips. His skin so hot I could feel the heat of his touch through the silk of my dress.

"Ivan."

"No more talking." He slammed his mouth onto mine. My thoughts scattered. My protests incinerated to ash. This. The heat. Him. I didn't want anything else. If I was going to burn in hell, I only wanted him to be the one to take me there.

"More," I mumbled against his closed lips.

"Beg me." He eased back, his eyes black as he peered down at me.

"Please."

"Yes." He refastened his mouth to mine. He thrust his hard tongue between my lips. Again and again until I mewed in his mouth. He crushed the silk at my hips and lifted it above my waist, finding the scrap of tiny lace that covered my pussy and little else. I gasped as he ripped it into two pieces. He discarded them, unfastened the shawl that I had loosely tied to my shoulders and tossed it behind him. My shawl became an unfurled triangle across the hood. That's when I realized what he planned. An anticipatory shiver rolled through me even before he grabbed me, lifted me and deposited me on the hood.

His eyes dark and gleaming, he grabbed the hem on my dress and yanked it up with one hand and worked open his fly with the other. I took the condom from him. I tore the package open while he stared down at me. My hair was loose around my shoulders. My breaths were short. My breasts moving up and down with each rapid one. The nipples were puckered, the silk sliding against the aching tips, but it wasn't enough. It was never enough with him. And right now I wanted to feel his rock-hard chest. I needed the weight of him bearing down on me. I reached for him. His head was bowed, his hair shadowing the stark hunger of his features. His body was drawn taut, his gaze intent. He groaned as my trembling fingers encountered the bulbous head of his erection and his piercing. I flicked it then licked my lips as I slowly rolled the condom on his steely length. He parted my knees with his firm grip. I was completely exposed from the waist down. My pussy smooth because of him, my cunt soft, my clit and the folds that surrounded it soaking wet. Even my inner thighs were slick for him. But I was unashamed. He was right. This was how it was between us. How it had always had been. How could I be ashamed of anything that was as beautiful as our mutual desire?

"Say it."

"Yes, Ivan. I want you."

"More." He glided his wet tongue along my neck.

"I need you."

"More." He pressed an open-mouthed kiss into my skin.

"Fuck me, Ivan. Please. I'm begging you."

"Yes, babe." He grabbed my hips, aligning and then plunging his entire sizeable length inside me.

"Oh Ivan," I praised. "You feel so good." My feet came up to find purchase on the steel hood. My shoes were who knew where. Probably somewhere on the ground.

His chest came down. I arched my back, grinding my tits and their hardened tips into the rigid planes of him. With one hand, I clawed at his shoulders trying to deepen the contact of his warm skin with mine. With the other hand, I found and grabbed his ass. I scored the flexed skin. I was desperate for more of his cock.

"Ivan, I need…"

"I know," he growled, and he gave it to me. He fucked me hard. He fucked me fast. He fucked me rough.

"Ivan, yes. Please don't stop." Eyes squeezed shut, my entire being was focused on where we were joined. I arched to meet each thrust. Deep. Deep. And deep again, he hammered into me. He began to chant my name. His piercing teased my clit each time he thrust in and out of me. The tension that had been spooling tighter and tighter, hotter and hotter, began to unravel. Pleasure peaked and spiraled outward. I screamed his name as it rocked my entire body. He groaned mine as it seized him. Heat and beauty, it shimmered over us both dousing us in the purest deepest magic.

CHAPTER forty-two

"Ivan drives me insane." I was trying to focus on Ivan's highhandedness at the venue and not on the way he had rocked me afterward.

"Insane in a bad way or a good way?"

"Bad," I grumbled. "Of course." Don't think about him letting you drive his car.

"Really?" Across the banquette table from me, Barbara scrutinized me. "I think he might know how to set you off for sure. But I think you're mainly just afraid of the way you feel about him."

"I'm not," I insisted. Only I was.

"If you're not then why did you run away? Why are we on the road well before everyone else? It almost seems like you might be scared to see him again. Afraid to try to work this out with him."

"How am I supposed to work it out when he's my best friend's ex?"

"Because ex is the operative word."

I narrowed my eyes at her. Why was she giving me such a hard

310   MICHELLE MANKIN

time? I had been working myself up for a good long Ivan bashing tirade, and she was breaking my momentum. "What about the Rock Fuck Club?"

"I don't know. That's a dilemma." Across the table from me, Barbara dropped her chin onto her folded hands. "But do you think maybe we could wait to figure this out until the morning? I'm beat."

"Alright, I guess." I glanced out the window. Pitch blackness greeted me out both sides of the bus, except for the periodic flash of a car going southbound in the other direction. We were on the causeway over Lake Pontchartrain. The bus would cruise along at highway speed over the dark water for the next twenty miles.

A jaw popping yawn returned my attention to Barbara.

"I mean sure. Of course, it can wait." I noted her slumped posture and weary expression. "I'm sorry I kept you up so late going on and on about him." I was going to have to figure things out. But she was right. It could wait until we arrived in Houston. Maybe I even wanted it to wait. It would give me more time to get my head clear. Too bad I couldn't take the Firebird out, roll down the windows and crank the music up loud.

"That was an intense scene between you and him," she commented, watching me carefully. "The thing with Cush, I mean. And I imagine it was intense whatever it was that messed up your hair and lipstick and rumpled your dress."

I didn't answer. Being fucked by him at the bridge had driven home his point about everything. I had reveled in his reminder. And I had been replaying it all in my head. His words and his actions. And I *was* scared.

"You coming to bed?" she asked as she scooted off her bench.

"Nah."

"Still not sleeping at night?"

ROCK *fuck* CLUB BOOK 3   311

"I slept in New Orleans."

"Napped like the dead. That you did." She patted my shoulder on her way to the bunks where the rest of the crew had already crashed. "Well, see you in the morning. Goodnight."

"Goodnight," I repeated. As she shuffled off, I opened my laptop and queued up *Tides of Conquest*. From his spot beside me, Mine settled as I stroked his fur.

"I know. It doesn't feel like home yet like the Enthusiasts' bus," I soothed, then stilled as that word choice hit me.

Ok, I backpedaled. What I meant was that it had only felt like home to Mine, because he liked all the guys paying attention to him.

You had someone paying attention to you, too. Attention like he gave you in the parking lot. Attention that makes you feel safe. Attention that makes you think maybe you could be…

I ended that thought.

"But you'll get used to it, Mine. I'll get used to it. It'll just take us some time to adjust. That's all." I put my headphones on. I stared at the screen, but I wasn't seeing the show. I was thinking about him. His words again. The outcome he thought was certain. What if it were?

My cell display lit up and danced.

Lying cheating arrogant prick calling...

Um, I looked away. Definitely ignoring that.

I stroked Mine's fur some more, returning my attention to the small screen and one of my favorite scenes where the dark knight finally admits his true feelings to his unlikely love and they make out by their campfire, but I couldn't focus on it. Unbelievable fluff really. I don't know why I liked the show so much.

Maybe because deep down you want to believe in those happy endings.

Maybe I just like the actor who plays Dante?

Woohoo, my dissenting voices were back.

Dante has gorgeous eyes and an amazing ass.

Ivan's better.

"Oh, fucking hell!"

"Oops." The cat gave me a disgruntled look. "Sorry, Mine." I stroked his fur. He put his head back down and resumed purring. I snapped my laptop lid closed and removed my headphones from the audio jack. I'd try some music instead. The song that immediately came on when I plugged my headphones into my phone was "Foreplay".

Double fucking hell.

My eyes burned as I replayed the day in St. George with Ivan in my mind. Us joking on the drive. Him holding me while I shared things I never shared with anyone. Him including me in his family. The incredible way it felt when we were joined in the ocean, in the shower. Then later how natural it felt to be working side by side, me on my editing, him on his guitar. Being in his bed while he slept. Driving his car. His wish for me.

I stared blankly out the window not even really registering the rain.

Maybe Ivan was right. Maybe he was right about a lot of things.

A lurch as the bus came to a sudden stop pitched me forward. The banquette table nearly sliced me in half. So did the realization of what my feelings were about Ivan.

Holding a hand to my stomach, I slid out of the banquette to check on the others.

"You ok?" Barbara came out to ask me at the same time I had turned to the back to check on her.

"Yeah." I nodded, glancing around at everyone else. "Y'all ok?"

"Yeah," Ignacio confirmed, his curly hair smushed on one side.

"Affirmative," Les said.

"You bet." Ernie nodded, straightening his skewed glasses.

"I'm good, honey. You?" Carla's dark cocoa brown eyes were narrowed in concern.

"Just bumped my stomach on the table. I'm going to go check on the driver." I turned to the front. His seat was empty. A glance out the front windshield made me stumble. There was a hunter green Firebird blocking our way, and a man I knew very well getting an earful from our driver.

"Stay," I told Mine unnecessarily before exiting. He had hesitated at the door. I didn't know a whole bunch about cats, but I knew they didn't like getting wet. I stomped through the pelting rain and shallow puddles straight to Ivan. He turned away from the driver as soon as he saw me. His gaze swept over me. His soulful brown eyes seemed large in his face. His masculine features seemed somehow harsher, and he looked even more irresistible to me than he ever had, even with his hair wet and plastered to his skull. Maybe it was just the rain, or maybe it was just me and knowing, right then and right there with a certainty that shook me to the core the way I felt about him.

I came up short, stopping in front of him, a foot away. I'd intended to shove him in the chest like he had shoved Cush. I was so mad at him for endangering us by pulling this stunt, but I was also feeling something else as I stared at him. My heart pounded hard with that other emotion. It screamed inside of me. It blazed from my eyes.

"What the hell are you doing, Ivan? You could have killed us! Killed yourself. What were you thinking?"

"God, you're beautiful. I just saw you, just had you, but it's not enough. It's never enough, and it feels like it's been a thousand years since I last touched you." He stomped straight to me. The couple of feet of distance between us eliminated, water splashed aside in his wake. He grabbed me and yanked me into him by my hips. "Mars, I'm sorry. I didn't know your driver would throw on the brakes so hard. But you must know if you run, I'll follow, and I'll catch you, every single fucking time. You're not getting away from me. Nothing and no one is ever coming between us again. And with guys like Cush throwing themselves at you, I couldn't allow another moment to pass with you thinking I was complicit in what Ty did."

"What?" I blinked through the rain at him.

"I know he tried to blackmail you about us. I saw the full playback from your interview of me tonight. I confronted him. You can trust me when I tell you he won't do anything like that again." He let out a heavy breath. "What you apparently don't know is that he had nothing to blackmail you with. Raven already knows. At least, she knows how *I* feel. When I called her and explained about your father, I also told her about us. Everything. I explained how it was all on me, of course. That I wouldn't take no for an answer. That I was the one always pushing you. She knows me well enough to get that."

"Even after I left you this morning, you tried to take the blame and fix things between her and me?" I asked the question, though I knew he had called. She had told me only part of it apparently.

"Yes. I didn't want you to be alone."

"Why don't you want me to be alone? Why would you care?" I needed to know his motivation. "In New York you were more than happy to come between us."

"Because I didn't know a lot of things then. Because you and I hadn't started on this journey then. And because I didn't realize one very important thing until now."

His hands rising from my hips to my face, he plunged them through the saturated strands of my hair and cradled my skull.

"I love you," he declared, and I trembled as he stared down at me.

"Ivan," I breathed, bringing my hands to his solid chest. I rested them there marveling in the sure rhythm of the heart that beat beneath my palm. He lowered his head, and I lifted onto my toes. I kept my eyes open, my gaze reflecting the wonder in his until our lips met. With my lids closed, I savored. The image of his face and the way he had looked at me. His mouth and the way he moved it on mine as if my lips were the finest he had ever tasted. His tongue as it pierced my lips. His moan. His breath. His hands in my hair. His fingers urgently tugging on the wet strands.

Then I gave it up. His mouth. His lips. His fingers in my hair. After all it was only a dream.

"Babe, what's wrong?"

"Besides what you just said and that kiss? A whole lot of things."

I watched his expression of wonder wash away in the rain.

"I've never had a guy tell me he loved me before." I removed my palms. No more steady rhythm. No anchor under my hands. The soles of my feet sank into the mud.

"I've never spoken those words to anyone before," he admitted.

"Well, this is unexpected. Give me a moment to catch my breath, so I can figure out what to say..."

His eyes narrowed. "Are you saying you don't believe me?"

"Well, I saw you kissing another woman tonight. A naked woman, Ivan. I think that pretty much calls into question the credibility of those three words."

"I thought you had rejected me. Rejected us."

"There was never an us."

"There can be. You said you would try. Are you forgetting all the time we spent together? All the talks? All the confidences we shared? Where's the beautiful woman I held in my arms, the one who smiled and laughed with me, the one who comes apart in my arms every time I get her there?"

"It won't work, Ivan. I keep telling you."

"Why?"

"Because I'm me. You're you. Because of my job."

"Because of what Tyler said?"

"I don't know, Ivan. Maybe he's right in a way. We're bad for each other. We're too much alike. Our jagged edges don't fit together. We just use them to slice at each other."

"I made a mistake, Mars. You made one when you kissed Cush. That had nothing to do with RFC. It was just an attempt to get back at me. True or untrue?"

"True."

"If you didn't feel something for me, then what was the point of that? I hurt you, Mars. I'm sorry. I thought I had to move on. So you gave me a dose of my own medicine with that asshole Cush? Believe me when I say I don't like anyone else touching you. After the way we connected in St. George, and after the reminder on my Firebird, I don't think you would like it very much if our roles were reversed, and I was starring in a reality show where you had to watch me hooking up with other women. Am I right?"

"You're right."

He nodded once, his expression softening. "I'm not infallible. You're not, either. No one is. But when you and I are together apart from all the madness, we're motherfucking magic. And I think just a chance at building on that is worth a risk. Take a risk on us, Mars. Let me be your guy. Anytime, anyplace, anyway, I won't let you down. Give me an opportunity to prove myself to you. I'll fill your days with smiles. I'll light up your nights. Love will smooth the jagged edges. Love and music. Together we'll replace the bad memories that trouble you when the sun goes down with good ones."

"We're just another catastrophe waiting to happen," I whispered.

"Or a fucking miracle. A chance for something great for both of us if you would take that first step with me. I love you. Doesn't that count for anything?"

"With your history? With mine?"

"So, you don't love me?"

I didn't speak, to confess or deny it. I swallowed repeatedly. I could barely look at him without my heart leaping out of my chest to cling to his.

"All the signs are there, Mars. You're protective of me. You defended me to Tyler even after I fucked up. But I guess you're too afraid. You'd rather leave me out here on this limb alone. Loving you, but not having that sentiment returned." His expression hardened. "That hurts babe. It cuts. And I think you get how deeply."

"Yes, I do." He meant with Hawk. How it had cut like a blade each time Raven's brother had gone out with someone else. Was that how Ivan felt? Truly?

"I would never leave you to stand on the sidelines to love me all alone. I get you, babe, and I've got you. No one's going to hurt you while I'm around. They won't even fucking dare to try."

"I'm sorry. I just can't give you what you want."

"You can. You're so brave, babe. So strong. Who else is better to understand you and love you than someone like me?"

And he was so determined. So certain.

"You just need to let me get close enough to your heart like you've allowed Raven. I promise you I'll keep it safe."

And there was the irony, the heart of the matter, the center of everything. He wanted me to give him access to my most vulnerable part.

"You shouldn't want anything from me." I tried again to make him see this was an impossible dream. "I'm not cut out for a relationship."

"I've only had the one. And I messed it up. But I learned from it.

And she and I were never like you and me. We're resilient. We have to be with the shit life's thrown at us. We can make this work, babe." His gaze was imploring as rivulets of water ran down the earnest planes of his handsome face. "We owe it to ourselves to try."

"I don't think...."

"Is this working for you?" he interrupted. "Taking hit after hit? Falling to your knees? Getting back up time after fucking time, only to stand alone? Defending everyone else? Protecting everyone else? Sacrificing your happiness for everyone else? With no one you can turn to in the middle of the night when it all becomes too much for you and you can't even sleep?"

"No." Tears pricked my eyes. He pierced my heart, sliced it right through the center with his insight.

"Not for me, either, Mars." He reached for me and framed my face with his wet hands. "It's not fucking working for me either, babe. It sucks, and that's the fucking truth." He used his thumbs along the underside of my jaw to gently lift my face. He lowered his. He pressed a petal soft kiss to my lips. A dewy kiss. A devastating one. All his kisses were. Then he plucked me out of the mire. Emotionally and literally as he swept me into his arms and carried me back to the idling bus.

He rapped on the door. It opened. He set me down on the first step. I stood there above him soaked to the skin, and he stood in the rain gazing up at me as if I were a princess in a tower. "I'll be right behind you, babe, in the 'Bird. I know you won't sleep. But I hope maybe while I'm out there driving, and you're sitting in here awake, you'll think about me. Because I'll be thinking about you. And hoping you'll realize that everything I've said is true."

CHAPTER forty-three

"Oh, my gawd!" Barbara exclaimed as soon as she saw me. "Look at you."

"Yeah, I'm pretty wet." I padded carefully across the slick laminate floor. "I'm heading to the shower." I noticed as I moved that the bus was in motion again. My heart skipped a beat knowing Ivan was out there in his Firebird escorting us. A dark knight on a rainy night only in a classic muscle car instead of on a steed.

"That's not exactly the way I meant it. You. Ivan. The way he is for you. A guy like him." She shook her head. "Damn, Marsha. Are you ever going to stop running away from him long enough for him to catch you?"

"Um, I...How did you..." I stuttered and stared at her. "Were you listening to us?"

"Duh, girl. That was something out there between you two. But I didn't need to listen. It's easy to see what's going on."

"Easy is not a word I would use to describe Ivan Carl and me."

"Probably not. But only because you are both equally hardheaded. Both banged up. Both scared. But I think after tonight, he wins. He's pretty ironclad determined."

"Yeah." My heart didn't just skip on that thought, it galloped. "Well, I better get in that shower." My teeth started to chatter.

"Oops. Yeah. You do that. And I'll mop up this puddle."

"Thanks, Barbara. You've been a great friend. And I've been pretty shitty."

"You haven't. Professionally, you're always appreciative of what I do. Personally, you've opened the door to your inner group and let me be a part of it. I've been an outsider all my life. It feels good, really good to be included. Even with all the drama. Nobody else made the decision to include me. You did that. That happened because of you. I love you, you know."

"What?" I turned back to look at her.

"You're not hard to love the way you think you are."

"Um, yeah I am. Armor on the outside and sharp edges in here." I thumped my chest. "No one gets in through the barbwire around my heart. You heard him."

"Yeah. But he said more than that, and if you listened more with that guarded heart of yours than only with your ears you'd hear better. You're far too generous and forgiving with others. And way to stingy with yourself."

My eyes rounded. I just blinked at her. She smiled slowly. "Get your shower, Mars. Oh, and call Raven. She's texted your cell about twenty times and called me nearly that many."

"Hey you." Raven's sweet voice echoed in my ear. I scooted deeper into the couch feeling warmth that had nothing to do with the blanket I'd found to cover my legs. "About time you called. Where are you?"

"Somewhere between Nola and Baton Rouge. It's good to hear your voice."

"Good to hear yours, too. Our bus is a little ahead of you now. We passed you. I was in the back lounge with Lucky, but the guys saw you and told me."

"Really?" My tone reflected my incredulousness. "In the middle of the night?"

"They're guys. More likely they noticed the vintage automobile. So, you wanna tell me about what's going on with you and Ivan?"

"Nothing's..." I started to deny it. I was a terrible friend regardless of what Barbara thought. How could I have forgotten Raven and how Ivan and I, any version of us, would likely hurt her.

"Honey," she whispered. "We gotta talk about this. I know we just got back to being us. I know I messed up with you. But I also know the carte blanche way you love me. Can you let me love you that way in return? Can you trust me enough to share the truth about what's going on?"

"I don't want to hurt you," I whispered.

"There's a reason why it's not a good plan to be involved with an ex of your best friend. I'm not gonna lie. My feelings about Ivan are convoluted. We were pretty serious at one time."

"I know."

"At one time. Not anymore. I don't feel the same way about him. But there's still some lingering emotions. They spilled over in New York. That's my bad." She sighed. "He played a vital role in my life at one time. He got me through a real rough patch.

"Yeah." My heart twisted tight.

"But I'm with Lucky now. He fills every bit of the spaces inside of me in a way that Ivan never could."

"Oh."

"Being apart from you was terrible, but it made me realize even more how important you are to me. And it was good in another way. It gave me some time and emotional distance to gain perspective." She let out another long breath. "So, honey. You and Ivan. From the beginning. Spill."

So, I did. I dug deep and shared with my best friend. Not the intimate sexual details. I skirted carefully around those. But I told her how Ivan and I had connected. How it had been so intense. Knowing me so well, she asked pointed questions that helped me sort through my thoughts better than I had been doing on my own.

"He wasn't like one of your hookups," she concluded. "You connected emotionally. He let you see his soft side. Because of that call from your father the first time you were together, he saw yours."

"Yeah."

"That's why you've been so conflicted and felt so guilty, honey. It's always been more than just sex with him. You see that, right?"

"Uh-huh." Now, I did.

"It scares you."

"Absolutely."

"Knowing him. Knowing you. I can certainly see why."

"You think?"

She ignored my sarcasm. "So tell me about the recent stuff."

"He's been flirty."

"That's Ivan, alright."

"Cocky. Annoying."

"Mmm, hmm. For sure."

"He's also been looking out for me. Sharing things. Including me in his family."

ROCK *Fuck* CLUB BOOK 3   323

"The band? He never did that with me, hon."

I knew that.

"That's significant."

I knew that, too. "He's also comforted me. A lot of times."

"I've seen that side of him."

Yeah, she definitely had. "He pushes me. A lot."

"I think he tried with me. To get me out of the funk I fell into after Hawk. But I only realized that recently. Perspective, you know. I just wanted to color him as the bad guy. Anger's easier to process than taking some of the blame. But he and I didn't work out for a lot of reasons."

"Wow."

"A bigger wow is what he's told me about you. He says you're beautiful, brave, strong like the Roman god of war you're named for. I think those were his exact words. He's in love with you, Mars."

"He told me tonight."

"He and I never exchanged those words."

I knew. She had told me, and he had mentioned it tonight before... "He said he loved me just now in the rain by the side of the road. He stopped my bus with his Firebird."

"Whoa. Memorable spot for a declaration."

"For sure."

"But dangerous." Her voice clogged. Mine did, too. Hawk had been hit and killed while waiting for a tow truck on the side of the road. "So, I hope he doesn't make another grand gesture like that. But we can't live our lives in a bubble trying to control our environment and avoid every potential danger, either. That's not living. That's just existing."

"I hear ya."

"Do you really?"

Yeah, that particular piece of wisdom went from my ear to my heart.

"I love you, Raven," I declared.

"I love you more." She stole my line. "And listen I can't tell you what to do with Ivan. But I can let you know whatever you do decide you won't be alone."

Tears brimmed. "Wish I could hug you."

"Wish I could hug you, too, honey. We'll make up for it soon. See you in Houston."

We ended the call, and I started to reach for my laptop, but my cell rang with another call.

Lying arrogant prick calling...

Um, maybe I needed to edit the details on that contact.

"Hey," I said. "Are you ok?" I glanced out the window but couldn't see the Firebird.

"Yeah, babe. I'm fine. Nice that you're worried about me. I'm right behind the bus. Driving me nuts, going so slow."

I smiled. I bet it did. "What's going on?"

"Not a whole fucking lot. Listening to music loud. What're you doing?"

"I took a shower. I was cold. You must be cold."

"I'm fine, babe. Don't worry about me. But my jeans are getting tight thinking about you naked in the shower. Remembering us naked in the shower."

"Yeah," I breathed.

"Fuck," he said. "Just your sigh gets me hard. Move onto another topic. Asap. Anything else."

"Well, I just talked to Raven. About you."

"Surprisingly, your tone doesn't make that sound like a bad thing."

"It wasn't actually. I think she's going to be ok with it."

"With what, babe?"

"With you and me."

"Motherfucking hell. I wish I could kiss you."

"Me, too. Let's change the subject. I don't have jeans issues, but my lady parts are getting a little restless."

"Lady parts? A little restless? Babe. Who am I talking to, and just how old are you?"

I giggled. "My pussy needs your amazing cock. Better?"

"Yes, and um, no."

I laughed.

"Love the sound of your laugh. Your voice. You, babe."

"I love you, too."

"Fuck me. She won't tell me when I've got her in my arms, but while I'm driving over the Mississippi River."

"Yeah, sorry about that."

"Don't be, babe. That you feel that way at all about me is a motherfucking miracle."

I giggled again. Instead of feeling scared anymore, I felt so light inside I was surprised I didn't float to the top of the bus and bump my head on the ceiling.

"I'll let you go, babe. A state trooper just pulled in close behind me. I might be in a no cell zone. But please call if you need me or just want to talk."

"You, too, Ivan. Be careful," I whispered as we ended the call. I set the phone beside me, so I could hear if he called again, and lifted my knees to my chest, wrapping my arms around them. On the couch beside me, Mine gave me a huffy look. I'd disturbed his slumber.

Murmuring an apology, I opened my laptop and restarted Tides of Conquest. This time I smiled softly as I re-watched my favorite episode.

Maybe it wasn't unrealistic fluff after all.

CHAPTER forty-four

"Hey, babe." A thrill shot through me at the deep sound of his delicious voice. "You're not sleeping, huh?"

"No. I thought we might talk."

"I'd like that."

"Me, too." I tucked the blanket around my legs. The bus air conditioning blew cold. But hearing his voice and knowing he was so close made me feel warm. Beside me, Mine added to the coziness, purring softly.

"What've you been doing?" he asked.

"Watching *Tides of Conquest*."

"You like that show?"

"Yeah."

"Knights and damsels in distress and all that shit?"

"I'm a girl, Ivan."

"Totally aware of that fact, Mars."

"So, I like the relational stuff. The fact that everything works out in the end."

"I can see where that would be appealing."

A heavy moment of silence ensued.

"You still think about him?"

I didn't need to ask who he meant. "Sure. He was a good guy. I was hung up on him for a long time. It was a tragedy to lose him. But when I'm with you, I don't think about him at all."

"It's ok to miss him, babe."

"Can't miss him all that much though, can I? We were never together, except that one time." I pulled in a deep breath and gave it to him real. "You were right. I idolized him. Built him up in my own mind. We didn't even have much in common besides Raven. I set my affections on him from afar, but I never let him see the true me. Never let him near my heart. Never shared with him like I've shared with you."

"Glad to hear that," he said softly. "I think it takes someone who's been where you and I have been to find strength and beauty where others only see the result of our pain."

"Yeah, he wouldn't have had a clue how to deal with someone like me. He never would have understood me the way you do. Even if I had shared the things I've shared with you. He never would have had the insight to tell Raven about my father."

"I didn't mean to overstep…"

"It's ok," I cut in. "I was mad at first, sure, but I realized afterward that she needed to know. That she would want to know. So, she can help me."

"That's Raven."

"Yeah." That was him too where I was concerned. "I'm guarded. It's harder for me to put my heart out there the way she does to let people close."

"Different backgrounds, babe. The situation with your parents. Your mom leaving. My old lady being how she was sending me off because I didn't meet her expectations. Those events have shaped us with sharper edges than people like Raven who grew up in a more nurturing environment. We learned too young that the love we thought was limitless from the people we should most trust was conditional. People like you and me, we've learned to fight, scrape and claw to get what we want. What we want to hold onto. What we want to keep."

"You sure you want to keep someone like me?" My question was whisper soft.

"I'm sure. I fell under your spell the first time I saw you. Your beautiful gold hair was loose around your shoulders. Your baby blues were full of shadows and mystery. You were wearing that leather dress. I wanted to rip it off your sexy body and then you started mouthing the words to my song. Like a goddess or a siren or something. You were so fucking into my music. You knocked me on my ass. I still haven't recovered."

"I don't know." I went for lighthearted since his words floored me. "You seemed pretty confident to me."

"Practice babe. Being who the people want to see. But that doesn't mean shit compared to the way you look at me."

"How do I look at you?"

"Like you want me. Like I might be the finest guy you ever laid eyes on. Like you want to hold onto me and never let me go."

"I do," I admitted. "You are. No one comes close to the impossible standard you've set. I don't want to let you go."

"From the first time, Mars, I wanted to be yours. And I wanted you to be mine."

Another long weighty moment of silence followed. I absorbed, then I formulated the words to explain. I wanted him to know everything. I knew he was strong enough to hold the things I told him. To keep them safe. To keep me safe. "It's hard for me to believe I can be worthy of love."

"Yeah," he agreed in a nonjudgmental accepting tone. I think he already knew. "I can see that. I understand it. And I'm here to show you, to prove to you that you are. However long it takes."

Wow. The rain, the kiss and the declaration following it had already melted my heart and made it malleable, but this conversation, his commitment, those words? They shaped and fully formed it. He was right. The debate was over. The outcome decided.

"What you said at the venue. In the rain. Right now." The sentiments that Raven and Barbara had echoed. "You're right. I've chosen, too. It's you for me and nobody else."

"I'm glad, so glad, babe."

"I've known it was you for a while now. I've been trying to convince Mine that we could deal without you. But he knew that was a lie." We were so much alike Ivan and me. Sharing the same insecurities from neglect and rejection made us so willing to sacrifice and see the good in others and so hesitant to believe in it in ourselves. "No more running from you. From us." I was worthy in his eyes, and he was certainly worthy in mine. Staying though I pushed him away. Protecting, defending and caring for me even if the enemy was mostly in my own mind. "I'm done with the RFC. I'll figure out a way to tell my boss when we get to Houston."

"Hey." Ivan's deep dreamy voice went in my ear and straight to my heart. I sat up straighter on the bus couch. He was the catalyst that jolted every single part of me instantly awake.

330   MICHELLE MANKIN

"Hey, yourself." Beside me as still as a stuffed animal, Mine continued his impression of a tabby colored pillow.

"You don't sound sleepy."

"You don't, either. Good thing, since you're driving."

"Yeah. Google maps says three more hours to go. "

"You going to make it?"

"Fuck, yeah I'm gonna make it. I get you on the end of this fucking long ass drive, don't I?"

"Yeah." A warm shiver rolled through me.

"I can't wait, babe."

"Me, either." I glanced out the window. The darkness was lightening. Pitch black had given way to shadowy grey at daybreak. We were on I-45 in the rolling hills south of the metroplex. "Did you see the Omni all lit up when we went through downtown Dallas?"

"Yeah, our skyline's pretty amazing. When the tour's over I'm taking you to my place."

"On White Rock Lake?"

"Raven tell you about it?"

"Yeah, just that you had a view of the water, a small recording studio and a huge four car garage in the backyard for your cars."

"I got the house for a steal. It's in a quiet neighborhood. Lots of old trees. The houses look different, not all cookie cutter."

"Sounds nice. Like you probably fit in except for the quiet part."

"The lots are large. The houses widely spaced apart. And obviously I've soundproofed the studio."

"You practice the stuff for your new album there?"

"Some. It's relaxing to be there. Like being on one of the band outings. A place I return to regularly to regroup."

"And create new music."

"Actually, my head's about to burst with six new melodies tonight."

"Really?" My eyes widened.

"For sure. Driving, thinking about you, it's got me fucking inspired."

"Tell me more."

He laughed. The sound went straight to my heart. Like his voice did, only faster. It made my toes tingle, and I was suddenly in the mood to dance. "You get nearly as breathy excited when I mention my music as you get when you're about to take my cock."

I smiled. "I love the insider stuff. It's a privileged peek behind the veil. To see the magic as it's made. Unwrapping all of the layers. I told you."

"You did. I remember."

"You get just as jazzed about conjuring the music and lyrics out of thin air," I guessed.

"I do. I process as I create. Emotions. Events. Life. Composing music is therapy for me the same way listening to it is for you. It's also where I dream. With my guitar, a steno and a pen the world can be whatever I want it to be."

"Tell me more about that. How it feels when you write a song."

"What exactly do you want to know, rock chick?"

"Everything." My eyes brightened, and the wings of my musical soul unfurled preparing to lift into the air on mystical currents. "Tell me everything."

I WAS ON THE edge of my seat. Well, the edge of the motor coach's couch when we hit the outskirts of Houston. The Cynthia Woods Mitchell Pavilion was in Conroe, a piney woods suburb north of the city.

I hadn't slept. But I wasn't tired. I had restarted *Tides of Conquest*, filled Ivan in on some important plot points, and we had talked about music. Something we were both passionate about.

The bus came to a halt, my emotion in my eyes I watched as his Firebird pulled into an empty space alongside us. I saw the driver's door swing open. Biker boots to the concrete, Ivan used the door as a prop rising to his full height behind it. I stared at him. So compelling, so impossibly handsome. Even with the rain and the long drive. The evidence was right there in front of me. His copper brown hair hoisted by the breeze. His unyielding visage. Muscle tee. Jeans. Wallet chain. Rings on his fingers. Steel in his spine. Total rocker cool. My body buzzing with anticipation, I managed to stay in my spot for a microsecond. Then I decided, 'fuck playing it cool,' when I saw him lift his shades onto his head and glance right up at me on the bus. I was getting me some Ivan.

My feet flew down the aisle. I hurdled Mine, who seemed to think that being in my direct path right under my feet was always the best place to be. I popped the door open in midstride and launched myself down toward the pavement bracing for a hard landing, but it never happened. Ivan was there. He caught me and twirled me in a complete circle before he let my feet touch the ground. Laughing, I wrapped my arms around his neck, and he wrapped his much stronger ones around my waist.

"Missed me, huh?" I heard and felt his low rumble of approval. It rolled through his solid chest as he crushed me to it. I didn't reply. Words weren't needed. I let my actions do the talking. I threaded my fingers into his thick hair. I tugged demandingly on the silken strands. He tipped his head down to me. I had a moment to register the sheer gorgeousness of his face and then his mouth was on mine, and I was experiencing it all. Him and his everything. His firm lips. The slight bite of his piercing. The deep possession of mouth as he parted my lips. His warm breath, his marauding tongue and his deep groan. The feeling of being claimed, of being his, rippled through me.

"Ivan." I tore my lips from his. My eyes fluttered open even as I my body suffered the trembling aftershocks of his kiss. "We need to get a room, and we need one fast."

"The bus is close." He glanced behind me.

"No." I jumped up into his arms and wrapped my legs around his waist, not caring that I wore a white sundress and the skirt hiked up to reveal my nude panties. I didn't care about anything right now but being with him and showing him how I felt. "That's too far," I decided. "Here, Ivan. Right here. Fuck me here. Hard. Against the..." My eyes widening, my words escaped me. Falling from the heights of passion to the lowest low, I unwound my legs from his waist. I slid down his hard body. I yanked down my skirt and the unseemly display of my undergarments.

"Daddy," I swallowed and took a big step away from Ivan. "What are you doing here?" He was in full uniform of course. He meant to be intimidating. DPD. Yellow patch. Badge. Tool belt. The works. The uniform had granted him access to the gated venue parking lot I was sure. Had he driven here last night right after his shift? If so, why?

I had taken great pains to avoid him. He strictly avoided me. The last time I'd had any contact with him had been over the phone. During Raven's season, I had called him after my car had broken down. I had been desperate and begged him for money. He had turned me down but had taken advantage of the opportunity to remind me what a terrible disappointment I was.

"I came here to see you. You weren't hard to find. I just looked on the website for that show of yours." His eyes the same blue shade as my own were narrowed with the usual disapproval. "Got to see a lot more than I bargained for. A lot more than anyone should. But then." His disdainful gaze swept over me. "That's you in a nutshell, Buttercup."

"You caught me at a bad time."

"It's always a bad time. From one to the next with you."

"Don't..." I got out, but he wasn't through. He was never through cutting me into tiny pieces he could grind under his heel.

"Don't speak the truth, you mean? The truth is you're a bigger slut that your momma ever was. And everyone knows about it now on account of that shameless show. Everyone is talking about it." Everyone meaning his fellow officers. He valued his job and his reputation above everything. "About you and all those men." I lowered my chin to my chest, shrinking inside myself. "Ne'er-do-wells the lot of them. Your favorite type. The only type that will have you. Like this one right here, no doubt." He included Ivan in a condescending glare. I hated for Ivan to see me like this, who I became, who I retreated into being, in front of my father. But I hated myself more. The old self-loathing bore down on me heavily, but suddenly Ivan placed his hands on my shoulders. Giving me his support. Support where I had least expected to find it. Love, too, from someone who truly understood me. A partner, Ivan stood tall and stayed steady not to spite me but because of me.

No, I wasn't on my own anymore. I was no longer abandoned. It wasn't just me facing my father alone. Something blindingly bright and achingly beautiful rose within me like the buoyant feeling I got whenever I listened to one of my favorite up-tempo songs but more, infinitely more.

"You need to stop right there." Ivan grit out the warning to my father and moved in closer behind me. His warmth washed away the chill on my skin.

"Excuse me?" My father's dark grey brows snapped together. He wasn't accustomed to anyone countermanding him.

ROCK *fuck* CLUB BOOK 3   335

"I'm through listening to you insult her. Marsha is an admirably strong, capable and courageous woman. No thanks to you, or the reprehensible way you speak to her or the abuse she has suffered over the years from your hands."

"I never…"

"You did, and you're the one who's shameful. I may not know a lot, but I know a father should be a refuge for his daughter. That he should protect and defend her until his dying breath. Not terrorize her mother so badly she disappears without a trace or treat a little girl so badly that you nearly broke her bold spirit."

"You don't know a thing about it. And I'll speak to my daughter anyway I damn well please." He refocused on me. "Marsha, you're coming with me. No more gallivanting. No more humiliating degrading behavior. I'll get your court transcriptionist job back. You'll come home…"

"No, sir. Actually, she won't. She won't be going anywhere with you. Her home is with me. A home is somewhere you feel safe and accepted. You never gave her that." Ivan's words were a pennant of truth that unfurled around us both. "You won't speak to her at all anymore. You won't even come near her."

"And who's to stop me. You?" The military shorn top of my father's head bristled with his agitation.

"If need be," Ivan returned.

Hands over the pummel of his pistol, my father moved forward, and Ivan met him, a tower of immoveable protection in front of me.

"I can have you arrested."

"You could, but you won't." I spoke up, moving beside Ivan, finding and brandishing the inner strength his faith in me had beaconed. His surety gave me the security I needed. His love redefined me. Our love was a new beginning. It made all the difference. It didn't crumble my world, it remade it. "Because you're a coward," I spit out that truth at the man who was a father in name only. "Only a coward would treat his family the way you have. Everything Ivan said is true. I'm not weak and broken. I'm strong, capable and brave. I'm not shameful. I'm beautiful, and my life has value just because I'm me. You're a weak, pathetic and deplorable person. And if you don't want me telling the world in great detail what a fucked-up excuse of a man you are for abusing me, your own daughter, you will go away right now and leave me alone."

My father stepped back. I had never seen him retreat from anyone. "I let you have power over me when I believed your lies. But no more." Ivan beside me, I watched as my strength and the truth I wielded slammed into my father. I stood up straighter realizing the validation I had sought in all the wrong places had been inside me all along. And as I came to that realization, my father seemed to diminish in size right before my eyes. "Don't call. Don't come around. I don't want to see you ever again."

"We have it all recorded." Barbara suddenly appeared. "Filmed it from the window above you in case he forgets." A rush of footfalls sounded behind Barbara. Ignacio, Les, Ernie and Carla exited the bus. Wearing firm expressions, everyone moved into place behind Ivan and me. My father shook his head in disbelief.

"Go away," I told him. "Don't ever come back. I have everything I need right here. With Ivan. With my friends who love and support me. With my real family."

CHAPTER forty-five

Not a damsel in distress in need of a champion.
A team.

My protective dark knight and me.

No, not my knight.

My modern-day badass rocker.

I spun around to face him after my father ducked between two other parked tour buses and disappeared.

"Sorry you had to witness that." I placed my hands on Ivan's hard chest, right on top of the flaming wings of the Firebird and tipped my head back to look at him.

"Witness what?" He aimed his still vengeful appearing visage down at me.

"My father and me. How I get flustered when he lays into me."

"You're embarrassed?" He sounded incredulous.

"Yes." I nodded.

"He's the one who should be embarrassed for being such a useless fuckwad. You on the other hand were a total warrior."

"Thank you." My lips curved in satisfaction. "It was a long time coming. But I'm still sorry you had to deal with him."

"We don't get to choose our parents."

"Yeah, I know. But what we do get to choose is who we want to have at our back when we get blindsided by them." I lifted onto my toes and pressed a grateful kiss to the outside corner of his mouth. "Sexy, strong, everything I want. Everything I need. In case you didn't already get it. I choose you."

"Anytime, anyplace, anyway, babe." He gave me his cocky half-smile, and I felt his hands settle warm and possessively on my lower back.

"Thank you for defending me."

"You did well enough yourself. I was just emotional support."

"Back to back, you and me," I told him. "I like that."

"You and me, Mars, we're a pretty formidable duo."

"I agree. But, I don't think I thanked you properly for, you know," I peered up at him through my lowered lashes, "your emotional support."

"No?" He cocked his head at me.

"Uh-uh."

"Do I get to choose the form of repayment I would like?"

"Sure."

"I choose naked gratitude."

Unfortunately, naked gratitude had to wait. Ivan got pulled away by Tyler because of some kind of crisis related to the band's upcoming performance. I used the extra time wisely.

While he went into the venue, I took one of the shuttles and checked into the hotel. I paid for an upgrade to a larger room separate from Barbara. When my man did get free from his responsibilities, I wanted us to have lots of room to play. Then I called the crew in for an emergency meeting of my own.

"Hey. First off, I want to thank all of you for being so supportive of me during my season and for coming to my rescue this morning with my father." I cast my gaze around the suite's seating area where we were all assembled.

"You didn't need to be rescued." In the khaki upholstered chair on my right, Barbara scooted forward, reached for my clasped hands and squeezed them.

"Thanks." I smiled at her and then the others as they murmured similar sentiments.

"Couldn't have been prouder." Ignacio leaned forward and nodded at me from his spot on the opposite end of the couch.

"Me, too." Carla echoed, on my left on the middle couch cushion.

"You set him straight." Ernie bobbed his head, opposite Barbara. His features as usual were shadowed by his favorite 'Sound Matters' ball cap.

"You are the ruler of the badass cosmos." Les smiled, a rainbow of flower power from his position on the ottoman directly across the coffee table from Carla.

"So, what's this meeting all about?" Barbara, as executive producer got us, mainly me, refocused on the task at hand.

"Tonight, I want y'all to get closing footage. It's going to be my last official night as the Rock Fuck Club star."

"Are you quitting?" Barbara guessed.

"Not quitting per se. I think there's more to be done to round out everything in my season." The theme Barbara had mentioned me needing to have? I had one in mind now. But I didn't know if I would ever get the opportunity to share it. "The Gods of Rock tour still has one last stop in Napa. But I'm done fucking anymore rock stars."

"That's not unexpected," Ignacio said.

"Have you told Suzanne yet?" Barbara asked.

"No." I shook my head. "I wanted to talk to y'all first. Run what I have in mind by you before I tell her. See if you think my idea is solid."

"Alright, shoot." Ignacio put his hands on his knees and leaned forward.

"Well something that happened with Ivan got me thinking. One of the RFC followers, a girl named Brenda is pretty in tune with the original concept Raven started out with. Something that focusing on some artificial construct like ten rock stars in each season may have detracted from."

"What's that, Mars? Barbara queried, her delicate brow scrunched.

"A woman's right to choose. A woman being in charge of her sexuality. What she wants, when she wants it, how and with who."

"For sure," Carla agreed.

"The ranking system is fine. That's important. I like mine, do or don't or stay the hell away. But a one to ten number system is fine, too. The next girl who comes along can decide for herself what she prefers. Because freedom to do so emphasizes the concept of the show."

"Ranking and reviewing the rock stars makes them cognizant of how they treat women. Not just as objects but as individuals with hearts and feelings." Barbara nodded. "It's an accountability thing."

"Yeah, because," I nodded back, "even if the cameras aren't rolling on them, the rock stars know if they're total shits the information's gonna pop up on the Facebook page. If there's validity, others will comment and corroborate." I hadn't talked to Raven yet, but I think she would be encouraged to see her idea working out not just on the grand scale on the show, but on an individual basis with sister supporting sister. I certainly was.

"So, you're planning to tell Smith to drop the stipulation in your contact that requires you to hookup with ten different rock stars."

"I don't think anybody *tells* Suzanne Smith anything, but I'm going to present it to her like I have to y'all and then see what happens."

"She might sue you for breach of contract." Les cringed.

"She might." I might end up in worse financial straits than I had been back when Raven signed up with WMO to rescue me in the first place. But I had learned from my best friend's example. She had sacrificed for me. At the time she and Lucky hadn't been a couple. They had just been two individuals on the cusp of realizing the potential they could be together. But even though no vows of love had been exchanged, that didn't detract from the magnitude of what Raven had done. She assigned great value to me. To being loyal to me. Some people were worth making that sacrifice for.

Ivan

"That's the way it's gonna be, Ty."

"Timmons went ballistic. She's not on board with us debuting a song that's such a departure from our heavy metal sound here. We could lose our contact."

"Then we do." I bit out, standing nose to nose with my best friend in the crowded hotel lobby. Several people turned to stare. I didn't care. "And we get a new one with someone else."

I had to sing that song tonight. It was about her. It was her and me. I had put off playing any tunes from the new album. But I wasn't putting off shit anymore.

"She's leading you around by your dick, man. Don't give her that power over you. No cunt's worth that."

I slammed my palms into his chest, turning the full force of my wrath on him. He still sported a black eye and sore ribs from sticking his nose in between me and her the last time. "The only reason you're still breathing calling her that is 'cause I know," I growled, my eyes boring into his. "I fucking lived the whacked shit Priscilla put you through. But no more Ty. I can't believe you would even want to fucking go round with me about Marsha again."

"If I need to, fuck yeah, I'm gonna go round with you again." His lips pulled back from his teeth. He didn't back down. Ty never backed down when he thought I was doing something stupid. Most of the time I loved him for it. Right now wasn't one of them.

I tried to reason with him. I didn't need a bloodied drummer on the riser behind me tonight. I needed my best friend. "I'm gonna put it all out there for her tonight."

"I don't even get a say?"

"No, man. Fuck no. Now listen." I pulled in a breath that did fuck-all to calm me, but I got a glimpse of her in my mind. Fucking beautiful this morning. Her golden hair skimming my hands. Her sunshine and summery scent filling my lungs. Like the goddess she was named for, she had stood warrior tall, her spine snapped straight, and she given it and then some to that worthless worm the way he deserved. A team she had called us. Fuck, yeah. Fuck anyone who got in the way of that team. Even Ty.

"She's gotta see. I want her to see. I want the whole fucking world to know what she means to me. Music is her love language man." I was giving mine to her in a way she would never forget. In a way she would truly understand. Love wasn't just words to me. It was actions. And this was the first one among many more that would prove to her that not only was she mine, she was my everything.

CHAPTER forty-six

"Hey, I need you," I said as soon as Raven answered her cell. "Where are you?" Warmth filled the center of my chest at her immediate ready response.

"You didn't even ask what I needed," I pointed out.

"You're my best friend, Mars. You need me I'm there."

"I'm in my suite." I gave her the number. "Bring Sky."

"She's with me now. We're just the floor above you. We'll be right down."

I imagined I could hear the flurry of footsteps on the ceiling above me. Even though I was nervous, I was smiling, and my smile widened even more when I heard the rap on my door.

"They're fast." Barbara's green eyes rounded. "I'll get it." She went to the door, and I stood in the seating area bracing for the inevitable questions.

"What's going on?" Raven came straight to me, her brows in a worried v.

"RFC chicks emergency meeting."

"Ahh." Her expression relaxed a little.

"You remember when you told me I needed to push back with Smith?"

"I remember." She nodded.

"You offered to give me moral support."

"Absolutely." She reached for my hand pressing our palms and fingers together before she intertwined the digits. Sky and Barbara were across from us. They moved shoulder to shoulder closer together. Yeah, we all knew the formidable executive well. And if one of us was in trouble we all were.

"'I'm going to attempt to push back now."

"What's this about? Or who?"

"It's about me. Mainly. But it's about all of us in a way. "At least I hoped that was the way Suzanne would see it. After all wasn't she a sister, too? I sucked in a breath and pulled my cell out of my pocket. "I'm gonna call her now before I lose my nerve. I'll put her on speaker."

"Miss West?" I had her personal cell. She answered on the second ring. "Hello. I was just going to call you."

Oh, peachy.

"Oh really? What about?" I exchanged a glance with the others. Had she already figured out about Ivan?

"Firstly, the background stuff on the other guys Raven was with. I like it. Asking them all the same questions about her. It's good. The redo on Ivan Carl is done well, too. It's stripped down. Real. We only used a tiny segment of it in the opening teaser on her season, but it worked."

That was surprising.

"However, what I don't understand is where you are going with your own season. You've been all over the map with the guys you've chosen so far. There are only two stops left. Not a lot of time to decide."

"Yes, about that. I'll get right to the point. I'm not fucking anymore rock stars, Miss Smith. I've fallen in love with one."

"Ivan Carl."

"Yes."

"Well, a hazard of the job apparently. That nevertheless does not exempt you from fulfilling your obligations."

"I won't fuck anyone else. I won't even pretend."

"You signed on the dotted line to do so. This is the Rock Fuck Club, not the Rock Love Club. If you think I'm not going to insist..."

"When you insist I fuck a certain number of rock stars you undermine my freedom, my right to choose as a woman. That's the concept of the show. A concept you said was important to you."

"It's extremely important to me, Miss West. However, the show is my show. You are only an employee. I'm the one in charge. I have the final say. And what kind of show would we have if our RFC stars are falling for someone after say the first hookup, for example?"

"Um, not a very good one."

"Just so. You have only three rock stars left to fulfill your contract."

"Two if you count Cush Diamond."

"Yes, well, I guess we could, and Mr. Carl can certainly be one. That leaves one remaining. Surely you can..."

"No."

"Are you refusing outright? Do you realize the amount of money we've invested in this concept? The cash outlay on your season alone?"

"I'm sure it's substantial. I'm not asking you to scrap my season. I just want you to consider being flexible about the terms."

"Ten rock stars. Those are the terms. You knew that going in."

"He won't like it. I won't do it to him." He had to know. He had to see that I chose him. Actions spoke louder than words. "I wouldn't like it if our roles were reversed."

"So this is your line in the sand?"

"He's my line in the sand. Yes."

"I'll be in touch, Miss West. I have a lot to consider. You can expect to hear from me sooner rather than later. In fact, count on it. Good day."

STILL REELING FROM MY run-in with the executive, I pasted myself to Ivan's solid side as soon as he entered the suite.

"Is everything ok?" His hands curved around my upper arms. The rings encasing his fingers pressed into my skin as he leaned back and searched my eyes looking for answers within them.

"It will be," I returned, hoping against hope, and betting on me and Ivan, plus the crew and the three women that had just left that somehow this would work out. There had to be a way for me to circumvent the remaining rock star left in my contract. Possibly—on the other hand, though it was a lot of money, I wouldn't compromise myself anymore. Not ever again.

"How much time do we have before you have to go back to the venue?" I asked the only rock star I ever wanted to fuck again.

"We have all the time in the world. Mars." Removing his hands from my arm, he slid them down my arms, gathering my hands in his own before he raised his gaze. "I want you." His expression was warm, and his chocolate eyes brimmed with the intensity of his desire. "I don't want anyone else. I want to be your only one. I want us to be exclusive. I want you on my bus with me. In my bunk and on the road with me wherever that road leads us."

I smiled. "I want that, too."

"Then that's the way I will make it. My world for you." His eyes began to flicker like a canopy of stars on a sultry summer night.

Pressing me backward into the entry wall with his body, he brought our gathered hands above my head and pinned mine there using his own.

"The bed this time for a change? Or right here against the wall? Your choice."

"I thought you were choosing this time." My words were spaced out to accommodate my shortened breaths. Excitement tingled throughout my body focused in certain areas. His hard chest to my breasts. His insistent contours to my compliant curves. His heat. His thick cock.

"Naked is naked."

I gasped as he ground his length into one of those hyperaware areas.

His gaze dipped to my parted lips, then rose, his eyes dark, his gaze heated. "And naked time with you means I always get what I want."

"Then take it. Take me. Any way you want."

"Now." He dropped one of his hands. "Here." He yanked up the hem of my skirt. He dove his hand underneath it. His fingertips skidded along my skin. My thighs trembled. My flesh heated like tires spinning on asphalt.

"Yes," I breathed when he reached the apex of my legs.

"Babe, you're so beautiful," he praised as my breasts rose and fell against his hard chest. "You're so wet. Your panties are soaked, and I've barely touched you." He ripped them down my legs. They glided to the floor of their own accord once he got them past the curve of my upper thighs.

"You've got me pinned. I'm under your control, and I like the things you do to me. Of course, I'm turned on."

He grinned, the half-smile. The arrogant one. My pussy spasmed beneath his palm. He swiped his thumb over my mound. I shivered.

He dipped a long finger inside me, sliding it in and gliding it out.

"Yeah, you definitely like me." The rumble of his voice made my nipples tighten to points.

"I can come on your finger." I licked my lips. He lifted his gaze to follow the motion of my tongue. "But I'd rather come around your cock."

"I love the way you talk." He lowered his head. He pressed his mouth to my lips. His wet tongue parted them. He slid his finger in and out of my cunt to the same rhythm his tongue fucked my mouth.

I moaned and sucked on his tongue. He ripped his mouth from mine.

"You're so sexy." He stared at me. His eyes dark. His gaze dipped to my chest and the cleavage the décolletage revealed.

"Ivan." My clit was throbbing. "Fuck me."

"Hell, yeah." He released my hands. I laid them on his strong shoulders as he unbuckled his belt. The pins and needles feeling abated by the time he lowered his jeans.

"Let me put the condom on."

"By all means." He gave it to me. I rolled it on slowly while we both watched.

"Hop on, babe." He ripped up my skirt, positioned and pinned me again, against the wall, not by my hands, but on his glorious cock. In and out he stroked while I held on for the ride. The wall banged against my shoulder blades. His fingers flexed into my ass cheeks. My white dress rode up around my waist, and his hips rocked as he plunged his long length deep inside me.

"More. Faster." I begged, reveling in the sensations. His thick cock. His piercing striking my taut clit like the lash of his hard tongue.

"Yeah babe." He gripped my ass tighter. He fucked me harder. I clawed at his shoulders. My cunt tightened around his cock.

"Yes. Ivan. Oh yes." I felt it coming.

"So good." He rasped. "So tight. So, fucking tight."

"Oh, Ivan."

"Oh, Mars."

"Yes, Ivan. Now." I moaned as it hit me.

So hard. So hot. My entire body scalp to toes tingled, it felt so amazingly good.

He groaned and erupted inside of me, gripping my ass so tightly it burned my skin.

Tremors shook my body. Shudders rolled through his. We tumbled through the fire melded together. In our passion. In our love.

CHAPTER forty-seven

"So how much time do we really have?" I asked Ivan as his hands smoothed over my naked soapy body in the shower.

"Right now?" His eyes on mine, his hands froze on the shimmering skin over my hips.

I nodded, and the warm shower spray pelting my shoulders arced around us like a watery cape.

"Not enough."

"Oh." My face fell.

"I know." He glided his fingers up my sides, stopping under my tits. He swiped his thumbs across the peaked nipples sending a zing of sensation to my cunt before he lifted his gaze. "I want hours and hours with you in that big bed in the other room. But we gotta set up early for a new song tonight."

"A new song?" An anticipatory shiver raised bumps on my skin.

He grinned his cocky half-smile. "Knew that would get your attention."

"Love your music, Ivan. Love you more. But I can't wait to hear some of the new stuff y'all have been teasing me about."

"Tonight's the night. I've written a song just for you."

"Me?" My eyes rounded.

"No-one else but you, babe. I'm a little nervous to debut it."

"You get nervous up there?"

"Oh yeah. It usually goes away after the first song. But yours is first. We're leading with it."

"I can't wait." I drew in a sharp breath. He'd flicked my nipples again.

"We practiced it once already." He lowered his head. His mouth hovered over mine. "Maybe we might have a little more time."

"HE'S DOING A SONG for you?" Raven asked, glancing up at the stage. The Enthusiasts' roadies were hurriedly setting up. The techs checking the guitars. The mics. Making sure the cords were taped down. A girl with violet hair and sapphire blue eyes wearing fingerless gloves worked on Tyler's drum kit. A female tech? She was gorgeous. Where had she been during the previous stops on the tour? I'd never noticed her before.

"He is." I nodded my head excitedly. "A new song. One that's going to be on their next album." My freshly washed hair swished around my bared shoulders. I had gone high drama rock chick for the occasion. Low cut v-neck camo shirt. Frayed jean shorts. Black strappy leather sandals with towering five-inch chunky wood heels. Silver chains for accessories. And the piece de resistance? A glossy black Marilyn Monroe style duster.

"It looks like they're almost ready. Where does he want you to stand?"

"I don't know." Sudden full-blown panic made my tone tinny. "We didn't talk about that. We got distracted." More than once. The shower. Against the counter. I fanned my flushed cheeks with my hand.

"Think, Mars. Did he tell you to stand to the side of the stage or in front of it?"

"He didn't specify. We're right beside the catwalk. Do you think it matters? Won't he see me here?" He had seen me that first time.

"I'm not sure. The spots get in their eyes sometimes with this kind of setup."

I started to tremble. The lights had lowered. The techs were gone. A puffy cloud of smoke rolled onto the stage. Ivan appeared on it.

And then nothing else mattered.

His eyes glistening like the richest confection, he strode to the center of the stage with a cordless mic in his hand. He didn't have his guitar. That was the first thing I noted. It was unusual for him. He was also naked from the waist up. Total swoon. His skin appeared to gleam. I wondered if he'd slathered in baby oil.

Um, I hoped we were getting together-together right after the show before it wore off. Slipping and sliding with Ivan in the sheets? Um, yes, please. I shifted my legs restlessly.

Grinning his panty-melting frontman smile, Ivan flourished a sculpted arm to the right. "My buddy, Arrow on the lead guitar tonight."

While cameras flashed, and strobes popped, the blond guitarist lifted his chin then lowered his head and unleashed a scintillating chord. In the crowd, girls screamed, and guys clapped.

Ivan brandished his other arm. "Jag as usual grooving on the bass."

His angled black bangs shadowing his green eyes the lean bassist smiled coolly and plucked a few funky notes.

"And up top where he belongs…" Ivan turned. "Ty the master of disaster on the drums."

Tyler's arms wind milled. The lights flashed to his frenetic beat. While the crowd ramped up, Ivan stepped from under the white pavilions and sauntered down the catwalk. He was barefoot. He wore no accessories. He didn't need them. He was sending a message. This song was him stripped down to the core. And it was me just as I was for him. I got it and everyone else did, too, as he sat down, threw his long legs over the side of the stage and he sang to me.

I've got the time, time for you
There's a place for you, you know it's true
If there's anyway, I'll see it through
Anytime, anyplace, anyway
It's you.

If you need anything, I'm your man
No matter what it is, I've got the plan
Believe in me, I understand
Anytime, anyplace, anyway
I can.

Nothing's gonna stop us, not even the rules
I live life my way, I ain't gonna lose
I always get what I want
Anytime, anyplace, anyway.

Now I've got you, won't set you free
Fulfill every dream, as you will see
The only one for you, and you for me
Anytime, anyplace, anyway
It'll be.

EPILOGUE

"Where are you taking me?" I bristled in Ivan's hold. Not a lot. I liked where I was. But a little. I didn't want him to think he could manhandle me and always get away with it. "I wanna go back to that big bed. Do the baby oil thing again. Then pick up Mine from Barbara's room." She was the designated cat sitter.

"Next night, Tigress. Next hotel. It's late. I'm beat." I could hear the amusement in his tone, but I couldn't see it because he'd blindfolded me with one of his handkerchiefs. A dark navy one. I couldn't see a thing. I only knew we were outside, somewhere near the venue. I could hear the crickets chirping and feel the balmy night air.

"If you're beat why are we out here?"

"Chick or Girl, you're a pain in the ass with all your questions."

"You like my ass. You mentioned it quite specifically. Several times tonight."

"You're right. It's amazing. I need to write a song about how amazing I think it is."

"Don't you dare," I huffed trying to squirm out of his arms. Not really. I only burrowed closer, pressing my soft cheek deeper into the smooth skin over his hard chest.

"Stop trying to make me want to fuck you again."

"I'm not," I disagreed, even though I was.

"You are. But I love you. Even if you're insatiable."

"I love you insatiably."

"I know you do. The scales were tipped in your favor even before you drew that line in the sand with your boss. But I'm glad you did that, babe. So glad."

"You sang your song to me. Your amazing song. Even though it might get you into trouble. Ty told me what your boss said."

"Ty talks to much." He pulled off the blindfold.

"We're in the parking lot." I blinked in the dark. "Next to your bus. We have to be in that thing all day tomorrow on the way to Napa. This is not my idea of a nice surprise, Ivan."

"We're not there yet." He adjusted me in his hold and opened the bus. He carefully carried me up the steps and through the front lounge.

"Why aren't you turning any lights on?"

"Because." He set me down. My body slid along his. Rugged contours against supple ones. His cock was rock hard. It gave an eager twitch. My pussy quivered.

"Ivan, are you sure you don't want to..." He had flicked open the curtain to the middle bunk. His bunk. "Oh..." I stuttered. My heart stumbled. "Oh my. That's pretty." There were twinkling lights, a web of them all over the ceiling. Our names together on a large leather storage pocket at the foot of the bed. Two sets of headphones linked together with a splitter and tied with a big red bow. "When did you have time to do this?"

"For you, I make time."

"Yeah." He certainly had. Tears threatened. "We're sleeping here tonight. Right?"

"Would you like that?"

"Yeah."

"Put the headphones on. I transferred your music to my iPad."

"You did what?" A tear spilled over, tracing warmth down my cheek that arrowed straight to my trembling heart.

"I told you," he reminded me unnecessarily, his expression and his voice soft. "I'd light up your nights and fill them with music."

"You did."

"Ear to ear, song by song, night or day, it's me and you making music and memories together."

"Yeah," I agreed, swiveling away from the beauty he had created for me to the beauty he was. "Record labels. WMO. They won't stand a chance against us."

"Whoever takes a swing at us, Marsha West, we'll swing back harder. It's you and me, babe. You and me against the whole motherfucking world."

ACKNOWLEDGMENTS

Otherwise known as I can't believe we did it.

Husband, my boys, Dr. Diane Klein, Brandee Price, Cassy Roop, Michelle Preast, Wander Aguiar, Matt, Lisa Anthony.

It's always *we* for me. No book of mine ever comes into being without help.

A lot of help.

Stylistic editor, copy editor, beta readers, formatter, cover designer, photographer, model, proofreader, and you the readers and book bloggers who love books and reading. The book community rocks!

The Rock F*ck Club series is special to me. In 2017, I decided I wanted to tell a no holds barred rocker story where the groupies are in charge. It was a crazy idea, but my author bestie Michelle Warren read the first three chapters and encouraged me to go for it. Then my best friend slash PA Lisa Anthony said play big with it or go home. Lisa also says it's her favorite series because she knows what it cost me to write it. The title alone I had to fight for. My hubby wanted me to call it Rock Fun Club. Others advised me to use a pseudonym. But in the end I felt I had to keep the title and the concept under my own name. After all, isn't being brave, bold and beautiful the point of the series?

As women we need to stand up for ourselves, what we like, what we want to do and how we want to do it. For me as a writer creativity is at the center of it.

So, I hope you enjoyed the story. I hope you tell others about it. I would love if everyone who reads it puts up a review to tell others how the story made them feel. And I hope most of all that you are brave, bold and beautiful in your own life. Stand up and speak up for what you like. In and out of the bedroom. Be your own best unique you.

If this is the first series of mine that you have tried, consider checking out my Tempest bad boy rock star series. Six books in total. It's a completed series with an uplifting undercurrent.

For a different feel, for beachy SoCal surfer rockers, try my Rock Stars, Surf and Second Chances series. Each book in this series features a different character in the band. And they are best read in order.

Next up: a Christmas 2018 surprise, a collection of unique rocker stories that I'm putting together with some rocking friends of mine

Then the next two books in the Rock Stars, Surf and Second Chances series. High Tide and Island Side. The custom covers we shot in Ocean Beach, California for these two are amazing.

Then Twisted Magic, the long-awaited conclusion to my paranormal rocker series set in New Orleans.

Then more Rock F*ck Club.

I can't wait to introduce you to the star of season three. She will be introduced in Marsha's and Ivan's Postseason Novella. She will crank up the hot in the series.

Follow me on Bookbub for release alerts: https://www.bookbub.com/authors/michelle-mankin

Made in the USA
Coppell, TX
05 October 2023